as we can discern, the sole purpose of human existence is to kindle a light in the darkness of mere being:

C. G. JUNG

ALL THE RIGHT PE

As fa
a lig

ALL
THE
RIGHT
PEOPLE

WILLIAM
WETMORE

Doubleday & Company, Inc., Garden City, New York

1964

*All of the characters in this book
are fictitious, and any resemblance
to actual persons, living or dead,
is purely coincidental.*

To Jonathan

CHAPTER I

My family has always lived in a place called Gravenhurst, Connecticut, which a lot of people probably feel is just our tough luck.

Gravenhurst happens to be near Century Park where you find rich people who don't like salt water. Living that close to Century is asking for trouble because right away everyone begins to wonder why you don't live *in* it. They know you must want to because that's where rich people who don't like the ocean live and you can be damn sure there's no ocean around Gravenhurst.

It all gets pretty tiresome. I mean Century isn't *that* great. As a matter of fact, I could tell a few tales which might not make it look quite so upper-upper. Like the time we had to pay . . . but it isn't such a hot idea to tell tales because they give the wrong impression and might make people think we really wanted to live in Century, rather than Gravenhurst.

Imagine such a ridiculous thing as that!

Anyway, what I've been getting at in twenty-five words or more is why we have always lived where we do. My family—the Clarence Woodruffs by name—own, publish, and edit the Gravenhurst *Daily Watch*. In fact I'd say my family *is* the Gravenhurst *Daily Watch*.

That may sound pretentious, but there's quite a responsibility involved. More than thirty thousand people live in and around Gravenhurst (including one thousand inmates at our brand spanking new and spiritually uplifting Federal House of Detention) and it's our job to give them "Your News as You Make it," as our slogan says. It is also our job to keep out all competitors which we do by blending a passion for progress with sound business sense. The passion for progress makes itself evident in an occasional editorial on urban renewal and the sound business sense is apparent in the fact my father owns most of the real estate on Main Street. Of course it was all inherited—the family's been around these parts since 1639 when the town was first settled—but Pa's managed to hang on to it and I guess that takes some doing these days.

What this all boils down to is the Woodruffs have had things pretty much their own way for the last ten generations or so and I suppose we're a fine example of the big fish in a small pond variety. We live by a lake on top of Woodruff Hill in one of those rambling, Early American farmhouses which has been renovated and added to so many times it really isn't early anything right now. But it looks early as hell and everybody in town calls it the Big House, except for a few wise guys who refer to it as the Bug House when the old man isn't around. I don't recall anybody ever calling it that to his face. We're all just a little intimidated by my father. Even Mayor Healy, though he likes to pretend he isn't scared of anyone. Even me. In fact about the only people around town who aren't are my sister, Abigail, who is a little crazy, and Bollard, the butler, who is similarly afflicted. Otherwise I'm sure they'd be just as scared as the rest of us. The best way to explain why this is so might be to tell a tale for which I'll most likely be shot. But my deep devotion to the truth, sometimes called gossip, compels me:

This goes back to a summer night about four years ago. It was just after my freshman year at college and I was being allowed to meet a side of my father from which Mother had heretofore spared me. He was celebrating something. I think we had just busted another union attempt to organize our shop. Pa wasn't exactly a liberal. Anyway, eight or ten publishers from around the area had been invited to share our victory over the downtrodden, a breed of people for which no one felt much compassion since, as Pa often put it, they were usually lying down in the first place. It turned out to be quite a celebration. By the time dinner was over most of our distinguished publishers were acting like frustrated strikebreakers and I'll bet a poll of the wives would have revealed a prohibitionist trend. All that saved the group from seeming pretty ordinary was a strong flavoring of dignity. Fortunately there was enough to keep an entire senate from toppling over the edge of propriety, so no matter how raunchy they got, somehow it was all right. But by far the most dignified and most raunchy of all—with the possible exception of Bollard, the winetaster—was one Clarence Woodruff. He is blessed with a profile which looks like somebody's founding father and gray hair with as fine a set of feathers as could be found anywhere in the world. Also he's tall and just a little deaf, a handicap for which he amply compensates by shouting, though no one is quite sure why. The effect is action, integrity, and thundering courage even though the intent, at least that night, was laughter, brandy, and mindless oblivion.

After dinner somebody told him there were lights across the lake at Mayor Healy's so Pa decided to paddle over and invite the mayor to join us.

"After all, I made the son of a bitch, did I not?"

So off he went, which is sort of crazy at his age, and I saw Mother wave Bollard after him. About a half hour later they still hadn't come back and I was dispatched. I don't know why. To drag the lake maybe. It turned out they weren't too hard to find. The publisher was in his canoe, paddling away to beat the band and singing, "I love the lassie with a big round assie," which happens to be a favorite of his, while Bollard sat on the dock, holding on to the painter and humming a quiet little tune of his own. Pretty soon Pa got tired and Bollard hauled him in and we all went back to call the Healys on the telephone. He was slightly bewildered, Pa I mean, but he didn't say anything.

A little while later Happy Healy and his wife showed up and managed, despite a façade of assurance, to suggest a peasant couple uncomfortable in the master's presence. They both had bursting, shiny cheeks and fat fingers and eager, reaching smiles which, despite the pretended assurance, made them look like children not quite at home in a new neighborhood. At the time—four years ago— that's about how they should have looked, for only one year before Happy Healy had been nothing but a freshman alderman from the Fourth Ward. As far as Pa's concerned, being an alderman is just about last rung on the political ladder. Especially if your constituency happens to be located in the Fourth Ward, better known as the Whiskey Ward or Irish Town, so Happy and his wife had no real grounds for assurance when they climbed to the heady heights of Woodruff Hill. But worse than that, it was pretty much of an accepted fact among those in the know that the Old Man put Happy in office and could just as easily put him out if the whims and fancies of Gravenhurst politics so directed. Apparently the Happy Healys understood this for their behavior implied a desire to entertain our publishing royalty rather than risk the insolence of friendship, and though I've heard it said that an Irishman's happy exterior often hides the cunning of a Sephardic Jew, it seemed doubtful that night. Pa went to work with the relentless rhythm of a stoker, heaping ridicule and mild abuse on the mayor and his lady, but the faster he shoveled the brighter burned their good humor until I began to suspect they would both pale and die without it. Frankly the whole performance got a little hot for me and from the looks on their faces some of our guests must have felt the same way. I know Mother did because she said "Now Clarence" from time to time but once Pa got going there was nothing anybody could do to stop him. That's the way he was—rough and ready and candid as a clenched fist—which is okay just so long as you can take it when your turn comes.

Later on Bollard managed to add brandy tasting to his many skills which led to a violent attack of hiccups while in the presence of our guests and qualified him to share in the endless supply of Woodruff wit. This took some of the pressure off the Healys for which I imagine they were very grateful despite Bollard's English ancestry.

"From now on, Bollard," Pa said sweetly, "shall we let our guests decide on the relative merits of each drink?"

"If you'd prefer it, sir," said Bollard. "*Urp.*"

"With the exception of Mayor Healy," Pa added.

"Beg pardon, sir?"

"As an Englishman," Pa explained, "you are better qualified to judge what is right for the Irish than the Irish are."

"Quite right, sir."

That was one time Happy Healy did not laugh, but it was too late in the evening for anybody to care.

Anyway, Bollard didn't last long enough to enforce the sceptered weight of British authority. He soon passed out in a bubble bath which might have proved fatal had Mother not personally removed the plug.

"Thank heavens for the bubbles," Mother said later.

That's a fairly representative glimpse of the Woodruffs at play, but only at play. For the outside world of Gravenhurst et al we try to cultivate a somewhat more austere image. Though I wouldn't say the slogan "Nice guys finish last" quite captures the Woodruff idiom, it is certainly an accurate expression of family doctrine. As a result Pa's managed to cultivate a fair amount of respect around the area, plus a liberal salting of genuine hatred which, when added to what's been accumulated by previous generations, comes to quite a fair amount. In fact, it's hard to believe I'll be able to contribute much when my time comes, but probably anyone can be a son of a bitch with practice. It really looks like a long, uphill pull for me, though. I went to one of those small, wilted ivy colleges in New England because Princeton, feeling itself no match for the rising tide of public opinion, agreed my record was pretty uninspiring. This was sort of too bad because Tommy Compton, the City Judge's son, went to Harvard. The Comptons are neighbors of ours and very close friends, so naturally we were not pleased when they managed to outpoint us like that. About all I learned at college was how to stick out my lower jaw in order to look more like a regular fellow than I already did and how to butter up football players. It wasn't much of a start for the future champion of Woodruff tradition, but Pa was a pretty good teacher so I figured things would work out all right.

As it turned out, though, it wasn't really Pa who taught me. It was a fellow named Jesse Rosenfeldt. Now anyone could tell Jesse was no Irishman. He was no gentleman, either; at least not so far as Pa was concerned.

Jesse arrived in Gravenhurst in the spring, just a year after I started working full time for the paper. We knew somebody unwholesome was around because Mayor Healy came running over first thing to tell us all about it. I happened to be in Pa's office at the time. It was my first close glimpse of the mayor since that night four years before, and I must say he had turned into a pretty impressive-looking politico, even though Pa didn't seem to think so.

"Something rather interesting has come up, Clarence." Pa bent his ear and Mayor Healy was forced to repeat the statement in a less statesmanlike shout.

"That seems hard to believe," Pa said.

The mayor risked a look of impatience.

"It could be quite important," he said.

"I'm sure it *is*, Happy, my boy," Pa agreed. "Why else would a man of your stature venture out on such a hot day?"

"Clarence, a fellow came in to see me this morning," Happy Healy began. "A Jewish fellow."

Again the bent ear forced an undignified repeat.

"God help us," Pa said. "Was he armed?"

"Please, Clarence," the mayor shouted. "I'm just telling you what I know."

"All right. What did he want, Happy?"

"It was more or less, uh, confidential, Clarence."

"Perhaps you'd better not tell me then," Pa suggested patiently.

I was in a far corner of the office, checking the early edition for mistakes and trying not to laugh.

"I think it concerns the *Daily Watch,* Clarence," Mayor Healy explained.

"Then perhaps you should tell me," Pa agreed.

"All right. If I have your word it will go no farther than this room until we know exactly what the man is up to."

By then I was suffering from silent laughter and didn't notice he was eyeing me with suspicion.

"Don't worry," Pa reassured him. "Larry's with us."

I lowered the paper just long enough for a stern nod. "Rather cut out my tongue," I promised.

But the mayor was not quite such a jolly old Irishman as I had been led to believe. He gave me an angry look and turned back to Pa. "The man said he represented a large industrial concern," Mayor Healy began. "A large industrial concern," he repeated. "From New Haven. Told me they were thinking of starting a plant here in Gravenhurst which would employ some two thousand people."

"What kind of industry?" my father asked.

"That's what struck me funny," the mayor said. "He refused to say who his principals were. Started off asking the usual questions about size of labor force, water supply, housing, and like that, but then he got to asking about your newspaper and looking in onto a lot of things didn't seem like they had much to do with heavy industry."

"He did, did he?"

"Things like what people in town thought of the *Daily Watch* and the Woodruff family. I had the distinct feeling, Clarence, that he was more interested in your paper than my town."

"Well, you can hardly blame him for that," Pa said.

"I was trying to do you a favor, Clarence."

"Thanks, Happy, I appreciate that. How are things going over in City Hall?"

"Oh fine, Clarence. Just fine."

"I understand you've been having a little trouble with one of your policemen."

"That's right, Clarence."

"Hear he's been offering the ladies a chance to trade his speeding tickets for some of their more intimate favors. Is that about the size of it?"

"That's about the size of it, Clarence."

"Did you throw him off the force, Happy?"

"Well no, we didn't, uh, Clarence. But he was severely reprimanded."

"I think he should be thrown off, Happy."

"Well, you know, he's Clem Harper's, uh, cousin, and, uh . . ."

"Clem is chairman of the Republican City Committee," Pa finished. "As a matter of fact I didn't know they were related, Happy, but you can't let politics interfere with a question of duty."

"I agree with you one hundred percent, Clarence, but, well, next year is an election year, you know, and Clem and I already have our differences."

"I suppose you have a point there, Happy," Pa agreed. "Although there might not be so many differences if you'd stop running around with those Young Republicans and stick with Clem and me and the rest of the people who put you in office."

"I've got to play both sides of the fence there, uh, Clarence."

"Just don't play one side while the other one's looking," Pa said.

Mayor Healy laughed. "Which about sums up politics, doesn't it, Clarence? Somehow you always manage to get that thumb of yours right onto the center of things."

Pa tried not to show his pleasure but failed by just a bit.

"Now about that cop," the mayor reminded.

"All right, Happy, one more chance. But if you don't throw him off next time I'll splatter it all over page one. Is that clear?"

"Oh, you don't have to worry about that, Clarence. You don't have to worry about that at all."

"Well good. And thanks for the information, Happy. I appreciate it."

"Always glad to help a friend, Clarence. Always glad to help a friend when the opportunity presents itself."

"Good way to be," Pa said.

"Which reminds me," the mayor began.

"What?" Pa asked.

"Which reminds me, Clarence, the wife called this morning. She's chairman of the Animal Sympathy League, you know, and the ladies are dropping out to the Landscape Inn this evening for their annual dinner and strategy meeting you might say and she was wondering if the *Daily Watch* could send a photographer. Get a picture and do a little story, don't you know."

"I guess that could be arranged, couldn't it, Larry?"

"We're pretty busy, Pa," I said.

"I know," Pa agreed. "But I'm sure this ASL business is a very worthwhile, uh, thing."

"I'll tell Ned," I said.

"Sure would appreciate it," the mayor said, and he was on his feet with a hand out for Pa to rise and shake.

"Thanks again, Happy," Pa said.

"Not at all, Clarence. Not at all," and he left.

"What was all that about?" I asked.

"Damn newspaper scout," Pa told me. "Probably wants to start a competitive paper, but he'll soon find this isn't the right place."

"He sure will," I agreed.

"That goddam Irishman's getting too big for his britches," Pa grumbled.

"Since when has the *Daily Watch* become such a defender of the ASL?" I asked.

Pa shrugged. "Who's defending it?" he asked.

"Well," I laughed, "knowing what you think about them and all."

"And just what *do* I think about them?"

"Pseudosentimental ghouls," I said. "That's what you called them last week."

"When they stick their noses in conservation," Pa admitted. "I don't see much point in protesting the annual slaughter of deer when one realizes the animals will starve from overpopulation if they aren't shot."

"How about when they try to get an eight-hour-day for work horses?"

"I hadn't heard that one." Pa hedged.

"And double rations for singing canaries?"

"All right, Larry. That's enough of that. Just see to it the dinner is covered."

I tried to laugh, failed, got up to leave.

"And don't say anything about this newspaper scout or whatever he is," Pa warned. "Not until we're sure."

I nodded and went out, careful not to slam the door. Even though Pa was a little deaf he hated to see a door slam. It was as though he knew the noise would drive him nuts if he *could* hear it.

As luck would have it, there was more than one reason for trying to talk Pa out of exchanging favors with Mayor Healy: I was assigned to cover the professional animal lovers.

Well, that's life. I hung around the office awhile, brushing up a
feature story on the new low-income housing project which everybody was feeling pretty grand about although I wasn't entirely convinced that building a perpendicular slum would really be such a
great improvement over the horizontal one we already had. Except, of course, that it would confine the eyesore to a smaller area.
I don't want to seem cynical but personally I'd rather live in an old-
fashioned slum than one of those brick chamber pots and let the
money be spent trying to eliminate the cause of poverty rather than
making it more palatable. But what the hell, that's none of my business. I wrapped the story up with a tidy little quote from Mayor
Healy about Gravenhurst fulfilling its pledge to set an example for
county, state, and nation, thereby keeping my personal opinions
down to a shrug. It was only four o'clock by then so I picked up the
phone not knowing just what I was going to do with it and ended up
putting in a call to Hal James, junior partner in James, Fenton &
James, real estate and insurance brokers. Hal was about the best
friend I had, as far as I knew, with the possible exception of Tommy
Compton who was sort of peculiar and therefore more neighbor
than friend.

"Hal? Hey, boy, it's Larry . . . Not much. New with you? No dice,
got a date with the sheep lovers of America . . . No, no, Animal
Sympathy League. You know, love me love my dog . . . Listen,
want to take a run out to the airport, put in some time? Okay. Half
hour. Meet you out there."

There was no hurry since I knew Hal would be late. In fact I
knew just about everything Hal would be, or thought I did. We
grew up together. Went to grammar school, junior high, even prep
school, and would have gone to college together except he joined
the Army and then went to work for his old man. As a result we'd
probably have been close friends whether we wanted to or not. Hal
was a funny guy, funny ha ha, a genius for getting into trouble and
making people laugh about it instead of getting them sore and I had
some talents in the same direction so between the two of us we
managed to stir up a fair amount of action right from the beginning.
I can remember when we were about four or five throwing the cat
in the cesspool and both of us falling in after it: *plop, ploop ploop.*
A lovely sight, among other things. And how on rainy days I used to
go over to Hal's place and we'd get all dressed up in cowboy suits
except one day we changed the game and stuffed the suits and

strung them up from a rafter in the barn and Hal's Aunt Martha came in and oh boy could she scream. And then later the tentative, tiptoeing, scared brave way we tried to show each other we weren't afraid of girls and managed to pick up two specimens of that peculiar species and lure them back to the house when nobody was there and dance on the lawn cheek to cheek trembling with the mystery of it but each afraid to toss in the towel until we were able to achieve a kiss or two and retire with honor from the field of sex. We were about twelve then and it was at least two years before we managed to match the accomplishment and at least two more before we surpassed it. And there were other shared memories, not all of them funny. Not to us anyway. Like the time we both fell in love with Nancy Burrows, a perky-breasted, round-eyed fisher of adolescents who played the two of us until we lay exhausted at her feet, writhing and flopping and saying things like "I wish it didn't have to be you, Hal" and "No matter how it turns out we'll still be friends, okay?" until we both got dumped by a blonde, marceled baggy-pants from California. And it wasn't very funny when little Al Hanna, the only other hometowner in our class at prep school, got leukemia and died. All he was supposed to have was a cold and Hal and I were on our way to the infirmary for a visit when he came out all dressed with a nurse on each arm and one of them clucking "You should have told us about this sooner" and little Al all gray-faced and abstract-looking, just able to give us a vague smile and half a wave before they hustled him into the elevator and down to his grave. At least that's the way it seemed. They took him to the hospital but we never saw him again, and only the week before the three of us had managed to stash away a fifteen gallon barrel of cider in an old well behind the gym. I remembered he was kind of dragging at the time but Al was so full of chatter and ideas you hardly had time to notice if anything was wrong.

Anyway Hal and I had been through most everything there was to growing up together so we were pretty close and for the last couple of months we'd both been taking flying lessons on the theory life was kind of boring if you didn't spike it with a little action once in a while.

Well, for once old Hal fooled me. His car was already there when I got out to the airfield. I discovered why the second I walked into the office.

"Tell you the truth, Pete," he was telling the boss, "I don't run

around with those rates tucked away in the old head bone . . . Hey
Larry, howsa boy . . . But you let me take those policies along this
after and I'll get a report out on 'em first of the week."

"Well I dunno."

"What d'you mean you don't know? Worst that can happen is you
get a free analysis of your insurance coverage. Something for nothing, boy. Whaddayou nuts?"

"Okay," Pete laughed. "But I got obligations to Jensen and Company so maybe you beat the premium even then I can't give you
the business."

"Obligations?"

"They helped swing a loan."

"Oh hell, we'll help swing a bigger one." Hal laughed.

"Yeah," said Pete, doubting.

"Come on, come on." Hal pushed, still making it a joke, not joking.
"Gimme the policies."

"Okay," said Pete. "Arright, arright. Christ, you guys are all alike."

Hal laughed again. "We gotta eat too," he said.

Pete ducked into another room. Hal rolled his eyes hungrily. "I
should have been a minister," he whispered. "Just pass the plate
once a week and no hustling. What a life."

I laughed for lack of anything better. Hal on the make was still sort
of a stranger to me. Even his looks were different. He was a big guy
with a lot of dark brown hair and his ears tucked back tight and a
heavy, gentle jaw and soft, easy-natured features. He looked right
to me in a blue button-down shirt bagging out over khaki pants and
a pair of loafers flopping on sockless feet. But in his insurance brok-
ing outfit Hal was all wrong. Like his classbook photograph: Dark
suit and earnest features and Rotarianesque poses draped over the
old Hal with such care I sometimes forgot he was there at all. But
that's life. Everybody has to play his little game and I didn't care a
hell of a lot what the façade was just as long as the underneath part
survived.

Pete came back and surrendered the policies. Hal glanced over
them with a professional air, but I knew from previous experience
what he was doing. Calculating the commissions. That's all.

"We'll see what we can do for you, Pete," he said, as though Pete
had in fact been begging for the privilege.

"Find me the dough for a nice new Tripacer," Pete suggested.
"That's what you can do for me."

"Who knows?" said Hal with an air of mystery which was probably well grounded in fact.

"Yeah," Pete said. "That's what I was wondering."

Hal gave him a big laugh.

"You out here to fly or just con me?" Pete wanted to know.

"Both," Hal answered. "If you've got anything will get off the ground."

"Couple of J-3s," said Pete.

"With or without wings?" I asked.

"With," said Pete. "To start anyway," and he came out from behind the counter, looking more like a sheep herder in his flight boots and leather sheepskin-lined jacket. It was about two hundred and ten in the shade but not hot enough for him to separate himself from either jacket or boots which was just as well. He might have turned into a grocery clerk without them.

"They're all yours," Pete said, thumbing through the window at a couple of Piper Cubs parked close by. "I hope you got plenty of life insurance." He shoved through the door and we followed him out.

"Not me," said Hal, sounding indignant. "I don't believe in that crap."

"No?" Pete asked. "I thought you guys sold anything just so you made a buck."

"General insurance," Hal corrected. "That life stuff's for the hucksters. Anybody wants it we'll sell it but personally I'll take mutual funds with term life thrown in."

"Yeah, what's that?" Pete asked.

"It's so you don't have to die to win," Hal explained. "I'll bring out a couple of brochures next time."

"Jesus Christ," Pete moaned. "Hooked again. Gowan, I can't afford talking to you."

Hal laughed and swung the tail of his plane around and climbed in while Pete stood by waiting to turn her over for him. I watched until they got the engine going, then waved and climbed into the other one. Hal was a natural pilot and Pete said I was too, though I'm not so sure. With me it was mostly trying to keep up with Hal. In any case we both soloed in only seven hours and were greasing them in on the landings every once in a while which is when you hardly know whether you're down or not it's so smooth, but all the same when I stopped competing with Hal and started thinking I could get pretty tense. Not Hal, he flew like a robot. It was fantastic.

Not that he never made a mistake but he was always ready to compensate for it even before it looked bad. Once I made up my mind to land, for instance, that was it and if the glide was off or the stall too high I just came right on bouncing in and only a sure crackup could make me gun it and take her around again. But not Hal. He was never committed, just played it as it came, gliding, gunning, compensating gliding again just so long as there was enough field left to play with and when he finally got down it was *just* so. You had a feeling his mind and body were all he had to work with. Nothing rattled him. I was about halfway to the take-off point when he came roaring by, just starting to lift off but not too busy to make the old Jap grin and mouth "Melican you die" before pulling up and heading into that long shuddering, painful climb which is the time I'm least convinced airplanes are here to stay.

I braked and hauled back on the stick and revved her up to the mark while the little plane kicked and buffeted and threatened to shake apart, then checked my carburetor heat, swung onto the strip, took a deep breath and committed myself with a steady thrust on the throttle. She hesitated, teetered, then swung into motion, gathering power and confidence and stability until the plane and I were one and sure and the tail was up and I could feel power enough to lift clear and before I knew it the hangar and main office were turning into toys. I banked and found Hal swinging to the east toward Gravenhurst and went after him, laughing and talking to myself and whooping with the release and sheer pleasure of being alone and competent and unafraid.

I came up alongside him and we tried some not very precise precision flying and faked a couple of short landings where you cross your controls and go down like an elevator and we flew along the outskirts of Gravenhurst clustered like a rash on the green, gold and brown flanks of countryside spreading to the horizon on all sides and before we knew it the hour was almost up, we had to head back. I waved Hal in ahead so I could watch him go down and banked wide giving him plenty of time to get out of the way, then followed, dropping down and cutting the throttle when I got parallel to the edge of the field and starting the wide bank into my approach. I could see Hal coming in nicely and was betting he would grease it for sure when a Tripacer dropped out of nowhere, landing crosswind and my chest wrapped tight with fear and I started yelling, "Hal, look out, look out, look out" and stared in horror as the planes bore down, overlapped, then miraculously continued their separate ways, seeming to settle down with planned precision.

"Holy smoke." I was too scared to swear and I came in behind them, jittery, jumpy, damn near catching a wingtip and cracking up myself.

When I got in Hal was just climbing out and the Tripacer taxiing in toward us.

"You see him?" I asked.

Hal shook his head. "Not until he got past me," he admitted.

"Son of a bitch," I said. "That was close."

Hal nodded, shrugged, started to laugh, then Pete came up and he put on the serious face again. "Pretty close, huh?"

Pete nodded. "You gotta watch out for that bastard," he said.

"Who is it?"

"Vanden Gasser," Pete answered. "He'll land on Main Street you give him half a chance."

State Senator Vanden Gasser, Wilbur C. Vanden Gasser, whose name and campaign slogan—Vote for Wilbur, he's a Gasser—were the most appropriate I'd ever known. I'd heard about the flying senator and knew him, of course, since he was a good friend of Pa's but this was the first time I'd seen the guy in action.

"Where's he been?" Hal asked. "Haven't seen that Tripacer around before."

"Hartford most likely," I said.

"That's right," Pete confirmed. "And I wish he'd stay there while I still got some planes left."

The senator headed our way lugging an overstuffed suitcase. He was little and leather-faced with a mouth full of snow-white teeth and when he grinned there was no doubt but you were face to face with a pocket edition of the archetype politician. What made him different, though, was most of the time his grin or frown of sympathy or pistonlike nod of enthusiasm were genuine, for the senator's hobby was campaigning. He really liked people and therefore his re-election every two years was as certain as the tides and of about as much interest to his inland constituency. Fortunately, however, he managed to conceal a brain, a sense of responsibility and an abhorrence for political expediency beneath the façade of good-fellowship and thus was not the archetype politico at all. That the electorate was unaware of these qualities made no difference, of course. They simply went on supporting him for the usual absurd reasons, sublimely unaware of the virtues he so carefully and justifiably concealed.

He came toward us squinting, then grinning with recognition.

"Honored to be met by our working press," he laughed. "Especially one with the presence of mind to bring along an insurance broker. How are ya, Hal?"

"All right," said Hal. "No thanks to you."

The senator raised his eyebrows and looked at Pete.

"You almost clipped him coming in," Pete explained.

"Clipped who?"

"Hal," Pete said, shaking his head. "You came in right under him."

Senator Vanden Gasser pushed his glasses up on his forehead and pinched the soreness on the bridge of his nose. "Never saw you. Never saw you at all, Hal."

"That's okay," said Hal. "Just so you keep missing."

The senator nodded, tried to smile. "Guess I'm kind of tired," he explained. "Too damn much going on." The sound of a car turning in caught his attention. "Uh oh, there's the better half. See you around, boys," and he started for the door with as good an imitation of briskness as you're likely to find anywhere.

His kids beat him to it, exploding onto the field like an army of Lilliputians and bearing him off in a scramble of chaos and chatter and mock protestation from the senator.

The three of us stood there grinning.

"Great guy," I said. "Only decent politician in the county."

"If he'd just learn to fly," Pete suggested, "we'd be all set."

Hal laughed. "Come on, I'll buy you a drink."

"Got an assignment."

"All the more reason."

I shrugged. "See you, Pete."

"When the Gasser's out of town," Hal reminded.

"Yeah, take it easy boys," and we wandered out.

"What time you supposed to be there?" Hal asked.

"Seven-fifteen."

"Oh hell, you've got plenty of time. Let's go by the club?"

"You're buying. How can I refuse?"

"We'll see about that." Hal shook his fist, tossed an imaginary dice roll. "Four sixes in one," he said. "Let's see you beat it, boy."

I rolled him back. "Aces. Tough luck, Tiger." We both laughed, feeling the easy warmth and security of a lifetime friendship, hopped in our cars and spun out of there with casual confidence. If anyone ever had life right by the balls it was the two of us.

We wound up the country club drive past the string of Oldsmobiles and Buicks and occasional Caddys which signified a golf tournament most likely and managed to find a couple of parking places left by some early departers. The clubhouse was of colonial design and already looked old as hell even though it was only built ten years ago so we were pretty proud of it. They'd picked a site with some good big shade trees: elms and maples and a couple of oaks which if you made the mistake of thinking they were planted when the place was built, added quite a few years so it was really very nice. I've even heard people from Century Park complimenting it, reluctantly, of course. The women call it "sweet" and the men "cozy" which may give the impression it's kind of small and I suppose maybe it is though all those enormous plantation pillars in the front entrance sure make it *look* big.

Anyway, we liked it. They'd been having a tournament all right. The place was stuffed with chitchatters and guffawers and big, circular, tight-lipped smilers. We nodded and waved and howdy-dooed our way through the Great Room and into the Oak Bar. The place was dripping with the bright colors of summer fashion plus, I'm ashamed to say, a certain amount of nondeodorized sweat. The bar ran full length and we stood facing a line of variously decorated backs and behinds; a medley of two-ply lisle knit shirts with action free, gusseted arm insets, wash'n wear with convertible rib-knit collars in Tamarack green, Tiger tan, Desert downy, and Yachting blue plus an assortment of other exciting new colors carefully designed and engineered to flatten the belly, bulge the bicep and otherwise make his lordship sexy as hell. At least until the moment of truth; that is the moment when he most needs to be sexy, being required to remove his clothes, let the flab flop and flump into bed with his by then somewhat nonplused lady love.

Well what the hell. I'm no reformer.

We squeezed our way to the bar with a volley of "Howsa boys" and "Not much, s'new with you" and the like and settled down mid a flow of all but incomprehensible golf talk.

I turned to Hal. "You on the wagon or something?"

"No. What's it gonna be?"

"Martini."

"Make it two," Hal announced. "Two martinis with a twist," he called. "And make 'em real dry, huh, Mac. Just a sniff, huh, boy, you know what I mean." He winked at me and reached for the dice cup. "Now. Prepare to meet your maker."

"Shutup and roll," I said, looking knowledgeable.

"Four fives all day," said Hal, disgusted. "But it's too good for you."

"Yeah?" I scattered the dice. "Four sixes. Congratulations, Daddy-o, you've just been made a host."

Hal groaned and reached for the bar chit. I laughed and lifted the drink with ritualistic care, lest any of it spill, and tipped it to my lips, serious, reverential, all my senses turned inward to the enjoyment of this belly-burning alcoholic communion.

"Ahhh," I approved. "Thanks a bunch, Hal boy."

"I'll getcha," he warned. "Just wait'll number two."

And he was right. Both two and three went on the Woodruff bill but I didn't care, in fact considered it a rare accomplishment to slide the old bar chit over and embellish it with *C W IV*.

I started to tell Hal about our newspaper scout, then remembered Pa's warning and realized the martinis were beginning to loosen me up a little. "Gotta go," I said. "Goddam sheep lovers'll lynch me."

Hal laughed. "Ah stick around. You can pick up the story later."

"Uh uh." I swallowed a belch. "Gotta go. S'quarter seven. Gotta pick up a camera." I happened to glance at the bar mirror and saw Lou Baine, our sports editor, standing in the door, rolling his shoulders like a fighter and wondering who he could con for a drink. "Hey Lou baby," I called. "Lend me your camera I'll buy ya drink."

Lou came over, short stocky, built and dressed like a Tuesday night bowler, not happy in the pastel sophistication of our beautiful Gravenhurst Country Club. "Buy me a drink," he said. "And I'll give ya the goddam camera."

"Got any film packs?"

"Two."

"It's a deal," I said. "You know Hal James, don'tcha."

"I dunno. Yeah, I seen you aroun', huh." Lou stuck out a beer-fattened arm for Hal to shake, then squeezed between us for anonymity, looked around, muttered: "Jeez, what a bunch a turkeys, huh?"

Hal and I laughed democratically.

"What'llya have?" I asked.

Lou shrugged. "Ah, rye'n ginger."

We ordered two more martinis for no good reason and when the chit came I reached for it seeing as Lou was my idea but Hal held up his hand in a gesture filled with largess and brotherly love.

"S'your funeral," I told him graciously.

And while we were finishing that one Hal asked, "How come you have to go to the whole goddam dinner just to take a lil' picture?"

And I couldn't think of a reason.

"I mean that's kinda silly, isn't it?"

"Kinda," and I managed to conjure up a mental image of all those animal lovers sitting around munching on overdone roast beef and telling each other what a shame it was for people to go hunting and killing things and all as though roast beef were plucked from a tree or something. As far as they're concerned it's perfectly okay to bonk a nice fat old unsuspecting Hereford bull over the head just so long as he's well marbled but shoot a deer and eat it, why Mercy, that's practically murder. Or shoot a dog that's known to have killed a bunch of deer, why sake's alive, dog's a man's best friend. Wipe your mouth, dear, it's all greasy.

"Hell with the sheep lovers," I announced.

"Attaboy," Hal agreed. "Tell you what, we'll drop down to the Napoli, have a nice big spaghetti dinner, bottle of dago, then run over to the dinner so you can get your picture. Okay? How 'bout it, Lou?"

"Suits me," said Lou. "I got nuttin' going."

"But don't let me miss that picture, okay?" I begged.

"Don' worry 'bout it," Hal assured me.

Pretty soon the athletes spotted Lou and began coming over to make sure he could spell their names and to explain just what it was other than incompetence which prevented them placing first so we got the hell out and went down to the Napoli, a chrome, plastic, and jukebox emporium with about the best guinea food in town. And some pretty good wine too.

I managed to soothe my aching conscience by frequently reminding everybody about my obligations to the Animal Sympathy League, an indulgence which didn't seem to interfere with their plans much and made me feel a whole lot better.

By nine o'clock, assisted by and assisting Messrs. Baine and James, I managed to put in an appearance at the annual dinner of the ASL.

Well boy, I don't mind saying it was anybody's guess what would

1

happen next. This Lou Baine was turning out to be quite a sport. I mean he was *loaded*. And Hal and I were a couple of wild men, as was well known, so I didn't envy those ASL people one bit. Anything might happen and I mean *anything*. We'd all driven out in my car, planning along the way how we could really screw things up at the dinner. It was going to be something! Nothing violent of course. Just some pretty funny questions like how did they feel about oral contraception for rabbits and was it true some of their best friends were coons and did anybody have any idea—in round numbers to be sure—how much wood a woodchuck could chuck if a woodchuck could chuck wood? Roughly. Oh we were in great shape all right. Just how Hal, being an insurance and real estate broker, would fit in to all this sort of stumped us until we fell upon the idea of selling travel insurance to ducks.

Ha!

Anyway, we got to the Landscape Inn, stumbled through the bar entrance, me in the lead, and headed for the banquet room. It wasn't long before I realized I was traveling alone and looked back to find the boys waving in a reassuring, be-right-with-you way. I dismissed them and kept on going alternately promising myself to carry on in reckless, devil-may-care fashion and trying to sober up.

I got there just as the final speaker sat down, giving me an opportunity to nod apologetically at Mrs. Healy, the chairman, after which I huddled in a corner waiting until she adjourned the meeting and deeply resenting the ASL for having caused my courage to falter. All those old biddies glowering at me. It was too much. But would Marlon Brando's courage have faltered? Paul Newman's? Certainly not. I resented the ASL all the more.

Then when the meeting broke I apologized quite soberly to Mrs. Healy, explaining that something rather unexpected had come up and discovering with some surprise that she hadn't expected me at the dinner anyway. Only afterward for a photograph and a little rundown of the evening's business. Therefore, as far as she and the others were concerned, I had not as yet been the least bit remiss. It was all very discouraging.

Then luck came my way. I spotted a row of stuffed animal heads at the end of the room—a moose, two deer, one fox, a bobcat—and subtly, rather smugly, gathered the Animal Sympathy League members under this assortment of hunting trophies for their annual picture. It was all too good to be true: A chance to be absolutely fiendishly game without their ever knowing it was intentional. What luck! I aimed the camera and almost laughed out loud at the thought of telling Lou and Hal about my marvelous *coup*. Then the risk of possible repercussions sobered me and I lowered the camera, sheepishly cutting all stuffed heads—at least the dead ones—from my shot.

Slack! went the camera.

"Hold it. Just one more please."

Slack! And I hurried over to be sure all the names were properly spelled.

"Mrs. Arnold S. Gould, isn't it?"

"Yes."

"And Mrs. Rutherford Bates, right?"

"Larry, you ought to know that," she giggled.

They live close by. She has a son younger than me. I've always wanted to ask how young Master Bates is but haven't been able to get up the nerve yet.

"And Mrs. Robert . . ."

"Hey Larry, where'sa mother humping shitpot 'round here?"

I turned. The silence was like stale thick soup. There was Lou swaying in the doorway, no-necked, sallow, squinting in confusion, baffled by my inability to answer.

"Gotta fine shitpot," he explained. "Gotta blow lunch." And as though to emphasize the urgency of his request, he vomited on the floor.

"Excuse me," I begged tactfully, made a dash for the staggering Lou and rushed him out the door in a trail of sickness and muffled cries of horror from the good ladies of ASL.

So we managed to upset the status quo after all, though not quite as planned.

The rest of the evening is hardly worth remembering.

Next day Lou was fired. Nobody seemed to know or care to mention that I had actually been with him. I guess Mrs. Healy didn't want to be known as a troublemaker. It was a tough break but there wasn't much I could do other than express my sympathies. After all, it wouldn't do for the publisher's son to beg special considerations for an employee whether it had anything to do with me or not. I'm sure Lou would have understood this but he left town so fast I never found out.

CHAPTER II

It was at least three weeks before we actually met Jesse Rosenfeldt, though we had managed to find out quite a lot about him. I was taken off police and general assignments in order to polish up my spying talents. It wasn't too hard to keep track of his activities around town, nor was it hard to verify that the newspaper was his main interest. Everywhere he went his questions inevitably got around to the *Daily Watch* and what people thought of it. And he went everywhere: the radio station, which was the closest thing we had to a competitor and could be counted on to tell all; most of the big stores; the schools; and just everyday people he happened to strike up conversations with on the street or in some diner or bar. He even managed to get one of our linotype operators loaded so he could pump him on the size of our shop and caliber of equipment. Needless to say all this was something less than ideal groundwork for a beautiful friendship between Jesse Rosenfeldt and the Old Man.

But the biggest news of all was about Jesse himself and his family. I happened to drop by Hal James's office one afternoon when he was wheeling and dealing with some New Haven real estate broker. It was a good thing I did. I mean it was a lucky break that New Haven guy happened to be there. We knew a few things about Jesse and his old man by then but most of it came under the heading of statistics. Just knowing it was a Rosenfeldt snooping around, for instance, told us plenty. Most everybody in the state's heard of Rosenfeldt Realty. But judging by the look on his face when I mentioned the name, this guy knew a little more than we did.

According to him, the Blockbusters, as they were called by a not very intimate circle of competitors, had quite a system going for them. In fact it was downright poetic if you didn't happen to be on the losing end. It seems way back about a hundred years ago Great-Great-Grandpappy Rosenfeldt discovered his infallible formula just about the time he'd made a few bucks in the import business and was scouting around for a new place to live. Apparently somebody pointed out to him the adverse effect his mere presence could have on certain residential property values and from then on Mr. Rosenfeldt was up to his neck in real estate. First he got himself a silent partner name of Hooker who claimed to be a direct descendant of Reverend Thomas Hooker, alias "Son of Thunder," one of the founders of the Connecticut Colony. Whether he was or not didn't really matter just so long as he agreed to move into one expensive, elegantly restricted Yankee neighborhood after another, handing each in turn over to Mr. Rosenfeldt for the final *coup de grâce*. This consisted merely of spreading the word that a Jew had somehow squeezed through the gates of Christendom, after which it was only a matter of time before neighboring property values for miles around went down flatter than the walls of Jericho. Communications not being quite what they are today, Mr. Rosenfeldt was able to work this gambit all the way from Greenwich to the Rhode Island border without ever being accepted, tolerated or otherwise abused. By the time he was through Great-Great-Grandpappy Rosenfeldt was just about the biggest real estate operator on the eastern seaboard, except for his son, of course, who turned out to be bigger, and his son's son who turned out to be bigger still and finally Benjamin Rosenfeldt, Jesse's father, biggest of them all. But by the time Benjamin came along, making money in real estate was almost as easy as printing it in the basement and he soon developed a taste for riskier forms of acquisition. Among other things, he liked to take an occasional flier at some highly speculative manufacturing, merchandising, or business opportunity which the average investor, for one reason or another, was afraid to touch. These projects, at least the ones which survived, were now managed by Jesse and his three brothers under a parent company called Venture, Inc.

Well, as it happens, the newspaper business is crawling with highly speculative investment opportunities these days. A combination of circumstances has conspired to put the squeeze on publishers across the country, and many communities where two and even three dailies once thrived are now down to one. As far as we're concerned that's fine. I mean there's nothing like having a monopoly even if it's a small one but, if pushed to the wall, I guess even we'd admit the *Daily Watch* gets a little sluggish sometimes from lack of competition plus a need to hold the line on spending. On the other hand, we weren't about to try anything new unless we absolutely had to. Why should we? I mean Pa knew as well as anybody else there were plenty of new typesetting and printing processes around, some of them pretty good, others not much better than our conventional setup, all of them representing automation in one of its lifeless, antiseptic forms or another. But with heavy investments in the old-fashioned, yet perfectly adequate equipment why should we fool around with something new? After all, just because it happened to be new didn't mean it was necessarily worth doing. It's the contents of a paper that count anyway, not the format, but even more important, there's an intangible factor in the newspaper business—something you could call spirit for lack of a better word—which feeds not on progress, but its direct opposite. Putting out a newspaper the way we do it is a daily drama steeped in five hundred years of legend and tradition. Its principal characters are the linotype machine, veins pumping molten lead, fingers delicately collecting, measuring lines of type, and the rotary press, belly full of newsprint, soul full of thunder. The setting is a back room reeking, shrieking with heat, sweat, steam, scrap metal, discordant noises, both human and mechanical. The supporting characters are a rugged breed of men who share one admirable flaw; namely a somewhat romantic (though by no means philanthropic) devotion to the printing trade. And well they might, it's essentially hot, heavy work and a man's job and fully as romanticized as war.

To trade all this in for a phosphorescent morgue filled with ticking automatons just so we could pay tribute to an abstraction called progress seemed kind of foolish to us. Sure the *Daily Watch* was old-fashioned, but you could feel it, you could hear it, you could smell it. It was *alive*.

Anyway, maybe I've protested too much, but that's why we haven't gone in for any of this new stuff. That plus the fact we were making money as is and had nothing to worry about on that score. At least until the Rosenfeldts started poking around.

When Pa first heard about them he thought maybe they were going to try out some of this automation stuff on us, but after snooping around a little we soon found out their motives weren't quite so complicated. A weekly tabloid had gone bust someplace outside of New Haven and the aggregate joys of finding himself a bargain and competing in a business no one else would touch with a two-dollar bill was just too much for Ben Rosenfeldt to resist. Also the chance of knocking over a couple more Yankees and getting his thumb into the state political pie might not have been entirely repulsive to him.

Whatever his reasons, it looked like the Rosenfeldts were in Gravenhurst to stay. For a while anyway.

In hindsight, it seems silly to have gone gumshoeing after Jesse, trying to find out what he was up to. As it turned out, all we would have had to do was ask him. He came right to the house one evening. Just sort of walked in. I guess he figured about the only way to get close to Pa was by sneaking up on him, which was pretty good figuring. Actually he hit it just right. We were having some of the Junior Chamber of Commerce over for drinks so all Jesse had to do was walk in and help himself. I noticed him because, having had the unequaled privilege of covering the Junior Chamber weekly lunches, he was the only guy there I didn't know at least by sight. But the Old Man had met almost none of them which was why we were having the party in the first place and I guess Jesse must have figured this out because he looked just as carefree as a puppy. Of course I didn't know who it was at the time, but he stuck out from everybody else for a number of reasons. In the first place, he was one of the ugliest men I'd ever laid eyes on, and in the second place, somehow it looked good on him. He had a prize fighter's nose which might have been Semitic once, but was now equally apportioned across both sides of his face. He was fat, the way a deceptively strong man is fat. Solid, squat, more mastiff than man. His eyebrows were heavy black and went all the way along the top of his face— not his forehead because he didn't have one—like the fenders and runningboard of a Model-T Ford. He had pie plates for ears and a lower lip that looked like a squashed pink marshmallow. And on top of it all he was noticeably short. Yet somehow, despite all this, he seemed a stack and a half above the rest of the people in the room, Woodruff family excluded of course. Partly it was the way he dressed. He wore a suit and a vest and a large gold watch chain with all kinds of fourteen-carat accomplishments dangling from it and he didn't seem at all inclined to ingratiate himself with Clarence Woodruff, the Third. Perhaps that's what set him apart more than anything. Almost everybody else in the room seemed to be drifting toward Pa and that carefully planned intimacy which would leave them wrenching their neck muscles with pleasure once performed. But not this one. He just drank and watched with the hint of a private joke twitching one corner of his monumental mouth.

Now as it happens, I'm not very good at walking up and speaking to strangers because, being from Gravenhurst, I've never met very many, but I would have risked it with this one. That is if he hadn't spoken to me first. At the time I was having one of those nice little talks with the community-minded which makes most newspaper people want to take gas.

"Say Larry, how'bout little coverage on our Jaycee exhibition out to the County Fair. Real swell job. Something special, you know. Lot of the boys put in extra time on this one."

"What is it?"

"Supposed to be a secret, Larry boy, but I'll tell you." It seems everybody has a secret in Gravenhurst which they're all willing to share.

"That's swell," I said.

"It's a display," he told me, his eyes popping with excitement. "A display showing the development of industry in Gravenhurst since the area was first settled."

"How about that," I said. Since Gravenhurst is primarily a produce center and has almost no industry at all, I welcomed an interruption.

"I beg your pardon, but aren't you Larry Woodruff?" It was one of those nonregional accents which, by a strange paradox, one usually finds at such provincial places as Harvard University.

"That's right."

"Well good. I'm Jesse Rosenfeldt."

"How'd you get here?" And I'm afraid it was admiration rather than annoyance which motivated the question.

"By joining the Junior Chamber of Commerce," Jesse Rosenfeldt explained. And he added, "I was desperate" in an aside which was missed by his fellow members.

"I doubt my father will be overjoyed."

"That occurred to me," Jesse admitted. "But I thought it might be worth a try. Anything to prevent bloodshed, ha ha ha, if you know what I mean."

I soon learned Jesse had a funny way of laughing—it was almost a bark—when dealing with something potentially unpleasant. Especially if there was any possibility he might be the source of unpleasantness.

"Then you're definitely going to set up shop?" I asked. By that time we'd managed to withdraw to a quiet corner of the room.

"Definitely."

"And you'll be what?"

"The publisher."

"How old are you?" I asked.

"Your interviewing techniques are fairly instinctive, aren't they?"

"Sorry."

"Thirty."

"That's pretty young for publishers."

"Especially when they have no newspaper experience," Jesse added.

"None at all?"

"None," Jesse confirmed. "On the other hand I've had some experience in the jungle of commerce and industry, ha ha ha, and one can always hire people with newspaper experience. Especially these days." I shrugged. "Now let's have another drink and celebrate," he went on. "Be nice to have a little friendly competition, don't you think? Put some life in that old poop sheet of yours."

"Perhaps you should meet my father. To get some idea just how friendly things will be."

"Now that would be splendid," Jesse smiled. "But let's get the drink first."

Having expected my introduction to bring sensational results, I was sadly disappointed. At first anyway.

"Well well," Pa said amiably. "So you're the fellow who's bringing big industry to Gravenhurst."

"Lying is something of a hobby with me," Jesse said.

"You're in the right business," Pa said. "Decided to start that paper yet?"

"Oh I thought we might give it a try."

"Fine, fine," Pa boomed. "Could use a little competition around here. Keep us on our toes. But how'd you come to pick this community?"

By that time Gravenhurst's busy builders had postponed their ounce of unction and gathered around the contestants. The heavy concentration soon attracted Mother.

"Oh we shopped around a bit," Jesse began.

"Excuse me, Mr. Rosenfeldt," Pa interrupted. "I'd like you to meet my wife."

"How do you do," Jesse said.

"This is Mr. Jesse Rosenfeldt," Pa explained. "Our future competitor."

Mother offered a nod and a smile, both tiny but not meant to be ungracious, only to shorten the interruption.

"Mr. Rosenfeldt was just telling us how he came to select Gravenhurst as the field of battle," Pa explained.

"It's all quite simple," Jesse said. "We surveyed some fifty small
cities, as I remember it, and Gravenhurst seemed the most likely
place for competition."

"Because it's a growing community, I suppose," Pa said.

"Actually not," Jesse replied. "It was because your paper seemed
like the easiest one to knock off."

That was the first time I ever saw Pa flustered. "We'll see about
that," he snapped and walked away.

The Jaycees surrounding us sighed as one man and drifted after
him. Only Mother and I remained.

"The last paper tried to compete with us lasted six months," I
said.

"But that was fifteen years ago," Jesse reminded me. "Times
change."

"It's a good paper," I said. "Everybody knows that."

"Depends on who you talk to," said Jesse. "A lot of people think
it's rather bad. My apologies, Mrs. Woodruff."

"That's quite all right, Mr. Rosenfeldt." Mother had a serenity
about her which seemed almost mystical sometimes. It was so powerful I'm sure she could have stepped into the middle of a street
brawl and had everyone sipping tea in no time. "But what interests
me," Mother continued sweetly, "is the importance you seem to
attach to whether our paper, as you so tactfully put it, is 'rather
bad' or not."

"I beg your pardon?" Jesse looked confused for a change.

"Your concern for the quality of our paper, Mr. Rosenfeldt,"
Mother continued. "I find it rather baffling."

"I find it rather essential." Jesse smiled.

"There are many other factors which we consider quite as important," Mother said.

Jesse began to look from right to left, as if he had just stepped off
the bus and discovered it to be the wrong stop. "Such as local tradition, I suppose, and community loyalty and things like that," he said.

"Precisely," Mother confirmed.

"Being a businessman," Jesse went on, "and not an anthropologist,
I wouldn't know about such matters."

"Precisely," Mother repeated.

Jesse realized he was coming unstitched and took the necessary steps to protect his nudity. "It's been delightful. But I must run along now."

"Of course," Mother said. "Do come again."

We exchanged nods, he and I, and then he ran away.

"Round one, Woodruff," I said.

"He seemed very nice," Mother said. "I hope he understood."

"I doubt it, they usually don't."

"They?" Mother asked, and again I found myself faced with the choice of risking controversy or running.

Sam Crawley, the fellow with the County Fair exhibit, showed signs of heading my way.

"Oh excuse me, Mother," I muttered. "There's something Sam and I have to talk about."

I turned away before she had a chance to raise her eyebrows.

"Say Sam," I said. "About that exhibit of yours . . ."

"Yes, well I did want to give you a brief summation of just what it is we fellows are attempting to achieve."

"Yes," I said, wondering why only seconds before it had seemed so necessary to avoid controversy.

"You see we feel us Jaycees have a moral obligation to demonstrate the hidden industrial potential of this pokey old burg . . ."

Anything was better than listening to this pink-cheeked, wet-lipped zealot.

"No sense being afraid to show our stuff," he continued. "After all, only way we'll ever attract the big boys is to show we're sympathetic to industry, understand their problems from our own experience and are willing to pitch in and work alongside 'em shoulder to shoulder." He had a shy, unsure way of looking up from under a set of wispy straw lashes to see how his spiel was going over. That he felt the need to do this was Sam's only saving grace.

"Like to have you talk to Hugh Godkin about this," he continued. "Hugh's special assistant in charge of exhibits."

"Like to," I lied.

Godkin was a little fellow about my own age, neatly packaged in wash'n wear suit and permanently noncommittal smile. He aroused in me about as much curiosity as would a carefully wrapped pork chop in the supermarket. I'd known him in junior high school but had lost track since. In those days piety was his primary concern, his father being the Presbyterian minister, and he therefore made everybody a little nervous. I remember his entering a bull session once to tell us sex was the most beautiful and sacred gift God had bestowed upon mankind which may or may not have been so but at the time was monumentally beside the point.

We talked much too long, Hugh and I. He was so sincere and so enthusiastic about the goddam Fair I was afraid to cut him off for fear he'd burst into tears, but finally the need for a drink gave me an excuse to take off and I kept right on going. The urge to get away from all those Jaycees was as pressing as a full bladder and once accomplished the relief was just as comforting.

I guess it must be pleasant sport to look down on a place like Gravenhurst from the Olympian heights of one of those supposedly liberated big cities I've heard so much about, but having to *live* in it is something else again. I mean what could be nicer than sitting in your lofty tower—or towering loft, as the case may be—and writing one of those definitive sociological exposés on the jerks who live someplace else? All that split-level crap, for instance. Being a hick from the provinces, I am unable to think of a fitting word to describe just how jolly it must be and so must borrow from the sophisticated vocabulary of a metropolitan nymph whose path once crossed mine: It must be "funzees." But I had to live in Gravenhurst, not study it, and so the theory everybody was nuts except me was not "funzees" at all.

CHAPTER III

I went up to my room, changed into old clothes and sneaked down the back stairs. Whenever things weren't going as they should in the social department I usually headed for the lake or one of the trout streams that drained it, or just out into the woods someplace. Then life wasn't quite so complicated. At least not for me because I didn't belong there and didn't have to worry about doing the right thing in order to stay.

That evening I chose the lake. It was about a mile square and the twilight calm left it cool and black and soothing as eternity. The only other house was Mayor Healy's and it couldn't be seen from the water, as per agreement when we sold him the lot, so the wilderness seemed real enough and I was almost never aware that it lay

only a few hundred yards from the chrome and clatter of Gravenhurst. Neither was the wildlife which inhabited those three or four
miles of woods along and beyond our northern shore line. It was
there that I headed, paddling slowly and gently in the hopes of
surprising a deer or two come to feed on the sweet, tender grasses
in the shallow spots. The splashing of a bass as he drove his prey
through the reeds sounded grotesque in the silence. A hawk left
his lookout, lazed through the soft evening air and disappeared. A
brace of native duck, flushed from their nesting place, labored in a
vertical, painful climb and the rhythm of my paddling linked me in
a timeless chain with past and future and the never-ending beat of
life which had touched the lake and left it forever changed yet
somehow always the same. Each ripple held a secret not to be
shared but existing nonetheless. My boyhood was hidden here.
Somewhere in the blackness were changes my life had brought.
Each stone I'd hurled to make rippling targets, each fish I'd caught,
each bird, snake, turtle I'd shot had altered the lake's existence to
an infinitesimal yet infinite degree. And in return it had altered
me, for here I watched life come and go and come again, unconscious, unconcerned, enviable. Yes, enviable, for in the lake's un-
consciousness lived only instinct, a mindless, spineless mass of
muscle and juice triggered by the immediate presence of danger,
desire, appetite. Here no longing lived, no anxiety, no threat of
inconsequence. It was a state of being which the people of Gravenhurst, myself included, seemed eager to recapture. The forbidden
fruit of self-consciousness, self-awareness, gnawed our guts and
though we did our best to ease the pain with a soft diet of affluence
and trivia, it persisted. Perhaps this was why I loved that lake so.
Somewhere in its depths lay the key to . . . well to eternity, maybe,
or oblivion, and I came looking for it every chance I got.

The lake was kind that evening but often it was not. I'd seen it
boil with the hatred of a summer storm, but worse still, I'd seen it
cold and hard and white with winter death, its crust flecked with
the bodies of deer brought down by dog packs in a gnashing, slavering pageant without purpose, for the deer were only killed, not
eaten. And I'd seen it in the early spring, gentle to look at but still
treacherous and rotten as old soup with the thawing death of winter-
time.

But that evening no death showed. There was only gentleness.
From the middle I could make out a doe and her fawn feeding

along the far shore listening only for the kind of danger which came yowling and yapping or tromping and swearing through the woods and not aware of the kind that slipped across water. I was less than fifty yards away before they began to notice me. First the fawn, curious more than anything else, watching and munching with mild interest. Then her doe, more careful perhaps but no more inclined to run; not until that fatal curiosity had been satisfied. Only twenty-five yards before the tails flicked and sent them tiptoeing to shore and finally into the rocking rhythm of flight. I could hear the high-pitched snorts of danger as their warning was picked up and passed along by other deer working their silent, secret way to water.

It seemed hard to believe I was less than thirty minutes away from the false frolic of Woodruff Hill. I could picture Pa hiding his boredom in smiles and occasional laughter while Mother cast a spell of warmth and understanding which would strip the fledgling boosters of their civic feathers and leave them yes-ma'aming and no-ma'aming like frightened children. It wasn't so very long ago that Mother's way of doing things had seemed stereotyped and silly to me but that was during those rebellious college years which even we provincials allow ourselves in moderation. Now that I was beginning to grow up—or capitulating, as the case may be—Mother's Olympic concern with the social graces didn't seem quite so absurd. A few social ants in the pants, or angst in the pangst as it's become these days, couldn't do any harm. Not in moderation, I mean. What bothered me a little was whether Mother's approach could be called moderate. Take the fact that my sister Abby, who was twenty, hasn't been around much the last few years. That's because Mother has been busy squeezing her through the social strainer. As a result, the most likely place to find Abby was down on Long Island or one of the other debutante hunting grounds where in the spring and fall of every year a relatively rare game bird known as the St. Grotlesexer can be stalked. Now the St. Grotlesexer, as many people know, is prized for a number of reasons: He is expensive to raise; selectively bred, though an occasional secretary bird has been known to damage the line; relatively hard to find; and despite complaints that his is an acquired taste, considered a great delicacy by those who are supposed to know. Thus it was natural for Mother, who might be described as something of a social gourmet, to send Abby in search of such a prize.

To put it another way, Abby was our bridge between Graven-

hurst Pond and Eastern Seaboard and Mother was determined not
to let her wash out. Pa thought it was a lot of hokum, as did Abby,
but Mother was determined, so that was that. Still, it would be unfair to call her preoccupation with the social climb immoderate because that kind of thing came naturally to Mother and she didn't
spend too much time at it. The whole business was more challenge
than pretension with her. Having mastered one area of social mechanics she couldn't resist looking for new territory to conquer.
Thus, once the Gravenhurst terrain had been explored and tamed,
it was natural for her to take a bead on the national scene.

Of course, having a daughter like Abby made things much more
challenging because she was kind of above all that. I don't mean
above in a superior way. Abby was the family poem. Everything
she said or did had the light lyrical quality of a dream. Socially
she was as unreliable as a spring day and I think Mother found that
exhilarating. When her morning coffee sessions for community-
minded ladies became tiresomely uncomplicated by social crises all
she had to do was be sure Abby was there. And when Abby performed predictably, Mother never seemed to mind. Instead she took
it as a challenge and set about rebuilding those walls of propriety
which her daughter had managed to collapse. I remember one such
session a few years ago. Abby was just home from boarding school
and looking deceptively innocent. She is little and has an impudent
little girl's face which helps perpetrate the fraud of innocence. I
happened to be in the house at the time, so we were both invited
to play "and you must meet my darling children." Everybody knew
me from working summers on the paper so Mother didn't waste
much time trying to sell them a bill of goods on my score. With
Abby, though, it was a different story.

"It's so nice having Abby home from boarding school," Mother
told the ladies. "She loves it there . . . Don't you, dear?"

"Oh boy," said Abby.

"But we miss her terribly."

"Where does she go?" someone asked cooperatively.

"St. Mary's," Mother said. "It's a rather intimate little school in
Virginia."

"We sent our Jane to Gravenhurst High," one of the more aggressive ladies said. "That way we have her to home."

"I envy you," Mother smiled sweetly. "But we wanted Abby to
see a little of the country, you know."

"Our Jane takes a bus trip to Florida every spring," the aggressive lady said. "She stays with her daddy's people in Fort Lauderdale."

"How lovely," Mother said.

"Mother, is Fort Lauderdale intimate too?" Abby asked.

"Would anyone like some more coffee?" Mother asked. "Good. Cream and sugar? Just black. But as I was saying, we do miss Abigail. And you, Mrs. Akers? One lump, I believe. Yet it's such an attractive school and Abby loves it so, we just couldn't bear to take her away. Mrs. Berry? No? It was a bit strong, wasn't it. But we're so proud of Abby, you know. She was just elected president of her class."

"Now that's nice," the aggressive lady said. "My Jane's class secretary. Tell me, dear, did you have to campaign and make speeches and like that?"

"Not exactly," Abby said. "There were only eight girls in the class."

"But how were you elected, dear?"

"We drew straws . . . And I lost."

"Ah ha ha hah," Mother laughed gently. "Abby, you're killing. Now run along, both of you. That's enough silliness for one morning."

And off we went while Mother happily set about repairing the damage. But that was quite a while ago and now Abby's a big girl, figuratively speaking, about to start her senior year of college, which is not to suggest she has become more conventional in her old age, but rather more adept at her old tricks.

I looked at my watch. It was after seven and Pa would have my head if I kept him from dinner which was just about his favorite sport nowadays. I turned the canoe around and headed back to my own world with a good deal more speed but far less grace than I had left it.

The very next day things began to change around the Gravenhurst *Daily Watch*. As might be expected Pa's reaction to Jesse Rosenfeldt was not a passive one and he wasted no time making the fact painfully clear. Pa worked hard, played hard, and expected everybody else to do the same. Of course we're not all built that way, but if you wanted to work for Clarence Woodruff, the Third, that's how it had to be. To me he was a real capitalist in the old-time American tradition. A slugger. So right away things began to shape up around our shop, just as Jesse predicted they would. It really didn't seem like there was much to be shaped up, but I guess even the toughest businessmen go soft when the nest becomes a little too well feathered.

Nothing could be done about the *Daily Watch* building itself, short of moving out. It backed onto the railroad tracks so we wouldn't have to tranship our newsprint, but that meant we weren't exactly in the town's prime location. City Hall was across the street which was a help to the reporters, but didn't do much for the architectural atmosphere. Just a gray, shapeless pile of stone droppings. And aside from City Hall, nothing but bars, diners, abandoned stores with some pretty sorry people living above and the political headquarters of State Senator Vanden Gasser. But it wasn't a depressing street. Maybe because I'd known it so long. I can remember way back when the railroad still maintained its passenger service and all the stores were full and there was a kind of nervous prosperity in the area because of the life-bringing train. It was an eager street then. Now it was grim, ugly, and tired. But when you've known something for a long time, how it looks or feels doesn't matter; it's still a part of your life and so you like it. Take the *Daily Watch* building, for instance. That was a mess. From outside it looked like the Hollywood version of a frontier newspaper office: square façade with GRAVENHURST DAILY WATCH in raised, gold-colored letters across the full length, peeled paint, and two big shop windows so ordinary citizen Jones could look right into the heart of his city's press. Only it wasn't the heart. It was just the advertising and classified department which may be the pocketbook, but certainly isn't the heart, so people long ago had given up that little pastime.

Getting to the editorial office was a real challenge because the floors were staggered and you were always going up and down stairs and when you got there the trip didn't seem altogether worthwhile. Not unless you'd learned to love it over the years like that dead street outside. It reminded me of some room in a cheap hotel. There was a sink in the corner with soggy gray paper towels stuck to it. The walls were of a cracked yellow motif, and it was small. Yet somehow nine old-fashioned wooden desks, at least as many people, a phone booth, a news ticker, and more typewriters than would actually function all managed to find room at the same time. Naturally this kind of a setup stimulated considerable confusion. But if the confusion didn't get you then the smell would. Partly people; the sour sick smell of nerves around deadline on a busy morning. Partly glue which had been slopped in haste over so much copy for so many years that nothing and no one had escaped its taint. Partly the dust and dry flannel smell of old newspapers. Not what could be called an efficiency layout, but the funny thing was you came to like it. I got a kick out of watching the faces of our new reporters when they first saw the place—just a little queasy, it seemed—yet after a couple of months they'd be treating the *Daily Watch* as a club; always dropping in at off hours to see who was around or to read the ticker or just kill time. I guess that's because working for a newspaper is very personal. There's no time for diplomacy and there's no defense against a badly written story. It's not like being in business where a lot of people usually work on the same project so when things get screwed up nobody knows who to blame. When you hand in a story that's it and if it happens to be bad, having the news editor read it aloud isn't likely to improve the style much. As a result, everybody has his sweet feelings hurt most of the time, or else he's hurting someone else's so even though you may be too busy to notice, when the battle's over a lot of blood has spilt and it's kind of nice to stop by when things are quiet so you can see what a dump the place really is and how stupid it was to get in such a sweat.

Also some of us come out of boredom. At least the young ones do; the ones from out of town who don't know anyone but each other. But for every out-of-towner there's usually a local reporter so I'm partly right; it's a club.

The permanent staff was headed by Teddy Pearson, our executive editor, a bald, pink cherub who oozed a chubby complacency more characteristic of booster than newspaperman. Then came Ned Polk, probably listed as Pollacko in the annals of time but Polk for the past two generations, who was a caricature of the rough, tough news editor and sort of a hero with me. There was Carl Robinson who liked to chase fire trucks, ambulances, state troopers, or any other agents of disaster so long as they were good enough to maintain speeds in excess of 60 mph. There was Jeff Collins, our ace political reporter, who could have left for bigger ponds but didn't because he was a local boy. And Meg Brown, the society editor who was always getting her copy mixed up and once put the headline NOW'S THE TIME TO DO IT RIGHT over a wedding story, rather than with the recipe feature for which it had been intended.

Then there was me, the summer vacation, general assignment hot-shot. Until last spring, anyway, when I became the year 'round general assignment hotshot and police reporter. But I couldn't really be counted as a permanent editorial staffer because Pa'd be moving me around from one department to the other until I finally learned enough to get invited upstairs as his assistant.

Then there was the not-so-permanent staff: has-beens deserted by fuzzy dreams, and will-bes, running, slipping, stumbling toward that big city daily with the "roll 'em boys" and the crusades and the rest of that nonsense. They looked after the school page and the farm page and the sports page and they helped out with politics, police, obits, and anything else that came along. But they'd all be moving on either because of ambition or incompetence so it didn't matter who they were because they were always changing, yet always the same somehow. Pretty smart boys, some of them. At least once they were used to things like Ned Polk's abuse which was pretty tough to get used to. Especially if you'd just come from the soft sweet encouragement of college and mother. But there were some awful jerks too. Jerks of all ages with about as much aptitude for the newspaper game as I have for childbirth. They were sort of sad, but saddest of all were the drunks, face down in undigested talent. That was the not-so-permanent staff.

Anyway, we were the first to feel Jesse's presence. Everybody on the paper would sooner or later, but our department led the list. Pa came down the day after he met Jesse.

"Gentlemen," Pa said. "I'm afraid we must start working for a living."

I was surprised this didn't get a laugh, even though he said "we."

"There is a competitive paper starting up here . . ." and he went on to tell about those living incarnations of evil—the Rosenfeldts—for the benefit of those who didn't already know. Then he laid out a program for more local news coverage, more feature stories, and more everything else. After he got through everybody was trying to figure just when we were supposed to sleep. It seemed like a pretty good pep talk to me, though, and I wished there were something I could have said to show we were all behind him, but being the publisher's son, any war cries out of me might have sounded less than spontaneous.

Pa had commandeered Ted Pearson's desk because he liked to sit down and sort of fit into things when he had something to say to one of his departments. Ted now stood behind him with his arms folded, looking more like a cupid in mid pout than a trusted lieutenant. "I don't think we should have any trouble, Mr. Woodruff," he said, rubbing his egg with characteristic concern. "Not if the fellows really pitch in and work."

"What?" Pa demanded.

It sounded even sillier the second time.

"Which means we're working for the *Daily Watch* twenty-four hours a day," Pa said. "Right, Ned?"

"That's right, Mr. Woodruff," Ned Polk said, but he spoke in the slow rumble of a distant storm.

"No extracurricular activities, no politics. Right, Ned?"

Ned Polk rolled back in his chair and studied Pa. "That's right, Mr. Woodruff," he said finally.

"Right," Pa shouted, and he banged the flat of his hand hard on the table before I had a chance to figure out what was going on. "What's more there's a two-month bonus for everybody if Rosenfeldt is out of business one year from today." Pa raised slowly to his feet and scanned the room with benign dignity. "The future of the *Daily Watch* is in your hands, gentlemen," he said and left.

I happened to walk out with Ned Polk. "The Old Man sure knows how to get people working for him," I said.

Ned looked at me funny, but didn't say anything. I guess he was thinking about that bonus.

"How 'bout a beer?" I suggested.

"Like to, Larry," he grumbled, "but I have some business with the mayor," and he lumbered through the rush-hour traffic in that heavy threatening way of his which made cars stop and wait in whispering silence until he reached the sidewalk.

I reminded myself to ask Pa about Ned Polk and his extracurricular activities, then for lack of anything better, walked around the corner to Chick's Diner for a little socializing. The place was, as usual, jumping, and for no good reason, except that it always had been. Carl Robinson, *Daily Watch* hero and champion of Gravenhurst's huddled masses, was holding forth on bingo night out to the Mohegan Engine Company.

". . . And then Joe calls B-12 and 'Bingo' cries Mrs. Malone after maybe eight, maybe ten numbers had been given. 'Uh oh,' says Joe. 'Somebody's cheatin' in this here game,' and Mrs. Malone, oh bruuuthur, was she ever steamed up so Joe has to explain all over again it's double diagonal and I'm tellin' you if you think Mrs. Malone's face was red you shoulduv seen *Mr.* Malone's."

Lots of laughs.

I gave him a wave and sat as far away as possible since it was only a matter of time before he'd begin reciting the entire guest list for the Mohegan bingo affair while his cluster of admirers stared in open-mouthed fascination.

In my determination to duck that dubious exercise in total recall I managed to sit right next to Hugh Godkin.

He didn't notice me at first, being so deep in conversation with the girl beside him, but I figured he would soon enough and decided to get it over with so's to relax and enjoy my coffee.

"Hugh, howsa boy?" I greeted.

"Well well, Mr. Woodruff, four, and how are you, sir?"

I winced. He was kidding about the Mr. Woodruff, four, stuff but only halfway. "What's new with your Jaycee exhibit?" I asked.

"Coming along," he said mysteriously. "Coming along, boy."

I nodded, even managed an encouraging wink.

"Hiya Larry," from the counter girl. "What'll it be?"

"You, Mary," I said. "On white."

"Toasted?"

"Suit yourself," I shrugged.

"Haw haw," said Hugh. "That's pretty good."

Mary and I both looked at him in mild surprise. We knew what was pretty good and what wasn't.

"You on white. Haw haw," Hugh repeated.

"The usual?" Mary asked.

I nodded and she turned to draw me a cup of black coffee.

"Apple or blueberry?" she called.

"Apple," I said, realizing with something close to panic that I would now have to make chitchat with Hugh. I don't know why but he hit me just wrong. He was too goddam good or something. However, it was neither the time nor the place to worry about that. I leaned across and nodded to his girl friend.

"Hi," I said.

She tried to smile, lost her composure and looked to Hugh for assistance. I wondered what it was I'd said.

"May I present Miss Amanda Simpson," Hugh offered. "My fiancée."

Miss Amanda Simpson's cheeks turned from pale gray to an unsuch a mob of interesting people. Elsa Maxwell was there and John Wayne and that charming Cyril Ritchard, but best of all . . .

She seldom got around to what the play was about because obviously nobody cared very much. Then there were some horrible ones about Abby or me and what cute things we had done as children. Yuk yuk. I finally had to edit those myself to avoid becoming the town clown.

Mother would be first to admit it was a pretty nauseating journalistic performance, but the good ladies of Gravenhurst took to it like addicts to their must dust so that was all there was to that.

Other areas of self-preservation included such matters as a promise by Pa to repair a certain store front which had been left peeling and paintless for several profitable years, or to reduce a rent commensurate with the reduction of living standards in a certain neighborhood.

By the time Rosenfeldt and his gang were ready to roll, the *Daily Watch* was more firmly entrenched than ever, as far as we could tell. In fact the day they printed their first edition we felt confident enough to carry the story, although I must admit putting it on page twenty-two under a number ten headline (which is not much bigger than an airmail sticker) was something more than an oversight.

NEW DAILY IN CITY
A daily newspaper published by Jesse Rosenfeldt, son of Benjamin Rosenfeldt, the real estate king, began printing in this city today.

Pa seemed to think that about covered the situation and most people on the *Watch* agreed with him. Nevertheless, there wasn't a one of us who didn't sneak out and buy a copy of the *Enterprise*, as Jesse and his father modestly called their little effort. Without even bothering to read it you could tell one thing right off: it sure was different! In the first place, it was tabloid size and inclined to let photography do the job, while we are standard and lean pretty heavily on the printed story. But the big difference was style. The *Daily Watch* is a classic example of the reserved approach to American journalism. A lot of people think that's too bad because it makes pretty dry reading most of the time, but we run a conservative newspaper devoted to fact rather than flair (sort of like the *New*

healthy fever pink. Her eyes dropped to her left hand where trembled the engagement ring, its modest diamond and setting looking like nothing so much as the eyestalk of a lobster.

"Congratulations," I said to one or both. "Where is your home, Miss Simpson?"

But the lost composure continued and I began to suspect it was a permanent condition.

"Amanda's from across the Hudson. Center Falls, New York," Hugh interpreted.

"Well, what do you know," I said, disgusted with myself for bothering. "And what brought you two together?"

"Amanda plays the organ for Father," Hugh explained.

"Isn't that nice," I said, straight-faced, and: "Awfully glad to have met you." I gulped, gobbled, paid, and ran.

Outside I felt better immediately. The town's soft summer rhythms simmered and cooked the harshness from reality until nothing remained but a vague and gently recognizable spattering of colors, faces, objects, sounds, all blandly reassuring from a distance, all confidence and comfort until a closer inspection revealed the various components in their separate tedium, insufficiency, and drabness. The trees lining Main Street were beautiful, not in themselves alone but because they sprang from cement, fed on dust, grit, urine, scraps of sunlight, and managed in their struggle to cast a spell of gallantry and hope. In the woods where they belonged one would have noticed only that they were a trifle scraggly. The cars, false-fronted buildings, traffic lights, billboards, neon signs, all of little consequence separately, together made that special aggregate which was Gravenhurst, Conn., not New Milford, not Gravenhurst, Nebraska, but Gravenhurst, Conn. A dubious achievement, perhaps, but an achievement nonetheless.

And the people, what of them? Also of no consequence separately? I suppose so. If they chose to be.

And if they didn't? Well, they could always leave town and go to New York or one of the other metropolitan achievement centers. Hal James and I ought to know. We'd talked that subject over often enough. Right from childhood on up, he visiting me or vice versa, lying flat on our backs in bedroom privacy and darkness, me with an arm curled tight across my face for increased seclusion and Hal the same way, talking until dawn grayed and the birds tattled about how someday we'd do something and be somebodies somewhere.

But always somewhere else. Never in Gravenhurst. With us it was axiomatic that to stay in Gravenhurst was to achieve a sort of permanent somnolence, an unquestioning reliance on instinct and custom, a loss of self.

Yet here we were.

I turned off Main and down Mill Street toward the slum section. Smells from the fish market rolled across my senses, sweet and powerful and somehow touched with mystery; a colored boy and three whites loitered on the corner, bored, trouble seeking. I started to cross the street, stopped in disgust and walked them down, eying each one back, being careful not to break the rhythm of my strolling gait, pleased with my performance and the fact that I'd made it without incident.

Then up Front Street, slightly unnerved by the sudden closeness of life; the rows of shacks so thin-skinned you could hear a bed squeak from across the street, porches bordering on the sidewalks their shadows filled with voices and laughter and secrets barely hidden, like pooping in a public lavatory, laundry pink and stained and unashamed lolling gently in the evening breezes.

I hurried on back to the crowded, light-flicking, traffic-filled order and routine of Main Street, got my car and went home where, except for Abby and me, and Hal on an occasional martini call, no one ever thought about Gravenhurst in terms of leaving any more, only of coping.

CHAPTER IV

Abby never took much of an interest in the Gravenhurst *Daily Watch* because, as she put it, "the damn thing's so clumpy," but when she got back and discovered a small-scale war looming on the horizon her attitude toward journalism changed considerably. She wanted to know all about Jesse Rosenfeldt, a name which was fast becoming dirty around our house, and even went so far as to ask a couple of questions about the *Daily Watch* which was not like her at all.

But at that stage knowing anything about the *Watch* was practically irrelevant. We were more interested in fortifying the ram-

parts of Woodruff good will and prestige, both aspirations in which Abby had a singular lack of interest. Pa's first move was to promote the Gravenhurst Urban Redevelopment Program which, to the surprise of almost no one, earned him banner headlines in the *Daily Watch:*

PUBLISHER SPARKS URBAN RENEWAL
Woodruff Seeks Federal Funds

Over the years Gravenhurst had not done much to help itself in such areas as urban improvement and industrial expansion. Consequently these were quite challenging and all-encompassing fields. Just about everybody in town could thank Pa for his noble and forward-thinking project. But the best part was whatever the town invested for housing projects in slum areas or the reconditioning of rundown business sections would be matched by federal and state funds. Now if there is anything the far-seeing citizens of Gravenhurst like it's getting something for nothing. And if they can't swing that then getting it at a third of the price is next best. Of course the fact Pa owned a good slice of the property proposed for redevelopment was not mentioned in the *Daily Watch* article, nor in subsequent editorials praising Clarence Woodruff, "Gravenhurst's man of tomorrow." In defense of family decorum, I must say Pa made a point never to proof read editorials about himself. Theoretically, therefore, they could be either favorable or otherwise without interference from above. However, I don't believe this theory has ever been thoroughly tested.

The redevelopment committee, though most important, was only one of many prestige pots Pa set boiling. Charity drives, school improvement drives, God-fearing editorials on why we should buy from our dedicated local merchants, nothing was beyond the vision of our enterprising little daily. Even Mother resumed her newspaper skills by reviving a long dormant weekly column on the New York theatah and assorted subjects of interest to Mother. Most of them went something like this: DON'T MISS DESIRE! New York: You really mustn't miss the charming production of Eugene O'Neill's *Desire Under the Elms* now playing at the Shubert. Your dear publisher took me the other night and it was one of the loveliest evenings I've ever spent in the theater. We dined at Sardi's and saw

York Times B.C. which is Before Cuba, and B.B. which is Before Birmingham) and we feel our writing style should reflect this policy. Believe me, it does. But the *Enterprise* was to conservative news reporting what the mouse is to the maiden aunt.

LET'S GET
CRACKING

the headline whooped, and underneath was a picture, obviously phony, of some kids rowing a boat at the intersection of Flint and South Streets. Well it just so happens the Gravenhurst drainage system isn't our proudest possession and after a bad thunderstorm things often do get a little wet, but you can get used to anything in time. It also happens that one Clarence Woodruff, better known as Gravenhurst's man of tomorrow, and State Senator Vanden Gasser are part owners of the property on both sides of the intersection and do not look with favor on property assessments for improvements in the drainage system. This fact was rather tactlessly brought out, it seemed to me.

"What kind of influence does it take," the *Enterprise* yowled, "to prevent this city from taking action in the face of so flagrant a need for property improvements? Perhaps Mr. Woodruff, publisher of the Gravenhurst *Daily Watch,* and State Senator Vanden Gasser can supply an answer for the property is theirs, though the responsibility, apparently, is not."

All very interesting, if somewhat unnecessary. But more to the point, it happened there was a third owner of that property: Ben Tompkins, president of Sunnyside Supermarkets, one of the biggest advertisers in town. Can't imagine why they'd leave him out, the bastards. The more we read, the higher our skirts were hiked. There was a tangletown puzzle, free advertising if your ad happened to appear in a certain spot on a certain page, an advice to the lovelorn column, and God knows what all.

But most shocking of all was the style. Bouncy, that was the only word for it. Bouncy and opinionated which in a factual news story just plain stinks. This kind of stuff:

"Gravenhurst Common Councilmen gathered round the old gavel yesterday eve for another display of pomp and circumstance. All business, including the proposal for automatic gates at the city's five railroad crossings, was carefully shelved by the artful dodgers . . ."

Compared with:

"A committee to study the proposed installation of automatic gates at the city's five railroad crossings was appointed last night by the Gravenhurst Common Council . . ."

Gives you a pretty good idea of the difference between our two papers.

Pa was so delighted not even the Flint Street story bothered him. He burst into the editorial office like a class secretary at his twenty-fifth reunion.

"I'll be damned," he shouted. "It's a campus daily."

Ned Polk crossed a growl with a belch.

The young transients made laughing faces and mental notes that this was an experience to be remembered.

Meg Brown, the society editor, giggled in the mistaken hope such masculine exuberance might be the forerunner of an indiscretion.

"And I promised you people a two-month bonus," Pa groaned. This time everybody laughed conveniently so Pa could rap himself on the head and leave in mock disgust.

Yessir, we all had a good laugh. Only Teddy Pearson was capable of a dissenting squeak.

"Awful," he said. "Absolutely terrible. But it's sort of peppy to read, don't you think?"

Nobody bothered to answer.

After Pa left we all hung around word-fencing with Ned Polk, trying to establish a basis of professional equality between him and ourselves, failing, not realizing he had no intention of establishing such a relationship.

"Hey, Skipper," from Carl Robinson who thought Skipper was *the* thing to call your news editor. "I see where Vanden Gasser's got himself a new Caddy."

"What am I supposed to do?" Ned demanded. "Put it on page one?"

"Ha ha," from Robinson. "No, I didn't mean you was to do anything. Ha ha."

"Ned Ned," his name was Ned Ned to Meg Brown. In her urgency to catch his attention and get it over with I never heard her call him anything else. "Ned Ned, my little girl's been asked to a birthday party tonight and I have the Daughters of Rebecca assignment at six and my little girl won't be . . ."

"Spare me the details," Ned interrupted. "Hey, Spaulding," he was the new sports editor, an eager, ivory-faced pachyderm hot from the *Yale Daily News* and already a little grim about having been passed over for a Pulitzer Prize. "You got anything on for tonight?"

Spaulding thumbed his notebook frantically.

"No," he confessed.

"Well you have now."

"Oh Ned Ned," said Meg. "I can't thank you enough."

"That's a relief," Ned rumbled, then got up, stretched, letting the flesh settle. "See you in the morning, girls," and lumbered out.

Jeff hopped up and started after him. "Say Ned, I've been meaning to ask you about the significance of Healy's decision to request a re-evaluation for . . ." But Ned had kept right on going and the details of Jeff's question were lost as he shuffled, scraped, and scrambled after the big man.

"Yes sir, a brand new Caddy," said Carl Robinson.

"Personally I prefer the MG," said Mr. Yale Man.

Harvey Davies, our farm editor, was scanning the *Editor & Publisher* want ads with grim determination: "Young, energetic, resourceful reporter for general assignment and feature work," he read. "Fifty thousand circulation daily, Midwest. Two years experience."

"Two years, my God," and an agony of groans from one of our newest arrivals.

"Anything for a society editor?" Meg begged.

"Thinking of leaving us?" I asked, instead of "Why, do you know any?" which had been my first inclination. Meg had fuzzy, puffed out hair like an unclipped poodle and a squatting, loose bladdered manner which triggered an almost irresistible urge to give her a boot from time to time. But she also had a husband ten years in the state hospital plus an unmarried, totally dependent sister who should have been in the same place but unmercifully wasn't, so I usually managed to resist the urge.

"Oh no," she answered wistfully. "Just dreaming out loud."

"Society editor wanted," the farm editor read. "For twelve thousand circulation daily in Gravenhurst, Conn. Must be young, resourceful, good photographer, careful of personal appearance." I guess he hadn't heard about the husband and sister.

Meg's face went all soft and trembly.

"He's just kidding," I said. "Or maybe it's for the *Enterprise*."

"No, I was kidding," Davies admitted, catching on.

"Ha ha," said Meg, and went back to her typing.

Ted Pearson came back in then. It was the first I knew he'd been gone.

"*Enterprise's* sold out," he said. "Can't buy one anywhere."

"Curiosity," I supposed.

"Curiosity killed the cat," Meg offered with false brightness.

"Who's the cat?" Ted asked.

All that guy did was worry.

"Well, I'm getting out of here," I said, in no mood to consider the *Enterprise* a threat to anyone but its subscribers and customers. "See you guys in the morning."

"Good night, Larry," said Meg Brown, girl guy.

"Night," chorused the others.

"See you," I said.

I took the long way home that evening. Partly because it was summer and I had a convertible, but partly because the long way went past Nora Compton's house and I always felt like seeing Nora when something good had happened. I guess we were all more anxious about the new paper than anyone realized because it sure was a relief to have the whole thing over with. Well, not exactly over with, but at least out in the open where we could see what we were up against—which wasn't very much apparently.

I drove out West Main past Chick's Diner and Lock's Department Store and the Palace Theater and the supermarket and the random box buildings which added up to Gravenhurst's business district.

"Eddie, howsa boy?" to the cop on the corner and "Watch it, Joe, I'll runya down," to a guy I'd known as long as time—my time anyway—and the unnecessary stop to let a lady and baby carriage go by. "Okay, lady, you've had your fun. Now push!" But that one I didn't say out loud. Then past the firehouse—the Phoenix Engine Company—and up Hill Street to the ridge with its rows of warm, ugly houses. Little houses full of little people and big problems where dreams and passions surged, battered, but seldom broke through the walls of propriety.

From the ridge I could look down on a town where thirty thousand people played the charade of life for the greater glory of God, despite an angry suspicion it was not God's glory at all, merely an ape's. But the town was almost hidden by trees and nothing could be seen but a smudged brick chimney and the top of the Compton

Building at Four Corners and a smattering of slate and shingles and tar paper and red-gold windows burning in the evening sun. God's greater glory had all but disappeared.

As I drove along the houses got farther apart and bigger, but most of them were just as ugly as their little cousins below. Cluttered Victorian afterthoughts with too many turrets and too many gables and the occasional absurdity of a stained-glass window.

The Compton house was like that. When I was inside it always seemed getting out might take a long time. In fact the very existence of such a place as "out" became doubtful. It was like living in a giant oak tree lined with purple drapes. Pretty dreary, but I was used to it, just as I was used to Railroad Avenue, and it didn't bother me any more.

Nora was home when I got there, but so were her mother and father and brother, Tommy, who had become something of a problem for me lately because he wanted to work on the *Daily Watch* and Ned Polk wanted him to work someplace else. Any place else, as a matter of fact. Having to share the *Daily Watch's* imminent triumph with so many Comptons had not been exactly what I had in mind but there didn't seem to be much of a choice.

The best word to describe Judge Compton would be gray. He had cold, sharp, ice-gray features, flannel-gray clothes, and paper-gray skin. Except for an undercurrent of meticulous petulance, Judge Compton's most striking characteristic was the complete absence of striking characteristics. He had a face that defied memory and I was always afraid lest we meet someday and I fail to recognize him. So far it had been no problem, though, simply because he was the only completely gray man I knew.

Mrs. Compton made up for her husband by being a bright and ugly yellow. She tied her hair in girlish ribbons and usually wore slacks which emphasized the impending collapse of her bottom parts and she was full of words.

Finding a color for Tommy was not quite so easy. He looked gray like his father, but I grew up with Tommy and I knew there were a lot of secret colors in him. At least there were once. Now he worked as a trainee at the Gravenhurst National Bank and dreary resignation was his predominant characteristic. But inside Tommy hid the many colors of a dreamer which would have been fine except the dreams always smeared and splattered on their way out.

As for Nora, she was pink, which may seem a little nondescript because there are many shades of that color and not all are pretty. To be specific, then, Nora was a pastel pink in those days which was fine with me. However, I can remember other days when she did not seem quite so soft and gentle and desirable, but that could be blamed on her mother mostly. Mrs. Compton was a real social climber. With her it was a religion, not a game, and although being the daughter of a Main Street jeweler may have offered justifiable cause, it sure didn't dull the mighty sword of her pretension. As a result, both Nora and Tommy showed the strain of battle. But while Tommy had been able to avoid much of the campaign by means of prep school and college, Nora had not and the very willingness with which she joined the cause did not always show her to best advantage. My sharpest memory of Nora's childhood, for instance, was a fat little poohbear face mounted upon an everchanging assortment of pink, frilly dresses. At first there had been no reason for this monotonous change of clothes. Later on, however, out of a spirit of cooperation more than anything else, we took to shoving little Nora into the nearest mud puddle in order to bolster Mrs. Compton's frantic costume changes with a sense of purpose. Nora responded by offering to tell our mothers on us, a threat which lost most of its punch after a year or two of constant repetition.

So far Nora's charm must seem pretty elusive. However, as her physical sugars and spices began to develop this very delicacy of upbringing made her as desirable as she was unattainable. Instead of mud puddles, we took to pushing her into dark corners. Judging by her past this might seem to have been a fairly unrewarding pastime. However, no amount of social pretension could hide Nora's true nature and we soon discovered to our great delight that a tiny beast of passion lay hidden there. A gift from the jeweler's past, I'd imagine. And though she managed to keep her desire shackled in the chains of etiquette most all the time, occasionally it broke free for brief but delightful romps in the garden of love. Perhaps it was only because we were neighbors, don't ask me what starts these things, but I soon discovered Nora's little monster preferred me above all the others. To say it loved nothing better than to jump into my lap, curl up and go to sleep might be carrying the metaphor to obscenity. However, that's about the way it was, and though my lap was not intended as a place to sleep, I'd be a liar to suggest it was used for anything more.

Whether this arrangement would lead to anything as permanent as marriage I could not have said at the time, but there were signs. I was fresh out of college and therefore of marriageable age. I was pretty much resigned to a lifetime in Gravenhurst for which Nora seemed particularly well suited. We each had social prerequisites acceptable to the other, and though our love was not the burning variety, we shared a certain fondness born of a lifetime's many intimacies.

It was for these reasons that I found myself at the Compton house that evening and though they do not seem altogether satisfactory, there were no better ones just then. Unfortunately, I must have walked in on the tail end of an argument because everybody was looking pretty sore except Nora who never let that kind of a thing bother her. "Good evening, Larry," Mrs. Compton lied, patting her face in an effort to drive away any traces of anger which might still show. "How *nice* to see you."

"Evening, Mrs. Compton," I said. "Judge, Tom. Hi, Nora."

"I see we have a new paper in town," Judge Compton said.

"Yes sir. Should make for a little excitement around these parts."

The judge made no comment which is a trick he must have learned to make people say things they hadn't intended. It always worked with me.

"Pa doesn't think they have a chance."

"Why not?" asked Tom.

"Have you read it?" I answered.

"Sure. It's peppy," he said.

"Tommy's done more than that," Mrs. Compton said. "He's gone down to that awful paper looking for a job."

"What's so awful about the *Enterprise?*" Tom asked. "You haven't even read it."

"Well, it must be awful to come pushing right in as if it owned the town when we already have a perfectly good paper."

"I won't permit it," Judge Compton said, apparently resuming his earlier argument. "Loyalty is what makes a town like this worthwhile. Loyalty to friends and devotion to the community. I forbid you to work for them, son, and that is final."

"Besides, what would the Woodruffs think?" Mrs. Compton asked. "Or anyone else," she added to dispel the hint of social abdication implicit in her concern for what the Woodruffs alone might think.

Tommy leaned forward and tried to be reasonable. "Father," he begged. "The *Daily Watch* won't hire me."

"Because they don't think you're cut out to be a newspaperman," the judge said.

"Aren't you happy at the bank, Tommy?" Nora asked reasonably.

Tommy fell back in his chair and was gray again.

"It isn't that Ned Polk didn't think he was cut out for it," I lied. "There just weren't any openings."

"Ned Polk?" the judge asked.

"Pa lets each department do its own hiring," I explained a little pompously.

"I didn't think this was your father's doing," the judge said.

"Of course not," said Tommy. "That would be disloyal too, wouldn't it?"

"We'll have no impudence in my house," Judge Compton warned.

"You don't have the right disposition for newspaper work anyway," his mother told him. "Why, sweetie, remember when you were writing that college thesis business? The idea of having to finish on a certain date made you frantic. Imagine all those deadlines and things . . ."

"Mother, please."

"Goodness," she concluded.

"Poor Tommy," Nora said. "It's so hard for him."

Something had to be done before they all began making sentimental testimonials to Tommy's incompetence.

"Hey, Tom," I said. "You ought to try the *Watch* again. We're sort of geared up for the competition and maybe another man would be more plausible now."

Tommy didn't look convinced. Or else he'd learned the judge's trick because he didn't say anything.

"I'll speak to Pa tonight," I promised.

No comment.

"Drop by the shop tomorrow afternoon," I offered.

"That would be fine." Tommy smiled.

"While we're still on the subject of loyalty, Larry," Judge Compton said, "would you have any idea what Ned Polk and Mayor Healy are up to?"

"Up to?"

"Up to," the judge confirmed.

"In what way?"

"That is what I was asking you," the judge said, but without any humor.

"No sir, I wouldn't."

"They seem to be in cahoots with what might be called the renegade wing of the Gravenhurst Republican Party," the judge explained.

"Oh yeah," I said. "Pa mentioned something to Ned couple of weeks ago about extracurricular activities, but I forgot to ask what he meant."

"It seems the younger members of the party would like to see far less of such men as Clem Harper, Vanden Gasser, your father, and myself."

"I didn't know Ned had anything to do with it."

"None of us did until recently," the judge said. "But he seems to have political aspirations."

"Poor Clarence," Mrs. Compton said. "Right in his own back yard."

"And judging by that story on your father and the senator's real estate ventures," he continued, "I'd say the *Enterprise* was similarly inclined."

"Sort of looks that way," I admitted.

"However, I'm sure Clarence will know how to handle the situation," Judge Compton concluded.

It was my turn to say something loyal, but I declined. "How 'bout some Ping-pong, Nora?" I asked instead.

"If you'd like to," Nora replied.

Playing Ping-pong was about the only way I knew of getting Nora away from her family. At least while we were in the house. When I took her out they never objected if we came home late. In fact they were a lot more tolerant about that kind of thing than most parents I knew, but at home they were early nineteenth century. It didn't make sense because obviously a lot more could happen to Nora in a car at night than right in her own house with the family all over the place. But that's the way they were. Sometimes it even seemed like they almost *wanted* something to happen. But they were just sort of naïve probably because while we were in the house everybody went crazy whenever we disappeared for a couple of minutes. Unless we played Ping-pong which they could hear us doing. Otherwise Mrs. Compton would have fits and start calling, "Nora . . . Noraah . . . Nora dear, what are you doing?" un-

til she could hear the old Ping-pong ball start *pickpocking* again and all was well.

I felt sort of foolish at the age of twenty-two courting a girl over the Ping-pong table, but we'd been "going together" since way back before I knew what that expression meant which may have been why Judge and Mrs. Compton still called us "the children" and treated us the way they did.

I followed Nora from the room, trying not to show how eager I was to get out of there. Tommy gave me a sort of wistful look so I told him it *was* nice to see him in case he had any ideas about joining us, and away we went, free at last. My ecstasy manifested itself in an indiscreet swat upon Nora's bottom which she didn't seem to appreciate much at all, but I did.

"Hey, you look great when you're mad," I said.

"That's lucky," she huffed. "Because I usually am when you're around."

I guess she really did look great too, though I'm not entirely sure. That sounds funny, but when you've known somebody as long as I'd known Nora you sort of lose your sense of perspective. Anyhow, other people said she was pretty, so it must have been true. She had light brown hair that got streaked in the summertime, by the sun, I'm pretty sure, and she'd grown up tall and sort of rangy which I liked for some reason. But it's hard to describe her face. Not that I can't remember it. Really. It isn't like her father's face, but I can't see it would help much to describe her feature by feature. I mean it's the over-all beauty that counts anyway, not just the way her face was put together. If I were asked to name the one quality which characterized her, I'd pick serenity. Nora exuded a ripe, patient, comfortable confidence which enveloped her whole being. I guess that was because she had always lived in Gravenhurst. She went to the local schools and the Community College which may not be America's greatest seat of learning, but we were all pretty proud of it. Gravenhurst CC is only a two-year deal but you can learn a lot in two years if you try. I mean a person gets out of something just exactly what he puts into it and the books are the same whether you read them at GCC or Harvard so it doesn't follow that Nora's stupid just because she went there. I mean, does it?

Anyway, she's always lived in Gravenhurst and she belongs to one of the best families—on the Compton side, that is—so I don't suppose her serenity, or complacency or whatever you want to call it, was too tough to come by. But Nora's never been a coaster, though. Anybody who doesn't believe me just has to ask her about literature to discover how true that is. She has a book on it which starts with Plutarch's *Lives* or something and runs all the way through Faulkner. Anybody will admit that's a lot of literature and she practically knows it by heart. Just name a book, practically any book at all, and she can give you the plot, the names of most of the characters, and the author. One, two, three, right off like that. She's a whiz at crossword puzzles too. Sometimes I used to think Nora might have spent a little more time trying to understand the stuff she'd read, but it was pretty impressive all the same.

It's hard to remember just when I first fell in love with her. When I was about fourteen, more or less, because until then she hadn't very much to waggle at the boys, other than her fat pink tongue. As a result, when we would all get together minus Nora to talk about *sex* which was a way of having kids if you didn't have enough will power to wait for the stork, I never thought of Nora doing all those things we discovered girls had to do. In fact, the only girl I could imagine doing them was Mary Kowalski who lived on a potato farm and had dirty blond hair and wore faded print dresses with nothing underneath. Of course, with Nora and most of the other girls around it didn't matter what they had on underneath. But it did with Mary.

Anyway, the summer I was thirteen Nora went away to a dude ranch in Arizona or someplace and I decided to miss her terribly. My project was so successful I finally took to visiting Mary Kowalski where the pain of unrequited love could be properly treated. I don't mean Mary was the village pump or anything like that, but she wasn't above a little funning and there was a frisky, teasing, close-pressing way about her which kept me constantly aquiver. Naturally, I assured myself this was all for love of Nora and to prove it I wrote long letters describing how much I missed her which wasn't easy to explain since exhibit A, namely Mary, could not be mentioned. But Nora must have got the idea because she wrote back and even managed to say she missed me too. When the Comptons finally returned I was the original lonesome piner and after two weeks of practically choking to death whenever Nora was around I finally managed to ask if she'd mind if I kissed her. More to get it off my chest than anything else. Well, she said she guessed she wouldn't, although I'm not so sure. Anyway, it was kind of a letdown compared to Mary. Sort of cold and dry and not at all what I'd led myself to expect. But we worked on it over the years and it got better.

Getting back to the *pickpocking* Ping-pong ball, we were just rallying automatically so we could talk without being diverted by the game.

"Larry?" she asked. "Did you mean that about Tommy and the newspaper?"

"Why of course," I said with more authority than was rightfully mine. "If we can find a spot for him."

Pickpock . . . pickpock.

"I don't think it's a good idea," she said.

Pickpock.

I hadn't laid eyes on Nora for almost a month which, considering we were not only neighbors but in-love-neighbors to boot, was kind of a long time. To tell the truth, she was beginning to scare me a little. I had only seen her on occasional weekends during four years of college and in the summers either I was too busy with the paper or she was away. It was as if by mutual agreement she had decided —and I mean in that way—by mutual agreement *she* had decided college years were bad years for courting. I don't know just why this was so. Maybe she felt my being away with a lot of new people and new ideas made me sort of suspect, so she chose to wait until the crisis was over and I could be thoroughly reindoctrinated in Graven-hurst lore. It never occurred to her I was the one who felt inade-quate. All the fresh new sophistication of college life was no match for the competent serenity Nora had acquired by simply staying home those four years and stitching herself more firmly into the community cloth. As chairman of the Junior League and a member of the Welcome Wagon Committee, Nora had responsibilities and position in town while I was still a college boy. A couple of times I had stopped by the house and found her entertaining a brood of matriarchs with such competence and maturity I was inclined to go out and play in the yard until she finished.

That's why it seemed foolish for us to be playing Ping-pong and even though it probably wasn't so, I sort of felt she was doing it to amuse me. But what really scared me was something else. It was the fact we were no longer children playing at love, sighing with unfulfilled passion and secret relief as the back-to-school time forced a periodic postponement of courtship. Marriage, not September, was the end to this new relationship and the decision, unhappily, was ours to make. That's what was so scary. And then to top it, here she was telling me, wife-like or mother-like or both, what I should or should not do for Tommy. It was just too much.

"So you don't think it's a good idea," I mimicked.

Pickpock.

"No," she said sternly. "I don't."

"Why not?"

Pickpock . . . pickpock.

"He's not the type," she said. "And it shouldn't be encouraged." Just then she blooped one at me and I couldn't resist the old grand slameroo. *Whock!*

"Oh, Larry! You're such a child really."

I fetched.

Pickpock . . . pickpock . . . pickpock.

I waited for her to bloop one again. She did. *Whock!*

"Larry, honestly." She must have lost a good seventy percent of her composure trying to duck that one and I refused to go chase it. Don't ask me why. I felt ornery, that's all. The way I used to feel with Mother sometimes when she thought it was bedtime and I didn't.

"Your turn to get it," I told her.

"Well, if you don't want to be serious, then maybe you'd just better go home."

"Come on, Nora, don't be so stuffy. I got it last time."

"That's not the point."

Now I knew what the point was a lot better than she did. Doing without people who like to run other people's lives. That was the point but I didn't feel like explaining it. "What is?" I asked.

"It isn't nice to make slams when you are playing with a lady."

"Oh," I said. "Nobody ever told me that before."

"Well, I think it's time someone did," she said. "Now go find the ball."

"Woof, woof," I said, but she was tiring me fast.

"Nora . . . Noraah . . . Nora, dear, what are you doing?"

" 'Aving a bit of intercourse, Lovey," I said just loud enough for Nora to hear.

Ah sweet love!

I was asked to find my own way out.

Maybe it was the look she'd given me. If so I wasn't conscious of it. Her words had been far from gentle, but whatever the reason I was reminded of a time when we were kids, Nora soft and pink and gap-toothed and the rest of us skinny, grass-stained smellies, kids on a picnic. Nothing specially relevant about that except somewhere along the line Nora found one of those little anchor emblems off some kid's sailor hat and we all wanted it, we boys anyhow, and she said she'd give it to her favorite boy of all and I was the pigeon. She came over all kind of humble and submissive and pinned the thing on my chest while the rest of them tittered and rolled their eyes and singsang "Larry's got a gir-el, Larry's got a gir-el" until I ripped it off and threw it at her feet. Right away I realized it was a terrible thing to do because Nora looked up to me and I'd let her down. Yet now, as though aware she no longer did, I felt only defiance and a hero's elation. More like a kid than a kid. Funny I should think of Nora and that anchor business all of a sudden. Except it's the only other time I can remember having crossed her.

CHAPTER V

That I felt so triumphant after my little rebellion was probably a good thing because Pa would be pretty far along on one of those magnificent celebrations of his and I'd need all the fervor I could muster in order to keep up.

As is often the case, our kitchen entrance was the one Abby and I almost always used except when we had company so that was where I headed. There were a number of reasons for this. In the first place, as children the kitchen had been headquarters from which most of our adventures originated. But now it was still a good idea because Bollard would usually be there or Mr. Quincy, the caretaker, or at the very least, Hilda, our cook, the silent wonder of the world, and by means of these three choristers one could usually find out what had been going on around Woodruff Hill. It was the best way I knew of discovering Pa's latest mood and thereby deciding whether to join him or head for the lake.

That evening all three of them were there.

"What's the matter?" I asked, for Mr. Quincy seldom came to the house unless something was. He was a New Hampshah fellah whose main job was to raise game birds and train our springer spaniels. If something went wrong in either of these departments Pa could be expected to throw a fit.

"It's them damn quail, Larry," he said. "Ain't got much up-stayuhs," and he tapped the side of his head for clarification.

"Bad news?" I asked.

"Eyuh."

"Well, how bad?"

"Hundred percent," he said. "They're all perished."

"Does Pa know?"

"Ain't told him yet," Mr. Quincy said.

"If yuh struck 'im across the face, lad, it couldna 'urt 'im more." Bollard claimed Liverpool origins and had a kitchen accent to prove it.

"Well, let's not tell him right now," I said. "Pa's celebrating tonight."

"Good gracious," Mr. Quincy exclaimed. "I might better run 'long home."

"Bleedin' coward," Bollard remarked.

"How'd it happen?" I asked.

"Took a fright," Mr. Quincy explained. "Fox or somethin'. Every one of them foolish creatures piled on top of each other 'til the entiuh brood smothered to death."

"Togetherness," I said. "It's a wonderful thing."

"Eyuh," Mr. Quincy agreed.

"Anyhow, let's save it for tomorrow."

"Whatever you think's right and propah," Mr. Quincy nodded, kept nodding.

"If you've a notion to live 'til morning, lad," Bollard said, "then take my wurd it's the right and proper thing to do."

"Likely so," from Mr. Quincy. "Likely so."

"Thanks for the good news," I said and headed for the pantry door.

"Not atall," I heard Mr. Quincy say. "Not atall."

I found Pa in the living room drinking martinis and eating fresh caviar with a spoon, a pastime which he once told me was the next best thing to sex. Abby was there too, sitting on a window seat and reading the *Enterprise* to find out why Pa was so pleased. She was frowning a little around the eyes and her mouth had an unsure look, like a child with some new toy it likes but doesn't quite understand yet. And Mother was sitting next to Pa, watching him consume with a fascinated pleasure. I don't blame her. Pa at play was always a spectacle.

"We've licked them already, Larry my boy," he shouted. "Have a martini."

"Thanks," I laughed. "Is it really that simple?" I kissed Mother and homed in on the bar, a colonial serving table which, for the benefit of Mother's community gatherings, didn't look like a bar at all until about six o'clock in the evening.

"Sure it's that simple," Pa shouted. "You saw the paper. What else could it be?"

"You're probably right," I said.

"Course I'm right. Must have insulted half the town in their first edition and that's fatal."

"I think it's fun," Abby said, which, counting our executive editor and Tommy Compton, guaranteed the *Enterprise* a circulation of at least three and maybe more.

"You do, do you," Pa roared. "Well, I may have you committed yet, young lady, so watch your step."

"Just be sure they don't get you first, Pa," said Abby. "Because if that happens you've had it."

"What?" Pa asked.

"Now Abby, don't be fresh," Mother smiled.

"I said," Abby yelled, "not if they get you first."

"Come here, imp," Pa commanded. "So I can wring your neck."

Abby stuck out her tongue and refused to leave her refuge. Pa glared at her with mock anger but she pretended not to notice. I couldn't help laughing, though if Abby had been my brother it's a pretty sure bet I'd have hated her. There wasn't much doubt who Pa's favorite was but somehow, being as she was a girl it didn't bother me so much. Abby was the enchantress while I was the family necessity and there was neither formula nor reason for comparison. At least so I told myself.

"Bollard," Pa shouted, but there was no response.

"*Bollard!*" That time it worked. Bollard came to the entrance of the living room and stood there without saying a word. He hated to be shouted at. At least he pretended to.

Pa stared at him for some time. "Bollard, you're a surly old bastard."

"Clarence, really!" Mother protested.

A smile touched the corners of Bollard's mouth. "Will that be all, sir?"

We all laughed except Bollard who knew it would spoil the effect and Mother who dared not risk a lapse of authority.

"No," Pa grumbled. "That's not all. Would you bring Miss Abby a split of champagne."

Bollard left without a word.

"Oh Pa." Abby ran and kissed him abundantly. "I'll never let them take you away."

"Thank you, Abby. That's extremely reassuring. But for your information, that newspaper which you and Mr. Rosenfeldt find so delightful is doomed."

"Why?" Abby demanded.

"Because in the newspaper business you cannot destroy the status quo without destroying yourself as well."

"How boring," Abby said.

"So's poverty," Pa laughed.

"Poverty with honor," Abby said. "That's the ticket."

At that point Bollard returned with the champagne and the subject of poverty in all its forms was discreetly dropped. I couldn't help wondering, though, whether Pa had maybe jumped the gun a little.

"How about that Flint Street story?" I asked.

"Dead issue," he shrugged. "That property's already included in our urban renewal program."

Well even so, the story didn't make us look too farseeing and progressive, but I didn't feel like throwing a damper on things just then. Even if I could.

"Oh, say, Pa, I almost forgot," I said. "Tommy Compton still wants to work for us."

"Polk thinks he'd be terrible," Pa said.

"Did he ever explain why?"

"Never asked him," Pa answered. "None of my business."

"I said you'd have a talk with him tomorrow."

"Fine," said Pa. "You can call him tomorrow and tell him I won't."

"He's thinking of going to work for Rosenfeldt," I said.

"Then why does he want to see me?" Pa asked.

"He'd rather work for us. It's sort of a question of loyalty."

"Loyalty," Pa scoffed. "Who can be loyal and work for that

damned . . ." He paused to select the proper epithet . . . "That damned Communist."

"Communist?" Abby asked.

"Anybody you don't like," Pa explained with mock patience, "is a Communist."

"Gosh," Abby said. "No wonder there's such a lot of them."

I knew better than to argue with Pa when he was in that kind of mood. Much easier to bring Tommy around anyway. Then the Old Man would see him. After all, Tommy was practically a member of the family.

"Larry," Mother said. "You'd better clean up before dinner. Grampa is coming."

"Oh my God," I said without intending to sound horrified. "I mean nobody told me," I tried to explain.

"Your mother didn't want to spoil things for us," Pa laughed.

I could remember when that kind of a remark used to hurt Mother's feelings, but she was accustomed to it by then and besides Pa really liked Old Gramps. He was the only grandparent we had left and everybody felt kind of sentimental about him. The rest had long since been reduced to those lacquered, brooding hang-jowled studies in righteousness which we knew as the family portraits. But except for being the last of his generation, Grampa Lindsay could list few distinctions. And this was so despite the efforts of his good wife who had loyally collected the many inconsequences of their life in a book entitled *Mr. and Mrs. Roger Lindsay—Their Life Together.* Needless to say the book had limited appeal, though there was some unintentional commentary worthy of a place alongside the finest in American humor. Gramps had been an executive in his day. Vice-president in charge of sales at the Gravenhurst Block and Supply Company "where courtesy counts." It was a position rich in the illusion of promise but Grampa seemed neither to notice nor mind that he had made the delicate transition from up-and-coming young man to loyal and trusted old-timer without any substantial improvement in salary. Perhaps this was because he became a vice-president instead. Gramps never was one for putting material considerations above honor. Whatever the reason, the result was a life of some drudgery for Mother, who was the eldest of five. Gramps and Gramma Lindsay were able to attain a living standard best described as abject gentility and since travel was their major social pretension, Mother often ended up holding the family bag for long periods of time. It was with their many and often tedious travels that *Mr. and Mrs. Roger Lindsay—Their Life Together* concerned itself and while most of the prose was pretty sticky, there were, as mentioned, some unintended bright spots.

Take the following:

"During our week in India, Roger had intimate relations with General Brantley, Commander in Chief of the British Forces there." (Names changed to protect the innocent.)

I often wished Gramma had been blessed with photographic aspirations rather than literary ones.

However, let us not abuse the memory of our dear departed. Let us abuse the living instead. Gramps, who was well into his anecdotage, had apparently arrived, for my room was right above the living room and dusty murmurings of glories long past, long separated from the dry chaff of pain now curled through the floor, settling around me in a dim dull film of yesterdays.

I changed and went downstairs and greeted him with the hearty, hollow enthusiasm one usually saves for the almost dead.

"Why hello there, Gramps," I said. "Thought you'd be in Paris by this time."

His lips worked back and forth in a series of smiles and subsequent recoveries to be on the safe side of some pretty unreliable bridgework. They made smacking sounds. "Why Larry," he said. "Don't think I wouldn't like to be."

I stepped back to admire him. Gramps was a pretty sporty dresser now that respect for old age allowed him to do more or less what he pleased and I always made a point of saying so.

"You look great," I told him. "Fit for the finals at Wimbledon."

More smacking sounds.

Actually the finals at Wimbledon was not quite where he belonged for though sporty enough Gramps could not be considered a model of fashion. He wore one of those tartan summer sport jackets—the Black Watch, I think—which would have been pretty nice if the young advertising bucks down at Westport and such places hadn't taken to wearing them to bed. However, what really eliminated Gramps from the world of high fashion was not that everybody else had one, but rather because he wore a clip-on bow tie along with a pair of robin's-egg blue slacks which did not match anything known to man. Otherwise he was doing fine.

Privately Abby and I used to laugh at Gramps but laughter was always a little disconcerting for his absurdity was ours partly and though the life which had been his to give now lay shriveled and dying, we owed him a measure of gratitude.

After I finished my slightly stilted display of good humor Abby came over to do her bit. Gramps had opaque brown eyes that sparkled with mischief or fear, it was often hard to tell which, and he fixed them on Abby with the steadiness of a hunted bird. It was as if he feared she might find something laughable in his fallow gallantry, though Abby never would have permitted such a feeling to show. She kidded him too, but in ways so manifestly flattering that Gramps actually seemed to purr with benevolence and gratitude.

I was about to join in just when Bollard announced dinner, bringing frivolity to a temporary halt while we pondered the prospect and swallowed anxiously. Eating was a religion with Pa and except when we had too much company, in which case the food would not be up to snuff, he went at it with solemn reverence. We never said Grace in our house. There was no need for it. The entire meal was a form of communion. Each taste of food, each sip of wine comprised an act of devotion, a gesture of thanksgiving. I hate to overdo this, but it's important to know there were other things in life, besides business, which Pa took seriously. One was eating, another was art. I think Pa would have contemplated murder to further either of these interests. As a matter of fact, he'd lost an old friend —a college chum turned expatriate—in order to gain our Swedish cook. Practically hijacked her from the friend's home during a trip to Europe and, as I understand it, among the eating peoples of the world, this is a crime far more capital than murder.

As to art, the interest was originally Mother's; therefore our collection tends to favor the impressionists. We have a Renoir, for instance. I have to admit it's a pretty small one, but all the same . . . And there's a Pissarro and a Monet and a lot of stuff by people I never would have heard of if we didn't have them at home. So as collectors go, Pa would best be described as primitive. Not that he liked the primitives. On the contrary, it's Pa's considered opinion Grandma Moses stole most of her canvases from a fourth-grade Thanksgiving exhibit. But as a collector he relies more on instinct than knowledge. He also has an eye for the bargains. Therefore, our walls represent some pretty cagey investing plus one or two somewhat bearish commodities. We have a couple of Reverons from Venezuela, or someplace, which were stumbled on during a Carib-

bean cruise when he happened to spot Reveron himself working by
the sea. Pa says you could tell right away the guy was great, but
we also have some of the least accurate paint hurlers in the business
so his instinct isn't one hundred percent infallible. It's pretty good
just the same, though, and Pa's about as proud of his collection as
he would have been had he founded the Gravenhurst *Daily Watch*.

Of course not many people in town know Pa's interested in art.
He doesn't think that would be such a good idea so when people
are around he plays dumb and says Mother's in charge of the artsy-
craftsy department. But occasionally I've seen him in the evening
sitting in front of a painting with a glass of brandy and a thoughtful,
almost sad expression on his face. Sometimes for long periods of
time because I've come by as much as an hour later to find him with
the same painting and the same almost sadness.

Mother, on the other hand, is primarily concerned with the
beauty of color and technique and is not subject to artistic brooding.
Unless, of course, someone has outplayed us by collecting a little-
known artist-turned-great whom she had overlooked. For instance,
when Mrs. Compton stopped referring to a painting she had picked
up in Paris for almost nothing as "a rather touching little study by
someone you never would have heard of" and began calling it, "My
Buffet," Mother found cause to brood. Actually almost any triumph
of Mrs. Compton's would cause Mother to brood, as conversely any
defeat would cause her to rejoice. This was all fairly friendly and
often supplied the meat of our dinner conversations. It was Mother's
custom to take advantage of Pa and his epicurean devotions by
doing most of her talking while he ate. This was likely to be her only
chance for between meals, even between courses, Pa managed to
outshout her. And if that didn't work, he simply pretended not to
hear a word she said until Mother finally gave up in a fizzle of
frustration.

This particular evening she was using her allotted time to fill us
in on the latest doings of the Nepotan Society, a very exclusive
ladies' club to which one could be elected only after Death had
joyously created a vacancy.

Well Mother was talking so fast and scoring so many opinions I
guess Pa felt she might carry the day so he stepped up the pace and
managed to consume his soft shell crabs plus half a bottle of Chablis
in half the usual time. That's something Abby and I don't see very
often. Even Gramps seemed awed by the performance.

Apparently the weekly name-to-be-dropped, otherwise known as guest speaker at the Nepotan luncheon, had failed to show up which, according to Mother, was a terrible shame because:

"He was that nice boy from Harvard who wrote a book about bombs or something and we did want so to meet him."

Because of this literary truant, culture gave way to scandal and the ladies apparently enjoyed themselves immensely.

Most of her news was pretty spicy, but I didn't happen to know the participants so it was a little hard to remember just who had done what with whom by the time she was finished. Also Gramps kept clouding the scene by attempting to trace the character defects of everyone involved back through the mists of time, only to bog down in hopeless confusion somewhere around the emergence of Neolithic man.

However, when she started in on Ned Polk's wife I was all ears.

"But my goodness, I nearly forgot the most important news of all. Apparently Sally Polk tried to commit suicide a few nights ago."

Pa sputtered and cleared for action with a long swallow of wine.

"Sally Polk," Gramps began. "Sally Polk, Sally Polk. Let's see now . . . Clem Harper's daughter, isn't she?"

"Yes Daddy." But Mother hurried on. "Emma Grady told me she and the doctor were awakened by a pounding on the door around two in the morning. Emma went down and there was Sally, dumb with shock, her wrists bandaged in a torn sheet."

"Now wait a minute," Pa interrupted, swallowing hard and fast but Mother only doubled her pace.

"Emma said there was nobody with her by the time she got to the door, but she could see a man walking down the street. She said the man definitely did not look like Ned . . . Isn't that awful," Mother concluded. "Who do you suppose . . ."

At that point Bollard's entrance forced an angelic silence and we waited anxiously for his none too hurried departure.

"Who do you suppose . . ." Mother began again, but that was as far as she got.

"Emma should have more sense," Pa interrupted. "Has she never heard there's such a thing as a code of ethics in the medical profession?"

"That's Dr. Grady's problem," Mother said. "Not his wife's."

"Blabbing professional secrets all over the damn town," Pa snorted.

"Darling, the Nepotan ladies have no secrets." Occasionally Mother's courage surprised me. Not even Abby and Bollard would have dared such defiance.

Pa demanded a repeat of her last statement and Mother obliged with a chilly smile.

"By God, if you want to gossip, concentrate on your own members," Pa advised. "Enough material right there to keep you going night and day."

"Clem Harper," Gramps said. "Wasn't his mother Mary Dickson?"

"Yes, Daddy, I think so. That's not true, Clarence, and you know it."

"What about Mary Tompkins and that bartender?"

Abby and I sat still as we could, lest they notice us and decide to change topics because of the c-h-i-l-d-r-e-n.

"Mary Tompkins is no longer with us," Mother declared.

"It sounds like the Capone Syndicate," Pa said. "Just don't get caught and you've got a legitimate business."

"Really, Clarence, you're impossible."

"All right," Pa continued. "Let's take another look at your . . ."

But Bollard was back and again we had to wait.

"As I remember it," Gramps began. "That Dickson stock wasn't . . ."

"All you know," Pa interrupted, "is she appeared at Dr. Grady's with a pair of cut wrists. Now what's all the excitement about? Couldn't she have tripped and fallen against a window? I imagine it wouldn't be the first time."

"That's exactly what she told the doctor," Mother nodded triumphantly.

"Well then?"

"Oh Clarence, it's much too pat an explanation."

Pa laughed, just a little unpleasantly, I thought, but he declined to continue the battle.

"Speaking of the Polks," I said. "I stopped by to see Nora this evening and the judge asked me what Ned and Mayor Healy were up to."

"Nothing if they know what's good for them," Pa shouted, and I decided my conversation opener had been ill-chosen.

Mother's next topic turned out to be in quite a different vein. The Nepotans had decided to "adopt" a bevy of underprivileged European children and that meant not only sending money every

month but exchanging letters as well which had the side benefit of
improving one's French assuming, of course, that one adopted a
French child, and didn't it seem like a worthwhile thing to do?

"*C'est une idée magnifique,*" Gramps said, though it didn't sound
quite like that.

"How much?"

"Only thirty dollars a month," Mother answered.

"All right," Pa said. "As long as you don't bother me with the
damn letter writing."

"Darling, you're such a sentimentalist," said Mother.

"What kind are we going to get?" Abby asked.

"Caucasian," I piped up. "They're the best."

Mother ignored me, but Pa laughed, which was why I said it in
the first place and the idea of Pa laughing at something I said made
me sort of giddy so I started giggling foolishly.

"Be quiet," Mother told me. "There's a boy from Cherbourg, but
I really can't decide. They're all such pathetic little things. One
wouldn't believe a child could survive what they've been through."

"We have needy children too. Right here in Gravenhurst," Pa
pointed out.

"Take me for instance." I hadn't meant to sound self-pitying and
tried to cover my mistake in facetious smiles, but somehow the idea
of her adopting a little boy—even by mail—made me surprisingly
jealous.

Mother must have noticed because she gave my hand an embarrassing pat. "Not like these children, Clarence," but she was talking
to me.

I turned away in confusion but Gramps saved the day with another French inanity and I was able to rest and recover in the babble
of inconsequence which followed.

But instead of offering solace my mind flickered back to a stormy
night when I was four or five. Back before understanding when
thunder was fear and to wake in the night was to share my bed
with monsters. I remembered lying still with fright, hoping to be
overlooked by the destroyer that crashed in the night, then racing
through the white flashes and leaping shadows to the safety of
Mother and Pa. I remembered the sweet relief of their closeness as
I climbed the soft mountain of bedclothes and the sharp, hard,
breath-stealing kick which sent me screaming to the floor. Abby had
gotten there ahead of me and did not intend to share the privilege.

I never blamed Pa for being annoyed. Screaming is no way to extract sympathy from a sleeping father. But I wasn't aware of such subtleties at the time and therefore resented his dragging me to my room and locking the door while Abby stayed behind, curled in their warmth and safety, and Mother, stunned with sleep, I suppose, failed to save me from injustice.

Perhaps if Mother had favored me we could have lined up two against two and made a good fight of it but she was, on the whole, fair to both of us which gave Abby a two-to-one lead right off the bat. Maybe more because, though Mother tried to be fair, I think her inclination was to indulge Abby more than me. Given the genteel drudgery of her own childhood, it was understandable that Mother would bestow little gifts of ease and forgiveness on Abby while I, as the heir apparent, received more Spartan attentions. But being understandable didn't make it any more welcome.

Well, as already mentioned, when Pa celebrated something there was no stopping him and the force of his elation soon pulled me free of my private confusions. By the time dinner was over we had all been swept up in the flood of his optimism and even Abby, despite her treasonous comment that the *Enterprise* was fun to read, now brimmed with the glories of conquest. But sharing a triumph with his family was never enough for Pa. He always did things in a big way and pretty soon his trusty telephone began to bring news of "victory" to the homes of our more intimate allies. Enough of them responded by appearing personally in various stages of thirst and a party resulted. Not a big one. Just Mr. Harper and Judge Compton and a couple of other trusties plus their wives, but under Pa's careful guidance they managed to produce a fair share of hubbub. Even the judge made a bid for conviviality though the results were somewhat strident, like a child performing before company for the first time. Of the whole bunch, Clem Harper was Pa's greatest drinking associate. Everything Clem did was designed to make him seem bigger than five foot five and this included laughing. My God, how he could hoot! Now there's nothing Pa likes better than a good laugh to follow most everything he says. At least after he's had a couple of drinks. So he and Clem made a great team. Not to mention a great deal of noise. Not that Clem Harper was Pa's toady. Far from it. He was a rough little character; a lawyer with plenty of formers under his belt—former corporation counsel, former city judge—and now chairman of the Gravenhurst GOP

Committee. Clem just liked to laugh because that was another of the things he could do bigger and better than anyone else in town. As usual, he found justification for this by telling as many dirty stories as he could remember but no one was shocked simply because the party, as was customary, had split in two with most of the ladies fluttering like dainty laundry in a far corner of the room. Only Abby stayed to share the man talk, standing firm and supple midst the heavy tobacco smells and rough wool laughter. It was a privilege she'd been allowed for several years and, since Pa condoned it, the men no longer were made self-conscious by her presence. There was something strangely appealing about Abby in that masculine environment. Though fragile and female, she held a place of her own which neither required nor got any courtly attentions from the men around her. She was like a woman at ease among horses. The effect doubled her sex appeal.

It was almost twelve before I could see any signs of calling it a night. First Gramps, who was something less than a key man in this group and not likely to start a trend, decided to wend his twittering, bewildered, robin's-egg blue way home. Then the ladies began to butt and tug the fringes until one by one their men turned into pumpkins and were dragged off bumpty bump.

Since I have an almost manic fear of missing something, it was two A.M. before I finally followed Pa upstairs and went to bed. Even Abby had folded.

And all I got for my pains was an invitation to play golf the next afternoon with Mr. Harper and Pa. You don't have to be good to enjoy golf but at least you should be steady. I was neither and profoundly wished the invitation hadn't happened. However, if I was ever going to be any good at my job I had to get to know men like Clem Harper and the sooner the better, so . . .

CHAPTER VI

I woke up early the next morning with a case of frazzled nerves and mild traces of hangover. A swim in the lake was the best remedy so I hopped into my bathing trunks and stumbled toward a watery salvation. The morning stillness of July hovered over the countryside with a gentle gauzy touch; a coolness which would soon turn to singeing heat. I followed the path down through hayfields clipped to stubble now and shining wet with morning dew. Robins pecking for treasures along the grassy trail stopped, swiveled their heads and flew. A band of crows raised from the fields and winged cawing for the woods.

I walked out to the edge of the dock, aware of nothing now; nothing but the cold black shock to come. The lake was still but for an occasional trout rise and iced with patches of prehistoric mist. I took a deep breath and fell forward in a dive which was almost unintended. Down past the grayness of light it took me and into a world black with lonely secrets. My mind became a part of that instant, its only concern being the sensations and functions of a living thing and again I felt that oneness with life in all its forms from the beginning to the end of time. Then my fingers touched the soft ooze of bottom mud and flinched in disgust; my lungs ached and I reached upward with long, clawing strokes until the surface burst in a spattering of spray and cool, clean-tasting air. I let myself float as long as the lake would hold me, then, as the sinking began, turned and swam crisply to shore. I tried to recall that brush with enlightenment but it seemed a long way off, buried deep in the mud with the larvae and soggy corpses of lesser living things. No longer meant to be mine for I was God's image again and cursed.

On my way to work I reminded myself to call Tommy Compton about that interview with Pa, but there was so much going on I forgot all about it. We went to press at one o'clock which gave only a fixed five hours to get all the copy in and it didn't matter whether there was a lot of news or none at all. We still had to be finished by one. I don't know why it is, but news always seems to break at once. Sometimes I used to suspect the county of a conspiracy to drive us all nuts. Why else would things start happening all over the area in entirely unrelated community compartments? Yet they always seemed to. By making my police calls early in the morning I could usually tell what kind of a day it would be. If there were more automobile accidents, or more knifings, or more burglaries than usual, then we could pretty well count on something big over in City Hall, or a sensational development in some trial at the county court which had been asleep for weeks, or a headline tragedy. There was no logical explanation for this. Not the slightest suggestion of cause and effect. What else could it be but a conspiracy? Or the moon. Someday I'm going to do a study correlating the community pulse with the phases of the moon. Someday.

Anyway, that morning was one of the bad ones, as the page one layout clearly showed:

HIGHWAY MISHAPS
CLAIM THREE LIVES
(#4 head, page one/with photo)

GUARD HURT IN KNIFING
Police Question Elderly Convict
(#5–72, page one/with drop)

UNION LEADER HELD
ON EXTORTION CHARGE
(#2–24, page one)

MAYOR TO SEEK
STATE FUNDS IN
HOUSING PROPOSAL
(#3, page one)

SCHOOL BOARD DEFIES PTA
IN HOT LUNCHEON HASSLE
(#3–36, page one)

DEMOCRATS HIT
HOUSING PLAN
(#4, page one)

And so on and on until Ned Polk had mercifully shouted himself hoarse, and most of the copy was slopped soggy with glue and Meg Brown stopped whining "Ned, Ned, can I use the YMCA photo or do you want it for page one?" and settled for the latest Betty Crocker recipe instead and there was a nervous stench in the air and Jeff Collins, ace reporter, looked more like the Easter Bunny and everybody else was carefully hidden behind a mask of activity except Ted Pearson who was leisurely pecking away on his daily editorial— this one happened to be on "Interesting Tombstones I've Seen in Forest County"—and except for yours truly who was rewriting the lead on that goddam knifing for the fourth time despite a cascade of instant abuse pouring from the news editor's oral aperture.

Then suddenly one o'clock was upon us and we were allowed to sit around in stunned silence wondering if Ned Polk meant half the things he said, but trying not to care much one way or the other because abuse was a right and tradition due all news editors and not something to be taken personally. At least so we told ourselves.

Pa called me up to his office right after deadline. "I thought Tommy Compton was coming in to see me," he said.

"I forgot all about it. We were pretty busy this morning. Besides, you didn't want to see him."

"Something's come up," Pa said.

I waited to see whether he wanted to tell me.

"Remember Harvey Healy, the mayor's younger brother?"

"Sure. Best reporter we ever had."

"Well, he's going to work for Rosenfeldt. The bastard."

"I thought he'd given up newspapers for real estate, because he had to make some money."

"And now he's giving up real estate for newspapers," Pa said. "Because he's going to be Rosenfeldt's news editor."

"Well, I'll be damned. Rosenfeldt must be paying him a fortune."

"That's right. What's more, he bought up Healy's company, merged it with Rosenfeldt Realty, and made that shanty Irishman a junior partner."

"Wow."

"Anyway, I don't want any more relatives of city officials working for the *Enterprise*. Otherwise we're going to start losing stories, not to mention our municipal contract."

"Wow."

"You're a big help. Now get Tommy over here this afternoon, but don't let on it's anything special."

"Okay," I agreed.

And that's how Tommy Compton became a newspaperman, or at least started working for the *Daily Watch*.

I had lunch that day with the Easter Bunny who was slowly turning himself back into Jeff Collins, ace reporter, by making as many knowledgeable comments on the local political scene as he possibly could, and with Ned Polk plus a couple of the migrants. In the morning excitement I'd forgotten about Ned's wife. It may have been true, but you certainly couldn't tell anything was wrong at home by studying the great man himself. Ned specialized in impressing people and he knew the best way to accomplish this was to reveal as little as possible. Nobody ever got anything out of Ned he didn't want to give, except possibly after he'd elbowed his way past a few stiff drinks. I couldn't blame him for being that way. I'd seen his paycheck once and for a married man of forty, even though he had no children, it could not be expected to bring much economic satisfaction. So there had to be other compensations such as power and prestige and these were what made life worthwhile as far as Ned Polk was concerned. Power and prestige rather than dollars and cents were the measure of his wealth and every step he took was for the purpose of amassing a fortune in this human currency of his.

Even his clothes, or perhaps especially his clothes, for appearances play a big part in the power game, seemed to contribute. He wore suits styled for turn of the century, high-buttoned, narrow-lapeled, suspendered and underneath the inevitable vest (also with lapels), sleeve garters and gold watch. His hair was black, thin, parted in the middle, plastered down and feathered round the edges where his hat, which should probably have been a derby but was a compromise of soft felt, had recently found its groove. This plus his bearing, the slow, authoritative way of answering questions, the hint of scorn when others were expressing their views, the trick of ignoring occasional questions and opinions as if they did not deserve the attention of a superman; all these factors combined to produce not envy, which is the rich man's reward, but fear.

As a result Ned enjoyed a life made rich by the patronage of political ambition and I would say he deserved every last favor of it.

I was impressed by Ned Polk, there's no escaping that fact. But it seemed to me, as heroes went, I'd managed to pick myself a pretty good one.

Being as how Ned was the way he was, I wouldn't have wanted to be in Tommy Compton's shoes. Not the least little bit.

I was in the editorial office when Tommy came through to see Pa, so I stuck around because he'd soon come down for a talk with Ned which would probably be an indication of his future treatment.

It isn't pleasant to admit, because Tommy was supposed to be a good friend of mine, but I didn't wait in the hopes of making life easier for him. I waited the way a fun-loving Roman must have waited for the next serving of choice Christian tidbits. I wasn't the only one either. An unusual number of staffers had found excuses to stick around that day and though hardly noticeable, there was, nevertheless, a hint of joyous expectation. We talked and read the paper and pretended having nothing to do was all a grand coincidence, but any sound on the stairs brought sudden silence. Only Ted Pearson seemed oblivious and asked from time to time "Doesn't anybody have anything to do but sit around on their fat duffs all day?" But though Teddy was supposed to be in charge, he only suggested and expected Ned to follow through and this time Ned said nothing. He just crouched, waiting, sniffing the hot blood of our expectation.

It's hard enough being interviewed for a new job but under these conditions the chore took on Homeric proportions and Tommy reacted in a clatter of confusion.

I suppose he had thought it would be smart to work up a few conversational openers and questions to keep the interview from falling flat. These began to tumble from his lips long before he reached Ned Polk's desk.

"Well this sure is a great day for me," said Tommy. "I mean it's a real thrill."

Now the *Daily Watch* is a newspaper, not a quiz program, so "thrill" might be described as the noun least likely to succeed.

Ned made no comment. Just left Tommy standing by his desk while he looked him up and down in feigned disbelief.

"Gee," Compton said. "I mean, yes *sir!*" He stuffed his hands in his hip pockets, did a sort of two-step twitch with his feet, and looked around the room with a high-flying smile that fluttered and fell. "Uhh," Tommy said, still standing. "Yuh." Then at last he shuffled around the chair and sat in it. Ned's eyes followed him down, full of pretended wonder, like a tough watching the rich kids come home from school.

Somebody snickered. Ned's jaw went out and his eyebrows lifted, as if he had misunderstood and thought the joke was on him.

Tommy's eyes strained from side to side to catch some flicker of understanding, but no one helped him. "Well," he said. "I thought maybe you could sort of kinda in a general way tell me what I'd be doing."

"Doing?" Ned asked.

"Well, uhhh, yuh," Tommy fumbled. "I mean what sort of things will I be covering, for instance?"

"Oh," said Ned. "Are you working here?"

Tommy nodded his head for some time, trying to get things sorted out a bit. "Didn't anybody tell you?"

"Why no," Ned lied. "I guess they didn't want to upset me."

"Ha, ha," Tommy tried to brave it out. "Well I know how you feel, Mr. Polk. About taking on green reporters, I mean. But I'll do my best. I really will."

"It isn't taking on green reporters I mind," Ned said. "We do that all the time. What bothers me . . ."

"All right," Ted Pearson interrupted. "Come over here, Tommy, and I'll fill you in on the details."

It *was* getting a little rough, I guess, but all the same we resented this curtailment of our afternoon pleasure.

I don't know exactly why Ned disliked Tommy so. I mean when he gave the rest of us a hard time it was usually with blustering good humor. "Woodruff, you feather merchant, how many times do I have to tell you? Not None of the suspects were. None of the suspects *was*. How can goddam none be in the goddam plural?" That was his favorite. Abusive, maybe, but good-humored too, while with Tommy it had been plain meanness. I don't know why. The only tangible reason was Tommy's father. Maybe being as they were political enemies, Ned didn't want a Compton right in his own camp, but that seemed a little farfetched. Of course, Ned and Tommy were entirely different types, one being a real man's man and the other sort of a poet's poet—at least from the standpoint of physical appearances. But that didn't seem like enough of a reason either. I suppose Tommy was sensitive looking to the point of effeminacy which irritates the hell out of some people. Especially when they're a little worried about their own sex instincts. But I never would have expected Ned Polk to react for that reason. Anyway he wasn't. Tommy wasn't. Effeminate, I mean. He was tall and thin with large soft eyes and black lashes. He had blond hair combed to the side, unfortunately, instead of straight back, which gave him the look of an English schoolboy and that happens to be just exactly the wrong look to have in Gravenhurst. And he was shy. And since we are getting down to cases he was effeminate *looking*. Only looking though. It would have helped if his hair didn't keep falling across his forehead, forcing him to sweep it back with long, tentative fingers. I told him so once, in the hopes he might try combing it straight back, but he refused. Primarily because I had suggested it. "I'll comb my goddam hair the way I want to," he told me. "And if people don't like it tough shit." Which doesn't sound very poetic, I'll admit, but Tommy was like that—at least he used to be—with me or anyone else he knew well. However, that was quite a while ago and over the past five or six years it seemed this redeeming spirit of his had been steadily on the wane. Tommy went to one of those small New England prep schools which was always raving about its ability to give the students individual attention. But according to Tommy, about all he got out of the whole ordeal was individual abuse. Apparently his headmaster took the discovery that Tommy was not much of an athlete as a personal insult and an affront to school tradition. As a result his scholastic success seemed shamefully inadequate and Tommy soon became obsessed with his own inferiority. Perhaps if he had taken a year off instead of going straight to Harvard he might have been able to shake loose from this feeling. As it was, any chance of building a new Compton image was neatly foiled by his prep school classmates who, either from habit or spite, were only too glad to inform all interested parties that "this Compton character is all right if you have any use for grinds." Since very few people did, at least in Tommy's potential circle of friends, the wit and spirit which crouched behind his scholarly exterior slowly atrophied and all but disappeared.

Once on a football weekend at Cambridge I asked a Harvard friend of mine if he knew a guy named Tommy Compton.

"Old Trench Mouth Tom? Sure I know him. That is, I know who he is. I mean to say hello to or something like that."

I asked if he knew where Tommy lived, but my friend, who claimed not to know himself, wasn't inclined to ask around lest people jump to the false conclusion he and Trench Mouth were on the verge of a budding friendship. In the end I had to go to the admissions office to find his address and when I finally tracked him down it was with mixed emotions. Tommy himself didn't seem so bad probably because I was a childhood friend and some of his old personality managed to bubble through the muck of rejection, but his room told a different tale. The only furniture was that provided by the college; a bed, bureau, desk, and two wooden chairs, bits and pieces which in themselves might have lent an air of monastic asceticism had they been the predominant motif. But they were not. In fact they were barely visible beneath scattered piles of soiled clothes, discarded milk cartons, dirty paper coffee cups, ashtrays piled to overflowing like tiny trash heaps, and other assorted signs of filth. To his credit, I suppose, there were also books, musty, dank, and forbiddingly long. Reference books mostly. Dull, drab triumphs in detail.

"Christ," I said. "What a pigpen."

"It could do with a little neatening up," Tommy admitted.

"Neatening up, my ass. It'll have to be burned."

Tommy laughed and some of his grayness seemed to flake away, but not enough to suit me and I took off first chance that presented itself.

Later on when Tommy had graduated and returned to Gravenhurst I didn't know what to expect. If he was the way he'd been at Harvard the Comptons would have to keep him locked in the attic or someplace. That much I knew. But it turned out he wasn't that way at all. Tommy returned to his Gravenhurst cage just as he'd left it; unassuming and gray most of the time but capable of brilliant color displays on occasion. It was a disturbing combination. He seemed to live inside the confines of his parents' obsession for convention without letting their shadows fall on his soul.

Thus within these limitations fluttered a wild bird of hope, but a frightened bird unhappy with its nest, unfamiliar with its habitat, fluttering fitfully and without purpose behind the walls of order.

Wanting to work for the *Daily Watch* constituted one of those fluttering dreams which Tommy entered with panic rather than precision and without thought for the predator. Yet there was the possibility a real struggle might bind him to reality and give some purpose to his confusion. This, right or wrong, was my justification for encouraging him to work for us, though I don't know why he wanted to. I really don't.

Tommy left as soon as the interview was over and I went after him sort of to boost his morale a little but there wasn't much I could do since it was almost four o'clock and time for our golf date with Mr. Harper. That's probably just as well since there wasn't much I could have said anyhow. Pa came out about then, welcomed Tommy aboard and told me to hustle it up so I asked Tommy why not come by the club around six or so and we'd have a couple and he said maybe he would.

Clem Harper was in the locker room when we got there, all dressed and ready to go, strutting up and down the aisles, apparently pleased with the bubbly sounds his golf spikes made on the cement, and joshing the boys.

"Ah ha," he greeted me. "Where's your old man?"

"He'll be right along. We left 'bout the same time."

"Beginning to think I'd been stood up. By God, I couldn't have survived that. One Woodruff maybe, but not two of them. Ha ha, Jesus Christ, that's more'n a man could bear."

Some of the other men looked up from their dressing with little hopeful smiles but Pa came in about then so they pretended not to notice.

"Ah there he is, the old son of a bitch himself."

Pa didn't go for this kind of stuff in public. "Is this gentleman with you, Larry?" he asked.

"What gentleman?"

"Ah yes, quite so," Pa said. "An understandable confusion."

"Well whaddaya know," said Mr. Harper. "Like father like son of a bitch."

The room clogged with vicarious pleasure and unlaughed laughter.

I retreated round the corner to my locker. Mr. Harper continued to laugh fortunately, but I noticed he changed the subject, went back to insulting the others in his explosive, irreverent, and totally indiscriminate way.

I took a deep breath of locker-room air, a sour but reassuring mixture of sweat from our clothes and shoe polish from the valet's cubicle; a potent blend of school days and affluence which I found to be just right. I shucked the drab cord jacket and flannels, my working colors, and transformed myself from the inside out, at least so it seemed, by donning a pair of salmon pink slacks, a blue knit sport shirt and a pair of richly polished and tasseled golf spikes. Once dressed there seemed little doubt I was not just an occasionally good golfer but an always magnificent one. I ducked out to the golf shop—empty now but for the pro's assistant, it was still too early— and bought myself some balls, cracking the cellophane and feeling their rich-textured newness.

"Going to be wanting a caddy or cart, Mr. Woodruff?" the assistant asked.

"I'll let Pa decide that one," I told him. "He'll be out in a minute."

"Sure thing," and he dragged my bag from its cubbyhole, sliding it over the counter.

"Thanks."

"Good luck" he offered and I nodded, half-serious, then went out and began practicing some approaches on the now empty eight-

eenth green. I enjoy playing golf though I'd probably enjoy it a lot
more if I were as steady and professional as I looked at that moment.
But the trouble is I don't enjoy it in a fun way, only a competitive
one. It doesn't relax me. On the contrary I'm as keyed up for a
friendly nine holes of golf as I used to be for the big football game of
the season back in the old school days. So while pretending to practice I was really giving myself a little sports therapy, trying to steady
down, concentrate, get myself in the right frame of mind for competition, or fun, as it's come to be called.

I couldn't beat Pa, he was in the low eighties just as sure as he
was playing, but I could maybe take a couple of holes off him. And
Clem Harper, well he was steady too but had no form at all, no distance. In fact you'd have thought he was batting clean-up for the
Dodgers to see him address the ball, so I figured on giving him a
pretty good game. I reached back and patted my hip pocket to be
sure the old wallet was there. Not that I'm a defeatist or anything.
I was planning to fill it.

Pa and Mr. Harper came out then, followed by two caddies and
only two.

"Shall I get a caddy?" I asked. "Or double up on yours?"

"Hmmm?" Pa asked absent-mindedly.

"The caddy," I repeated. "We're only playing nine holes, shall we
double up or what?"

"Oh, I thought you'd probably get a cart," Pa said, then turned
back to a previous conversation. "There's no doubt about it, Clem,
if he pulls the convention he'll be elected. Vanden Gasser couldn't
miss in the popular vote. But the convention," Pa repeated. "There's
where we could get in trouble."

"Which reminds me," Mr. Harper said. "You know he's upset as
hell over that goddam Flint Street real estate story."

"Fiddlesticks," said Pa. "That's a dead horse."

"Nevertheless," Mr. Harper insisted, "he was all for flying home
and fighting it out."

I was beginning to feel a little left out and, so as not to, ducked
into the golf shop and ordered up a caddy of my own. Three big-
timers, three caddies, that's the way it struck me.

When I reached the tee Pa was saying: "All right, Clem, dollar
Nassau and I'll spot you a stroke a hole though it sorely grieves me
so to do."

"Oh it does, does it," Mr. Harper laughed. "Well I'd be quite content with two strokes a hole if you'd prefer."

"No no," Pa cooed. "That wasn't quite what I meant."

They both laughed sort of routinely and Pa turned to me, getting ready to make a similar arrangement, I supposed.

"Why don't you show us old men the way, Larry," he said, a trifle patronizingly and I went into a slow burn, realizing they weren't planning to include me in the competition. That's no mood for golfing so I tried to take hold and force myself to concentrate on the mechanics of the game and forget about everything else.

I teed up, stepped back, took a deep breath, two practice swings, neatly brushing the grass on each one, addressed the ball and walloped it two hundred and fifty yards straight down the fairway. How do you like that? I asked them, but silently. If I wasn't going to be included let it be because I was too good for them, not vice versa, as they must have thought. Or Pa, anyway.

Mr. Harper was next; knees flexed like he was playing for a low pitch, he corked a slice about a hundred and fifty yards but without enough distance to get him in trouble.

"Can't do you any harm," said Pa, then followed us with an easy, mechanical two-hundred-yarder.

Pa and I were both on the green in two and in for a couple of pars which is real news for me and Mr. Harper came chugging along for a five and a split counting the one stroke handicap.

"Well what's that for you, Clem, old boy?" Pa asked.

"Five."

"Four for me," said Pa. "Even up, eh?" He forgot to ask how I'd done.

As he stepped up to take his honor on the second hole I let him know. "I believe the honor's still mine."

"I beg your pardon?"

"I believe it's still my honor," I repeated.

"Oh really? But I had a four."

"So did I," I informed him.

"You didn't, well for heaven sakes. Well done, Larry. Well played, old man."

But the effort it took to cross him left me rattled and I sliced one into the rough on the short second hole.

Pa stepped up, serenely unaware I'd been abused—if I had been— and put one on the green for a sure par. This was the kind of hole

Mr. Harper could handle even though it took a driver to do it. He was straight as an arrow, and right up alongside Pa.

They started off together while I headed down to the right in search of that lousy goddam slice.

"What about Ned Polk?" Clem was asking. "Just how serious are his political ambitions?"

"How would I know," Pa laughed. "He's your son-in-law."

"And your news editor," Mr. Harper replied, laughing too but with an edge to it.

It was the kind of conversation I should be getting in on but they kept right on going and I couldn't catch Pa's answer.

"Get a line on it?" I asked the caddy.

"Just to the right of that big maple," he said.

"Good. I forgot to watch it." I'd been too sore, as a matter of fact.

But it wasn't to the right of the big goddam sonofabitching maple. It wasn't anywhere at all, as far as I could see. I took a nine iron and started scything the heavy grass, more to let off steam than find the goddam ball.

Pa and Mr. Harper were on the green, putting.

"Mannerless bastards," I seethed, then tried to get control. "They didn't mean it," I told myself. "Just too busy talking. Mannerless bastards all the same," I concluded.

"Here it is," said the caddy.

I took a furious five-goal cut and knocked it ten feet, still in the rough.

"*Swell*," I told myself. "Just *great*." Then managed to get a fairly decent shot up short of the green and putt out in five. It didn't matter. Pa and Mr. Harper were already on the third tee.

"Ah there you are," said Pa cheerfully. "We've already driven."

I determined to show them my heels that trip and had managed to get possession of enough self-control to do it. I was just addressing the ball with the kind of grim concentration which often works with me when Pa said: "Now remember, Larry, don't try to kill it." And I laced into that little white son of a bitch so furiously I went one way and the ball another in a good-bye slice which was, if nothing else, quite remarkable.

"Oh that's bad luck," said Pa, as I started to set up again. "Why not drop it out on the fairway," he suggested. "Save you losing another one."

"I'd just as soon play by the rules," I said and smirked.

He raised his eyebrows and gave Mr. Harper a mock "uh-oh" and I belted another one into the woods.

"Maybe I can find it," I said.

They both smiled at the humiliations of youth and went about their business.

"Well anyway," Mr. Harper said, "I told the judge it didn't make any difference if the man had future possibilities or not. What patronage there was had to go for past services not future ones. Otherwise the whole damn system's gonna break down sooner or later."

"Absolutely," said Pa, "absolutely," and they both walked on past me, neither one very interested in my little absurdities.

From then on it was just as well they ignored me. By hole number eight I'd managed to lose six balls and the club which, in my opinion, seemed most responsible for it all. I didn't even bother to play in on number nine after knocking two more in the water hole. You'd think everybody'd have been pretty disgusted with me by then. But they weren't. Nobody'd noticed.

"Well, Larry, that was lots of fun," Mr. Harper told me. "Good talking to you."

"Yes, I think you'd be quite a golfer," Pa said, "if you just made up your mind to settle down and practice."

I nodded, whipped. "Thanks very much. It was lots of fun."

"Now," said Mr. Harper. "How'd we come out, Clarence?" And they wandered off together, totting the score and hee-hawing like a couple of conspiring kids.

I started to follow them in.

"Hey, Larry."

I turned gratefully. It was Hal James, on the putting green, still in his business suit, practicing.

"Don't tell me you've been playing golf," he kidded.

"No," I admitted. "I don't think so."

Hal laughed. "Lose some dough?"

"No," I said, embarrassed to explain why.

"Well then it couldn't have been too bad."

"No."

"Come on. I'll putt you for drinks."

"Wait'll I take care of the caddy and get changed." I went over and paid up, finding it a little hard to look my boy in the eye.

"Thanks, Mr. Woodruff. Want me to take a look for your club?"

I looked around nervously, afraid Hal had heard. "No thanks. I'll find it tomorrow."

"Okay," he shrugged, looking kind of superior.

I slid my putter from the bag and turned away. It's good to have a little money so you don't have to worry too much about guys like that. I wondered if maybe I had a lot of money I wouldn't have to worry at all, then went in and showered, changed, got out fast.

Hal seemed cool, relaxed, almost aristocratic out there putting in his business suit, a gin and tonic parked on the grass beside him.

"Hey hey," he said and gave me a big wink.

"How come you're so cheerful?"

He shrugged. "Drink a hole?"

"Sure."

We played around, almost even, Hal maybe one drink up, maybe two, kidding each other, ticking off the town and its troubles with amused if slightly contemptuous sophistication. Pretty soon I was feeling properly superior again.

"Guess what," said Hal.

"What?"

"Picked up the Kramer Lumber and Supply account this after."

"No kidding! You personally?"

"Me personally."

"Wow. What's it worth?"

"Three thousand a year."

I whistled. "As much as that, huh?"

Hal nodded with reverential ceremony. "They're a big outfit," he said, eying me gravely. "A mighty big outfit."

I was still making a lousy seventy-five bucks a week. "Well the least you can do is buy me dinner," I said.

"All . . . right," he agreed expansively. "I'll do just that."

"And put it on your expense account," I added.

"Hand me the *Daily Watch* insurance," he laughed, but only with his face, "and maybe I will."

"Keep your shirt on," I said. "One of these days."

He rubbed his thumb and forefinger together and winked which was in reference to an earlier conversation we'd had about splitting the commission.

I winked back and felt pretty shrewd.

"Come on," Hal said. "I want to show you something."

He led me around to the parking lot and pulled up in front of a brand-new 3.8 Jaguar sedan. "How do you like that?"

I had to admit I liked it a lot. "How much?" I asked, hoping to dull his triumph a little.

"Less than three thousand counting the trade-in."

"Terrific," I had to admit.

"Come on, I'll give you a ride," he said and we took a run around the block while I succumbed to the rich smell of new leather, the sight of polished wood finish and the distinctly pleasant experience of being stared at enviously.

"You're really moving, boy," I told Hal.

"Oh hell, she'll do over a hundred when I get her broken in."

"No, I mean you. You personally."

He laughed with a rich, almost gaudy sense of confidence. "Well, it's a crummy little town. But you can still make a buck in it all right, all right."

"'Member when we used to talk about getting out, doing something different?"

"Not on your life. Not when there's dough like this to be made."

"No, I guess not," I had to agree.

Hal swung back into the country club drive just as Tommy Compton was getting out of his car.

"Hey, I almost forgot," I said. "I'm supposed to meet Compton for a drink."

"That nut? Boy, hasn't he changed."

"He's working for us now."

"Poor you."

"Ah Tommy's all right."

"He's sprained his head muscle from thinking too much," said Hal. "Otherwise he's fine."

I laughed and leaned out the window. "Hey Tommy," I called. He looked around, halfway up the club steps. With the glasses and surprise all over his face he looked more like a heron or something than a human being, much less friend. But then he recognized us and laughed and waved and came toppling down the steps and looked okay again.

"Hey what in the world is that?" he cried, gamboling around the Jag. "A hydrogen bomb or what?"

"It's a dancing girl," Hal mumbled. "Better watch out."

"Come on," I whispered. "Don't be a prick."

Hal shrugged. "Jaguar," he said. "Three point eight liter."

"Boy," Tommy whooped, trying to muster enthusiasm and succeeding, as far as I could tell. "What a meat wagon."

Well it wasn't quite that, but what the hell, he was trying.

I laughed for him and we climbed out. On the way in Tommy nudged me: "Aren't those columns about the most pretentious-looking things you ever saw?"

I pretended not to have heard.

There were only a couple of people out on the terrace so we set up camp in a far corner, watching the few golfers play in, feeling a little too overheard until gradually the twilight and the drinks helped us pull the universe in close around us and relieved the self-consciousness.

Hal leaned toward me, glanced over his shoulder once for confirmation or effect, asked: "See that fella putting the eighteenth?"

"Yuh."

"Know who he is?"

"Uh-uh."

"What fellow?" Tommy asked.

"Fellow playing the eighteenth," said Hal.

"Where's the eighteenth?" Tommy asked, running his fingers through his hair.

"Oh for Christ sakes!"

"Who is he?" I asked.

"You oughta know," Hal said. "You're supposed to be a newspaper reporter."

"Oh I see," Tommy said. "You mean over there."

"Who?" I asked.

"Admiral Stewart," he said. "Admiral Sam Stewart, USN retired."

"Bully for him," I said.

"You know who he is, don't you?"

"No. Who is he?"

"Admiral Stewart," Tommy whispered confidentially. "Admiral Sam Stewart, USN retired."

I couldn't help laughing.

"Very funny," said Hal. "Yuk yuk." He could get kind of pompous sometimes. "Admiral Stewart just happens to be Mr. Big in the motel business, in case anybody's interested."

"What's he doing here?" I asked.

"I assume you've heard of Interstate Inns, Inc.?" Hal hinted.

"I guess so," I said.

"Well with the Route 19 bypass just completed, wouldn't you think it might have something to do with building a motel somewhere along there?"

I laughed. "You might," I admitted.

"If you thought about it at all," Tommy added.

Hal raised his eyebrows. "Seeing as you're *both* newspaper reporters, it might be a good idea."

"*Okay,*" I said. "Take it easy."

"He's also a former assistant secretary of defense or something," Hal went on. "And not exactly a nobody."

"Why not?" Tommy asked, apparently feeling his gin a little.

Hal gave him the crumbling look but Admiral Stewart was just strolling along the terrace on his way to the locker room so there wasn't much could be said.

"Afternoon, Admiral," Hal called. "Have a good game?"

The admiral looked up, squinted, recognized, grinned the way sailors are supposed to grin; all weathered and leathery and wind-wrinkled which was fine except he wasn't weathered and leathery and wind-wrinkled in the slightest.

"Oh, hello there, Hal. Not too bad," he said. "Good enough to take your old man."

At that point Mr. James was close enough to recognize and greet. Large and pink and cozy as a barber he came up the steps and fondled us, one by one. "Hello, little darling," he said to me, and "Hi, sweetie," to Tommy. "How's your daddy?" Then he introduced us to the admiral and, to my horror, they both sat down.

"What will you have, Admiral?" both Hal and his father chorused and then, laughing at the coincidence, both raised their arms and flailed for the waiter.

"Gin and tonic," said the admiral. "Got addicted to it in India, I'm afraid," and he chuckled in a modest, reminiscent sort of way.

The Jameses ordered for us all.

"When were you there?" Tommy asked cooperatively.

"During the war," Admiral Stewart replied and raised his head to display a half-moon smile at once patronizing and seemingly patient.

"Admiral's a real expert with a capital E on Far Eastern affairs," Mr. James explained.

"Middle Eastern," the admiral corrected.

"Middle Eastern, Far Eastern," Mr. James laughed. "It's all Gooks-ville to me."

Hal laughed.

The admiral said nothing.

Tommy seemed embarrassed.

I watched the admiral, and tried to decide which way to jump.

"Have you been there recently?" Tommy asked.

"Oh yes," the admiral confirmed. "I travel all through the area couple of times a year. India, Burma, Thailand, Vietnam, the works. Keep an eye on things for Uncle Sam, don't you know." And he laughed at himself, as only a truly important person can afford to do.

"How's it going?" I asked. "I mean the fight against communism and all that."

"Terrible. Absolutely terrible," the admiral informed us.

"How so?" Tommy asked.

"How so?" the admiral repeated in astonishment. "They're mopping the floors with us all over Asia. That's how so."

Both Hal and his father looked at Tommy and shook their heads. I wondered what they knew that I didn't.

"Yes, but why?" Tommy insisted.

"How old are you, young man?" the admiral asked.

"Twenty-two."

"Well you should know the answer to that one. Where'd you go to college?"

"Harvard."

"Uh huh." The admiral now seemed to understand. "Well, for your information, young man, the Communists happen to be playing for keeps."

"That's absolutely right, Admiral," Hal agreed.

"Looks like Harvard didn't give you the whole story," the admiral suggested with a wink which Mr. James fielded and fired back at him. "Otherwise you'd have known that."

"Seems to me," Hal ventured, "we ought to cut off the foreign aid, let 'em see what it's like without old Uncle Sam."

"Not exactly cut it off," the admiral corrected, "but earmark it for military purposes and administer it with our own personnel. After all, we're primarily interested in protecting U.S. interests and that's what the military's for."

"Exactly, Admiral," Hal agreed. "No I didn't mean cut it off entirely. Just stop wasting it on a bunch of people can't appreciate it."

"Quite so," the admiral agreed.

"Hal makes a point of keeping up," Mr. James explained.

"And I suggest you do the same, young man," the admiral advised Tommy.

"Yes sir," Tommy agreed. "But don't you think the way we gave the money makes us partly at fault. I mean just to hand it over either for military or civilian uses without any strings attached?"

"Of course," the admiral bellowed. "It was our fault to trust the bastards. That's one mistake you don't see the Communists making. When they want something they go right out and get it and the hell with how it's done."

"We could learn plenty from those bastards," Hal opined.

"Better to learn it now," his father put in, "before they shove it down our throats."

"You're goddam right it is, Everett," the admiral agreed. "All this bunk about human rights and self-determination. Lot of hooey. Might makes right and that's that."

"But surely," Tommy slogged ever onward. "Surely we don't have to sacrifice moral principle simply in order to assure the proper administration of our foreign aid."

"Moral principles," the admiral snorted.

"Moral principles," Hal echoed.

"No such thing in international affairs," the admiral explained.

"Not so far as the Communists are concerned," Tommy agreed.

"Not so far as *any*one is concerned," the admiral corrected.

"Then what are we fighting the cold war for?" Tommy demanded.

"Power," the admiral announced. "World domination period, new paragraph."

"Huh," said Tommy, but lapsed into loss of confidence and silence.

"This is a serious business," the admiral pushed on. "No place for all this idealistic claptrap."

"There's *got* to be a place for it," Tommy insisted. "Mankind has never been content to live for very long without it."

"Mankind, huh," the admiral snorted. "This is war, boy."

"Listen to the admiral, Tom," Mr. James advised. "Here is a man who knows of what he speaks."

"Well I don't know," Hal said uncomfortably. "Tommy's got a point, I guess."

"He has a what?" Mr. James demanded, not sure he'd heard right.

"Excuse me," the admiral begged. "Got a little phone call to attend to."

Hal, looking both relieved and annoyed, sulked in his drink. At least he'd risked an opinion, though, and that's more than could be said for me. But the trouble was I didn't know what I thought, it was all so goddam complicated. One day you read one set of facts and conclude this; the next day another set and conclude that. The hell with it. Just trying to figure out what was going on in Gravenhurst kept me busy enough.

"Looks like we may have a little story for your business page," Mr. James was saying.

"Oh?" I asked.

"Interstate Inns, Inc., has decided to build a first-class luxury motel and restaurant on the bypass. Going to see if we can't cut into the borsch circuit."

"Attaboy, Pop," Hal trumpeted.

"Yes sir, we're gonna give those Jew boys something to think about and that's a fact."

I supposed congratulations were in order but could think of nothing suitable.

"Give you a call when the deal's finalized," Mr. James promised, then rose importantly. "Better go find the admiral, get on home before Mother has a fit." He gave us each that special smile and strode off, truly the monarch of all he surveyed. Through the French doors I saw him stop, fumble for his glasses and peer around him, then step out again, masterfully.

"Well maybe the admiral knows what he's talking about," Hal said. "But it sure sounded like hogwash to me."

"That's absolutely right, Admiral," Tommy mimicked.

Hal looked at him hard, then down at his drink. He didn't say anything for a while, then: "I feel like getting laid tonight, how 'bout you guys?"

"Sure," I agreed too quickly. "Why the hell not?"

Tommy didn't say anything, but I knew he'd chicken out and, having made only one trip to the Fun House myself, I didn't feel like kidding him about it.

"We'll have a nice dinner right here," Hal decided. "Bottle of grape, the works. All on me, see, last of the big spenders. Then we'll have some fun, okay?"

"Is the fun on you too?" I asked.

"What are you, a client or something?" Hal laughed.

"Let's have another drink," said Tommy, dry-mouthed. "On me," he added too late to seem casual.

We did. In fact we had a couple more. Meanwhile the terrace began to fill with Friday evening and we became less and less capable of conversation. Curiosity took over and we began peering around us through the twilight gloom.

Then I stiffened as Nora came in followed by that girl, what was her name, Amanda Simpson, and Hugh Godkin and who? Oh my God, Clammy Sammy Crawley. Nora, my love, can't you do better than that? I hadn't seen her since the great Ping-pong debate. She spotted me and gave a little nod and I rolled my eyes but she wasn't amused.

"Boy, Nora sure can pick 'em," Tommy groaned. "Present company excluded," he added graciously.

I was about to thank him when Hal asked how Abby was.

"Fine," I told him.

"Haven't seen much of her this summer," Hal mused.

"Been playing the big leagues. But she's home now."

"What big leagues?" Tommy asked.

"Uhh Guuud, dalling, you know."

"That doesn't sound like Abby," Hal remarked.

"It isn't," I had to admit. "It's Mother."

"But does she like it?" Hal asked. "Abby, I mean."

"Sure. Why not? It sounds like a ball. But she's not too impressed, if that's what you mean."

"No, I didn't guess she would be," Hal said.

"You given up on her?" I asked.

Hal looked surprised. "Given up? We're just a couple of old buddies."

"Sure," I said.

"What else could we be? I can't compete with your father."

"And that's supposed to mean?"

"Listen," said Hal, "I took your sister out for two years. Spent a fortune on her and never got to first base. At least I've earned the right to say she's in love with her old man."

"Let's eat," I said.

"Couldn't even take her to the movies without feeling I was busting in on the two of them."

"Come on," I insisted. "I'm starved."

"Okay," he shrugged.

To get from terrace to dining room we had to go past Nora's table so I groped frantically for a suitably clever remark.

"Hi," I said, falling some distance short of the mark. "Having dinner?"

"We've already had it," Nora informed me, or was she scolding?

Hugh Godkin stood up very formally. "Say Larry, I'd like you to meet my fiancée, Miss Amanda Simpson, Mr. Larry Woodruff."

"Yes," I said. "We've already done this."

"And Mr. Hal James," he continued, unphased. "And Mr. Thomas Compton." He remained standing, thoroughly composed though I couldn't see why. "Well," he said, "you fellows out on the town, eh?"

Hal winked to keep him happy and we sidled away.

I saw them leave when we were halfway through dinner, Miss Amanda Simpson and Mr. Hugh Godkin, arm in arm like wedding-cake dolls, and Clammy Sammy following Nora in fits and starts as she stopped here and there to say a word, completely unaware of the discomfort this caused him as he stood, waiting, alternately trying to smile and square his shoulders, failing at both. I knew how he felt.

Tommy said almost nothing from the time Hal suggested a trip to the Fun House. I couldn't decide whether he was apprehensive or simply planning his escape. One thing, he was sure pouring down the booze and I began to suspect he meant to go through with it this time. If so I couldn't blame him for being a little nervous. I was too and I'd already been there once.

But at least I managed to hide it and Tommy's evident inability to do the same stirred me to contempt rather than pity. A little self-confidence was all he needed. Look at Hal: always in complete control of himself socially. Maybe Tommy had more brains than the two of us put together but that should have made him more skillful, it seemed to me, rather than less.

On our way out, a couple of courage-pumping brandies later, Tommy allowed as how he thought he'd ride over to the Fun House with me.

"But we don't come back this way," I said.

"S'all right," he said. "I'll pick up the car tomorrow."

"Doesn't make sense," I shrugged.

"S'all right," he insisted with a touch of dissonance. "S'all *right*," and he jumped in the car before I could make any more objections.

I wasn't about to let Hal get away from me in that goddam Jag so we took off with a screech and I hung right on his tail as we wound and whined down a set of older and older country roads. We were going too fast to talk. Especially with the top down.

"Larry," Tommy shouted.

I nodded grimly, taking a curve wide and dragging out of it with a heavy foot.

"Larry, what's it like?"

"What's what like?"

Hal started pulling away from me on a straight stretch and boy I really had to haul ass. The engine raged and my hair lashed in the wind, stinging like sand. Tommy forgot what he was saying. I could tell his eyes were on the speedometer, fascinated. It touched ninety, then fell off as I caught up and slowed to turn onto a dirt road. The race was over then and we bounced along at a more reasonable speed.

"Being with a whore," Tommy said.

I laughed. "Just like being with anybody else," and the confidence skimmed from driving and drinking spared me the realization that I had no way of knowing whether that was so or not.

Tommy lapsed into silence again as we turned in at an old farmhouse. From the outside you could see nothing unusual but a thin strip of light around the shaded windows. This wasn't to fool the cops. They knew all about it anyway. Just to be sure some good citizen didn't get suspicious and file a complaint.

We pulled up by the side door, let the attendant take our cars past the house and into the barnyard parking lot out of sight of the road. Hal was hot to trot.

"This country living," he laughed. "It's the greatest."

"Hmmm boy," I agreed. "Smell that clean country air."

"We ought to come out here more often," Hal said. "Good for our health."

Tommy didn't say anything, but he stuck good and close.

"Yes sir," said Hal. "Gonna get me little Susie tonight."

I couldn't remember mine's name.

Hal went up and knocked on the kitchen door and pretty soon there was some shuffling and the door opened and a woman all frazzle-headed like a farmer's wife stuck her head out.

"Sorry to bother you," Hal said, keeping his face in the dark.

"But my car broke down up the road and I was wondering if we could use your phone."

She squinted at him, then whooped.

"Can't fool me, you young devil," and waved us in.

"Finest quail farm in America," Hal told Tommy confidentially. "And poor old Mother Murphy runs it all by herself."

Mother whooped again but her eyes were on Tommy.

"May I present Mr. Thomas Compton," I said. "Mr. Compton, Mother Murphy."

"No," said Mother Murphy incredulous. "Well isn't that the nicest thing." She was round and fat with pretty-baby features deep set in the suet like a pastry face painted on a large white cake. "Well now you just make yourself to home, young man," and she took his arm and Tommy kind of leaned into her like he thought she could help. Then she led us to the pantry where we were fitted out with a grotesque and varied assortment of Halloween and comic masks, a tradition partially responsible—but only partially—for Mother Murphy's place being known as the Fun House.

Hal traded in his pussy-cat mask for a bunny rabbit on grounds that it was more appropriate. But Tommy and I, not feeling ourselves regular enough customers, settled for Mother Murphy's first choice; a woodpecker for Tommy and a sort of caveman for me, though it might have been anybody.

"There," said Mother Murphy. "Bunny, Birdie, and Baboon, don't you make a handsome trio."

"Baboon?" I asked, a trifle miffed.

"Baboon," Mother Murphy confirmed. "The girls have decided he's a baboon." I wondered how many people had worn this face before me. We were then led through the cellar door, down to her locally famous Forest Room and there deposited at the bar.

"Could I please have Susie?" Hal begged, temporarily awed by the sudden plunge into this sultry, night-blooming existence.

Mother Murphy gave him a reassuring wink and left us.

We were in a fine brick cellar, properly aged and tempered in a country tradition originally intended for Mason jars and cider barrels, apples, potatoes, and onions slowly stewing in their bins, but now hidden under Mother Murphy's sure instinct for the garishly elegant. Through the gloom emerged glass-topped tables with gold-painted iron filigree and black imitation-leather chairs clustered around imitation gas lampposts similarly adorned and faintly glowing and the bar itself a long golden rampart festooned with plaster cupids and curlicues and backed with mirrors and racks of liquor including an unusually varied assortment of exotic, mouth-wrenching cordials. Mother Murphy would not be a likely choice to redecorate the White House, but the very outlandishness of her décor was strangely suitable in the Forest Room and a welcome diversion from the patrons. Ah yes, the patrons, an awesome collection of shapes and sizes all masked as weasels and ferrets and stoats and frogs and bunny rabbits and rats and mice and pigs and ducks; in short every conceivable representative of barnyard, boondock and bog, each facing his female-type human being across the golden festoonery. Seated in back were the reasonably discreet married men, seeking the security of darkness and solitude. The bachelors generally gathered at the bar, or wherever they pleased, and the truly discreet, the solid citizens, made no public appearance at all, but arrived by taxi and crept straight to their beds where, like eager children, they awaited the mothers of sin to come tuckums in and bestow that special good-night copulation.

Besides ourselves there were four or five other masked men lounging on the bar with their whores in various poses of casual innocence, an effect achieved, perhaps, by the very unwhorishness of the whores. If I'd seen them anywhere but Mother Murphy's it would never have occurred to me they were more or less than sterling examples of the average American woman. This was fine with me. If I couldn't have Nora, I could have somebody just like her and without any more effort than it took to reach for my wallet and relieve it of twenty-five bucks. What's more there was no chance of being rebuffed; in fact no risk at all beyond the possibility of a raid and everybody knew that was out of the question as long as Mother Murphy permitted the local champions of law and order to pinch her fruits for free from time to time.

We stood at the bar trying to appear casual and unconcerned but Tommy managed to spoil our best efforts by alternately staring in open-mouthed fascination and commenting on what he saw.

"Look," he babbled, "there goes someone now," as a casual chipmunk ushered his parttime mate through the den door, as it was called, that is the door leading to the upstairs bedrooms.

"What'd you think?" Hal demanded. "They were gonna do it right here?"

Tommy swallowed hard and, not being sure what he thought, swallowed hard again.

The melody of "dancing cheek to cheek" curled from three or four carefully placed speakers.

We ordered drinks from a large, black bartender, half of whose face was arched in permanent surprise (or was it scorn?) at the antics of his masters while the other half rested in quiet contemplation. It was a medley of expression which aroused both irritation and envy in me.

Then Mother Murphy returned, followed by a threesome of girls who queued and waited in various hip-hitched postures of rest and mild boredom, like women in front of a first-run movie house.

"Susan," said Mother Murphy, "I believe you've met Bunny Rabbit."

"Yeah?" Susan asked, rolling a piece of gum from one side to the other and resuming her chew.

"Hello again," said Hal.

"And Paula, this is Mr. Woody Woodpecker."

"Vell, how do you do," said Paula, a slightly deteriorated European with vague blond hair and well-boned features incorrectly mounted on a lumpy body.

"Very nice to know you," said Tommy in his best dancing-class style.

"And Anita, Mr. Baboon."

Our eyes locked as though we were strangers passing on a crowded street, each briefly and unintentionally caught in the other's web of hope and fear.

"Hey," I said. "How are you?"

"Very nice," she assured me.

"And now I'll leave you nice young people," said Mother Murphy.

Well, I guess we all sort of wished she hadn't done that. I mean we needed somebody to start the conversation going.

"You're Spanish or something?" I asked Anita.

"From Cuba," she said, pronouncing it Kuba, but being pretty good at languages, I knew what she meant.

"Hey no fooling," I said. "Did you hear that, Hal? Anita's from Cuba."

"Is that so," said Hal.

"And where are you from?" Tommy asked Paula.

"Hong-gary," said Paula.

"Well well," I said. "We owe the Communists a real debt of gratitude."

"Do not be so modest," said Paula and for the first time expression filtered into Anita's pale brown cheeks. I could be thankful for that at least.

Hal put his arm around Susie and drew her away from the others. "How you doing, Sugar Baby?"

"Oh it's you," she said and allowed herself to be withdrawn, much as a Pomeranian might allow itself to be trundled away by an overprotective mistress.

"How long have you been in this country?" Tommy asked.

Paula took a long drag on her cigarette and hissed. "Ten years."

"Like it?" Tommy asked.

She shrugged. "Inter-*esting*," she said.

This line of conversation didn't seem to be getting us anywhere. "Care to dance?" I asked.

Anita cocked a shoulder in acquiescence and backed up to the dance floor, waiting, empty-faced again.

We danced cheek to cheek or forehead to jaw, to be precise. Her scent had an oily substance; sweet and sweaty. She pressed hard against me, grinding. There were others dancing. A large fat fox and a skinny owl. We all three stared, dead from the neck up. Her grinding had a woolly, unpleasant feel. I pushed away.

"You know, I'm not really a baboon," I said.

"Como?"

"I mean you don't have to dance like that."

She laughed and we came together more gently and it was easier to pretend. I murmured absurdities designed to shroud the truth and conjure, at least in me, the suggestion of romance. When we were finished dancing the possibility I could be in love with Anita did not seem altogether absurd.

As we approached the bar Tommy was saying: "But what else could we have done? I mean without starting a world war."

Paula shrugged, looked a little out of sorts; not at the substance of Tommy's question so much as the time and place of its presentation. Then she moved close to him so the dress formed a kind of curtain and did something low down with her hidden hand. Tommy's eyes rounded and his jaw fell.

"You like to dance?" Paula asked and whatever it was she kept right on doing it.

"No," Tommy said. "Well yes, I mean if you'd like to," and Paula led the way with Tommy right behind her, looking a little rattled but otherwise all right, except he found it necessary to walk sort of bent over.

Anita laughed. "You want Anita does that?"

"No," I said too loudly. "No," I corrected. "Not like that," and she seemed to understand, coming close in a romantic rather than obscene way and I felt a sultry, apache-like confidence. "How 'bout little drink?" I asked.

"Gin tonic," she said and winked, as though at the thought of what alcohol would do to her virgin purity. Or so it seemed. We both turned to the bar, her hip pressing my thigh; our backs a wall to hide behind, and I ordered.

Hal pushed by, gave me an elbow. "See ya," he said. Susie looked around to see if he would stop to talk, then led him by the hand, more guide than lover. Hal kind of crab-walked to keep up. I turned back to Anita and the drinks. She was facing me and I saw her breasts, soft and brown, gently cupped. She watched my eyes and laughed and I turned back to the drink for fear she'd do something whorish.

"After this," she said, nodding at her glass. Then leaned over and whispered in my ear. "Like lovers," and her tongue probed more like a hungry lizard and I struggled to hold the image.

When we turned to leave I saw Tommy had already been led away. Well, they'd just have to wait. I wasn't planning to be rushed.

Hal was just coming down the stairs, maskless, hand shielding his face, as we were going up.

"It's me," I said.

He dropped the hand. "See ya," he said. "Got a golf date in the morning," and he kept right on going out the back door. It couldn't have been ten minutes since he'd left the bar. Bunny Rabbit sure suited him.

I followed Anita down a dark hall.

"It's number eleven," she said. "I'll be right back."

I kept going, shuffling, squinting, trying to see the room numbers without eavesdropping, found eleven, opened it and stared through the door as a bare-assed woman came down hard with a whip across the back of a kneeling and similarly unattired gentleman caller.

"Oh God," he groaned happily.

She came up for a second stroke, saw me, shrugged and let him have it again.

"Ahhh," said her contented friend. "You're killing me."

I closed the door in a hurry.

"Psst." It was Anita. "That's seventeen," she said, and so it was.

Well what happened during the next few minutes has been pretty thoroughly documented by better quasi-journalists than myself so it shouldn't be necessary to go into detail. However, perhaps I should note there was no immediate postcopulative guilt, no feeling of dissatisfaction, no self-recrimination, nothing of that. We had managed to retain enough of the romantic aura for which I in my piety felt a need so I was able both to perform and enjoy the performance as well as my limited experience required. In other words, the animal in me was well exercised, well satisfied and without conscious recognition of this, for *I* was a human *being*, after all, I felt as content and unconcerned as a full-bellied babe.

It was a short-lived contentment, however, for no sooner had I dressed and transformed myself back to Larry Woodruff, sated citizen, than I began to wonder what was wrong with me that I should gain such pleasure beyond the boundaries of propriety. Pretty soon I felt guilty about not feeling guilty and was thus ready again to face and understand the outside world. I said good night to Anita, adjusted my mask, and was off to find Tommy when a door swung open in sort of a hurry and out popped Hugh Godkin without his mask, looking a trifle preoccupied as though the one thing he wanted to do most was get as far away from the Fun House as possible. Not recognizing me, he turned fast and beat it down the hall. I took a look over the door. It was number seventeen all right.

I was in the bar a half hour before Tommy came in looking as placid and content as I'd felt. Paula was right with him.

"My God," I said. "Where you been?"

Tommy shrugged, seemed baffled. "Where was I supposed to be?"

Paula laughed and rolled her eyes. "Vas like Olt Faithful," she said.

Tommy looked away with a mixture of pride and embarrassment, as though he'd just won a prize for excellence in English composition or something.

"Where's Hal?" he asked.

"Went home."

"Went home? What for?"

I started to say something when Mother Murphy came over and whispered to Paula. She looked a little confused, then turned to Tommy.

"You come see Paula again," she said. "I haf telephone call," and she hurried off.

"Come on," I said. "Let's go home," and I managed to get him out the back door before Paula returned with her next customer.

CHAPTER VII

About a month after Rosenfeldt got his newspaper going something rather unusual happened. We received an invitation to come for lunch and spend the day at his place across the Connecticut state line in Putnam County, New York. Pa, of course, thought the man had either lost his mind or wanted to make a deal and of these two possibilities only the second interested him in the slightest. But he soon decided if Rosenfeldt wanted to talk deals so early in the game, then the odds were pretty good another couple of months would finish him off. Pa much preferred a clean bust to compromise.

Actually the assumption he was ready to talk compromise at that point didn't seem very likely to me. The *Enterprise* wasn't doing badly from what I could tell. Of course a lot of it was due to curiosity but I'd heard people make such cracks as "It's about time somebody gave Old Man Woodruff a run for his money," which didn't do much for the old self-complacency. Also their editorials had continued to display political tendencies favoring Young Republicanism around Gravenhurst. This policy, while predictable enough in itself, was especially insidious so far as the *Daily Watch* was concerned. Not only did the presence of a liberal point of view tend to force us further to the right than we cared to be, but far worse than that, because of Ned Polk it threatened to split us wide open. Having a news editor who openly sympathized with the competitor's politics could be modestly described as a tricky situation. Even an honest effort by Polk not to let his political beliefs influence the *Daily Watch* might be unconsciously subverted to the liberal cause. Such subtle assistance as the headline play given certain political stories, for instance, could definitely give aid and comfort to the enemy and who could say whether it was intentional or not? In either case there would be an element of suspicion working like sand in the well-oiled gears of our editorial machinery. While Pa expressed complete confidence in the firm foundations of Graven- hurst's old guard Republican leadership, I doubt very much that he wanted to test them too strenuously.

All in all it was not a promising setup and since Jesse claimed to be a businessman, not an anthropologist, we could only assume it was all Harvey Healy's doing. This made things even worse, for now the mayor, who had proved to be something of a fence-jumper any- way, would be influenced by an articulate brother and a powerful press as well as those forces which had already managed to lead him astray of his political makers.

As a result of these developments there didn't seem much chance anyone in the Woodruff family would take Rosenfeldt up on his little invitation, Pa's mood being mild indignation and at best a poor climate for compromise. However, one must never risk a predic- tion of Woodruff policy without considering sister Abigail. The more Jesse annoyed Pa, the more Abby wanted to meet him. It wasn't that she liked to see Pa in difficulties. On the contrary, she simply assumed he was indestructible and intended to savor our victory as fully as she could.

That night she came into my room after I'd gone to bed. After she'd gone to bed too, which wasn't such a good idea for Abby mis- takenly assumed brothers were related to cocker spaniels and she never wore anything but a nightie on these nocturnal visits. I knew it was terrible of me to think the things I did, but I didn't know exactly what could be done about it.

Abby had ice-black hair which was long and straight and cut in bangs like a little Egyptian princess. It almost looked goofy with her button-brown eyes and baby face, but almost is not quite. In- stead there was an enticing suggestion of lost innocence which made men who treated her in a patronizing manner because she was Clarence Woodruff's little girl, feel very foolish indeed. And she had a quick little body which curled up tight as a kitten when she sat down and always seemed to move about on tiptoe in an eager, reaching way.

I was reading a dead book full of journalistic knowledge I would rather not have had to know when in she hopped.

"Hey Abby, for God sakes, get dressed," I shouted, meanwhile trying to take my own advice.

"Don't be silly. I'm just a child."

"If you're just a child I'd better have a chat with my psychiatrist."

"And your very own sister too. Shame, shame." She laughed and curled up on the other bed in a half-kneeling, half-sitting position, apparently unaware one strap had slipped everlastingly far off her shoulder.

"Hey," I said, flicking a finger at her exposed side.

"Tities," she said. "Want to see?"

"Abby, for Christ sake."

"Ten cents a glance. That's a song, isn't it?"

"Not quite."

She pulled up the strap and threw herself full length on the bed in order to sight along her arm and trace the cracks on the ceiling. She seemed to have forgotten I was there.

"Can I do anything for you?" I asked with a real effort at sarcasm.

"I remember taking naps in here when we were kids. I used to spend the whole time trying to make faces out of all those cracks."

"It seems to me you spent the whole time asking a lot of goofy questions."

"And getting a lot of goofy answers."

I picked up my book and tried to start reading again.

"'Member telling me you were Superman?" she asked. "And I was Lois Lane or whatever they called his girl friend?"

I refused to answer.

"I believed you too," she said. "That's how dumb I was. Until you and Hal threw Mother's cat in the cesspool and proceeded to fall in after it."

I refused to answer.

"Remember?" she went on. "I knew Superman never smelled like that."

She rolled over and I could feel her looking at me, and my eyes started working the same line over and over like a busted typewriter. She knew it and started laughing.

"Now let us consider the possi . . ." she said. "Now let us consider the possi . . . Now let us consider the possi . . ."

I gave her a long sigh and put down the book. "Close," I said. "But not quite. Actually it was 'for a better understanding of modern journalistic . . .' But that was a real nice try."

"Thanks," Abby said, but she kept right on staring.

"Perhaps you'd like to paint me?" I suggested.

She thought about that for a while. "I don't think so Larry. Your ears are too big."

It's true, they were. And what's more, I was a little touchy about the fact because, as Abby had already taken the trouble to explain on several occasions, they made me look clumpy. Like the *Daily Watch*.

Again I made no comment.

"You should wear your hair longer," she said. "Then they wouldn't stick out so."

Well, I suppose we could have joked around awhile with that little gambit, but I just didn't feel like it. Not because I'm so touchy about my looks. Nobody could have survived the list of nicknames I've been subjected to and still be sensitive. I happen to have the same button eyes Abby does which, when combined with a helmet of thick brown hair and those goddam ears, suggests a number of counterparts in nature, most of them fuzzy little creatures not known for the nobility and stature which a Woodruff male would like to think he possesses. Therefore, though I'm not particularly sensitive about my looks, even though they resulted in my being called "Wombat" at college, I'd just as soon not devote too much time to the subject.

"All right, Abby, would you mind?" I asked with attempted authority. "I'd like to go to sleep now."

"Don't be silly. I came to talk."

"About what?"

"About Jesse Rosenfeldt."

"Don't know anything about him," I lied.

"Yes you do," she insisted. "You've met him."

"Just for a minute."

"Well, you've spied on him too."

"How'd you know about that?" I asked, mildly annoyed and surprisingly, mildly ashamed.

"Pa told me. Of course, he didn't call it spying. That's my contribution."

"And a worthy one it is too," I said, again trying out my sarcasm.

"Well if you won't tell me anything about him," Abby concluded, "then I'll just have to go see for myself this Sunday."

"So that's what you're up to."

"Yup."

"Don't let Pa catch you. He might not be amused."

"Why not come along?" Abby laughed.

"Me? You're crazy."

"Know thine enemy," Abby said. "Even the Bible tells you that."

"*Love* thine enemy," I corrected.

"Oh," she said. "Well even so you should get to know him first."

"I already know him."

"Not that well."

"Neither one of us should go, Abby, if you want to be serious."

"Why not?"

"I don't know. It's . . . it's disloyal."

"Oh Larry, you're such a clump," and she bounced out just as suddenly as she appeared.

Obviously I was right, but Abby had an insufferable knack for making the right thing look foolish. I told myself it was high time she grew up and began to assume a little responsibility once in a while; a conclusion which proved so satisfying I was soon forced to lay aside my book and succumb to that smug, complacent sleep which only the truly righteous are permitted to enjoy.

But it didn't turn out to be quite so complacent as I'd hoped. Dreams have a way of going on about their business without stopping to consider the obvious, or at least apparent, contentment of the dreamer. Thus I was dragged from my comfortable psychic rocking chair, dumped onto a train and carried off toward someplace terribly important. I always knew where but never why. It was a dream I'd had often and while the means of transportation shifted from train to car to bus to plane, even to bicycle, boat, and subway, it always called for a similar anxiety: Would I get there? Yet there was never any doubt at the beginning. On the contrary, only the greatest assurance that I would. I never missed the damn thing, whatever form of transportation it turned out to be, always settled back with confidence, expecting to arrive shortly and without incident at Gravenhurst or college or New York or wherever it happened to be. But sure enough, just as I had emitted a long, curling, comfortable sigh and prepared to thumb brainlessly through the latest periodical, everything would begin to go haywire. The train would stop where it shouldn't, lure me out to investigate, then with a snort of impatience, more of a sneer really, leave me gaping on the platform. The plane would be forced down at an unknown field, necessitating a private pilgrimage by cab, limousine, subway, boat, or bicycle in search of another plane to wherever I was going and usually ending up at an airline board of directors meeting to plead my case. Happily, I always got there in the end, but it seemed sort of unfair that a routine trip should turn out to be such an Odyssey and such a prosaic Odyssey at that.

Next morning I hit the deck early as usual and did a couple of pushups, knee bends, situps right away quick before I was awake enough to realize what little inclination I had for exercise. It's a pretty good system. Sound in mind and body and all that stuff and it doesn't really bother me that the dictionary gives "solid" as a synonym for "sound." I also took a cold shower which was a habit of mine because I subscribed to one of those strong-man courses once and the strong man told me you should always take a cold shower in the morning because it made you virile or something equally pressing.

As a result of all these activities, I was the last one down for breakfast which isn't always the case, but it happens. Only Abby still lingered in the dining room and apparently she was no longer there for feeding purposes because all she did was lean on her elbows and grin at me in a way which suggested she knew something I didn't.

"Where's Pa?" I asked in hopes it would stop the leering.

"In the living room," Abby said, "reading the papers," and her grin got worse.

"What's going on?"

She shrugged and I tried to ignore her. Bollard came in with my eggs which at least gave me something to do.

"Good morning, Bollard."

"That's your opinion," he told me and left.

I started to read the paper when the hall steps creaked a warning Pa was on his way out.

"See you in a couple of minutes," I called as he went by the dining-room door. That stopped him and he backtracked enough to stick his head in.

"'Fore I forget. Abby thought it might be a good idea if you two kids went to that Rosenfeldt thing. See what's going on. All right so long as your mother and I don't go." And he was gone.

Abby gave me a big fat wink. "What d'ya say, sport. Pretty good idea, huh?"

"I'll have to hand it to you Abby. You're a real operator."

"Of course you don't *have* to go. I mean not if you don't *want* to."

"Thanks."

"But you do want to, don't you?"

"I guess I do," I admitted. "Jesse's a pretty interesting guy."

Somehow it was hard to realize this fellow Jesse, whom I'd met and been impressed by, was also a demon named Rosenfeldt who happened to be the sworn enemy of small-town publishers, orphans and decent-thinking people the world over. I was a little apprehensive about which one would be our host that Sunday when we went calling on Jesse Rosenfeldt, the combined form.

Abby and I were both excited at the prospect of our outing. It was a perfect day, humming hot and ripe with promise the way August can be. And I knew even without looking that the corn fields were blue-green with late summer and the orchards crouched heavily on the soft land, waiting their time. Even the roads seemed slower.

On the way over we swapped theories about how things would be at the Rosenfeldts. Based on what I already knew, it seemed logical they would live in something like a castle; a stronghold. On the outside we imagined turrets and battlements and acres of close-clipped lawns while reaching into the distance, as far as the eye could see, row upon row of huts, each brimming with Blockbusters specially bred to bring immediate and total economic disaster wherever they might be dispatched: Jews for shipment worldwide; Arabs for Israel; a shock troop of black Africans, indigenous or otherwise, for the more obstinate neighborhoods; perhaps even a Baptist missionary or two for special assignment in Ghana, the Congo, Kenya, and points East.

And inside the castle, stone. High-vaulted ceilings, great slabstone floors and a fire so big, so vicious, that it inspired fear rather than comfort. We realized it was August, but there had to be a fire. In the middle of all this, dwarfed but unbowed by the magnificence of their wealth, would be the Rosenfeldts. Momaly, Popaly, Jesse, and the rest nibbling their mid-morning bagels and sipping hot borsht. Admittedly there are people in America better informed on the traditions of Jewish family life than Abby and me. However, be that as it may, Popa would be summing up the week's financial transactions with Jesse close at hand to make occasional corrections.

"No, Popa, not U. S. Steel. That was last week."

Which would make Popa, now nothing but parchment paper and chicken bones anyway, slump further in his high-backed, Victorian chair and lament: "I'm losing my grip, Jesse."

To which plump Momma who was by the fire, rocking contentedly and humming an ode to Zion, would exclaim: "Ooh Hoo hui, such a bizness."

And so on.

Also we talked about Pa and the newspaper battle. Since Abby's very existence was rooted in her acceptance of Pa as a sort of superfather, she recognized no threat in Jesse. To her the outcome of our teacup war was perfectly obvious and she therefore saw the whole performance as nothing but entertainment. She considered Jesse's departure shortly before the final curtain as inevitable as the ultimate downfall of the villain in a Victorian melodrama and whether the winds of fate blew with humor or pathos in the meantime was a subject for amused speculation, nothing more. She would have preferred to imagine it all as a titanic struggle between two beautiful gods, but when I told her Jesse was more of a gargoyle than a god she easily altered her canvas to a struggle between good and evil. And being a nice clean-cut all-American girl, Abby knew perfectly well who the winner would be.

As it turned out, our predictions with regard to the Rosenfeldt living standards somewhat missed their mark. That such might be the case became more evident as the road became less so. Having made the adjustment from macadam to dirt, we soon found grass the predominant construction material, and I was just beginning to wonder what might be next when our Rosenfeldt castle emerged from the shadowy confusion of a pine forest. Actually it was more A-frame than castle.

I don't know why it never occurred to us Jesse might have his own house. Except because we both thought of leaving home in terms of marriage, maybe, and Jesse wasn't married.

A trout stream lurched past the house and just as we were beginning to wonder where our host was, he scrambled out of it, wearing blue jeans and sneakers and a loose white sweat shirt, all of which were dripping wet.

"Hi," he said, trying to wring out his shirt without taking it off. "Just been moving some rocks around to make the fish more comfortable."

"You have?" Abby asked. "That sounds crazy."

"This is my sister, Abby," I said by way of an explanation.

"It probably is," Jesse admitted.

"My sister, Abby?" I asked. "Of course it is."

"No, I mean crazy," he laughed.

"Then how come you do it?" Abby wanted to know.

"I think it improves the fishing," Jesse explained.

"No," said Abby. "Really?"

"Sure," Jesse insisted. "Trout are like people. Make 'em comfortable and they'll swallow anything."

"I thought you were just a businessman," I ventured.

"I'm learning." Jesse laughed and it was that funny, threatening laugh of his. "I'm learning."

There was a silence.

"Any trouble finding the place?" he asked.

"No," I said. "Thought we were lost a couple of times, but it turned out we weren't."

Abby stood staring up at the pine trees that hung big and black around us. "Do you live here all alone?" she inquired.

Jesse laughed. "Most of the time."

"Don't you get lonely?"

"No," he assured her. "At least if I do it hasn't occurred to me yet."

"How romantic," Abby said. "Imagine being out in the wilderness like this all year round." She tore off her scarf in a gesture of release and concentrated on absorbing the atmosphere.

"Never thought of it that way," Jesse said.

"You didn't?" Abby was becoming suspicious. "Then why do you live here?"

"I built it to get away from my family. They were driving me nuts."

Abby laughed. "Boy that's romantic. About as romantic as a horse's behind."

Jesse didn't say anything. But I could see he was studying her with a funny mixture of curiosity and admiration and that great ugly, wrinkle-browed face of his looked more like a mastiff than ever.

"You built it?" I asked, thumbing at the house.

"With help," he acknowledged. "But I built quite a lot of it."

"That's amazing," I said.

Jesse must have watched me grow more incredulous as my eyes took in such items as size and weight of the frames and the huge stone chimney. At least we were right about that part. There must have been an enormous fireplace.

"I didn't put the frames in," he apologized. "And a fellow helped me with the chimney, the plumbing, and things like that. But I did most of the rest myself."

I turned to say something to Abby, then looked away quickly so as not to draw Jesse's attention. She had the expression of a child at the zoo, having just discovered the hippopotamus. I realize it's unkind to compare a mastiff with a hippo, but the similarity did exist and I hasten to add fascination was her predominant feature.

"It must have been very interesting," I said defensively, lest Jesse think we'd forgotten he was the enemy.

"Oh yes," he admitted vaguely. "But let's go inside. Making drinks is what I really like to do."

"Where do your family live?" I asked on the way in.

"They have a summer place near here. Restricted neighborhood. No Christians," and he laughed, either at himself or our embarrassment. I couldn't tell which.

Inside was a big living room as high as the house itself with a wrought-iron balcony at one end where the upstairs bedrooms must have been. This was reached by climbing a circular iron staircase which I assumed he stole from a lighthouse. The walls were split pine with the bark still on—like the outside—which was smart because it gave the effect of a log cabin but also left space for insulation. Under the balcony, but off to one side, was the fireplace acting as a sort of divider between the kitchen-dining section and the living room. I couldn't see details beyond the balcony, but the impression was of heavy, low-hanging beams, coarse plaster, and rough plank furniture. It took getting used to which I might have been willing to attempt bit by bit, had Abby not thrown me off.

"Lordy," she shouted gleefully. "A fireman's pole."

Somehow I'd missed that. Abby made a dash for the stairs and sure enough, running down the middle was a brass fire pole. I must have given Jesse a startled look, because he shrugged. "It's something I've always wanted."

Abby let out a whoop and down she slid, skirts flying. Frankly it looked like pretty good fun so I had to have a try. Then Jesse demonstrated his morning descent which was executed with no hands, thus permitting him to tie his tie on the way down. I decided to save that one for the next lesson.

"Gosh, you really are nutty," Abby said with such naked admiration that Jesse was forced to stare at his hands in embarrassment and pleasure.

"I do my best," he said bravely.

Hard as I tried, it was impossible not to like him, which was why we never should have come in the first place.

I wandered around looking at things while Jesse changed, fixed drinks, and told us all about the house. He was a photographer by hobby which explained why the walls were thick with photos. Good ones, too. Skiing shots full of action, slum scenes full of crumbling sadness, beach scenes with sharp shadows and soft bodies. The usual stuff maybe, but all good and since it was only supposed to be a hobby you couldn't ask for more.

What Jesse liked best, though, was a collection of framed portraits which he called his "Success Studies." I didn't recognize any of them. They were all around Jesse's age and looked like cover candidates for a junior edition of *Time* magazine.

"I've always been curious about what makes one man more successful than another," Jesse explained. "Assuming their talents are relatively equal."

"Have you figured it out?" I asked.

Jesse shrugged. "These men all have one very obvious common trait which I believe will one day make them succeed."

"Ambition?" I asked.

"Partly," Jesse said. "Yet a lot of people have that and never amount to anything."

"Self-confidence?"

"No. It's more than that. Or less, if you will. Energy. That's what they all have."

Not having much, I'd hoped for something subtler and therefore easier to claim.

"Tremendous amounts of energy," Jesse went on. "So that while the average man puts in one day's work, they put in two. Simple."

"I'm afraid that lets me out," I said. "I'm lazy as hell."

"Well perhaps I'm wrong," Jesse yielded, but he did not have the kindness to protest my modesty.

"What kind of success are you talking about?"

"All kinds," he said. "Political, economic, social, artistic. Everything."

It was a pretty good theory, but my instinct was to disagree. I don't know why. Maybe because there were so many people around Gravenhurst who'd gotten to be pretty successful without all that much work. I wasn't sure just who in particular. Judge Compton, maybe, Ned Polk. Lots of people. Anyway I presented my rebuttal for Jesse's inspection.

"Take another look," he said. "I'll bet most of those guys are respectable but not successful."

That's a distinction we don't make in Gravenhurst.

"Mind you, this isn't the way *I* want the world to be," he added. "It's just the way it is."

We drank gin and tonics partly because it was hot and partly because it was all he had and we talked about Gravenhurst which Jesse seemed to have sniffed out pretty thoroughly. More thoroughly than we, apparently.

"Did you know Clem Harper kept a mistress over in Fairview?" he asked.

Not knowing annoyed me so I pretended I did. "How did *you* find out about it?"

"I don't remember," Jesse hedged, garnishing his bad memory with that barking laugh. "Must have just picked it up, I guess."

"Boy," said Abby, "I wish I could pick up little tidbits like that. The kind of scandal suitable for my delicate ears usually culminates in the news that Mrs. Thingamajig entered a store bought mix in the cake bake contest."

"Perhaps if you're a good girl Santa will bring you a nice fat scandal for Christmas," said Jesse.

"Oh goodie."

"Just so it isn't about the Woodruff family," I qualified, but Jesse gave no sign such an idea might have occurred to him.

"That would be carrying coals to Newcastle," was all he said.

Jesse liked to cook and had designed his fireplace so the kitchen side was a charcoal grill. We had something he'd learned to make in Argentina, consisting of small steaks and chops and sausages and a lot of doodads which tasted pretty good if you didn't try to figure out what part of the cow they belonged to. And he made a wine punch which had a Spanish name and was therefore a lot classier than the California guinea red he made it with.

We had a good time and learned a thing or two about Jesse in the having. He had gone to school in Europe for a couple of years, then to Harvard and Harvard Business School which isn't all that special

—even to a provincial like myself—except by the time he was finished Jesse was only twenty-one. Thus for the past eight or nine years he had been hopping around the world helping the old man set up new companies. Every time a venture was started he or one of the brothers would go with it for about a year until things were running the way they should, then pull out and go on to something else. As a result Jesse had been thrown out of one country for refusing a government kickback in the sale of some locomotives. Not, Jesse hastened to add, because he had anything against bribery itself, but because it would have compromised future operations. He had run a drilling equipment company in Venezuela, a trucking outfit in Thailand, an insurance brokerage in Argentina, a soft-drink bottling works in France, of all places. It seemed he had done just about everything there was to do in the business department and all before the age of thirty.

"You ought to be up on that wall with the rest of those guys," I told him.

"Who me?" Jesse gave his funny laugh. "Impossible. I'm a member of the Beat Generation just like you and Abby. You know, the Apathetic Americans."

"Who says so?" Abby asked.

"Well, I'll tell you," Jesse said. "Everybody says so, but let me give you a specific example." He leaned forward and put a spoofing serious expression on his face. "I was down in New York a couple of weeks ago, feeling kind of left out, don't you know, because everybody was talking about the Beatniks and since I wash and take aspirin for my hangovers, that meant they weren't talking about me. Now nobody likes it when he isn't being talked about, so I went for a walk in Central Park to forget my troubles and after a while I came upon some children playing jacks. They all had tired little puckered faces and wild fun-gorged eyes. I asked what they were doing out in the park all by themselves.

"'Waiting for our momies and daddies,' an aged little girl told me.

"'But where've they gone?' I asked.

"'To make the world safe for Democracy,' the little girl said . . .'"

I interrupted with a hearty laugh so Jesse'd know I was with him all the way.

"'To make the world safe for Democracy,'" Jesse repeated. "'That's wonderful. And what are you going to do when you grow up?'

" 'We're going to make it more comfortable,' the little girl said. 'If we ever get found.'

" 'Good for you,' I said. 'That's a very worthwhile thing to do, I'm sure.'

" 'It's because we're such rugged individualists,' a little boy explained.

" 'I can see that,' I said.

" 'What have *you* done?' the little girl asked, accusingly.

" 'Nothing yet,' I admitted. 'After all the grand gifts you and your momies and daddies have given the world, I'd sort of like to take my time. You know. Just to be sure my selection is worthy of a place alongside yours.'

" 'You ought to do something,' the little boy said. 'It's naughty not to.'

" 'Worse than naughty,' the little girl said. 'It's apa . . . apath . . . apa . . .'

" 'Apathetic?'

" 'That's right,' she said. 'It certainly is.' "

"And what's little Jesse going to do when he grows up?" I asked.

"Show the other kids how clever I am," he said.

"Is that enough?" I asked.

"No," he admitted. "Nowhere near."

Abby still had fascination spread all over her face like strawberry jam, but she managed to laugh and look embarrassed afterward. We'd finished lunch by then so she decided to take her confusion elsewhere, got up, kicked off her shoes, and went outside without a word. We both watched her padding along by the stream like a sweet little fawn. Jesse didn't give me any of that "My but you have an attractive sister" stuff, but I knew what he was thinking. Abby had the kind of face that would look terrific on a pillow. The idea sort of chilled me, but it was true.

We talked about the newspapers while she was wandering around and I found out Jesse was interested in a lot more than just whether they could put us out of business or not. He'd managed to stir a lot of idealistic tidbits into the soup as well. In the first place Jesse claimed to be disturbed over the monopoly status of small-town journalism with its dull fare of news arrogantly ground out by such family-owned community tyrants as the Gravenhurst *Daily Watch* and he wanted to prove competitive journalism could still be maintained at the small-town level.

That was ideal number one. Ideal number two concerned news-paper style. Jesse claimed the United States was plagued by two ex-tremes of journalism—the Hearst Method which was ninety percent depraved entertainment and the Times Method which was ninety percent lifeless fact. He believed both were wrong. The first for obvious reasons, the second because fact without opinion was not only boring but inconclusive. You had to offer the reader a point of view, otherwise the facts slipped through his mind like water through a greased pipe. Unless the reader becomes personally in-volved, Jesse insisted, you can't hold his interest and the only way he can become personally involved is through reaction to an opinion.

I told him that was the trouble with nineteenth-century American journalism when we had all crusade and very little fact which he agreed may have been true, but didn't mean complete elimination of opinion was the only alternative. There's a big difference, he said, between forcing ideas down people's throats and simply holding them up so every man can judge for himself.

"Theoretically you may be right," I dodged. "But it's not so easy in practice."

"Being able to cope with this kind of challenge," Jesse said, "is what gives a newspaper the right to call itself good. Sticking the old editorial nose up in the air may make a paper respectable, but doesn't mean it's worth a damn."

"There's always the editorial page," I said.

"What good is it if you're too bored to read the news?"

"How 'bout the *New York Times?*" I asked. "No good?"

"I'm talking about the Times Method," Jesse said. "The Ochs Method, which is what most small dailies have adopted. Not the *New York Times* as it is today. Look at what they did in Cuba and Birmingham, for instance. Right or wrong those stories were matters of opinion."

"Mostly wrong," I said. "If you ask me."

"That's where the challenge comes in," Jesse said. "Reporters who write only what happened don't have to be especially well informed. But reporters who also give you their opinion of the news and its significance better damn well know what they're talking about."

"Like the article you printed on the Flint Street drainage sys-tem?" I asked. "How come you forgot to mention the property was owned jointly by my father, Vanden Gasser, *and* Ben Tompkins?"

"That's a good example," Jesse conceded. "We made a mistake. Nobody knew Mr. Tompkins was a co-owner."

"Really? I thought it might have been because Ben Tompkins was head of Sunnyside Supermarkets and quite a potent newspaper advertiser."

"No," Jesse insisted. "That was an honest mistake."

"Too bad you didn't print an honest correction."

Jesse laughed. "I'm a practical idealist."

"I'll bet you are. Anyway, how's the paper going?"

"Not too badly." Jesse smiled. "Not too badly at all."

"I guess more people are reading than ever before," I said. "Because our circulation hasn't dropped off any."

"Let's say your distribution hasn't dropped off," Jesse corrected. "But it seems to me an awful lot of *Daily Watches* get left on the newsstands these days."

I should have known whether this was true, but didn't. "You're a born optimist," I said.

"That makes two of us."

"Well maybe Gravenhurst's big enough for both papers," I offered, which was pretty charitable of me, but the least I could do after such a good lunch.

"It isn't," said Jesse.

Just then Abby walked in and took the edge off things.

"Why do men always look like they've been caught with their hands in the cookie jar whenever you interrupt a business discussion?"

"I don't know," Jesse answered. "Maybe they have been."

"Clumps," Abby concluded. "Just a couple of clumps."

"There you are," said Jesse. "A lady with real insight."

"Come on," Abby said. "Let's all go down and catch a trout or something. I saw lots by the bridge."

"Okay," Jesse agreed. "On condition you both stay for dinner so we can eat them."

"Hey terrific," from Abby. "Will we really catch any?"

"For you," Jesse said, "those trout will leap right into our hands."

"I was just down there," Abby reminded him, "and they weren't doing too much leaping."

"Well don't worry," Jesse said, "if they don't I'll use worms."

"That unsporting," I protested.

"But it works," said Jesse. "Besides, Ernest Hemingway used worms and what's good enough for Ernie is good enough for little Jess."

"It looks like a nice day for fishing," I said.

"It is," Jesse said. "It's a nice day for fishing all right."

"Yes," Abby nodded slowly. "The fishing will be good today."

"You are right," Jesse said. "Today there will be much fishing."

"Just because the poor guy's dead," I said. "Don't start knocking him."

"What better time?" Jesse wanted to know.

We went fishing.

Well Jess, or Jesse, rather—there I go calling the son of a bitch Jess as though he were my best friend or something—anyway, Rosenfeldt only had one rod rigged so I started out while they sat on the bank kibitzing and laughing and finally forgetting about me.

I'd started downstream and was fishing up with a dry fly toward that bridge pool where the trout were supposed to be so comfortable. But it didn't seem likely I'd catch anything. It was all too easy and mainly I was just getting a little casting practice, watching the line shiver, lash, and loop out over the lower end of the pool, putting the fly on the surface in a gentle cartwheel, taking the slack, then casting again.

And in an instant the rising trout, line taut, striking, fighting a hooked fish and the walls closed in around us and it was just the fish and me and a brief announcement to the world beyond us.

"Hey Jess, hey Jess." Oh come off it, stop calling him Jess, and we were alone again, just old fish and me. He running, tugging, holding off and running again, a good trout, big enough to strip a little line off the reel, and me watching, keeping the line stiff, "Come on, baby, come on now," left hand like a harpist's working on its own, nimbly, and without a net I steered him toward the shallow water where he wriggled, trembled, back and dorsal high and dry, then a quick tug and he was flopping on the pebbles, "gotcha," and I pounced, smothering his flops, getting a good grip, hand trembling, as single-purposed as a cat and with no time out to admire his sleek, fat-bellied beauty. I cracked his neck, stuffed him in the creel and scrambled to start fishing again.

"Nice-looking fish," said Jesse and I was returned to civilization, slightly self-conscious, slightly absurd.

"Yeah, yeah," I agreed. "Nice-looking fish," and went back to my preying.

I got five out of there, all of them nice fat ten- to twelve-inchers and Jesse hooked onto three in a little pool above the bridge so we were all set for dinner and I felt proud as a kid with a string of perch; prouder than I'd have been with that goddam Kramer Lumber and Supply account. Just why I couldn't have said; except I guess maybe there's a lot going on inside which you just can't break to saddle and sooner or later it's got to bust loose. When I'm hunting or fishing it's all right but I wouldn't have liked it to bust out anywhere else.

Later, by a remarkably simple strategy of eliminating all traces of quinine water, we switched to martinis before dinner. Well now I like my martinis four to one and that's all there is to it, but I have to admit the absence of vermouth was hardly noticeable and after one or two not missed at all. But things got a little crazy. Not wild but just sort of nicely nutty; the way it is when you go camping or cruising or something like that. The usual touchstones of order and propriety got lost in a pleasantly scented haze of gin and we were strangely alive. Three human beings in total communication without fear or concern for the consequences.

After a while we got to talking about what it was like living in Gravenhurst especially when your name happened to be Woodruff and the stories came tumbling out so fast Abby and I almost got sore at each other in our impatience to go on from one to the next.

"And then," said Abby, "Mother came over and told me 'You've got to behave yourself, you naughty girl. After all, it *is* a country club dance, you know,'" and she got to giggling at the thought of Mother saying that. "'Oh, is that so?' I said, and I marched right down to the swimming pool and dove in-whee-clothes and all."

"Oh for heaven sakes," Jesse encouraged.

"Yes I did, and do you know what? Our whole group marched right down and jumped in after me. Well if you don't think Mother was fit to be tied."

"But what could she say?" I laughed. "All the right people were doing it."

"And then," Abby began again . . .

"And then last summer," I hurried to interrupt, "they sent me over to City Hall to photograph a robbery suspect and the guy got sore and kicked the camera out of my hands. Well you can guess what the headline was: Suspect Attacks Publisher's Son, that's what it was and the robbery kind of took second place."

Jesse laughed. "People are nuts."

"And you think that's bad," I hurried on. "You ought to hear the kind of things Pa . . ."

"How 'bout another martini?" Jesse interrupted.

"Sure, can't stop now. The kind of things Pa gets away with. I mean, y'know, he and Clem Harper and Judge Compton are sort of in political cahoots. Nothing crooked or anything but nobody gets into public office without their support and I don't guess we suffer for it in a business way. Well anyway, Pa was addressing the Republican City Committee at a campaign dinner back when Mayor Healy was just running for office and what does he do but introduce the candidate as 'Our man Friday.'"

"I'll be damned," Jesse laughed.

"And do you know, instead of being horrified, the slobs laughed."

"Sure," Jesse agreed. "I'll bet they did."

"Isn't it awful?" Abby sputtered. "But that's what it's like around here. I mean being a Woodruff and all."

"Now why would you want to ruin all that for us?" I kidded.

"Ruin it?" Jesse asked.

"Well you're trying to put us out of business, aren't you?"

"Oh I wouldn't do that," Jesse tch-tched in a spoofing kind of way.

"Oh yes you would, too," Abby insisted, apparently proud of the fact. "But Pa won't let you."

Jesse produced his barking laugh and changed the subject.

Then after that we had our trout dinner and sat around for a while until Jesse got the idea we should go skinny dipping in his favorite trout pool which we did, me feeling part naughty, part foolish, part wild and Abby the same, I'd guess, from the way she sort of jumped in quick and hooted and scooted back to the gin bottle for reinforcements. Jesse seemed completely at ease. There's no real reason why he shouldn't have been. It was plenty dark enough. But all the same, I could tell he was just sort of ambling around bare-assed and chatting away as though he were at a cocktail party. I couldn't help admiring or maybe even envying the way he could do what he had to, like being a businessman and all that, and then turn right around and do what he wanted to all just as relaxed and easy as you please.

It was almost midnight when we finally got out of there and it's a lucky thing I'm a pretty good drunken driver.

Abby and I managed to sober up a little on the way and as we did the notion we'd maybe talked too much began to haunt us but I said what the hell, so had Jesse.

"How?" Abby asked.

And so help me, I couldn't recall. "Well I'm sure he wasn't just pumping us. He's too nice a guy."

"No, I guess not," Abby agreed, but though she may have been convinced, I wasn't and pretty soon the hungry suspicion we'd been made fools of began to gnaw away at the day's pleasure until nothing was left but a raw mass of humiliation and I began to drive crazy until Abby got sore and we had a good fight and I felt better.

That night I had this dream I was walking down the street, going somewhere very important when an old station wagon loaded with crazy people pulled up alongside and I could see Jesse and Lou, our ex-sports editor, and Anita all yelling at me to come along, they were going to have a real blast and all the people on the street turning around to see what I'd do and who my friends were and I got scared, started running to my very important appointment, whatever it was, and when I got there it was just a little shack stinking of raw sewage and filth and when I looked on the name plate, all big and brassy, to see whose house it was, I saw my own name and when I went inside the whole place began to congeal. I don't know how, but space and all; everything began to solidify, crushing me, and suddenly I realized I was dreaming but it didn't matter, dreaming or not, if I didn't wake up I'd be dead.

Well I woke up all right. On the floor. And I still believe I'd be dead if I hadn't. Or maybe I was dead.

CHAPTER VIII

Pa's reaction to Jesse's declared idealism was predictable. Almost too predictable, it seemed to me. It contained an element of bluster which tempted me to laugh, and laughter at Pa's expense was a pastime I had not grown accustomed to at all. Possibly my imagination was playing tricks. Pa'd never struck me as the blustering type. He was much too sure of himself and with good reason, it seemed to me. I'd just seen and heard a little too much of Jesse, that was all. To me being young meant a time for watching and respecting while the old bucks showed you how. But to Jesse it was a time for getting things done and everything about him seemed to suggest the old ways should first be scorned and then destroyed. That sure wasn't the way I had been taught. When I found myself in a strange place—like college, say, or even the woods, or anywhere out of my element—my solution was to sit tight and watch how things worked. Not Jesse, though. He just looked around, sniffed the air a couple of times to get his bearings, and took off hell-bent for destruction after whatever crossed his path.

Just then he seemed set on destroying Pa and even though I was in danger too, the idea of hamstringing such a mighty prize filled me with an excitement which, I'm ashamed to say, was strangely exhilarating.

Pa was in his office when I told him about the Blockbusters' new dedication to principle and after a brief cooling-off period he began to show me some facts and figures which helped explain his blustering anger. Apparently Jesse's self-claimed financial triumphs were true. Our circulation had dropped off by about a thousand a day— ten percent—mostly from newsstand distribution, but what was far worse, the advertising lineage was down some seven percent and that, since money rather than circulation was immediately involved, wasn't funny. Pa's being angry with Jesse was in character, but his reaction to those reports was not. Despite a fighting reputation, he didn't look the least bit warlike at that particular moment. He looked hurt.

"Under the circumstances," he said, "you'd think people might give us a bit more moral support."

"But aren't they just buying out of curiosity?" I asked.

"It's the advertising. That's what I don't understand."

"Well, I guess you have to expect that."

"What?" he demanded.

"I guess you have to expect that," I repeated.

"Why?" But he was really asking that time, not challenging.

"I don't know," I admitted. "Maybe people really want two papers in town. Or maybe since the *Enterprise* does have some circulation they feel obligated to give Jesse—I mean Rosenfeldt—some of their advertising. You know, purely for sound business reasons."

Pa didn't say anything for a while. He seemed to be patching up a flattened spirit. "Well by God, I'll show 'em which are sound business reasons and which aren't." He got up and plonked his old-time straw boater on his head and managed to look like himself again. It was a relief. Maybe I'd looked forward to finding a weakness, but having found it I felt embarrassed. Like a fledgling Peeping Tom who hadn't really expected the lady would take *all* her clothes off.

Pa gave me a wink on his way out. "Time we improved some of that Main Street property anyway," he said. "Here, have a cigar." He pulled one out of his breast pocket and tossed it at me and I laughed at the way he was. Like a kid sometimes. Sad as a painted clown one minute and happy the next. Sure, I laughed and felt the old admiration seep back, though I couldn't for the life of me figure out what that Main Street property had to do with running a newspaper. I mean everybody knows a favor done is a favor earned, but it wasn't what you could call the direct approach of a noble crusader.

I stayed in his office for a little while after Pa left, as I had done several times before. Never had the fact it would be mine someday pleased me. It implied change, the heavy step of time. If his office could be mine then it could be someone else's too. My son's, perhaps. Perhaps not. Either way was all the same to me. I didn't like being a duck in a shooting gallery. Pop up, ride along—*bang, bang, bang*—pop down and it's all over. The hell with that. I wanted things as they'd always been. When I was a boy my father told me what to do and I did it. And now that I was on the edge of manhood he told me what to do and I did it. The things he told me had become more complicated, maybe, but essentially the system was unchanged. And that's the way I liked it. The day I'm alone in the publisher's office is the day tradition stops for me. Along with it come such honors as sitting at the head of the table, deciding where to send the kids to school, and what kind of a car to buy next year, and whether the boy should be encouraged to come into the newspaper business and so on until all of a sudden it's my turn to pop down. No thanks. Being the keeper of tradition rather than its beneficiary was not what I had in mind. Not me. I'd just as soon let things go on as they always had with Sunday lunches dependent on Pa's good will and "Dammit, Larry, don't mumble" and all the rest of it.

On my way out, I trailed a finger absent-mindedly along the bound copies of earlier *Daily Watches* which filled the bookshelves. It appalled me to think of the lifetimes my finger flicked across in those few seconds it took to reach the door. Nor would the addition of my own life to the collection of stale newsprint and leather lengthen our insignificant ripple in time by more than a few paragraphs. I could see it all now. Simple as pie. Dip into the files, change Third to Fourth and the job's done:

> Clarence Woodruff, the Fourth, owner and publisher of the Gravenhurst *Daily Watch,* died today. He was —— years old. Known and beloved throughout the area for his many contributions to community improvements, Mr. Woodruff was recently appointed chairman of the Gravenhurst —— Committee. He also played an active part in etc etc etc.

If only Pa and I were not so thoughtless as to marry women with different names, for I assumed I would, there being no other Alice Lindsays in town, belong to committees with different names and produce female children with different names, the *Daily Watch* might perfectly easily use Grandpa's obituary for both of us. But that's the way we Woodruffs are. Rugged individualists one and all.

Down in the city room things were jumping. I guess city room sounds somewhat pompous for a small-town daily. But you couldn't very well call it the small-town room, could you? Or the tank-town room, or the jerk-water room? So city room will have to do. Anyway, things were jumping.

"Been in conference, Woodruff?" Polk asked me.

"Sorry," I said. "What's going on?"

"I thought we'd try putting out a newspaper," he announced. "The boys just weren't happy with needle-point."

I didn't respond. If he wanted something he'd tell me soon enough.

"Senator Vanden Gasser cracked up his plane," Ned said. "He and three of his kids are dead."

"Oh Jesus. Which three?"

"Now how would I know? Call the Wolftown troopers. They're on it."

"All right."

"And listen," he added, "I sent Scoop here"—he thumbed at

Tommy without looking—"to get some snapshots of the family from Mrs. Vanden Gasser, but all he came back with was the heebie-jeebies. So you hustle over and get some photos in time to have engravings made."

"All right." I looked at Tommy. He was hunched over the typewriter, pale, sick white, appalled and limp with shame. He just sat there staring at his machine. There was no paper in it.

I know it's horrible and nothing justifies busting in on people at a time like that, but the trouble is, as the cliché artists have been telling each other for a long time now, somebody has to do it because that is what newspapers are for. I remember the first time I had to. A boy had been drowned and I was sent over to get a photograph from his mother. Happily nobody could see what was inside me that day. Of course I felt sorry for the woman. I wanted to and did. But I didn't know her or the boy and there were stronger emotions than pity in me. Partly fear. Fear that I wouldn't get the picture. Fear the woman might become hysterical and complicate an already hectic morning for me. There must be nobler Woodruff blood flowing somewhere. Partly it was a feeling of cheapness, because my problem and the paper's problem amounted to nothing but self-justification and really *was* cheap alongside that woman's tragedy. But worse still, it turned out she wanted to talk which really threw me. The picture was no problem at all. She produced it right off. But something deep inside had to tell me all about the boy. I guess she felt the telling was all that remained and maybe having one more person know about her son would make him live just a little more. Whatever her reasons, I couldn't wait. Deadline, you see. Terribly important. Oh yes indeedy.

"Well, yes ma'am, I'm very sorry all this happened and all."

"Oh and he was a very strong swimmer, you know. Yes he was. Why his father taught . . ."

"Yes ma'am, I'm sure that's true, but you see . . ."

"Yes, his father taught him to swim and he was just like a little fish. Really, you wouldn't believe it unless you . . . saw . . . him. Oh, my God."

"Yes ma'am, but you see, I'm afraid I'll have to be going." I dangled the photo at her. "We have to get this printed, you know," and I ran away.

Sweet Jesus, that was a day to forget. I thought about going back to see her sometime, but I only thought about it.

Anyway, that's something you don't get used to, but you get numb after a while so I went to see Mrs. Vanden Gasser and I got the pictures. Good, too. One had been used for a Christmas card just the year before and showed the whole family. See what I mean? You get numb.

I also got a clue to what happened. According to his wife, the senator had got wind of a campaign by the *Enterprise* to retire him from public service. It was more than that Flint Street stuff. They were really after him, apparently, and he'd been up most of the night with Clem Harper trying to figure out what to do about it. Then that morning he took the kids for a joy ride, as promised, but looking kind of punchy, according to Pete out at the airport, and on his way in he misjudged the approach, came down too soon and lit right into some telephone wires. Well, if that was an example of how Jesse intended to revive small-town journalism I wasn't too impressed. Senator Vanden Gasser was the only clean politician I'd ever come across. Anyway, Jesse got his way that time. The senator was retired.

But since Senator Vanden Gasser was a public servant, we were unable to concern ourselves for very long with the personal tragedy involved. Naturally we managed to produce our proper share of murmured commiserations on demand. But the real news, as far as we were concerned, was what would happen to Gravenhurst's political scales now that a sizable weight had been removed. Wilbur Vanden Gasser belonged to the Woodruff-Compton-Harper system of weights and measures and unless he was replaced with like kind and quality things could get a little tippy for the old guard.

Ned Polk didn't waste any time trying to figure out which way the scales were shifting. In fact he wrote the political story himself which he only did when the consequences were so delicate they couldn't be victimized by the subtle distortions of less experienced political observers such as Jeff Collins or me.

Ted Pearson took over as news editor and right away the high-pitched excitement which Ned maintained subsided to a kind of humdrum efficiency. Well, not right away exactly, but fairly soon after Ned and Teddy Pearson exchanged a few words which weren't too friendly.

"Would I what?" Teddy asked.

"Take the desk," Ned said. "While I follow up the Vanden Gasser story."

"You mean permanently?" Teddy asked.

"I mean today," Ned growled. "That's what I mean, today."

"Oh," said Teddy. "I thought you might have had something more permanent in mind."

"Did you?" Ned said, but that was all. He simply got up and stood over the executive editor's desk until his superior scurried away. That was all if you discounted the rage which stained his neck a stormy red and turned his knuckles white as chicken bones. It was such incidents as these which left me wondering whether I'd ever know what was going on behind the listless façade of Gravenhurst politics. The story Ned wrote offered little in the way of enlightenment, other than the noticeable absence of comments from such political stalwarts as Judge Compton and Clem Harper. The only people he did quote were Mayor Healy and three or four other characters whose contributions to the community, so far as the old guard was concerned, were pretty questionable. And Pa, of course, though I have a feeling he too would have been overlooked had he not taken the trouble to send down a statement. Even so it wasn't what you could call a balanced story. Since Pa hadn't expected any political speculation until the grave cooled a little, his statement was purely a testimonial and sounded pretty hollow alongside the practical commentary of Mayor Healy and his cohorts. But lest anyone attribute heartlessness to these forward thinking citizens, Ned was careful to pad their comments in the soft accents of deep mourning. Such adjectives as tragic, untimely, and sorrowful joined ranks with dedicated, noble, and farseeing to warm the cold, hard skin of underripe speculation.

Naturally Pa was none too pleased, but there wasn't much he could do about it because that day, by strange coincidence, a copy of the first edition was late reaching his desk and the paper was already out when he discovered Ned's story. But just in case this wasn't enough, the *Enterprise* came through with a real ballbreaker. Under Harvey Healy's by-line came the news that Ned Polk was one of three or four outstanding citizens mentioned to succeed Senator Vanden Gasser. The mayor's brother neglected to inform his readers exactly *who* had mentioned Ned Polk but that wasn't too hard to figure out. Harvey Healy, most likely.

Just how mad all this made Pa I really couldn't say, because instead of coming down and sounding off in his usual fashion, Ned was invited upstairs for a little private chat.

I didn't see Pa the rest of that day. Suffering Tommy asked me
to stop for a drink in the evening and I accepted, but only on condition we went out for dinner someplace because I couldn't stand
the idea of sitting around with the gray judge and his wife, talking
about the plane crash and having a tch-tch party. Besides, it occurred to me Nora might come along which would offer a nice
uncompromising chance to tell her how sorry I was about my despi-
cable Ping-pong manners. It worked out fine. Nora could have dinner
with us. In fact it even seemed like she *wanted* to and wasn't mad
at all. Too bad the same couldn't be said for her father. His usual
petulant whine had risen, to an indignant screech which, out of
loyalty probably, concerned itself more with Ned Polk's betrayal
than Pa's laxity. However, there were occasional overtones, leaving
the strong suggestion Judge Compton's loyalty couldn't stand much
more abuse from Pa. I was delighted when we finally left the Compton house.

I expected Tommy to be pretty depressed after his perfect failure
so it didn't look like light laughter would dominate the evening.
On the other hand, Ned gave me a by-line on the plane crash—my
first one on a lead story—so I was looking forward to playing the
combined role of hero and amateur psychiatrist in front of Nora.

We went to Frank's Place, a little bar and grill which was so
crummy people thought it had atmosphere. It was near the paper
and had become a hangout for reporters and politicians and off-duty
cops and a woeful, yapping, leg-lifting, face-licking pack of patronage hounds who spent their lives chasing political possums up the
power tree.

I liked taking Nora there because everybody knew me. But it was
more than that. Frank's Place was unique for two reasons. First
because of Frank himself, who was the self-appointed destroyer of
local tradition, social custom, self-esteem, pomposity, professed virtue, and all remaining forms of personal histrionics. Second because
the migrant reporters, their wit sharpened by loneliness, and the
local boys, their self-confidence bulging with the hot air of togetherness, were natural-born antagonists. You couldn't get bored at
Frank's. Something was bound to happen. The place was nothing
but bad lighting and bad photographs of patrons past and present
and wooden booths with the inevitable carved initials and the me-
mentos of pain and passion customarily found in a small city's vitals.
The yellowed headline MAYOR SHOT BY MADMAN, the night-

stick snatched from a long-dead cop by a long-dead drunk in one of Frank's historic barroom brawls. But at least you couldn't get bored.

When we arrived it was still pretty early, but there were signs. Frank was behind the bar talking to a patron. "Three manhattans and you're dead."

"Your ass," from the customer, but that was all he needed—just a little challenge—to keep him there all night. And Frank knew it.

Somebody on the telephone. "Don't wait dinner, honey. Jus' wait."

A subtle shift in juke-box selections favoring such musical splendors as "Hound Dog" and "Got along withoutcha before I metcha, gonna get along withoutcha now."

Frank spotted us as we came in. "Hey, we got the Ivy League tonight," he shouted. "Whatsamatter, you miss the turn for Century Park?"

I gave him a grateful wave. It was a real honor to be abused by Frankie Bourbon, self-declared pretender to the throne of France. Someday when I'm a big man in Gravenhurst maybe I'll be able to smart-talk him back. Wouldn't that be something!

There were plenty of booths unoccupied because most of the people were still clustered around the bar working out the kinks, so we took one and settled in for the long pull.

Nora always looked a little disapproving when I took her to Frank's, for which she couldn't really be blamed. But I figured it was good to get her away from all the coffee and righteousness once in a while. Not that I have anything against charity work. I mean somebody has to do it and as long as you really have something to give and don't do it just to make points for the Junior League or to rub up against some old bag who can do things for you socially, I guess it's all right. But a little change now and then never hurt anyone.

Frank came over to take our orders.

"What'll it be, gang? Ginger ale for the entire crowd. Live a little. I'll add some lemon peel and we'll have a real high-class party."

Sometimes he could get a little tiresome, but I never heard anybody say so. Not that Frank was big, but he had a tough mouth which embarrassed the sober people and outran the drunks.

"Nora?" I asked.

"Tom Collins," she said.

"Christ, it's a party," said Frank.

"Martini," I said.

"Me too," said Tommy.

"Oh my!" said Frank.

Nora looked prettier that night than I can ever remember seeing her. I tried to figure out why and decided it was because she seemed just a little puzzled and unsure of herself. She had a soft, almost frightened quality which was a relief after the no-nonsense competence her face usually reflected. Also she'd been getting some sun and her skin was honey brown, her hair touched with gold, and her whole being somehow hungry, yet gently passive; proud, yet with a touch of desire. It was pleasantly disturbing. I'd never seen her look so human before.

But the real surprise was Tommy. He seemed genuinely relieved by his convincing exhibition of what the unpromising young reporter is supposed to do.

"I thought you'd be glum as hell," I told him.

He just shrugged and didn't seem to think it worth discussing.

"What happened?" Nora asked.

"Oh I fouled up as usual," Tommy admitted. "They sent me out to get pictures of the children from Mrs. Vanden Gasser and I couldn't go through with it."

"I should think not," said Nora. "What a gruesome thing to do."

"Now wait a minute," I objected. "Somebody had to."

"Did you?" Nora asked. "I saw your by-line or whatever it's called."

"Yes."

"Oh Larry, how could you?"

"Well what did you expect?"

"A little peace and privacy for Mrs. Vanden Gasser," Nora replied.

"That's the way I see it," Tommy said. "You can't feel ashamed of being decent."

"Cut it out," I said.

Tommy laughed. "I guess that's not the real reason," he admitted.

"What is?"

"You'll think I'm crazy," Tommy said. "But somehow it was a real relief to make such a complete hack of an assignment and live to tell the tale."

"You mean things can't get any worse?" I asked.

"That's right."

"Well that's a crazy way of looking at things," I agreed.

"You're just sorry you had to do it," Nora said.

As a matter of fact I was sort of proud of doing it, but didn't dare let on. "Oh I'm a real criminal," I said instead.

Nora chose to ignore me.

"Don't feel too badly," Tommy laughed. "You couldn't help it."

"Were they really mad at you?" Nora asked him.

"Ned Polk was pretty annoyed," Tommy said, apparently boasting.

"Well I guess we ought to celebrate," I suggested. "I mean not everybody can screw things up as well as you."

"That's right," Tommy agreed. "Bartender."

The idea of addressing Frank as "bartender" made me shudder.

"Whaddya know," Frank said. "After all these years Frankie Bourbon, pretender to the throne of France, finally gets a title."

"Could you make them a little drier next time," Tommy asked.

Frank said nothing. He just stared from behind the bar and tongued his cigar.

"What's the matter with him?" Tommy wanted to know.

"He's not the bartender," I explained. "He's the owner."

"That's the trouble with this country," Tommy said. "Everybody *owns* something."

"I know. It's awful, Tommy."

After a while Frank brought the drinks.

"I apologize for my rudeness," said Tommy. "Nobody told me you were pretender to the throne of France."

To my surprise Frank laughed. "Don't get in a sweat. It ain't well known."

"Well it should be," Tommy said. "I mean it's the kind of thing people like my sister here consider very important."

"Hey, where'd you find this character?" Frank asked me. "He's sick."

"Up to the state hospital," I said.

"Yeah, they got some good ones," Frank nodded.

"That's right," Tommy said. "Take me, for instance."

"Do I got a choice?"

"Now I think I'm Robespierre."

"Who?" Frank asked.

"Robespierre," Tommy repeated. "Maximilien François Marie Isidore de Robespierre."

"Is it a broad?" Frank asked.

"It's one of the guys who put the finger on Louis the Sixteenth," I said. "You know, Uncle Louis."

"No kidding," Frank said. "Whaddya wanna be him for?"

Tommy shrugged. "It's a living."

"Real sick," Frank said. "Who is this kid?"

"Tommy Compton," I said.

"The judge's son," Frank said. "That figures," and he walked away.

Having always treated Frank with a respect reserved for members of the football team, I was somewhat awed by Tommy's performance. As I've said before, he could act kind of crazy, but seldom when strangers were around.

"What's come over you?" I asked.

"I told you. I'm a new man."

I looked unconvinced.

"If you'd really like to know," he said. "I'll explain."

"That would be great."

"It's because I've come to the conclusion newspaper reporting is a snap."

"Wonderful. Then maybe you'll learn how to do it."

"Maybe. But I'd hoped it would be more of a challenge."

"You've only been doing it a month. That's a little early to tell."

"Long enough to know it's just like bricklaying."

"Meaning?"

"The writing," he said. "You just pile words into little pyramids of fact. There's nothing to it."

"Journalism isn't a question of writing," I argued. "It's a question of gathering the news, sorting things out and being sure it's put together right."

"Well, I wish somebody'd taken the trouble to tell me that," Tommy said. "I want to write."

"Are you going to quit?"

"I don't know. It seems like sort of a waste of time for a writer."

"I knew you wouldn't like it," Nora said. "You're too sensitive."

"I want to write," Tommy said again.

"You don't know what you want," I said. "You're like some bird caught on a screened porch."

"I didn't expect you to understand," Tommy said.

"Fling flanging back and forth," I continued, "until he busts his neck."

"Very picturesque," Tommy said, "but not true."

"Are you really going to quit?" I asked.

Tommy nodded, but doubtfully.

"I can't wait to see Ned Polk's face," I said.

"Maybe I'll tell him tomorrow."

"Be sure I'm there. It would be a shame to miss the show."

"I'm not afraid of Ned Polk. He's just a lot of noise."

"Well here's your chance to prove it. Ned and his wife just walked in."

Tommy choked but recovered nicely.

I watched Ned Polk working his way down the row of stools—bar stools—making his presence known. He had a system of tapping someone on the shoulder, then not saying anything so the man who had been caught by surprise would be forced to make the greeting. In this way he seemed to gain an immediate advantage, judging by the look of relieved pleasure on his opponent's face once Ned Polk's approval, in the form of low-down belly laughter, had been granted. Throughout this performance, his wife, Sally, trailed him doubtfully. Few of the men at the bar spoke to her. In fact, few of them saw her. Ned had a habit of standing touching close when he addressed a man. As a result his victim was apt to see very little during the encounter. Some of them spotted her as she moved by and said hello in a sheepish, apologetic way because she was Clem Harper's daughter and you never knew when a little politeness might pay off, but most had already turned back to their drinks. They missed something, so far as I was concerned. Sally wasn't beautiful the way most women seem to want to be beautiful. That is, she didn't dress to please her own sex. But she had a hungry look, all thighs and sadness and soft warm skin. And she carried herself with a careless pride which scorned those who failed to appreciate her, but roundly rewarded the rest of us.

Yet she wasn't all animal. Just as Nora owed her beauty to that touch of desire on a canvas otherwise dulled by the gray colors of Gravenhurst convention, so Sally owed hers to the touch of gray. Only in her case convention did not seem to be the cause. Resignation perhaps, but not convention.

None of us had spoken throughout the entire performance. It was a bit of the Old West, Hollywood style. The fastest gun in the territory had just stepped into the Last Chance Café and we wuz wonderin' whether young Tom Compton, little known gunslinger, would choose to provoke the legendary desperado.

Well, as it turned out, he wouldn't. The tension must have been too much for Tommy because by the time Ned reached our booth, gunslinger Compton had reverted to type. He was unable even to meet the big man's scornful stare. His eyes rose, hesitated, then fell, like dead birds.

Ned stood over him for a time while the eyes struggled but failed to rise. "Scoop drowning his sorrows?" he asked me.

I turned a smile loose, hoping only Ned would see. There were moments when it occurred to me fear, rather than respect, motivated my admiration for Ned Polk.

Unfortunately, Sally witnessed my fulsome grin. She watched me as long as she could stand it, then let her eyes wash softly across Tommy's downcast cheek.

"How's the future state senator?" I asked, which may sound pretty courageous except I meant it to be funny and couldn't have been more surprised when Ned loosed his contemptuous gaze on me. He finally turned and rumbled off with Sally trailing, not meekly, but with whipped disgust.

"Goodness, what a brute," said Nora.

"Oh he doesn't mean it," I said. "Half the time he's just kidding."

Tommy looked up and there was a tiny smile to mock me. "Keep telling yourself that, if it makes you feel any better."

"I didn't see you starting any revolutions," I said, but Tommy just laughed at me.

"Poor Sally," Nora said. "So sad looking."

"I wonder why?" And I reminded myself to take a look at her wrists before the evening was over.

"I can think of some reasons," Tommy said. "But let's all have another drink before the party gets heavy."

"I thought we were going out for *dinner*," Nora said.

"Oh sure," Tommy said. "Just one little drink to whet the appetite."

"My appetite's about flooded already," Nora protested.

"Well let's finish it off," I said and held my empty glass for Frank to see.

"Is there a den mother in the house?" Frank yelled, which made everybody turn to laugh except for the one or two who were our age and preferred to remain as inconspicuous as possible.

Frank brought the drinks and we ordered steaks all around which he said we could have if the cook had any to give.

"Don' worry about it. You don' care watcha get. That's right, ain't it? Nobody comes here to eat, so you take what I got. All right? Sure it's all right."

It was usually good, though. Whatever he brought.

Some people had moved into the booth behind us and their conversation kept mixing with ours.

"Jack Croton's wife died, you know," somebody said.

"Well, she was an alcoholic anyway."

"So was Jack."

"You don't have to tell me. Only thing Jack could handle was a knife."

"Yeah, he was real good at that."

"This is a great place," Nora said. "Really!"

"What's the matter?" Tommy asked.

"Just listening in on a friendly little talk," I said.

Tommy craned his neck for a look at our neighbors, then waved and smiled.

"You know them?" I asked.

"Sally," he said.

"Goodness, talking with those people?" Nora asked.

"No no," Tommy said. "She was peeking over the other side." He twirled his glass thoughtfully and admired the rings it made on the wood. "How old is Sally?" he asked.

"Don't know," I answered. "Ned's age, I guess. Thirty-nine or forty."

"She looks younger," he remarked.

"I don't think she is. She and Ned went to Gravenhurst High together. That's where it all started."

"How romantic," said Tommy.

"The American Dream. Captain of the football team going with the beautiful politician's daughter."

"The politician's beautiful daughter," Tommy corrected.

"I'll bet Mr. Harper was pleased," Nora sneered.

"As a matter of fact there was a little static," I said. "According to Pa that's how Ned started working for us."

"How?" Tommy asked.

"Well you know Pa." But nobody seemed to find this explanation sufficient. "I mean as far as he's concerned a man should be judged on his merits, not his pedigree, so when Ned came looking for a job Pa not only gave him one, but told Clem Harper his future son-in-law looked like a real go-getter.

"And that's why Mr. Harper gave the happy couple his blessing?" asked Tommy.

"I didn't say that. But Pa thinks it might have helped."

"Say now, your father's a real champion of the Common Man, isn't he?"

Whatever I was about to reply was interrupted by the arrival of my sister and Jesse Rosenfeldt. Of all places for Abby to be seen with him, Frank's Place was about the worst. That was my first reaction. The second was what in the world was she doing out with him anyway? In Gravenhurst we believe in putting first things first and obviously what other people thought took preference over all other considerations.

I toyed with the hope they might pass us by which was only wishful thinking in a place that small. Besides, it would look pretty strained and give people even more to talk about if Abby and Jesse sat alone. Better a little fraternizing with the enemy than a family divided, so I gave them the big hello as casually as possible.

"Well well," said Jesse. "Instead of a round table full of wits we have a square table full of . . . No, no, that would be neither kind nor accurate." He waved a protesting finger at himself. "Be a gentleman, Jesse," he scolded. "What would Mother say?"

Abby laughed and pushed him into our booth.

"Join us," I suggested.

"We have," she said, and banged herself in beside me. "Hi," Abby greeted. "Hi, hi, hi," then she giggled and sighed and looked at us one by one, trying to discover what it was she'd forgotten.

"How do you do," Jesse said to Nora and Tommy. "My name's Jesse Rosenfeldt but I wouldn't hurt a fly."

"My eye," I said. "This is Nora and Tommy Compton."

"I knew there was something I was supposed to do," Abby said. "I knew it, didn't I, Jess?"

Jesse nodded in that sage way people who have been drinking too much use to conceal an oncoming belch. "Abigail's a smart girl," he announced. "*Urp*—I was surprised."

"I'll bet somebody doesn't think so," Abby singsonged for my benefit.

"Takes one to know one," Jesse said.

I decided a switch to highballs would be better for the long pull.

It was around ten o'clock by then and the metamorphosis which usually gripped Frank's Place was complete. Either through an electrical or personal deficiency, the atmosphere had grown noticeably dimmer. Music, loud and pointless but for its beat, clogged the air. An elbow slipped off the bar and its owner very nearly followed, but managed to recover, explaining it all by loud "Ha ha, that's one on me" noises. Somebody said "Christ, I lit the wrong end." "You shouldn't smoke them goddam things," he was told.

"So I got ten bucks on Gallant Man and what does 'at monkey do but pull up 'fore he's across the finish."

"They outa send them jocks ta school."

"Sure I had Ike. I ain't guessed wrong on a presidential election in over twenty years."

"We get a call see. There's trouble over to the Fun House. Me and Mike was on duty that night. I'm driving, see, so we get over there in jig time and there's this who-er out in the snow with nuthin on but her keymona and she's beatin' the life outa this gray looking, mousey little guy. No, I ain't tellin' ya who it was. You'd be surprised though. Huh? Sure you know him. Ain't a day goes by what you don't see him. Anyway, we break it up and she says the little bastard won't pay unless she does some tricks. 'I ain't that kind of who-er,' she says. Huh? Na, we coun't take 'em in. I mean whaddya think? The guy's a respectable citizen. Besides, them girls take real good care of us Christmas, if ya know what I mean, so we don' wanna make no trouble."

Jesse noticed I'd been listening. "The only difference between a cop and a crook," he said, "is one works on a salary and the other on a straight commission basis."

There's some truth in that, but it's not the kind of crack you want to make at Frank's Place. "Where'd you two have dinner?" I inquired, craftily changing the subject.

"National Distillers," he said. "Excellent roast of bourbon. You should try it."

"I'm doing all right. Thanks just the same."

"Nothing at all," Jesse said. "Nothing at all." He called Frank and ordered another roast for himself and one for Abby and topped it off with a nice little chat about how you couldn't be expected to stay sober in a place like Gravenhurst to which Frank heartily agreed.

"I didn't know you and Frank were buddies," I said.

"Oh we're old pals," said Jesse. "First place I came to when my father banished me to Gravenhurst. Can't blame me for that, now can you."

"Gravenhurst's not that bad."

"You're numb," he told me. "Ask Frank. He'll straighten you out. Frank's a destroyer jus' like me."

"What's that mean?" I asked.

"Tears down today to make room for tomorrow," Jesse explained. "Or maybe jus' tears it down period and to hell with tomorrow."

"Oh. A theory."

Abby gave her beast a pat on the head. "Jesse's a nice doggy," she giggled. "Let him have his fun before Pa peppers his behind."

"Don't mind me," Jesse said. "Mother tells me I'm too critical and since I was criticizing Gravenhurst, it seemed like a good idea to give a—*urp*—reason. Not the right one, necessarily, but at least a reason."

"What's the right one?" I asked.

"For criticizing Gravenhurst?"

"Yup."

"Because it's a dump," Jesse answered. "Forgive me, Mother."

Tommy, who looked like he'd been trying to decide whether Jesse would like him or not, finally got in the act. "Hurray," he said. "A prophet at last."

"Prophet," Abby said scornfully. "Who needs a prophet to tell him that?"

"What's wrong with Gravenhurst?" Nora asked, her voice sparkling with startled indignation.

Jesse reached for his flattened nose.

"Don't worry," Tommy said. "Nora has no punch at all."

"All right," Jesse said. "Then the trouble with Gravenhurst is . . . Ah, the hell with theories."

"I suppose it was just some more keep-up-with-the-Joneses talk anyway," Nora sniffed.

"Oh no," Jesse contradicted. "I'm all for keeping up with them. It keeps the slobs hopping."

"Who are the . . ." Nora tried to say it but the purity of her upbringing forbade such vulgar words. "Who are they?" she corrected.

Frank was back with the drinks and our steaks.

"Tell her, Frank," Jesse said.

"A slob," said Frank, "is a person who can do anything anyone else can do only half as well."

"In other words?" Jesse prompted.

"Almost everybody."

"A lot you know about us," Nora sniffed.

"That's right," Jesse admitted. "A lot I know about you." He paused, fingered his drink, shifted gear. "Anybody know what Gravenhurst means?" he asked.

Nobody did.

"Grab means grave in German," he said. "Graben, ditch or clearing, maybe. Horst, woods. So there you are."

"Where?" I asked.

He shrugged. "It's a grave or a clearing in the woods," he said. "That's what Gravenhurst is."

"Which is it?" I asked. "There's a difference."

"That's your problem," he shrugged.

I started to point out it was looking more like a grave every day, thanks to him, but Abby beat me to it. She was in one of her what-the-hell-do-I-care moods.

"Yak yak," she said. "Who needs it?" She got up and kicked off her shoes and tiptoed back to the shuffleboard. A couple of reporters she'd met once or twice were playing against two patronage hounds. I could hear a reporter needling the opposition.

"Hey we better take it easy, Pete, these guys already owe us more beer'n we could drink in a week."

"Don't worry," Pete said. "The Gravenhurst Republicans'll pick up the tab."

"Yeah, but who's gonna pick up us?"

Which made one hound growl and the other lift his lip and both flub their next shots. After that game the canines quit in a flurry of neck flexing and pants hiking so Abby got a chance to play and I volunteered to be her partner.

You might call that stage three in Frankian development; when the groups start overflowing into each other, making one big cock-eyed family. Before we finished the first game Nora had come over to kibitz and so had Sally which made it impossible for me to tell Abby what a jerk she was. I looked around for Ned and found him leaning into a group of men down at the other end of the bar, talking and shaking a finger and generally making up for that lousy paycheck he got every week from the *Daily Watch*. For a guy with political aspirations, Ned sure didn't waste much time with the happy family man routine. He seemed to use Sally like a dog uses his bone. Worrying her to death when she was within reach and forgetting all about her when she wasn't.

I took off my jacket and spent most of the time between shots with my eyes closed, just rocking to the music and yelling *"euuh"* now and then which couldn't have been too delightful, but it amused me. Sally must have got a little bored, though, because the next time I looked around she was sitting down with Tommy and Jesse, just watching them talk and smiling a little bit from time to time. It's funny how sometimes you can tell people have met before. I don't know why that is. Maybe because they don't try too hard with each other. They just take it easy and shuffle the conversation back and forth without any real effort. That's the way Jesse and Sally were. Having the instincts of a gossip, my first reaction was to wonder about Sally's cut wrists and whether there really was a man with her; a man named Jesse Rosenfeldt. But seeing as Jesse had barely had time to unpack when that incident took place, I decided the possibility was an interesting one, but highly unlikely. They were much more apt to have met under legitimate circumstances. Perhaps Jesse had been invited to the Polks for dinner and a little friendly political chat with Ned. Though I wouldn't exactly call that legitimate business, it seemed the more likely explanation.

However, by then I was too far gone to care a whole hell of a lot what was going on behind the black scaffolding of Gravenhurst's noble and forthright press. Things were flying and I was everybody's brother and life was good and cloudy.

Abby, on her part, was setting the pace for the ladies, so feminine disapproval became a pretty unacceptable virtue that night and even Nora got a little loaded. Not silly like Abby, but sort of dopey. Serious and loving and earth-momma looking. Full of giving and quick to smile, but confused and halting, as if she couldn't quite figure out how to distribute all the sweet, everloving compassion that was in her. I considered suggesting she organize a charity drive and give it all away in dribs and drabs, being sure nobody got enough, until there was nothing left but an enormous feeling of self-satisfaction. But I didn't tell her. I'm a good-natured drunk most of the time. Instead, between turns at the shuffleboard, I would stand close to her and sway and smile and tell her not to worry because she was a good kid at heart, which served to confuse her even more and remind me how drunk I was getting.

Jesse came over about that time and made some crack about whether it was the right season of the year to be in rut.

"Very funny," I told him. "Where's Tommy?"

"Took Sally home."

"Oh," I said, then came to. "He did what?"

Jesse shrugged. "She knew Ned wouldn't take her."

"You're dumber'n I thought."

"Thanks." Jesse handed me his empty glass. "How 'bout buying me a drink while I go take a wee."

I went over to the bar. Ned had his arm around some guy and was mauling him in a friendly kind of way.

"Old Jimmy," he was saying, "you're a regular goddam clown, aren'tcha?"

Jimmy managed to look half-pleased because his little joke had apparently succeeded, and half-panicked. Ned had a way of getting his hands all over people when he was drunk. I guess he didn't mean anything by it, but there was something obscene about all that fleshy corpulence enveloping a man.

"So anyway," Ned continued, "we get this three-day pass, see, and I don't know which of us is hotter to trot, me or this big-assed Marine who wants me so bad she's ready to wet her pants."

Somebody said, "Hey, take it easy," and he lowered his voice. About that time he spotted me.

"Whatsamatter, Junior, your girl run off and leave you?"

"Mine's right back there," I said. "Where's yours?"

"She's right over . . ." His eyes searched up and down the booths, then over to the shuffleboard, then back to me. "Where the hell is she?" he roared.

Maybe I'll learn to keep my trap shut some day.

At first I thought he was only kidding. In fact, for a second it looked like he might go back to his drinking and forget about Sally, but only for a second. Suddenly he pushed back from the bar and people fell away like flies from a mound of offal disturbed by its own rot.

"Where the hell'd that slut go?" he shouted. "Anybody see?"

No one answered. If they knew they were too surprised to speak.

"Whore," he roared and slung his glass at the floor. The place went damp with nervous silence. Only the juke clanged on unconcerned.

"Take it easy. Take it easy," and Jesse came wandering back with a look of bored contempt on his face. "She was tired and the Compton boy took her home. What's all the excitement about?"

Ned looked hard at Jesse and his face fell away from hatred to slack-faced shame. "Scoop Compton," he told himself and laughter began to *huh huh* deep down inside, rising and quickening until it finally discharged into the room. "*Ha ha, huh huh huh,* she sure can pick 'em." His words and laughter splattered over us. "The one kid in town couldn't get laid in a whorehouse." Ned shook his head. "Scoop Compton," he repeated. "Jesus H. Christ."

"See what I mean?" I asked Jesse. "Ought to take better care of your candidate."

"Thanks," he said, looking a little shaken for once. "I'll try to remember."

I looked around for Nora. She must have seen and heard Ned's charming performance, but the look on her face made me wonder. She was just leaning against the back wall with Abby and those two reporters, staring out at the world. But while the others had an anxious look about them, Nora had the dumb staring, wide-eyed look of a tourist who has been told the natives are friendly and simply refuses to accept any evidence to the contrary.

Ned pushed his way back to the bar. "So where was I? Oh yeah, she outranked me but I told her 'What the hell, honey, you can be on top if it makes you feel better.'" Another spasm of laughter and the flies settled back to resume feeding.

I couldn't make the adjustment to normalcy quite as smoothly as Ned and the others. Jesse was leaning against the bar with his back to me and his head bent, thinking, trying to figure out which way to jump next, probably, so I wandered back to see how Nora was getting along. It was after two and I began to worry about the next morning with that dumb, fume-heavy chill which was my kind of hangover. I played one more game of shuffleboard and made laughing noises, but the party was officially over. At least I thought it was. We were just getting ready to leave when Tommy came pitpatting through the door, swiveling his head and stretching his neck and blinking and hesitating as he tried to figure out where we were. The flow of words stopped and people turned to watch. Ned leaned his back to the bar and followed Tommy with his eyes, huh huhing and shaking his head and muttering "Scoop Compton. Jesus H. Christ."

Tommy finally spotted us and flapped over quick as he could. "What's going on?"

"Ned was wondering where you were," I told him.

"Oh. He was, huh." Then he wriggled his way into the midst of our little group. "He was, huh," Tommy repeated, but he was unable to turn around and face the possibility Ned might still be staring.

"We ought to go home," I said. "It's kind of late."

Since nobody disagreed, I put my arm around Nora and aimed her for the door, Tommy following. The fresh air revived us a little so we said good night to Brother Compton and took a drive down by the lake. It was a night to make lonely people ache. The moon was almost full and its pale light splashed across the fields, settling on the woods and houses in a fine phosphorescent mist.

"Does your father know about that dreadful Mr. Polk?" Nora asked.

"Know what?"

"That he's insane."

"Oh he was just a little drunk," I assured her.

"Huh!"

I could remember coming out to the lake as a boy, just to sit and let the soft, gentle monotony of darkness rock my wishing dreams of love. I would lie on the grass and yearn for a time when there'd be someone next to me. Someone sweet and hesitant to accompany me in a love symphony more touching, more delicate, more gracious than life had ever known. Then soon the someone girl was Nora and my dream brightened with the promise of reality. And now:

I drove up to the dock, gunned her a couple of times to clear the carbs. *CaaROOM CaaROOM—Cra Cra.*

Yanked the emergency on full. *Creeee—YACK.*

Doused the lights . . . Flipped the radio . . . *Zoooeeee zup zup zup* . . . to Lonesome Stan, the All Night Record Man.

"Our next cool slice of jumpin' stuff known to all you real gone kittens and cats as Mambo Rock is dedicated by Tearing Teddy Stang and the rest of the gang at the Fourteenth Street Social Club to Mary Jane Peterson, Mirabel Pollock, Connie Rodriguez and Stella, the Fella, Francini. Spin it, Man."

We were about ready.

I lit a cigarette because we wouldn't be needing both my hands for a while and I put an arm around Nora and I kissed her on the neck and we sat like that for a while. Not saying anything. Not doing anything. Just frozen in time. Since our love rite went only so far we had to stop like that every so often to make things last. Then after a while the cigarette started to burn my fingers so I flipped it out and let my lips wigwag up her neck and along the cheek. I could feel her turning just ever so slightly to meet me and the idea of her doing that—I mean wanting to kiss me too—got me kind of excited. Then we kissed and twisted our necks around a lot and held onto each other. Pretty soon I let my hand slip off her shoulder and across her breast which I kneaded conscientiously since, according to past experience, the treat wasn't apt to go on for very long. But that night she didn't seem to mind. Still pretty loaded, I guess, so I decided to push my luck and let a hand slide down across her belly and out onto her left thigh. I knew she'd stop me pretty soon, but I kept on while the going was good until my fingers reached the hem of her dress and I could feel the zipper coolness of her nylons. I was just getting ready for Nora to protest my manly exuberance when she moved toward me a little. By mistake, I'd imagine, and the hand was forced up her thigh without my meaning it to be. Then all of a sudden my fingers reached over the rim of her stocking, touched soft warm flesh, and recoiled in shame. But Nora hadn't said anything to dampen my ardor. I thought maybe she'd fallen asleep so I kissed her again to be sure and whispered something about being sorry. But she kissed me awful hard and pressed my hand against her thigh and I—oh Jesus—I didn't know what to do. This wasn't part of the ritual and I was boiling inside with an imagination geared to lesser forms of excitement, so by then I was about ready to . . . Well, gee . . . I mean I wasn't used to this at all, not with a nice girl and everything. But I couldn't stop. What would she think if I did? So my hand kept creeping and creeping and touching and touching and . . . Oh Lordy, what was that? But worse still, I could feel her thighs spreading instead of snipping shut like they were supposed to do and her hand started across my hip and I knew exactly where it was going.

I was so excited it was almost too late already. "Oh Nora."

"Oh Larry," she said, as though I'd remembered her birthday or something.

"Nora."

Then with a trembling, crying sigh she rolled herself on top of me and held tight and began to moan. "Oh Larry, I want you, I want you, I want you."

We pressed each other hard until I knew it really *was* too late for me, but didn't know how to break the news. Then I pushed her away and solemnly announced: "It wouldn't be right this way, Nora. It wouldn't be right at all."

She stared at me hard for a while, then shook her head. It was as if I'd awakened her from a sound sleep. Then she slid off and sat church still, staring straight ahead, dumb with the shock of her messy passion. I leaned over and kissed her on the neck again to complete the cycle.

"Oh Larry, I'm so ashamed."

"Don't be."

"Thank you for being such a gentleman."

"Don't mention it."

I flipped off the radio and released my emergency brake. *VRUP.* Turned the ignition. *Ararararararrreeee Ararararararrreee AraraROOM ROOM ROOM.*

And away we go.

During the ride home I remembered my boyhood dreams of love in which passion had been a dim and misty melody never to be compared with the grotesque, clumsy, barnyard orgy we had just climaxed so unnaturally. I began to wonder about the physical reality of sex which so many modern writers, dedicated to the doubtful virtue of recording their times, feel obligated to describe. In the first place, it seems unlikely that sex is a phenomenon peculiar to the twentieth century. But more important, I can't help but feel these same fictional journalists have proven beyond a doubt that the intricate, subtle, overpowering web of loving is charred and destroyed under the glare of physical description. It is the essence of passion which transforms reality to a dream worth dreaming, worth recording, not the act.

When we reached Nora's house she didn't wait for me to see her in. She only kissed with quick, cold shame and hurried off. I couldn't blame her. It was a pretty terrible way to carry on; letting her hand wander around like that and rolling on top of me almost like she was the man or something.

I mean, after all, I guess I could take care of myself. Especially after Anita and it wasn't as though she were my first whore or anything so there was no need for Nora to be so *aggressive*. I mean it's not as though I didn't know what to do. Just because Nora wasn't a sure thing like Anita doesn't mean I was scared to try. Nothing ventured, nothing gained. Everybody knows that.

All I needed was a little time.

Boy, I don't know what got into her head. We'd been going together for practically ten years and I never saw her behave like that before. I felt ashamed for her—truly ashamed—and that's a fact.

It surprised me a little to find Abby still out when I got back. If there was a party or something like that she could keep going all night, but the festivities were pretty well over when we'd left Frank's Place and it wasn't like her to visit some lovers' lane and play car-hopping games with Jesse or anyone else. That sport she left to her talented brother.

I was lying in bed wondering whether Jesse might be man enough for the job of winning her away from Pa when a car wound its way up our driveway and sat idling longer than is usually considered adequate for discharging passengers. Finally I heard Abby's voice good-nighting and the car engine surged and the outside noises returned to normal.

Then, as was the custom, there soon came a rapping, rapping at my chamber door.

"Tis some visitor," I muttered, "tapping at my chamber door—"

"Only me and nothing more," said Abby, which was about as complicated as our cute little literary games ever got.

"What's up?"

"Oh nothing. I just felt like talking."

"That makes one of us," I said, which wasn't quite true. There's nothing I like better than talking the whole thing over after a slightly confused and stimulating (alcoholically speaking) evening.

"Don't you want to? I mean, don't you *really* want to?" She bounced on my bed a few times to make sure I wouldn't doze off. "Cause I could always leave."

"I doubt it."

"And come back later," she added.

"I guess this is preferable," I laughed.

She sat on the edge of my bed, leaned back on her hands and communed with the wall. "He's quite a guy," she said finally.

"Ned Polk?" I kidded.

"No, stupid, Ned Polk is a beast. But now you've mentioned it, why doesn't Pa fire him?"

"For politicking?"

"Sure. He can't do that. It isn't right."

"I guess not," I agreed. "But Pa's got no one to take his place just now."

"It'd be better to have no one."

"Did Jesse say anything about him?"

"No. Why should he?"

"I've got a hunch the *Enterprise* put Ned up to it."

"Really? Hey, that Jesse's pretty smart, isn't he?"

"I'll say. He sure got rid of Vanden Gasser in a big hurry."

"Vanden Gasser? What's Jesse have to do with that?"

"Nothing directly," I admitted, then changed the subject. "So you had a good time, eh?"

She looked at me with a half-smile, then looked away again. "Oh pretty good," she admitted, then repeated, "He's quite a guy."

"I'm glad," I said. "Because when Pa finds out he'll shoot you."

"What does Pa care about things like that?" she huffed. "Appearances." She huffed again.

"Pa's a little touchier about Jesse and the *Enterprise* than he usually gets."

Abby laughed. "Pa'll do all right. Don't worry about that."

"Then you weren't impressed by Jesse after all?"

Again the hesitation.

"What *did* he have to do with the plane crash?" she insisted.

"Nothing really," I repeated. "Vanden Gasser was under some pressure from the *Enterprise*. It could have been a contributing factor."

"Or could not have been," she said, looking impatient.

"Maybe not," I admitted. "In any case, it was unnecessary."

She didn't say anything.

"Think he's the man to whip Pa?" I teased.

She shrugged.

"Think you could fall in love with him?"

No answer.

"I mean what with his being Jewish and all."

She turned on me, scrambling to defend a cause. "What's that got to do with it, I'd like to know?"

"I was just teasing you."

"Well it's nothing to joke about, and maybe I'll just marry him to prove it."

"It's a little early for that. Besides, I thought people got married for other reasons."

"Let's talk about something else," she suggested.

"Like for instance?"

"Like for instance how's the *Enterprise* doing and all that?"

"Pretty well. Pa's really worried."

"Why? He's had problems before."

"I don't know," I admitted. "Maybe because it's the *Daily Watch* this time and that's our bread and butter."

"He's had newspaper competition before," Abby persisted.

"Once, and that was a local group."

"So?"

"Well, most people around here are just a little scared of Pa, you know, and that always helps. Also he knew them personally and had a pretty good idea just what it would take to scare off each and every one. All he knows about Jesse is there's a multimillion-dollar real estate empire behind him and I guess that's enough to bother anybody."

Abby thought for a while, but apparently it didn't do much good. Her mind just didn't work logically when Pa was involved. "Pa shouldn't have to worry," she said. "Pa shouldn't have to worry about anybody or anything."

I didn't try to set her straight, but yawned instead.

"Okay," she laughed. "I get the idea."

"Sorry," I apologized. "The working press and all that."

"Too much bourbon's more like it." She slid to her feet and started for the door, then turned. "While I'm thinking of it, when are you going to stop taking out Nora Compton? She's such a drip."

"I've just been wondering the same thing. Good night."

"Good night, Larry. I'm glad you have."

"Good night, Abigail. I'm glad you're glad."

"I'm glad you're glad I'm . . ."

I slung my pillow and she ducked out the door.

It was good to know Abby agreed with me about Nora. I mean women are pretty intuitive about other women, I've discovered.

CHAPTER IX

Sleep must cure almost everything because by next morning the shame of my failure with Nora had lessened to exasperation and I even managed, though for admittedly brief moments, to recognize certain humorous aspects of the whole outlandish performance. That Nora apparently believed my restraint was motivated by propriety rather than spent passion helped a great deal. So did Pa, who was in such a rotten mood I didn't have much time for self-analysis. Apparently Abby, still convinced Pa would be above such pettiness as a concern for public opinion, had already told him about being out with Jesse. He was enraged and still mumbling "absolutely unforgivable" when I arrived at the breakfast table. I don't know just why, but somehow it seemed to me a description of Ned Polk's behavior might shift the burden of shame from Abby and me so I gave Pa a quick rundown while Abby volunteered some of the more colorful details.

"He called her what?" Pa shouted.

"*Whore*," Abby repeated.

"Absolutely unforgivable," Pa said, but he meant Abby's language, not the performance of his news editor. Drunkenness was one thing; betrayal followed by unladylike behavior quite another.

It seemed to me Pa was taking the whole business a little too seriously and I was wondering why when he volunteered an explanation.

"You're as bad as everybody else," he told us. "No sense of loyalty at all."

"Now Clarence," Mother soothed, "the children simply didn't realize you cared that much."

"Cared," Pa sneered. "Cared. My God, they should have been with me yesterday."

"What happened?" I asked.

"I had a little talk with some of our leading merchants," Pa said. "To find out whether they could be persuaded to withdraw their advertising from Rosenfeldt's so-called newspaper."

"And?" I prodded.

"Obviously they told me it was impossible. Why else would I be in such a foul mood?"

"Why, impossible?" I asked.

"Business reasons, ostensibly," Pa said. "Some said because the rates were lower which is obvious in view of the fact circulation is lower too. And there were one or two who explained they just liked to keep the old *Daily Watch* on its toes. But most claimed it was their policy to split the advertising on a circulation basis. Policy hell, there hasn't been a competing paper in town for fifteen years. Where'd their damn policy come from?"

"Jesse," I suggested.

"Were those the only reasons?" Mother asked.

"What?"

"The only reasons," she repeated.

"Oh, you know how it is," Pa conceded. "Some of them complained about mistakes we'd made in running their copy and about times we neglected to print the names of their damn wives and children in connection with some foolishness or other."

"That's the usual stuff," I said.

"Course it is," Pa agreed. "Made me damn angry. Matter of fact I told one fellow if he could run the paper better than I, by God, why didn't he?"

"That's telling them, Pa," Abby said.

"What'd he say then?" I laughed.

But Pa didn't seem any less anxious. "Said he'd already done me one better," Pa confessed. "Said he'd *found* somebody who could run a paper better than I and that was where his advertising went."

"A real crank," I noted.

"Ungrateful lout," from Mother.

"I wouldn't ever again let him advertise in the *Daily Watch*," Abby said. "Then let's see how his business does."

Pa just grunted and Abby looked bewildered. The battle had been joined but Sir Clarence seemed unable or unwilling to mount his fiery steed and vanquish the forces of evil. I shouldn't mock her. It's horrible when an idol starts to crumble. Not that Pa was crumbling really. But I mean, after all, he was just a man, a pretty exceptional one, maybe, but that's all, and if I could pay lip service to the fact of his mortality, whether I believed it or not, then why couldn't she?

"Anyway," Pa went on, "I don't want either of you seen with

Rosenfeldt again. It gives the impression we don't mean business."

Abby tossed her head. "Since when is my private life hitched to the fortunes of the Gravenhurst *Daily Watch?*"

"Since right now. Besides he's not the sort of fellow you should be going out with."

Abby's face was a blend of horror and disbelief. "What's that mean?"

"Well, uh, he's not your sort, Abby." Pa sounded appeasingly pompous. "He's a bit older. Belongs to another world, dontchou know. Not your sort at all."

"Do you mean because he's Jewish, Pa?" Abby asked.

Pa stalled. "What?"

"Because he's Jewish, Pa?" Abby repeated.

"Abby, you know I've never encouraged intolerance in this house."

"You've never had to before."

"Now Abby," Mother said, "your father doesn't mean that at all. He's only interested in what's best for the paper . . . and you."

"I'll see him whenever I please, Pa," she said.

Pa looked evening tired and, though he tried, was unable to answer.

I thought that would be the end of it, but apparently Pa's failure to meet her challenge hurt Abby more than anything else he'd done. We sat in shamed silence for an endless time. Then she gave a little gasp.

"Excuse me," she said, and ran away but we could all hear the hollow sobbing so clearly she might as well have stayed.

"Say, uh, Pa, could I ride down to the office with you?" I asked.

"Hmmm? Oh sure," he agreed without caring.

He looked so beat I thought a little company might do him good. It was very seldom I felt I could do anything to help Pa. My help was something he usually did without, but though Abby may have been the disillusioned one, it was Pa who had done the falling, and even though he'd taken a bit of a tumble in my own eyes, too, I was willing—in fact, eager—to help pick up the pieces. I don't know just why. I didn't secretly hate my father or any of that stuff, but being allowed to see his vulnerable side was sort of a privilege. It was like going backstage after the performance and saying hello to the hero, only to find him a little smaller, a little paler, a little more human and therefore likable than he had seemed under the triumphant glare of spotlights. Now Abby would have found such an experience disillusioning, but for me it was a welcome revelation. It offered the hope Pa and I, since we were both mortals after all, might one day remove the altar between us.

We talked a little about Ned Polk on the way to town.

"He's a coony bastard," Pa told me. "But without money or brains enough to keep pace with his ambition. We'll trap him one of these days."

"Then he really is after Vanden Gasser's seat."

"You're damn right he is. Polk and Harvey Healy and Rosenfeldt have been in cahoots for a month now, but Wilbur's death means it'll be just that much sooner."

"Does he have a chance?"

"Well," Pa chuckled, "the county executive committee has to decide who fulfills the unexpired term and our old friend Judge Compton's chairman of the executive committee, so . . ."

I laughed, but the car swerved suddenly and I realized Pa was still far from serene. He had a white Lincoln Continental which usually handled like a well-schooled hunter. Pa could anticipate road conditions and the Lincoln could anticipate Pa so the two of them usually cantered the highways in a clean symphony of control. Usually. But that morning was a hodgepodge of sudden braking, gunning, swerving, and bad timing until he finally pulled over to the right and limped into town with the normals, the dulls, and the drabs.

Apparently Pa was more worried about Abby than anyone else that morning because when we reached the parking lot he settled back in his seat for a couple of minutes, trying to get his problems sorted out.

"See what you can do about that sister of yours," he said finally. "She's got to realize ideals won't do her much good without a *Daily Watch* around to pay the bills."

"Is that a possibility?" I asked.

"Benjamin Rosenfeldt seems to think so, or he wouldn't be here."

"But if it's such a lousy paper, how'll he ever kill the *Daily Watch?*"

"The bastard's got plenty of money. He could just keep popping away until we bleed to death."

"You make it sound sort of hopeless."

"Well I don't know," Pa said. "If we can hold our own awhile and prove his competitive skills aren't as invincible as he's been led to believe, why . . ."

"Maybe he'll go play someplace else," I concluded.

"That's right."

"I hope so."

"Come on," Pa said. "Let's get down to the office before Ned Polk puts out an extra that I've decided to close the *Daily Watch* and retire."

"Aren't you kind of worried about that?" I laughed. "I mean not about that exactly, but for all you know, Ned might run a story endorsing himself for state senator."

"I doubt it. Even his own supporters might find that a little tough to swallow."

"But I mean something similar."

"He's a good man," Pa said. "Besides, I've got nobody to replace him right now."

By the time we got to the office I was feeling a bit queasy from the night before. My head ached with nagging premonitions which were probably only due to hangover nerves, but caused my fingers to jump from whatever they touched and turned the back of my neck cold damp with sweat and pain.

As a result of my own aches I wasn't especially aware of any changes in city room politics until later in the morning when the world around me began to filter in. Fortunately it was a slow day and we were permitted to limp through our assignments without too much effort, but after a while I began to sense something was out of line. Something more than the fact of a slack day. It was as if a customary diversion, some rather enjoyable interruption in the daily routine, had not taken place. Then I realized Ned Polk wasn't splattering Tommy with his customary dose of bilious abuse. Applying the shrewd deductive powers of a highly trained newsman, I soon figured out why. Tommy wasn't there.

When I handed in my next story I asked Ned where he was.

"He's got a headache," Ned said. "And it hurts so bad he can't type."

"Oh?"

"That's right," Ned went on. "I don't know how we'll get the paper out without him, but you just pitch in, Larry boy, and do the best you know how."

The funeral was early in the afternoon, but I didn't go. The idea of all those Vanden Gassers, one big one and three little ones, laid out like a mess of trout was more than I could face. Instead I drove home with Pa, then later on went over to the Comptons' to find out what Tommy was up to and see Nora. It was a bad time because the house was stuffed with committeewomen scheming to do some poor bastard a good turn. But worse yet, some of them had brought their children along so the place trembled like an overladen tree with the bittersweet fruits of forgotten passion. It gave me a funny feeling to see Nora in amongst all that pretended chastity. I knew there wasn't a woman in the place who had not lost herself in desire at least to the degree Nora had. And I could suspect others of a lot more than that. But theory and suspicion are not fact, and it was fact which fed my mind with distortions. I imagined Nora in a room filled with women like these. Looking like them. Talking like them. Heavily dulled like them. A great, vaulted room obscenely decorated in pink satin and glowing with soft, fleshy lights and an expectant, silent joy coloring the ladies' eager cheeks, much as though an execution were about to be performed. I could see Nora stepping primly to the center of the room where she would doubtless perform a precious ballet in touching tribute to Mr. Somebody's dancing classes. But instead she would begin suddenly to writhe and pulse her thighs and arch and shake and quiver her breasts and moan. Sad, hungry, animal moans. Eyes closed, hair swinging loose, rocking with the rhythm of desire. And the women watching, frozen in a dry chill of righteousness until the passion was driven out and she was allowed to join the other expurgated virgins.

All fantasy, but fed on fact. The fact of Nora lost in her body, pressed hard against me, hot-panting in the unlikely but often used discomfort of a car seat. It was difficult to imagine the other ladies similarly indisposed and I felt Nora had no right to masquerade as one of them. But looking back on it, the shocking fact is I was ashamed of the passion in Nora. Not proud. Such was the horror and paradox of my precious Puritan morality; having screwed a few whores made me a goddam prude.

Nora certainly didn't seem to be sharing my inhibitions. She was acting just as pure and sweet and sexless as the rest of them; which I failed to interpret as a clue to the rest of them, and it was impossible to believe she had any memory at all of the night before.

It certainly was not a good time for courtship and the first opportunity found me whispering something about an urgent meeting with Tommy. She followed me into the hall. I heard her call and looked around and there she was, padding along with that forward leaning, loose-wristed efficiency of hers which was absolutely sexless as a pitpatting partridge, yet strangely appealing. I followed her around the corner where nobody could see and she gave me a great big kiss. Nora was almost as tall as I was. Her eyes where my eyes were. Her lips level with mine. Her shoulders, my shoulders, her hips, my hips. Her thighs, my thighs, and so on with occasional biological differences. Somehow I lacked a feeling of masculine dominance.

"I love you," she said.

"I love you, too," I said, because it would have seemed naughty not to. She nodded appreciatively and let go of me.

I found Tommy in his room, looking like the old Trench Mouth Tom of Harvard undergraduate days, and I knew right away he was between jobs. First he wanted to know if Ned seemed mad at him.

"No more than usual," I said. "Why?"

"Oh I don't know," he said, but too casually. "I thought he might still be mad about my taking Sally home."

"No. Should he be?"

Tommy seemed miffed. "Well I did take her home, after all, and we were alone, and it was nighttime."

"That's right," I agreed.

"Don't you think that could have made him sore?"

"I don't know. Did you screw her?"

"Of course not."

"Then why should he get sore?"

"Well I might have," Tommy said hopefully. "And besides I hadn't heard that screwing a man's wife was the only way to make him jealous."

"I guess not," I conceded. "What's Sally like?"

"She's wonderful," he sighed.

"What do you mean by that?"

"Oh, she's very warm." He paused. "And understanding."

"What'd you talk about?"

"Me mostly," he admitted. "And my wanting to write and why Ned doesn't like me."

"Why's that?"

"She said he's never liked sensitive people very much. She said you can practically tell who's artistic and who isn't by whether Ned dislikes them or not."

"Well, I'm glad to know you're so artistic, Tommy. I mean now that it's been firmly established."

"You know what I think?"

"No," I said. "What?"

"I think he's a homosexual."

"You do? Boy he sure is a big one, isn't he?"

"What's that got to do with it? They come in all sizes."

"I just wouldn't want to get caught spreading a rumor like that," I said.

"Who's spreading a rumor? I'm just telling you what I think."

"Where'd you get the idea?"

"I don't know," he admitted. "Sally, I guess. She seems kind of hungry. I don't mean he never takes her to bed. Sure he does. Like a swatter takes a fly. But it's all taking, I'll bet. Another way of playing with himself."

"If he's a homosexual," I said, "how come he doesn't like you?"

"What makes you so testy today?"

"I don't know. You coming to work tomorrow?"

"No. I'm quitting."

"I figured you were."

"I've decided to go to New York," Tommy said. "And take some creative writing courses at NYU."

"The call of the Beatnik. How thrilling."

"That's what I expected," Tommy said. "One day I'm a two-bit cub reporter and everybody thinks that's fine. The next day I try to do something worthwhile and everybody thinks I'm a bum."

"It's a tough life," I said. "What are you going to do day after tomorrow?"

Tommy looked confused.

"The next job," I said. "After you get tired growing a beard?"

"There isn't going to be any next job, Larry," he said.

"Yeah, well maybe not," I said. "Anyway, I'll see you, kid. I've got to get home."

He didn't bother to say goodbye, but I couldn't have cared less. I was sick of his shilly-shallying ways, all justified by a kind of private pilgrimage in search of the truth. Why couldn't he work like everybody else?

I was halfway down the stairs when he yelled after me.

"Hey, Larry, let me borrow your car for an hour. Okay? Mine's in the shop and I've got a couple of things to do."

"Sure," I told him. "The keys are in it."

That's the funny thing about growing up with somebody. Even though each one thinks the other's a jerk, you go on asking and doing favors as if friendship were thicker than blood.

The ladies were still at it so I snuck out like a frightened child and headed for home. It was early September and the first touches of death in a masquerade of gold and red and false promise clustered in bronze patches on the otherwise green trees. A chill whispered close about me and the fields and gardens lay dry with a summer's giving. Only pumpkins and squash and a garnishing of tomatoes remained.

There weren't any houses between the Comptons and us. Only hayfields and pasture which had been part of the first Woodruff dream come true. It was no longer a real farm, but we kept a couple of horses and a cow. There was usually a pig or two and chickens, but their value was more esthetic than nutritional. Just gentle reminders that the land was there, not to be forgotten. The dogs were our main interest. Springer spaniels raised for bird hunting. They signified fall for us. We might never have known the time of year, but for the sight of a springer dancing across the frost-brushed fields like a big fish trying to spit the hook.

I went over the wall where the road curves away to meet our driveway and took a short cut across the fields. It led me by the old tennis court and I stopped there for a look at the past. We still played, but not the way we used to. Just Abby and me from time to time. Or friends of ours. But I could remember when that court was the social center of Woodruff Hill. When the dead red clay was studded with the color and chatter of summer life. When Bollard ran the gin and tonic brigade and the kids got Cokes with half a lime squeezed in and Pa and I took on all comers because he was that good and somedays I could play morning and afternoon without once throwing my racket. I could see the white metal tables and orange umbrellas. Women and laughter and bent straws. Sometimes a girl—Nora, maybe—to come and stare and ruin my serve. Brown legs and straining tendons and clumps of sweaters in little cashmere piles. It could have been yesterday, yet all this was gone for some time now. Three, four years. A quiet, anxious drift to the golf course where breaths were not so apt to shorten; hearts less inclined to pound. Meanwhile my generation, as yet uncommitted to the joys of family life, frolicked too far afield for the discipline of a tennis date.

I wandered past and down a shallow hill where the pasture gave way to brush and bramble and clumps of swamp grass as high as my head and scraggily fingered sumac. Here were the pheasant pens, their wire boundaries almost hidden in the heavy growth. Inside the regal stupidity of the proud cock pheasants blended with the dull brown stupidity of their hens in a parody of community living. Yet stupid simply because of their confinement. Once freed it took a good dog to break the mystery of their cunning. I've hunted alone for hours and never seen a bird, then covered the same fields with a dog and flushed five or six. The birds may be just as stupid, but it doesn't show so much outside the pens.

I crossed a wall back into the pasture and followed the wheel ruts to the barnyard and down toward the house. The dogs picked up my presence and started their God-awful yapping so I went over and stuck my fingers through the wire to give their noses something to do. I used to help train them and still did when there was time. One of them, Triumph, I considered mine. He was almost all white with flickers of black on his muzzle and low on his flanks and legs. Beautiful to watch him work and he could hunt almost the whole day without tiring. I unlocked his run and crowded my way in and wrestled him awhile, singsonging it was almost time, we'd be going out in a week or two and trying to hold him down until the wriggling stopped and he lay still with his tongue flopping coyly and his eyes waiting to play some more. Man's best friend now. But like Cerberus there were two other heads; one of the hunter, cool methodical, efficient; one of the killer, frenzied, wild-eyed, tearing the legs off a deer and leaving it in the bloodied snow to bleat the agony of slow, spastic death.

After mauling him awhile I ran for the gate and almost made it before he was all over me again. I laughed and told the whole bunch of them to shut up for God's sakes, and heaved an apple against the wire so it splattered and sent them all tails down for inside safety.

Then I headed down to the house and in through the kitchen as usual. Bollard was there in his shirt sleeves looking old as the forgotten past.

"Matter? You sick?"

"Um old, lad," he said. "And that um sick a being."

I laughed for lack of a better reaction. "Pa home?"

Bollard just nodded. He had no neck and when his head moved there was no indication that muscle and the subtle shift of bone had been involved. It was more like the movement of a button release on a suitcase.

"Bad mood?" I asked.

Bollard stuck out a hand and wobbled it back and forth. "So so," he said.

"Well!" I shrugged and smiled and left. I looked back and saw his eyes following me, but except for motion they were dead. Bollard was as much a part of my life as Pa and watching his spirit flake away was just as depressing as Pa's disintegration. According to family legend, my grandfather and Bollard met during the fall of '29 in a Wall Street bar where the two of them managed to solve America's economic ills, at least to their own satisfaction. Since we've always been a money-in-the-mattress family at heart, Grandpa could still afford to indulge in love for his fellow man, and did so by hiring Bollard. Actually he started out as handyman, but his predecessor complained so much about Bollard's uppity ways that Grandpa was finally forced to fire the predecessor and promote Bollard to the butlership, a position for which he was not absolutely suited. However, as a reliable source of humor and jury-rigger in time of crisis there was no one to beat him. Also he was a practical joker and loved to abuse our more pretentious guests, so Bollard more than compensated for his defects.

One of his favorite jokes, for instance, was to appear in a guest's bedroom much too early in the morning with a glass of hot water graciously placed upon a silver tray. The guest, of course, hadn't the slightest idea what was going on, but rather than display an ignorance of etiquette in the presence of a Britisher, he usually downed the revolting offering without question. Bollard would then return the glass crisply to its tray, bow, and make the following request: "Yes, sir. Thank you, sir. Will that be the right temperature for your bath, sir?"

If the guest laughed, he was immediately reclassified as unpretentious. Otherwise he was likely to suffer future indignities. In either case, the deed was done and vicarious pleasure rippled through the House of Woodruff.

Pa was probably in the library working, so I went upstairs with the idea of taking a bath and maybe a nap because the night before had not only caught up, but neatly passed me by and I was feeling mighty low. Unfortunately Mother heard me coming up the stairs and called, "Is that you, Larry?" which meant she wanted to see me about something.

Mother was sitting at her dressing table when I walked in, applying the finishing touches before dinner. She had on a coral pink, quilted dressing gown which was very simple and the sort of thing she usually wore for dinner when we had no company. Yet somehow, despite its simplicity, or perhaps because of it, the dressing gown suggested extreme elegance. This was due partly to Mother and partly to a very good dressmaker. I don't care what Madison Avenue sings the suckers about being chic on a budget, you can usually tell who's being chic that way and who isn't. It was difficult for me to bracket the words Mother and economy. Apparently she was determined to avoid all reminders of her girlhood with its starched, home-stitched pretension. Even when entertaining women whose means were obviously limited—such as the wives of *Daily Watch* department heads—Mother made no effort to hide her expensive tastes. However, though expensive, they were simple. To indulge them frankly and honestly seemed much more honorable than a patronizing rush to the attic for something glum and shabby whenever the less fortunate headed our way. As proof, most everybody in town liked her except for the usual counterrevolutionaries who would have spewed black envy no matter what she wore as long as Mother crowned the top of Woodruff Hill.

I went over and gave her a kiss, then retreated toward the large canopied double bed on which I'd spent a good part of my life.

"Have a good day?" she asked.

"A nothing day," I told her, which is the way most days are on a newspaper or anywhere else, I guess.

I made a lunge for the bed. Its old bones groaned and Mother looked around, her mouth bristling with hairpins and anxious silence, her fingers running to keep the upswept hair in place.

"Made it that time," I laughed.

She removed the hairpins long enough to say, "Honestly, Larry." Then she replaced them, tried to smile so I'd know she wasn't really cross, and went back to her work.

I couldn't help behaving like a child in that room. It was a womb of memories, most involving childhood and I was reduced to about age ten the instant I crossed the threshold. As kids Abby and I were allowed in almost every day, usually after Pa had left for the paper, to help Mother consume her breakfast. Those were the breakfast-in-bed days which lasted only until we were old enough to manage ourselves in the dining room, but they were times of great luxury for me. I can remember nothing better than a lump of sugar soaked in lemon juice, the bed's soft, semiconscious comfort made even more desirable by the hard shock of Abby who could not yet lie still, but could at least go away from time to time, and the crisp, reassuring telephone voice of Mother getting things done. And the sad time of suspense when the nurse came to steal our pleasure.

"Shall I take the children, ma'am?"

"They're all right, Nelly. Let them stay awhile."

And the sweet joy of reprieve.

Or Christmas Day, with our stockings hung and bursting secrets and Pa wondering what we could be doing in their bedroom at such an ungodly hour and the two of them watching with bemused, sleepfed patience and soft, sentimental, faraway eyes as we made our joyous Yuletide mess.

And the times not so long gone when I was home from prep school and would lie on the bed just as now, full of confusions Mother could never begin to understand, but always managed to cure with a quiet concern which made school seem a long way away and everything about it trivial.

I suppose Mother has changed over the seventeen years or so which make up my memory time. But if so I couldn't tell. To me she seemed the same. Probably if someone pointed a gun at me and suggested I describe those marks of age which must have come to her, I could do it. The laugh wrinkles round her eyes were deeper and I'd given up warning that frowning would put lines on her forehead and under her chin was just the gentlest hint of collapse and her waist had slackened, grown soft. But to me all this was merely change and not a sign of age at all. Her beauty remained, as it had always been, fine and soft and smiling, yet with elegance and grace enough to distinguish her from the apple pie mommas who hugged and squeezed and kissed like jealous children to show all the world how great was their love. I'd hate to count the number of times some friend's mother has told me, "We haven't got much money, but there's a lot of love in our home," as if money and hatred, poverty and love were part of some sort of mystical equation. Well, let them think so if it made their poverty more honorable, but I'll stick with the long-suffering rich where love is sweet smelling, delicate, fine as golden thread and worth thirty-five dollars an ounce.

I lay on the bed, watching and wondering what Mother was up to. Now that I was supposedly a man, I found her difficult to be with sometimes. Part of me still yearned to curl up in dependency, while the new man, choking with disgust, searched for a more adult relationship.

"There's something I want to talk to you about," she said when her hair had taken all the fixing it could stand and she was free to think of other things.

"Wassat?" I asked, for the ten-year-old was still in control.

"Your father. I'm worried about him."

Despite his uncertainty that morning, it would never have occurred to me to worry seriously about Pa. Of all the people I knew, Gravenhurst's Man of Tomorrow seemed the least likely candidate and I suspected Mother might do better to tend the social chores and let Pa handle the business.

"Oh I don't think we have to worry about Pa. He usually manages to come out all right." The power of my understatement was extremely satisfying, but I might have enjoyed it more fully had the sound of Mother's hand slapping the top of her dressing table and the sight of three angry faces staring from the mirrors not distracted me.

"Honestly, Larry, must you be so fatuous?"

"Huh?" I was eight years old by then and slipping fast.

"Do you realize how serious this newspaper business is?"

"Sure. I'm not like Abby."

"What does that mean?"

"Well, I know Pa's only human. And things aren't going so smoothly for the moment."

"That's edifying."

"But I still think he's too tough for the Rosenfeldts."

"What makes you so sure?"

"Well, I mean Pa's one of the biggest men in town. You can't take that away from him."

"And Benjamin Rosenfeldt is one of the biggest men in the state," Mother said.

"I guess that's so," I admitted, "but competing with the *Daily Watch* is a local battle fought on Pa's territory."

"Have you asked people what they think of the *Enterprise?*"

"Well I just sort of assumed . . ."

"Or how they feel about the *Daily Watch?*"

"I've heard some things."

"You should have," she said. "Generally people are rather pleased about the whole thing. They think your father's had things his own way entirely too long and wouldn't mind in the least if he were deposed."

"Oh I can't believe that," I said. "People say those things, but in a pinch they'd never let us down."

"Reassuring. If true."

"Besides, Pa's a pretty tough nut on anybody's terms."

"Larry, you apparently don't understand. Pa's had a survey made of local opinion and it isn't at all comforting. In fact, the results give one a feeling Gravenhurst's been waiting for an opportunity like this quite some time now."

"I haven't seen the survey."

"It's downstairs. You can read it after dinner."

"What about the business side of things? Does it cover that too?"

"As well as could be expected. The Rosenfeldts haven't been too free with their financial reports."

"Well how's the *Enterprise* doing in dollars and cents?"

"They're still losing a lot of money," Mother said. "But the gains are awfully impressive."

I nodded with unearned wisdom. "Pa'll lick 'em, you just wait and see."

Mother sighed, then came over and sat next to me. "Darling, I love your father very much. He's a fine man with many wonderful qualities. But he is not the one thing both you and Abby seem to think he is. Your father is neither a captain of finance nor a crusading publisher. He's a nice man who has inherited a good bit of money and managed to enjoy himself without losing it all."

"Mother, I just can't believe that."

"Nevertheless it's true. And while we're at it, the fact that you consider him a mere superman while Abby, in her innocence, considers him a god is not such a gratifying sign of sophistication as you seem to think."

"Maybe not, but I still can't believe Pa's what you say he is."

"Think about it awhile," she said. "Being nice isn't so terrible."

"It is if you think you're something more."

"Which is why we're having this little talk," Mother said.

"Why?"

"I don't want your father to be hurt."

"Would you rather he grew up to be a sissy?"

"Larry, there isn't time for that sort of false pride right now. Let's accept your father the way he is and see if there isn't some way we can help."

"All right. I'm sorry." Jesse's story of the aging children with their tired, puckered faces sprang to mind and I shuddered.

"First of all," Mother said. "About this Rosenfeldt business."

"Yes?"

"I think we should avoid reducing things to the level of a personal feud."

"How?"

"By you and Abby continuing to see him."

"That's fine with me. But it's a little rough on Abby."

"Why?"

"She's sort of interested in Jesse, isn't she? I mean you can't fool around with that kind of thing just because it helps the *Daily Watch*."

"The best way I know of making Abby do something," Mother said, "is to tell her not to."

"I guess that's so all right."

"And second of all," Mother said. "We've got to do something about Ned Polk."

"What can be done about him? He's the only news editor we've got."

"Not quite. I've already had a chat with Ted Pearson."

"Teddy Pearson, the bald-headed pigeon," I laughed. "My God, his own shadow sends him cooing for safety."

"He's a very tenacious little man," Mother said.

"Oh come on."

"Really. You don't know him, Larry."

"I know all he does is sit around pecking out editorials on the joys of gardening or some such junk as that."

"You know almost nothing," Mother corrected. "He was an excellent news editor in his day. Give him a cause to defend and he'll hang on for dear life."

"I haven't noticed much of that lately."

"Because of Ned. Your father has always been partial to Ned's swashbuckling kind of journalism, and Teddy Pearson knows it."

"Suppose that's so," I conceded. "What makes you think he'd want to be news editor? After all, it's a demotion."

"I don't think he would," she said.

"But I thought that's what we were talking about."

"No."

"Then who?"

"You," she said.

"Me? Mother, you're crazy."

"Why?"

"I don't know the first thing about it."

"Ted's going to teach you."

"When?"

"On Ned's day off."

"Does Pa know about this?"

"No," Mother admitted. "There's no reason why he should."

"My God, who runs this paper anyway?"

"Now don't worry about that. I've arranged for you to have lunch with Mr. Pearson tomorrow and see what he has to say."

"*You* have?" I asked, astonished.

"Yes," she confirmed. "*I* have."

"All right. But I think Pa should know what's going on."

"He will. Just as soon as you're ready to show him."

"I'd better get cleaned up . . . It's almost time for dinner."

Mother gave me a kiss and a pat on the hand which meant I shouldn't worry too much about all this. Therefore I didn't.

CHAPTER X

That night Abby came by my room for another one of her little chats which didn't surprise me half as much as the fact she had taken the trouble to put on a wrapper and to knock before entering.

"You busy, Larry?"

"What do you care?" I laughed.

"Oh," she said. "I guess you are. I'll come back later."

"No, it's all right. Really. Come on in."

"Okay. If you're sure." She poked around the room for a while, not saying anything, just letting her eyes run over my photographs which were intended to suggest the presence of a former schoolboy athlete and did, provided you didn't look too closely. I was usually buried somewhere in the back row.

"Can you find me in any of them?" I asked, a little sheepishly.

"Oh sure. I know where to look."

"That's too bad."

"No it isn't. At least I know where to find you."

"Meaning?"

"Suppose I thought you were the captain or something. Then I'd always be looking in the wrong places."

"You sure would."

"Like with Pa, for instance. Who'd ever expect to find him under a rock?"

"Now, now. Things aren't that bad."

"No . . . They're worse."

"Pa's just protecting our interests."

"That way?" she asked. "I'd rather not have any."

"What way?"

"Worrying about Jesse and me. Keeping up appearances and all that disgusting business."

"Oh I wouldn't worry about seeing Jesse," I said lightly. "Pa was just upset."

"But did you see him crawling when I asked if it was because Jesse was Jewish?"

"No I didn't," I lied.

"Well he was," Abby said. "He was crawling like a snake."

"Listen, Abby, Pa's trying to be practical. The *Daily Watch's* in trouble and he's got to do something about it."

Abby sat down at my desk and stared out the window so I couldn't see her face. She was hunched up and looked cold as ice. "Well I don't see why he has to fight this way. It's so grubby."

"That's the way life is. You might as well face it."

"If that's the way life is, then why didn't somebody let me in on the secret a long time ago? Instead of . . . Oh God, I'd rather not even talk about it."

"Instead of what?"

"I don't know," she said and shrugged. "Stringing me along, I guess. Encouraging me to think Pa was so great and just being Abigail Woodruff was so great and smiling and chucking me under the chin all the time because I said such cute little idealistic things."

"Well, you didn't expect him to tell you he was a fraud, did you?"

Abby turned around with a heavy sigh. "No," she said. "I didn't expect that either. Oh, I don't know. I don't know what I expected," and the tears began to flow while she stared blankly, seemingly unaware she was crying. "I just didn't expect to see Pa crawl," she said. "Not ever. Not ever, ever, ever," and she gave her complete and sobbing devotion to those first unconscious tears.

I went over and she pressed against me, holding tight and sobbing as if I were some inanimate, comforting stuffed animal.

"Don't worry Bones," I said. "You'll get over it." The use of her childhood nickname, almost forgotten now along with the jumble of knees and elbows and explosive, headlong laughter that was Abby as a little girl, didn't help matters any.

I was beginning to wonder if she'd ever stop when suddenly she did. Coldly, carefully, with compulsive eye dabbings and nose wipings she withdrew from tears to bitter resignation.

"Jesse may be a Jew," she said. "But at least he's real."

"So's Pa."

"Sure . . . a real fake," and she marched out of the room.

Well, I'd witnessed Abby's romantic histrionics before so this didn't worry me much. Besides, there were busy days ahead and I had other things to think about.

It turned out Mother had been right about Ted Pearson. In fact, if anything she'd underestimated his eagerness to be rid of Polk. As a result Ted wasn't satisfied with working me in on Polk's day off. He had me coming out to his house at night going over dummy layouts and taking dry runs until I was about crosseyed with the chores of news editorship. What with all that, about all I could do for Abby was thank God she'd be going back to college within the month. The change of scene plus a two-hour drive couldn't help but slow Jesse down a little.

Being so wrong about Teddy Pearson scared me because I realized it was only one of many basically faulty judgments collected over the years. Ned, the coony trader in human currency; Pa, the proud, indomitable stag; Mother, the social tycoon whose talents had once seemed wasted in committee absurdities; and now Teddy, the booster. All were shifting their patterns, yet not altering the basic elements of their nature at all. It was as if my view of life, once so fixed, smug, and safe, had suddenly turned out to be a giant kaleidoscope and I, somewhat sickened by the shuffling confusion, yearned for an end to the spinning, flicking, nightmarish abuses of my comfortable landscape. Yet I had to admit some of the new patterns were improvements. In fact, all of them were, for even Pa and Ned Polk, while losing that clean simplicity of a hero's silhouette, had gained in depth and detail.

Nevertheless, it was frightening to be so wrong about everybody and I was less willing than usual to surrender my preconceptions of Ted Pearson. The evidence was fairly torrential, however. Even Ted's physical appearance seemed to harden under the promise of a fight. He was still, outwardly anyway, the booster. Yet even this convenient epithet seemed to be jiggling loose and threatened to settle into some completely inconvenient pattern. He usually wore a bow tie, which may not give the Booster look to every man but it did to Teddy. And the shoulders of his suits, reflecting their master's concern for the dictates of *Esquire* and *Look* magazines, had dwindled from robust to sophisticated during recent years, and of course his shirts were festooned with the latest button requirements. But it wasn't with physical props alone that Teddy Pearson deceived the world. He also *talked* superficialities much of the time. What's more he could never steer completely clear of a certain envious curiosity with regard to life on top of Woodruff Hill. Once, for instance, I wore a shirt which not only buttoned down in front, but in back as well. That is, it had one of those little inexplicable buttons on the back of the collar. Teddy found this absolutely spellbinding and though he was careful to bury his fascination in sarcasm, I noticed a month or so later he had taken the precaution of buying a couple of those very same style shirts for himself. Then too, if I happened to stop by his house for a drink he was usually capable of saying "I don't know what you drink up there on the Hill, but all we got's rye," or some equally unnecessary crack as that. Yet beneath all these preoccupations with convention, Teddy seemed to conceal a living thing, its many facets functioning in rich profusion. He had plans for the paper, for instance, which weren't revolutionary, but more than Pa had produced in recent months. He wanted to put in tube routes for home delivery to solidify *Daily Watch* circulation. He wanted a second edition for country subscribers so advertisers could choose their markets and reach the readers they needed at reduced rates. He wanted to tone down Ned Polk's preoccupation with politics and bring more general news to the front page. But there was a lot more to his secret side than concern for the *Daily Watch*. For one thing, he had a terrific, though somewhat biting, sense of humor. He called Tommy Compton an "intellectual without portfolio" which about wrapped that boy up for the season. Then once when I started in on a little harangue about how the *Daily Watch* should do more to promote Pa's Urban Renewal Committee because it was a good thing for the community, Teddy bent an ear and looked around with such agitated concern I finally had to stop my sermon and ask what was wrong.

"I thought I heard the gentle thunder of platitudes," said he.

And as for members of the Gravenhurst Country Club who happen to have achieved the loftiest peaks of our social climb: "Genteel Bumpkins," said my former Booster.

He also turned out to be president of the Gravenhurst Players, a fact I, with my lofty neglect of local culture, had either forgotten or never known. It was all very confusing.

Perhaps none of these newly discovered dimensions were remarkable but they certainly served to liberate Teddy Pearson from the narrow cliché of small-town Booster. I was beginning to suspect that lost American Dream we've been searching for so conscientiously (and ever so smugly as well) might not really be lost at all. Hidden, buried perhaps, trapped in our separate souls, but not lost.

I began to suspect all this the afternoon I drove out to the Pearsons' for my first lesson in news editorship. They lived about ten miles out of town on Pioneer Ridge Road in a development called Colorado Heights. The house was late Tudor Garage on the outside and early vinyl within. I could see only one distinguishing feature in the entire room: messy bookshelves, so it's no wonder he had me fooled. Nevertheless, we got some work done and while the atmosphere may have been a little too neo-genteel to be true, I don't suppose it was any worse, really, than what I found at home that evening.

Hal's Jag was parked in the drive and as I was going down the hall his voice came trotting out to meet me.

"Yes sir," he was saying. "But the Homeowners policy *includes* your personal property feature. The whole deal wrapped up in one convenient package."

"You don't say," said Pa. "Well now, why hasn't Jensen and Company put me onto that?"

"Well, I guess they just haven't gotten around to it," Hal supposed, then spotted me. "Hey Larry," he said. "Howsa boy?"

"Hey hey," I said. "You hustling my poor old Papa?"

"That's about the size of it, eh boy?" Hal forced his face to laugh.

"Yes indeed," said Pa. "Your friend Hal here's quite a persuasive young man. Got me so interested in certain insurance matters I decided to bring him home for dinner. Talk a little business."

"Yes sir," Hal continued. "And as far as that other matter is concerned, if you'd let us have a look at the properties I believe we might be able to recommend a few preventative measures could bring you some sizable rate reductions."

"Now that's very interesting," Pa professed. "Might just do that, Hal, maboy, might just do it and see if you can deliver the goods."

"Just give us the chance, sir. That's all we need."

Pa winked. "That's what I like," he said. "Young man who isn't afraid to get in there and fight."

"I'd better get changed," I said.

"Good boy," said Pa. "And while you're up there tell that sister of yours to hurry up, I've brought home a handsome caller."

Hal chuckled. "Well anyway a caller."

"That's more like it," I laughed and went upstairs.

"Hey," I called, knocking on Abby's door. "Love awaits below."

She opened up. "Love does what?"

"Awaits," I said, thumbing down toward the living room.

"Jesse here?" she asked.

"Uh-oh, wrong number. It's Hal James."

"Oh. I thought you said something about love."

"Well you never know."

"Sometimes you do." Abby turned and padded toward her closet, dressed but shoeless and with a simple country look still, despite the elegance of her clothes. I waited and watched her ankling into high heels, suddenly transformed from peasant to princess by that simple adjustment.

"Still sore at Pa?" I asked.

"Sore? Who's sore?" And she marched to her jewelry box, plundered it for necklace, earrings, brooch.

"Weren't you?" I wandered to the night table, tried to be casual.

"Not sore," she corrected. "Disgusted."

"Hey, what's this?" I asked, picking up a book. "*Jewish Culture in America.*" I managed to produce a long, teasing whistle.

Abby said nothing.

"Well?" I asked.

"Well what?"

"The book."

"You already answered the question. *Jewish Culture in America.* Was there something else?"

"No, I guess not," and I turned to go.

"Hal James," she laughed. "What'll he think of next?"

"He's here on business," I said.

"Sure thing," she said. "And I'm Donald Duck. *Quack quack.*"

I gave up. Come to think of it, Pa wasn't in the habit of bringing people home on business, but then Hal was an old friend, after all, so why not?

On her way down Abby knocked, cracked the door and hissed: "Hurry up, for heaven sakes. He's your friend."

I don't know why she never liked Hal. Maybe the idea of going out with someone she'd known all her life just sort of bored her. Unless, of course, the escort happened to be Pa.

By the time I got down it was almost dark and seemed like midwinter. Bollard had a small fire going for show and they were all sitting at that end of the room in their winter positions; most everybody drinking bourbon except Abby who had a glass of sherry to kind of show she wasn't going along with Pa's little plan, if he had one.

I said "Hello again" and Pa told me to help myself, I had some catching up to do and I started to say no I didn't because I'd been out to Ted Pearson's, but managed to catch myself, and then joined the little circle for a round of pitter-patter talk.

Hal asked how the *Enterprise* was doing and Pa said all right if you discounted the way they did business, and Hal laughed and said what could you expect from a bunch of kikes but we weren't really worried, were we? Abby laughed and said of course not, Old Clarence always made out all right, which was her usual routine except this time she added: "One way or another," which Pa and the rest of us pretended not to notice. Then we had our customary little talk about the weather, and about that time dinner was announced.

Somewhere along the line Hal asked whether Pa and the boys had somebody picked out to replace Senator Vanden Gasser and Pa looked kind of mysterious, said things were under control as usual.

"Ha ha," said Abby, too loud.

"Are you feeling all right, Abby?" Mother asked.

"Of *course*, Mother. I'm just fine."

"Well you seem a little pale, dear, that's all." She leaned over and pressed a palm to Abby's forehead.

"Mother, please," she sizzled.

"But you *do* seem a little out of sorts," Mother insisted.

"That doesn't mean I'm *sick*, Mother. You're always hoping people are *sick*." Then she paused, added: "As though that was the only time you knew how to help them."

"Abby!" Pa warned.

She shrugged, lapsed into silence. Mother stared in confused concern.

"Larry?" Pa asked. "Did I tell you young Compton quit?"

"Well I sort of heard about it," I said.

"I'll be damned," said Hal. "That boy's not all there."

"How do you mean?" asked Abby.

"He just started," Hal explained. "And then he quit."

"I didn't know it was a sign of insanity to change your mind," Abby said.

"Well now, you'll have to admit it's a little unusual," I reasoned.

"I don't see why," she said.

"Done any flying lately?" I asked Hal.

He shook his head. "Gotta go up pretty soon. Getting a little rusty on those crosswind landings."

"Yeah," I agreed. "They're pretty tricky," but nobody took us up on our bid for heroism.

"What's Tommy going to do?" Mother asked.

"Go to New York," I said. "He wants to be a writer."

"Uh oh," said Hal. "A.C.–D.C."

"Really?" asked Abby. "My I'll bet you know a lot about it, don't you?"

"Listen," Hal threatened. "I know enough."

"A.C.–D.C.," said Mother. "I never heard that expression before."

"It means he's a homosexual," said Abby.

"Really, Abby," Mother disapproved.

"Mr. James of James, Fenton and James said it, Mother," Abby pointed out.

"Well I didn't mean it exactly that way," Hal protested.

"But that's what it means, doesn't it?" Abby insisted.

"Ha ha," said Hal. "Yeah."

I tried to be reasonable.

"Not everybody's A.C.–D.C. because he wants to be a writer or an artist or an actor or something," I said.

"Yeah, well," said Hal, which meant if there'd been any exceptions he hadn't heard yet.

"Oh come on," I said. "You don't mean that," but he just looked at me with squinted, accusing eyes and rolled his dessert spoon ponderously as though the Woodruff electrical system were also under suspicion. My only alternative was to laugh and wave his look away. After all, I held no stock in defending causes, rebellions, and the like. Not when they threatened friendship, for I had little enough of that, God knows, having been sent away to prep school and college and thus funneled from the main stream of Gravenhurst life. While I couldn't agree with Hal about Tommy, I could at least steer clear of the subject. It sure burned me, though, calling him a fairy and all, even though he *was* a little strange maybe.

The telephone rang then and we all waxed silent, wondering which of us had been honored.

Bollard came in. "Miss Abby," he said. "Telephone."

"Oh?" asked Abby. "Who is it?"

"Mr. Rosenfeldt."

"Oh!" And she hurried to the hall phone which wasn't very private.

While Hal introduced Mother and Pa to the inner joys of building a new motel on the Route 19 bypass, I eavesdropped:

"Hello? Oh yes, hello . . . Nothing, just having dinner. No no, it doesn't matter, we were finished really . . . Tonight? Well I don't know. I mean we have company. Well no, I don't see how. I mean it's sort of late to be calling and I . . . What? What do you mean conventional? Me? Well it *is* late. I'm *not* doing things by the book . . . All right, just for that I will. Yes right now. I'll meet you there."

Then Abby marched back in. "Gotta go," she announced.

"Go?" Mother asked. "But we haven't finished dinner, dear."

"I know. But this is sort of special."

"That's enough foolishness," Pa commanded. "Hal's here. Now you sit down and behave yourself."

"Love to," said Abby, aiming at Hal. "But I've got a date with a kike," and she left followed by a stream of ultimatums from Pa.

I'd have been impressed if she hadn't sounded so hesitant over the phone. When you counted that, her performance seemed more bluff than brash, as though she were trying to prove her independence rather than simply enforce it. I had a feeling Abby had to leave in a hurry before her mind changed; thus it was flight rather than defense of principle and totally unrelated to her behavior before Pa's fall from grace.

"Dammit to hell," said Pa. "I won't stand for that sort of thing." Though he had until now.

"Oh dear," Mother said. "When Abby gets her mind made up there's just nothing we can do."

"We can apologize to Hal," Pa said. "It's disgraceful."

So Abby'd been right.

"I thought Hal was here on business," I said.

"Now listen here," Pa said, and shoved back from the table so violently the candlesticks nearly toppled. "I'll have no impertinence from you, young man."

I squirmed.

"Whether Hal was here on business or not has nothing to do with it," Pa hissed. "Can you understand that?"

"Yes sir," I mumbled, and I did, too. Good manners mean a lot to Pa and to Mother. It's one of the ways they use for figuring out who was created equal and who wasn't.

"And now if you'll excuse me," he said, and marched from the room.

"Really," Mother sighed. "You'd think he'd know better than call right in the middle of dinner."

Then we made little sallies of unconcern for Hal's benefit.

"Shall we have coffee here or in the other room?"

"Oh let's have it in the other room," I said.

But we needn't have worried. Hal seemed completely untouched by the scene, as though it hadn't happened at all, and went right on chattering about that goddam motel of his and what a top-notch fella the admiral was after all.

Mother played along through one cup of coffee, then excused herself, tried the den and, finding it empty, followed Pa upstairs to bed.

Hal and I looked at each other, kind of half-smiling. I felt the old understanding coursing between us and guessed maybe we'd have a couple of drinks, sort of talk the whole thing over.

"Well," he said, "think I'll take a run out to the Fun House. Feel like coming along?"

"No," I said, "I sure don't."

And after that he couldn't leave soon enough to please me.

CHAPTER XI

The *Daily Watch* does not publish Sundays so we used to get away around noon Saturday which wasn't bad considering we also got a day off during the week. The only hitch was a stand-by list which meant about once a month a couple of us had to stick around the office all weekend in case something important broke. It wasn't much of an inconvenience because you could usually switch around if you had a date or something on your duty day. However, when Tommy quit I got left with the Sunday bag which was just one more reason why I was fed up with the Great American Writer. He hadn't wasted much time, I'll say that for him, because he was off to New York City that same weekend on an apartment hunt or pad hunt or whatever it is great American writers nest in. I was surprised his family had gone along with the idea, because, after all, they'd be financing it, but Tommy explained that the writing side of his future had been kind of played down in favor of a lot of talk about going for a Master's degree. Apparently Mrs. Compton rated scholarship pretty high up the ladder so everything was just dandy. I suppose she pictured Tommy languishing in some faculty club where the gossip was traded in classic rather than common jargon; where everyone was careful to assume scholarship and intellect were synonyms; and old friends, especially envied ones, who happened to be treading less ethereal paths, were discussed with a gently condescending air.

I sometimes wonder why the American scholar who is often so contemptuous of his low-brow brother, finds it difficult to accept the low-brow's contempt of him. It seems like a pretty fair swap to me.

However, I'm sure Mrs. Compton wasn't too concerned with that aspect of Tommy's future and neither was I. Actually, having to take his duty worked out fine because the only thing going on that Sunday was the Little League playoff which I would have gone to anyway and which was more fun to cover than simply to watch because I could wander around taking pictures and telling all those pint-sized heroes to get the lead out and show some class.

Also Ned Polk coached one of the teams and that usually led to a pretty colorful afternoon. Ned worked with kids a lot. It was sort of a hobby with him. They called him Old Fire and Brimstone—Brim for short—because of the way he taught Sunday school. But the name fit no matter whether he was coaching the YMCA swimming team or the Little League or whatever, because Ned believed in mixing sport with Scripture. It may seem a little out of character for someone like him, but Ned was a narrow-gauge Catholic and he'd have been the last one to notice. It was usually quite a show. His Little League team, officially titled the Gravenhurst Grackles, better known as the Mackerel Snappers, usually did more praying than ball playing, but Ned had managed to win the series three years out of five which is enough to make a fellow wonder about the Protestant Reformation. Before every game the whole team huddled out in the middle of the field for prayer meeting—"Pray together and you'll play together," he used to say—and not a one of them could step up to the plate without crossing himself. Earlier in the season, as a matter of fact, the shortstop had adopted this practice every time a hot grounder came his way. It took a real duster off the side of his head to shake this devotion to ritual.

There were those of us who secretly criticized his holy coaching, but it was difficult to say so without being called a Communist or something. I've heard Ned speak at Rotary lunches and the like in defense of his technique. It's nauseating: "I tell my boys 'Boys, you can't lose with God up there on the pitching mound'."

That sort of stuff is pretty tough to take. Especially on top of a civic lunch. But as I've said already, nobody ever did anything to stop him.

Actually it was fine with me because I enjoyed his coaching performances which seemed to combine Holy Rolling with some of the more abusive characteristics of our late Senator Joseph McCarthy. It was a real experience to watch Ned and God root those little snappers round the bases.

I took Nora with me, which was a mistake though I couldn't figure out why. Something about her that day affected me the way thunder and lightning affect cattle. Something ominous and inevitable about the way she took my arm. Something pat and just a little dreary about her beige skirt and blouse and pink cashmere sweater thrown round her shoulders, buttoned. It seemed she had crept in and enveloped me. I was being furtively digested and might be all gone very soon. Well, not all gone exactly, because I would become a part of her. Mr. and Mrs. Nora Compton. It was too bad she had that effect because the day was fresh and crispy and I wanted us to enjoy each other the way people in love are supposed to. Part of the problem was my work. I mean we got to sit in the dugout with Ned and his boys which was sort of a novelty, but I kept having to run around taking pictures and checking vital statistics. It was the kind of thing I usually liked doing, but that day was no fun at all because I could feel Nora tugging all the time, trying to choke down every tasty morsel of me. I had forgotten that she might not be feeling too partial toward Ned Polk after his performance in Frank's Place. Also, possibly the thrill of being on the inside, watching from the dugout, was canceled out by the limited social life down there amongst the gee whizzers. But the possibility her tugging might be justified didn't make it any more endurable and I had to concentrate hard on the game and local color so as not to let her get me down.

It's quite a sight, Little League baseball is, primarily because of how seriously everybody takes it. I mean here you have a bunch of kids no longer than their bats, spitting luck on their hands and knocking the clods from their spikes, lifting and tipping their caps, and eying that left-field fence with grim arrogance. In other words, doing about everything the pros do except on a smaller scale. And up in the stands proud mommas and poppas watching with crossed fingers lest their pint-sized DiMaggio drop an easy one or whiff with the bases loaded or otherwise disgrace the family name.

And the poor coach. Failure to put some kid in, even if it meant losing the game, was tantamount to a punch in the eye from Papa or, if Papa happened to disagree with the direct action approach to life's little iniquities, from Mama.

That's how serious Little League baseball was in our town. So serious, in fact, that construction of a first-class stadium replete with dugouts, horseshoe bleachers, a scoreboard, and other assorted status symbols took economic preference over everything but the celebration of Jesus Christ's birthday.

It was top of the ninth and Ned's boys ahead by five runs which is nothing in this league, but we were feeling pretty confident. I'd managed to get some good pictures; one of a kid sliding into third, hat in hand, with the ump calling him safe as if the world would end if that call weren't right (which for the umpire, anyway, might easily have been the case), and another of somebody's old man out on the field, raising hell over a bum call against his son who was out a mile, far as I could see. So I was pretty well through for the day and had no alternative but to devote my complete attention to Nora. She was at the opposite end of the bench from Ned, not quite caring what the Lilliputians were up to, which annoyed me because I'd rather have sat next to Ned where you could hear what was going on.

I happened to be wearing a fairly sloppy seersucker jacket and sports shirt and I hadn't been sitting down thirty seconds before she felt the need to lean across and adjust my collar. It was a matter-of-fact bit of repair work which implied a definite sense of ownership, yet I couldn't for the life of me understand what made her think there had been a sale. I wondered whether she had twisted our unlovely interpretation of love in a car into some kind of symbolic pre-marital rite during which the fact of Mr. and Mrs. Nora Compton had emerged.

"What's the matter?" she asked.

"Nothing, except I can still dress myself all right."

Granted it was a childish performance and Nora treated it as such by not bothering to answer. That annoyed me even more, but it also put me in check where I remained until the game ended with victory for the Vatican and gave me an excuse to jump up and run around and pretend I'd come without my mother. Ned was being mobbed by proud parents and it struck me as a great shame Sally wasn't around to share this moment of glory.

"Good going, Ned," I shouted.

He nodded, smiled, fondled his first baseman's curly blond head, and said: "With the help of the Lord," for the benefit of his admirers.

"How come Sally isn't here to enjoy the great triumph?" I asked.

"Couldn't make it. She went down to New York for the weekend."

"Hey what's going on? Everybody's taking off for the city these days."

"What?" But fortunately someone else had been yelling at him.

"Nothing," I lied. "It's too bad she had to miss it."

"Oh sure," Ned agreed. "Too bad, all right."

By any reasonable measure, the fact that Sally and Tommy were in New York at the same time was the purest coincidence, but I have a weakness for melodrama which can probably be traced to the days of radio soap opera so naturally I suspected the worst.

After the game we went back to Nora's house, by mistake, and I got roped into one of those Sunday night pick-up suppers which are sort of fun in your own home but deadly anywhere else because they require considerable practice. Each member of the family team must run run run to do his little chore and the insinuation of an outsider usually reduces this ordered efficiency to the utility level of a dropped clock. Perhaps I should have known the Compton system well enough by then not to foul it up, but I didn't. Mrs. Compton, with all her pretty bird flitting and nervous efficiency, reduced me to spastic incompetence and it was all I could do, usually, not to fall down.

Funny how people can get your goat like that. It's almost chemical. Mrs. Compton had no awing characteristics. No great wit, charm, or warmth. She had no special talent for contempt or ridicule. In fact, minus that bright yellow feathering of nervous activity, she'd have been as dull and gray as the judge. Yet somehow she had always held sway over me with the absolute authority of an Egyptian queen. I suspect her secret was too much orderliness. As a child I was always being hustled from one place to another in a program of efficient harassment which inevitably turned me dumb with confusion. The Comptons themselves suffered similar indignities so there was nothing especially pathetic about the way she abused poor Larry Woodruff. With propriety as her sledge she staked out the boundaries of family etiquette and not a Compton dared leave the compound. Even the judge was a captive and I often wondered how much this confinement had contributed to his successful, or at least respectable, career. The compression of his nature within such narrow limits made his impact small but hard as a frozen turd. How he would have managed without her will never be known since Mrs. Compton guarded her brood with bitch loyalty and hated to let any one of them out of her sight for very long.

It was not a good way for Nora and I to spend the evening. I felt cornered enough without adding Mrs. Compton to my addled fears.

We all sat in the kitchen—all but the departed Tommy—while Judge Compton trotted out a big news story I should be careful not to overlook. To the judge a big story was anything which placed him in a favorable light and usually had little chance of making the front page, or any other page, for that matter. So I prepared for a long, cold evening during which my contributions would never amount to more than an occasional "Is that right, Judge," or perhaps an "Ummmm, I see what you mean."

This time, it seemed, the judge was interested in sharpening the blunt edge of his political profile with a little human interest. A fourteen-year-old girl had been arrested for shoplifting at one of the local supermarkets. She had picked a rainy day so it would be all right to wear a coat and I guess the store detective must have thought he was witnessing a virgin birth. According to the police report, this tough little chippy had sashayed into the store with her nice flat body making its presence known despite the baggy coat and about a half hour later she was seen waddling out as if she'd never make the hospital. Now even detectives are smarter than that. Within minutes she had given birth to one canned ham (Danish), a small frozen turkey, a loaf of bread, some Camembert cheese ("Jeez, I din't mean to take that stuff. It smells rottin") and assorted canned goods. Not a bad haul.

I remembered her case. She'd been pulled into city court a couple of days before and had denied all charges. Just for the hell of it, it seemed to me. And now she was at liberty, awaiting a hearing. The whole thing was slightly unusual so I'd given it the lead—without naming the girl, of course—in an otherwise dull roundup of drunks and speeding charges for my daily court story. But other than that, there didn't seem to be much to it. Just a punk little girl headed for Juvenile Court.

Not at all, said the judge. She was a sweet, gentle child forced to steal in order to feed a consumptive mother and an alcoholic father and Lord knows what all in the sibling department. A hearing was scheduled for the next day and the judge had already made arrangements to put her on probation in the custody of none other than the judge himself.

"What are you going to do with her?" I asked, not meaning it to sound quite that way, but glad it did.

"She is going to come and live with us," Mrs. Compton said. "To help with the housework."

"Mother!" said Nora.

"That's very nice of you," I ventured.

"Mother," Nora repeated. "What about me?"

"She needs our help," Mrs. Compton said, for the press's benefit, judging by the quick look which came my way.

"Where is she now?" I asked.

"With her family," the judge replied. "I was hoping, Larry, you'd be able to get out there and take some pictures so the people in this town will be able to see for themselves just how dismal life really is for those less fortunate than ourselves."

"Well Monday morning's a pretty bad time for us," I lied. "But maybe we could follow up the hearing with a feature story."

"I think you should," Mrs. Compton said. "I think *something* should be done about this kind of . . . thing."

"Oh so do I," I agreed, though it was unlikely she'd have been such an eager beaver had the idea been Mother's.

"And I think it might be good for *Daily Watch* prestige," she purred.

"Maybe we could tie it in with our urban renewal drive," I said. "You know; no slums, no human tragedy."

"Fine idea," the judge agreed. "Fine idea. Give me a call in the morning and let's see what we can work out."

"Yes sir, I will."

"How long will she be staying?" Nora asked, and there was a stickiness in her voice.

"Now dear, it won't be as bad as all that," Mrs. Compton soothed.

"After all, Mrs. Compton, charity begins at home, doesn't it," I said.

"That's so true, Larry. So true," the judge agreed. After that the conversation went dead again.

I left as soon after supper as possible and that tantalizing sense of freedom joined me, bringing both pride and shame along with it. Pride in my ability to escape them still and shame in the realization it was only the absence of action, the evasion of decision, which brought these gifts of freedom. I was also ashamed of not knowing whether I loved Nora, for I was certainly not *in* love with her, or whether all the dreams and clumsy passion and affection were nothing more than the habit of convenience.

Partly because of this confusion I was afraid to marry her, but also I think it was impossible for me to conceive of romantic love in Gravenhurst. Though I understood satisfactory arrangements leading to comfort, contentment, and chronic inconsequence were often made between men and women, I did hope some shadow of romance might soften the glare of expediency and free me from sowing my seed in the dreary soil of custom and convenience. I don't know why Gravenhurst ranked so low in my esteem as a setting for courtship. Perhaps because everything about it and everyone in it, including Nora, were so familiar to me.

When I got home Pa and Abby were wandering around, admiring his paintings, contemplating changes and both apparently totally recovered from his fit of pique over her little defiance. This shouldn't have been too surprising since the incident was a couple of days old, but the funny part was there'd been no actual reconciliation. There never was in our family. Things just went on as if nothing had happened in the hope, I suppose, that the causes, once properly ignored, would have the decency to go away.

CHAPTER XII

Next morning I told Ned about Judge Compton's human interest story, but he didn't seem too interested at first. "So the judge's started offering candy to little girls," was all he said.

Feature story or not, the hearing still had to be covered so I took off for City Hall around nine to see what was going on. It was a good idea to check in at police headquarters and grab-ass with the boys just to be sure they'd remember to call in case anything important ever came up. I got a kick out of those guys. Before they made me police reporter it was hard to convince myself a cop was a human being. I mean the ordinary citizen only sees one when he's making an arrest, or walking his beat with an air of bewildered authority, or screwing up traffic at his favorite intersection. Yet headquarters was like the locker room at a public golf course. A lot of guys horsing around. Especially the detectives who were old salts and always practical joking the uniformed cops. They reminded me of Hal for some reason. You could see a guy who had looked pretty impressive on his beat acting like he'd dropped his pants at rush hour when those public eyes got through kidding around. And it was funny the way they handled prisoners. I don't mean right after an arrest. Then it could be pretty rough. But the next day or so, after the guy had been booked and the cop's job was pretty much over. Unless the prisoner was a pervert or some other kind of social unmentionable, an atmosphere of brotherhood would settle over the lockup. Give them a good old-fashioned burglar and it was more like a class reunion than an arrest.

"Hey Pete, remember the time we gotcha on the Johnson break?"

"You wuz lucky."

"Whad they giveya, two years for that?"

"Ah . . . I wuz out in six months. You guys."

I asked one of the detectives what time he thought the hearing would begin.

"What hearing?" They were always playing dumb that way. I think it was because half the time they really *didn't* know the answers, but by playing dumb *all* the time you could never be sure.

"The girl," I said. "The shoplifter."

"There ain't gonna be no hearing," the detective said.

"Huh?"

"No hearing. No hearing so there's no story so whaddya asking me questions for?"

"Maybe I can find somebody who's not so cute," I said.

"Ah, she skipped out," he said. Another example of the Gravenhurstite and his unkeepable secret.

"No kidding," I said. "What's the judge say?"

"He's kinda pissed off."

"I guess he would be," I said. "Maybe we should have a little talk."

My counterpart at the *Enterprise* was just coming out of the judge's chambers when I got there.

"What's going on?" I asked.

"Nothing," he said, the lying bastard.

"Morning, Judge," I said. "Little trouble, eh?"

"Oh, I guess it isn't too serious," he said with a false confidence I found absolutely charming.

"But she's jumped bail. Isn't that pretty serious?"

"Not jumped bail exactly," the judge said. "She's only a child. I imagine it was just a little misunderstanding."

"Got any idea where she might be?"

"Her parents seem to think she may have gone to stay with a friend." It all seemed a little too genteel to be true.

"One of the boys checking it out?"

"Well, uhh, not yet actually. I thought we'd have a look for her after court is adjourned."

"We?"

"Yes," Judge Compton said. "I don't want the child to feel she's a common criminal."

"Bit unusual, isn't it?" I was damn sure he hadn't cleared this through his wife.

"Yes it is," he admitted. "And I'd rather you didn't mention it in the paper just yet."

"Oh I guess we can sit on it awhile." I didn't really expect anybody to be very interested. "What about the *Enterprise?*" I asked.

"They, uhh, don't know anything about it just yet."

"Well then don't worry, Judge," I promised. "We'll wait until things straighten out." I suppose it was flattering of him to think I could control such matters.

"Appreciate it, Larry."

I nodded, displayed a professional smile and left. There was nothing else on the docket except the usual drunks and speeders so I took their names and headed back to the paper.

"Whaddya got?" Ned asked me.

"Nothing much."

"How about the judge's shoplifting girl friend?"

"Hearing's been postponed."

"Yeah? How come?"

"They couldn't find her."

"You mean she jumped bail?"

"Oh I don't know as you'd call it that," I hedged. "The judge thinks she may have misunderstood, but he's going out to look for her himself later."

"What?" Ned asked. "The *judge* is?"

"When he gets through court," I said. "Nothing to it."

"Nothing to it? My God, Woodruff, you'd run the second coming under births."

"Well, I sort of promised we'd sit on it until he had a chance to work things out."

"Swell. And did you assure him the *Enterprise* would sit on it too?"

"They don't know anything about it."

"I'd just as soon not take that chance," he said.

I guess he'd just as soon not miss a chance to drop one on the chairman of the county executive committee either, but I didn't suggest that.

"Okay," Ned said. "Play it this way, see." And he rattled off a lead which could under no circumstances have been considered flattering to the judge.

"Well it's kind of breaking a confidence," I said.

"Listen," Ned said. "Compton's a judge, not a child psychiatrist. He's got no business chasing that little slut all over town."

"I know, but . . ."

"Goddam dirty old man."

I could see Ned was working up the same kind of fury he had displayed the night Tommy took his wife home, so I decided not to press the issue.

"Okay," I said. "Okay."

As the morning unwrapped the Compton story got worse and worse. In the first place they found the girl right away. Her name was Mabel Crump and the detectives already knew something about her because this wasn't the first mistake so after asking around they finally dug her out of an old tenement near Flint Street. She was stretched out, flat-assed asleep in a room owned by some young punk who didn't happen to be around. According to the detectives, she must have taken on half the town, but according to Mabel it wasn't like that at all. She said it was awful. There was poor Mabel, poor Mabel said, sitting home alone, trying to be good when this bad man came to the house and made her go away with him.

"And what about all them balloons on the floor?" one of the detectives asked her.

"I wonder what they're for?" Mabel had asked. "Oh dear, oh dear, what have they done to me?"

Then she began a lot of weeping and wailing which nobody but the judge found very convincing. However, since *he* did, it was obvious the detectives would never get a conviction and this distressed them deeply. To the average law-enforcement officer an arrest without a conviction is life's hollowest mockery, and they felt the judge was about to do them a cruel disservice. In retaliation they gave us all the information we could use and then some.

I had to admit it turned out to be a pretty good story, but there was no doubt it made a fool out of Judge Compton in the bargain. It also made page one. I was a little miffed because Ned gave me a by-line despite the fact he had rewritten most of the story to make the judge look like even more of an old fanny-pincher than he already did. My lead had been "The usual routine of City Court was interrupted today while Judge Edgar Compton and city police joined in the search for a teenage girl who failed to appear on shop-lifting charges." But Ned changed this to read "The usual routine of City Court was reduced to chaos this morning when Judge Edgar Compton turned in his robes for a policeman's badge and went forth grimly to make his first pinch.

"The object of his search: A comely fifteen-year-old girl who failed to appear for a hearing on charges of shoplifting. Judge Compton is believed to have taken a personal interest in the suspect . . ."

I dropped by the court that afternoon to offer the judge my personal regrets but he was in no mood to accept them. God, he was mad. Even grayer than usual, but with a frigid, righteous anger holding little promise of an early thaw. He was back on the bench when I saw him which gave his fury a certain undeserved dignity.

"I see your father is king-making again," he said.

"Doing what?" I asked.

"I suppose you are unaware the county executive committee meets tonight to discuss our replacement for the State Senate."

"As a matter of fact, I was," I admitted.

"And your father was too, I'm sure."

I shrugged.

"I suppose your father was also unaware this little story of yours might suggest a basic falling out between myself, as chairman of the committee, and the Gravenhurst *Daily Watch*."

"Pa knew nothing about it. The story was on the street before he had any idea . . ."

"Are you suggesting," the judge interrupted, "that your father is incompetent?"

"I am not."

"Then how could he have failed to approve such a story?"

"Well Pa doesn't approve . . ."

"Unless, of course, he is taking rather a more personal interest in his news editor's political future than either Clem Harper or I realized."

"It has nothing to do with that."

"Really?" the judge mocked. "In any case, Mr. Harper and I have had a little chat about his son-in-law's political ambitions and we've decided they seriously handicap Mr. Polk's usefulness as news editor on the Gravenhurst *Daily Watch*."

"Well frankly," I said, "so do . . ."

"We feel, therefore, that your father could best assure us and the other committeemen of his political loyalties by letting Mr. Polk go."

"Pa will do as he sees fit." I was damned if I'd agree with him.

"I'm sure he will," Judge Compton said. "And I am equally sure he will find the loss of Mr. Polk far more fitting than the loss of his municipal contract and that considerable amount of commercial advertising which our more conservative members control."

"If you think Pa can be influenced by that kind of stuff, you've got another think coming."

"I've no doubt your father is a man of principle." The judge smiled at the magnificence of his wit. "With interest, of course. Now, if you will excuse me."

I started out. "Oh, just a minute," he called. "Need I point out Nora is as hurt and upset as we and no longer looks forward to your little visits?"

"What a hardship," I said and managed to slam the door on my way out.

Back at the office I ran right smack into another storm. There was a note on my desk that I was wanted upstairs. Pa was fit to be tied. But he was mad at me, not Ned.

"What kind of irresponsible schoolboy reporting is this?" he wanted to know.

"That's not the way I wrote it."

"Now listen, Larry. None of that," he warned. "I've already discussed this with Ned."

"What did he say?"

"Mad as he could be," Pa said. "Told me he'd only had time to skim your story and hadn't realized how insulting it was."

"That's not true, Pa. He rewrote the whole goddam thing."

"Let's have no buck passing. You know how I feel about that, Larry." But he said it kindly, as if he wanted me to accept this interpretation, it being the less complicated of the two.

"If that's the way you feel, Pa, then I've got some more bad news."

"Now what have you done?"

"Me?" I asked, but what was the use? I told him about the judge's and Clem Harper's decision.

"Clem would do that to his own son-in-law?" Pa asked. "Oh I doubt it. I'll have to have a little talk with Clem."

"I was hoping you'd tell them to go to hell."

"Clem Harper?" Pa asked. "And the judge? Why, we're old friends."

"I guess that's so, Pa. Well, unless you've got something else on your mind, I guess I'll . . ."

"Uh, just one more thing, Larry. We're running a withdrawal on that court story tomorrow. I think you should write it."

"Why me?"

"Good discipline. Next time you'll think twice about indulging these sophomoric tendencies."

"I thought I told you I didn't write the story, Pa."

"Let's have no more of that. Write the withdrawal and submit it to Ned."

"No, Pa."

"You refuse?"

"Yes," but I was scared stiff.

"Very well, then. If that's the kind of loyalty I can expect from my own family, I'll write it myself."

"All right, Pa. If you want to. And while we're discussing loyalty, thanks for yours."

I was out the door before he could answer me. This was a side of Pa I hadn't met before the other night when Hal came to dinner and the possibility it was because I'd never seen him faced with a crucial decision filled me with the terror of disillusionment. Despite Mother's preparations, and my own lip service, I couldn't truly accept the idea Pa was not a man of action at all, but only a frightened child wearing tradition's uniform.

It was about time I got mad at somebody and Teddy Pearson, who could have prevented the whole mess, after all, seemed the most likely target. Somebody said he'd just left so I took off after him and managed to catch up about at Frank's Place which was as good a spot as any to get mad. It was still early and there was nobody there yet. Just gloom and the smell of stale beer and Frank.

"How come you let him run that goddam story?" I asked. "Give me a beer, Frank, okay?"

"Sure it's okay. What am I, your mother?"

"You want anything?" I asked.

"Rye and ginger," said Teddy.

"Now, how come?"

"I thought that would finish Polk," Ted said. "What's wrong with your old man anyway?"

"I don't know. He thinks it's my fault."

"The hell he does. He just refuses to blame Polk."

"Why?"

"Because then he'd have to fire him."

"So?"

"Do you realize," Ted asked, "that your father's never fired anybody as long as I've known him?"

"Sure he has. What about Lou Baine?"

"I fired Lou. You know why your father lets the department heads do their own hiring?" I shook my head cooperatively. "So they'll have to do their own firing too."

"Why?"

"I don't know. Just can't do it, I guess. He did fire one guy, the janitor, about ten years ago. For stealing from the petty cashbox, I think. Only it was more than that. The guy was a drunk, an incompetent, he drove everybody nuts. We'd been trying to get rid of him for years but your father would just smile and say we couldn't do that because he was a nice old fella and had been around such a long time. The fact that he drove everybody nuts didn't seem to bother your old man much. When we caught him stealing, though, there was no alternative. But do you know what happened?"

"What?"

"He was back in a week."

"How come? Did he give Pa a line?"

"Nope. Matter of fact he was indignant as hell. Said he'd been taking a little bit from the cashbox as long as he could remember. That he only took so much and no more. Said he'd been around for fifty years and never thought to see the day a Woodruff treated him like dirt. Your old man felt so bad he hired him back with a raise."

I laughed.

"It may be a weakness," I said. "But you have to admit it's a pretty charming one."

"That kind of charm is half fear," Teddy said. "And you can't run a newspaper with it."

"Well anyway, your little plan didn't work, so what now?"

"Let Polk play out his hand," Ted said. "If he gets himself further committed to politics he'll have to resign from the paper."

"Judge Compton and Clem Harper want Pa to fire him too."

"Well that's a help," Teddy admitted. "But your father won't get around to it for a month or so and Ned will have to make his move before then anyway."

"You've got it all figured out."

"I know how badly Ned wants that Senate post."

"How come Clem Harper gives him such a rough time?" I asked. "I mean, his own son-in-law and all."

"Clem knows what kind of son of a bitch he is."

"And Pa doesn't?"

"That's exactly what I mean," Teddy said. "Your father decides how he wants to feel about somebody or something. Then he proceeds to feel that way and to hell with the truth."

"Okay, let's forget Pa for a while."

Ted shrugged.

"Let's have another drink instead."

"One more," Ted agreed. "Then I have to get home."

"About five more before I'll be able to make the trip."

"Don't worry about it," Teddy laughed. "Your father's a real nice guy."

"I know it," I said. "But he doesn't."

"Huh?"

"Nothing. Do us again, will you, Frank?"

One of the detectives came in about that time. "Hey scoop," he said. "You missed the hearing."

"What hearing?"

"Judge's girl friend. Six months probation in *his* custody. Ain't that cute?"

"Solves the domestic problem," Teddy said.

"Ah ah, that's a good one. Gimme a beer, Frank."

"It's a big deal," Frank said. "Flatfoot makes an arrest he's gotta celebrate. Gimme a beer. Big deal."

"Hey, you a wise guy, a what?"

They moved down the bar, their conversation blurring with the juke and distance. Nothing reached us but a muffled intensity which, by the very fact we couldn't hear what they were saying, gave the impression of significance.

"Just to change the subject a little," I said, "how do you think the competition's going?"

"Lousy."

"Why?"

"It must be," Ted said. "We haven't done anything to improve things."

"Like?"

"Like I talked to your father last week about the tube deliveries out of town and a few other things and that's the last I've heard of it."

"I'll ask him tonight."

"Yeah, do that," he said. "The sooner you figure out how to run this paper, the better its chances."

"Who, me? You're crazy."

"Who else? There's nobody running it now." Ted pulled out his wallet. "Here, take it out of this," and tossed a bill on the table. "I have to get home."

Frank came over when he saw I was drinking alone. "Hey," he said. "Mayor Healy was in here last night. You got troubles with him?"

"Probably," I said. "We got troubles with most everybody else."

"He was pretty loaded," Frank confided. "Made a few cracks about your old man. You know what I mean?"

"Yeah, I know what you mean. Thanks, Frank."

"Don't mention it. Anything happens to the *Daily Watch,* I lose my best customers."

"Well I'll see you, Frank. I gotta get home."

"Yeah, take it easy."

I got home to find Pa was no longer upset. Instead he had settled down to a reckless serenity which I found far more disturbing. And this despite the judge's refusal to come to the phone plus Clem Harper's warning that the committee would likely be split down the middle with the young membership riding hard on the heels of our mistake. It may seem a little illogical to measure the *Daily Watch's* success by the strength of its political ties, but the fact is there was no better way, and with Pa showing a deficit balance in this department, we had plenty to worry about, not much to measure.

Even Mother, whose customary role was to soothe the angry warrior, seemed more disturbed than usual but no amount of prodding could stir Pa's complacency. In fact the more we tried the more unconcerned and downright expansive he became. Abby was off to college in a few days so Pa spent most of his time doling out parental clichés about getting down to work and finishing strong despite the scornful apathy with which they were received. Obviously Abby was not responding; was in fact mired in private confusion, but Pa droned on his genial, platitudinous way until around about dessert when our refusal to play his game reduced him to sulking silence. Then suddenly, but without explanation, he got up and marched from the room, leaving us to decide whether we had bored him, betrayed him, or simply been forgotten. We were in the living room later, trying to carry on in normal fashion, but obviously crippled by his inexplicable behavior, when back he came like a spoiled child who knew he'd been naughty, but never doubted an ability to charm praise from punishment. It was as if we had been playing charades all along and Pa had only left to prepare his act. He came in smiling for our attentions and recited a little tale about Mr. Quincy, the caretaker, and his opinion of Bollard's drinking capacity.

According to Mr. Quincy, when a desire for drunkenness touched Bollard's soul all he had to do was "run 'round a sow-ah apple tree."

We all laughed on cue which pleased Pa and permitted him to return to his study, leaving us generously compensated for his disturbing behavior—at least so he seemed to think.

The performance was repeated about an hour later, this time with an offer for my benefit that we release a few pheasant in the morning and have some shooting before work. Naturally I was delighted and again we were left alone to contemplate his mischievous ways.

About that time Clem Harper called and I could hear Pa talking in vague, hospitable tones which, from their subject matter, obviously belied Mr. Harper's mood.

"He did, Clem? Well, well, well, that's quite a son-in-law you've got there . . . How's that? . . . Ha, ha, well a miss is good as a mile, Clem, my boy . . . Yes, the judge told me. Been thinking it over. Hate to lose a good man like Ned, though . . . Oh, I wouldn't like to lose a good newspaper either, Clem . . . This weekend? Why I'd love it, Clem. You know I'd never turn down a trip with you boys . . . Nice to talk to you, Clem. Looking forward to it. Good night now, Clem. Good night, old man."

If I hadn't still given Pa credit for holding an ace or two up his sleeve, I'd have suspected he was losing his mind. He came wandering in afterward.

"Clem Harper," he said. "Invited the judge and me to spend the weekend at his place in the Catskills. Nice fellow, Clem."

"How'd the meeting go?" I asked.

"Hmm? Oh, sounded pretty spirited. Committee's apparently deadlocked with Mayor Healy on the fence as usual. Ned's right up there, though. Seems like it's between him and old Pop Tompkins."

"It almost sounds as though you're rooting for Ned."

"Well, I like to see a young man like Ned get ahead."

"And what kind of young man is he?" Mother asked.

"Oh I don't know," Pa said. "Rough, tough go-getter. Kind of fellow made this country what it is today."

"Like you, Pa," Abby said, and her smile seemed real enough.

"I'd like to think so, Abby," Pa said. "I'd like to think so."

"Maybe the *Daily Watch* ought to back the Young Republicans," I said. "If they're the ones you admire."

"I didn't say that," Pa said, smiling. "I didn't say that." And the simple fact he hadn't told me to shut up made me worry more about the future than most anything which had happened so far.

"I thought you implied it," I said, still trying for a rise.

"I don't think so," Pa said. "Got a certain responsibility to the old guard. Ben Tompkins is a good friend of mine. Good client, too. Beside the point, of course, but worth mentioning. So are Clem and the judge. We've helped each other along through the years. Guess we ought to stick together now."

"Then you're going to fire Ned?" I asked.

"Oh well, that seems a little extreme, don't you think?"

"Then what *are* you going to do, Pa?"

"We'll have a little talk this weekend. Give a little bit here, take a little there. Get things all straightened out."

"Sure."

"Guess I'll turn in," Pa said. "Got to get up with the birds tomorrow. Ha ha."

"Okay," I said. "See you around six-thirty."

"Fine. Night night all," and he was gone.

Abby and I were too stunned to discuss Pa's performance, but Mother seemed to take it more or less in stride.

"Is he all right?" I managed to ask.

"Oh yes, dear," she said. "Your father's just a little tired."

It would have taken all night to find a common ground between the three of us on which to discuss Pa, so after reassuring each other with sympathetic noises we all went to bed.

I lay awake for a while, worrying more about Abby than Pa. I didn't know whether Jesse loved her or not, but if he did then the beast was devouring his own tail for the more he destroyed of the Woodruff myth, it seemed to me, the less chance he had of winning Abby.

Next morning I was up even earlier than necessary, routed from sleep by the excitement of hunting. Not just hunting, but the entire ritual. Morning with its soft gray silence questioned by the waking birds. The rough wool scratching, the heavy comfort of a boot and the house still choked with sleep, sighing. I went downstairs as quietly as the creaking would permit and out to the kitchen with its old canopied gas stove and wooden icebox big as a garage door. I put the coffee on, started some country sausage, and waded through sleep to a decision on the eggs. Should I wait for Pa or start them now? And without the help of reason, suddenly there were eggs cooking. And equally suddenly there was Pa. Not the publisher, but a man who hunts. A big yawning, easy man no longer riddled by the cancer of tribal refinements.

We yawned at each other and sucked the coffee's heat through our lips and fingers and we ate too fast, trying to make it last but in a rush to get out.

The kitchen door shook and Mr. Quincy came in, a hunter too, his gun broken, cradled, sleep smiling gently on his face. He poured a cup and sat down.

"Thought we'd try Triumph," he said. "And Maizie. They're working well together."

"Good," Pa said. "And the birds?"

"Released a half dozen. Seemed to scattah pretty good."

"Into the swamp?" I asked.

"Couple did. Pretty dry though. Others worked 'cross the big field."

We nodded and were silent.

Outside the morning air cleared the sludge of sleep. Fall had crept in on stiff, cold toes. A touch of early frost clung to the stubble of cut hay and summer's rapture seemed to be fading. It was almost time for football, cider stands, pumpkins, and falling leaves.

We walked up to the kennels and stood in the midst of bedlam while Mr. Quincy wrestled and whistled the two dogs into some semblance of obedience. Then we cut round the pens and down through the swamp first. I loaded, hearing the familiar slump as each shell fell into place and the finely worked click of a good gun. We spread abreast with Mr. Quincy and his angry whistle in the middle. It was tough going. Half the time you couldn't see the dogs in the heavy bearded growth that hid the swamp. They seemed to be working close and well, though, crisscrossing in eager, leaping patterns. Every once in a while Pa would yell "There he is," and the gun would start for my shoulder automatically with the cold damp barrel a reminder of years past; the beginnings of tradition. But each time it was only a dog he'd spotted and I'd begun to think of other things when a big cock pheasant flushed wild, *clang clang clanging* his frightened challenge as he burst on the morning.

"Yours, yours," Pa yelled, but he was way out and starting to settle in so I held my fire in hopes we'd put him up again later.

"Kinda rusty," Pa said. "Kinda rusty."

"We'd left them in the pen," Mr. Quincy said. "Young fellah might have got one."

"I was watching your dogs," I said. "So naturally I never saw the bird."

That made us all even.

"Larry's got a point there," Pa chided. "Flushed wild, Mr. Quincy. Flushed wild, all right."

I laughed, more at the excitement of his kidding than anything else. You can watch a person change without realizing how extreme it is until something brings him back to normal and allows you to compare. Pa had been gradually softening over the months like a chocolate soldier abandoned in the sun. So gradually I had almost managed to adjust to the loss of shape. But tradition's hands worked gently now, restoring—at least temporarily—the pride and spirit I had known before. Perhaps nothing could be done to obliterate the discovery Pa was soft inside, but at least he looked himself again.

We got no more action from the swamp which meant the birds had likely picked their way through and taken cover in a long-abandoned hayfield on the other side. The dogs worked in leaps, ears flying as they attended to business with startled efficiency. Then Triumph slowed, sniffed, went frantic and plunged at a clump of brush, causing it to discharge a hen and another cock. The birds flew straight away, one angling to the left the other right. The bedlam of flight, the pounding heart, the click, the crash of gunfire and two bits of lost life crumpled, careened, and socked the soft ground. The dogs plunged, disappeared, performed some canine calculations, soon were on the way back, their sad eyes a hypocrite's tribute to the prize each bore. Then off again, bounding, happy, pleased with the day.

We stayed out another hour, managing to drop five birds which was pretty good for the first time out.

"Well," I said. "Not so rusty after all." I was carrying two of the birds and could feel their dead weight pressing in the back pouch of my shooting jacket.

"Luck," Pa said. "Pure dumb luck."

"Mine or yours?"

Pa smiled and broke his gun. "I'm surprised you felt it necessary to ask."

His mood was so good I forgot myself. "Say Pa, Ted was asking about those tube routes."

"The what?"

"You know. His idea for home deliveries."

"Oh yuh," Pa said, and the vagueness began to seep back.

"What do you think?"

"Well, it needs study."

"It sounded pretty good to me."

"All Pearson's ideas sound good until it comes time to pay for them."

"But we have to do something."

"Hmmm," Pa said. "Well thanks, Mr. Quincy. The dogs looked just fine."

"Eyuh, doin' all right."

"Guess we'd better get to work, eh Larry?"

"Sure." I followed him through the kitchen, looking vainly for a chance to continue the conversation.

"Morning, Hilda," he said. "Bollard. Had good shooting."

And into the dining room where Mother was holding court alone. We lined up for morning kisses and sat down to a quick cup of coffee while she told us what good boys we'd been to bring home so many birds. Right away the clothes felt itchy, out of place, and slightly absurd. We sat for a while, sipping coffee, still pleased with ourselves. Then Pa asked: "Seen much of Nora lately?"

"Yeah," I said. "Off and on." I couldn't remember his ever having asked me that before.

"Lovely girl," Pa said. "Hope she doesn't share her father's sentiments regarding the house of Woodruff."

"So do I," I said automatically. "But I've heard she does."

"No indeed, you couldn't ask for a sweeter girl than Nora."

"Clarence, what are you up to?" Mother asked.

"Up to? Nothing, dear. I was just thinking. Larry's not too far away from the big day, you know. Awfully nice people, the Comptons."

Abby came in about then.

"Too bad Mr. Harper doesn't have a son," she said. "Good morning, Mother."

"What's that, Abby?" Pa asked.

"I said it's too bad Mr. Harper doesn't have a son," she repeated. "We could have a double wedding and solve all your problems."

"Apologize to your father, Abby."

"I apologize," Abby parroted.

But Pa remained genial. "Not a bad idea. Better that than marrying a kike."

I choked, ducked, nearly burned my nose in the coffee.

Abby was too shocked to reply.

Pa smiled quietly, pushed his cup aside, got up and left.

"Serves you right, Abby," Mother said. "If you must insist on baiting your father."

"Oh, was that my father?" Abby asked. "I didn't recognize him."

"Abby really," Mother sighed.

"Don't worry. I could never find the guts to marry Jesse. Not now anyway."

"I wasn't worrying about that," Mother said. "I was worrying about your rudeness."

"Well, why shouldn't I be rude?" Abby asked. "After all, look what Pa's . . ."

"I'd better be going," I interrupted. That was about all I could stand.

"Oh Larry, before you go," Mother called. "I have a favor."

"What is it?"

"It's this student exchange program, you know."

"No, I don't."

"Oh, you do," she said. "The children from Europe who come here to school every year. They're landing in New York Saturday and I'd love it if you'd go down and take some pictures. You know, do a nice feature story for me."

It seemed like a lot of work for nothing, but the idea of getting out of Gravenhurst for a while sure appealed to me.

"Okay," I said, and hurried off before the argument resumed.

I felt depressed as hell. Having Pa so much his old self one minute and a conniving trader in human favors, hatred, and abuse the next was worse than a steady decline. It didn't matter whether Mother had been right in warning me Pa was not the captain of finance and industry we liked to think he was. I longed for the days when he at least looked like such a man and I hated Jesse for forcing the sweat of truth through Pa's disguise. After all, what's the point of competition if all it does is destroy? Maybe the *Daily Watch* *wasn't* the greatest little daily in the world. What difference did that make? Good or bad it was a bulwark of order which had weathered pretty well in the winds of time. And there were a lot of people besides us who had found comfort in its shelter. As a newspaper perhaps it was only an intricate tower of order built to honor and protect itself. And perhaps that's wrong; order for order's sake, I mean. But honorable or not a great many people had crept behind the walls of our complacency and I saw no purpose served by the *Daily Watch's* demolition. To destroy order simply for the sport of it and with no guarantee of providing something better seemed just as pointless as to enshrine it.

Hal dropped by the office around deadline time wanting to have lunch and while realizing I was supposed to be slightly peeved at him, I couldn't remember exactly why, so we had lunch. Anyway, what good's a friend if you can't get sore at him once in a while and vice versa without throwing the friendship into a tailspin?

Oh yeah, Hal went to the Fun House that night after Pa'd invited him to dinner, which was what I'd been sore about. Preferred screwing to talking the whole thing over with his old buddy. Well, you couldn't exactly blame him for that. Not these days, anyway. Not when it's been confirmed beyond a reasonable doubt that screwing cures everything from acute pathological depression to the low blood.

And maybe it did at that. Hal was in a pretty good mood. In fact he was always in a pretty good mood. After a couple of martinis I asked him, "How come you're always so goddam happy?"

He waved his martini glass at me.

"I'll bet you have bad dreams," I said. "Like maybe the Fun House has been closed up or something."

He shrugged, sort of laughed, cocked his head like a puppy.

"Don't you?" I insisted.

"Nah," he said. "I haven't got time for that stuff."

CHAPTER XIII

I had planned to call Nora on Tuesday to see if I was persona grata yet or not, but Pa's little suggestions made my lip curl every time I reached for the phone. Thus it was a couple of days before I finally got around to making a date for Friday night. She sounded sort of hesitant, but finally said she guessed she could make it since the family would be away. The suggestion that, had the Comptons stayed at home, I might not have been so welcome came as something of a shock, despite the judge's warning. Snubbing Woodruffs was not an everyday Gravenhurst indulgence, but I managed to keep my head and ask where everyone was going. The judge, of course, was off to a summit meeting with Pa and Mr. Harper. And Mrs. Compton, it developed, had planned a trip to New York to pry into Tommy's affairs. I pointed out that Nora and Mabel Crump would therefore be left alone together and wouldn't it be fun? Fortunately, that humbled her a little.

It was sort of amusing to find Nora and Mabel alone in that great Victorian hodgepodge of a house. The Comptons had no full-time servants, ostensibly because Mrs. Compton valued her privacy, but actually because she drove them away with pretentious abuse. So there they were, alone together, Good and Evil Gravenhurst style, and my secret preferences were not altogether clear. In fact, I wasn't even sure which was which. Nor could I help but feel a touch of jealousy for those gentlemen of the other night whom Mabel had so generously entertained. She had the vacant, antiseptic beauty characteristic of southern waitresses or, at its most refined, airline hostesses, nurses, and the Misses Rheingold. Not antiseptic morally, of course, but only so far as sexual performance was concerned. There was an air of clinical detachment about her which spoke of sex in terms of bored submission, contraception, untimely trips to the bathroom and raised skirts. But she was available apparently and I guess nobody'd kick her out of bed, though some might prefer to bat her around a little first on the theory that fear was better than no emotion at all.

They made an unusual pair, Nora and Mabel, and I couldn't help but wonder what had induced the judge to bring her home. Since he was something of a prude, I wondered if he got secret pleasure out of having her around. Then too, there was the challenge of saving her soul and the resulting satisfaction of knowing he had made somebody else's life as dull as his own. But all the same, to leave her in the house alone on the assumption, I suppose, that the warm, cozy Compton atmosphere could not help but reform her wanton ways was to assume a great deal. At least so it seemed to me.

Therefore, we left her with some misgivings, but I must admit she seemed fairly harmless, standing in the doorway and advising us to "Have a ball, huh" with those rhythmic, cud-chewing jaws and tired eyes.

We went to see the movie at the Palace, despite a nagging suspicion Mabel would not have approved.

The flick was one of those Tennessee Williams deals which started out about a guy with some A.C.–D.C. problems who couldn't sleep with his wife without getting loaded first and ended about a guy with some A.C.–D.C. problems who couldn't sleep with his wife without getting loaded first. But an awful lot went on between drinks so I guess it was a pretty good movie. The critics had said it was very artistic so naturally I had to like it. Nora said it wasn't very uplifting, but some of the symbolism was quite well done. I knew enough to steer clear of that topic, having taken her to see the Gravenhurst Players' production of T. S. Eliot's *The Cocktail Party* some years back. She'd studied all about it before and I mean a guy couldn't scratch his foot without Nora saying, "Look, look, his stigmata's itching" or something so whenever she got onto symbols and stuff like that I knew it was time to change the subject and quick.

"Seen anything of Sam Crawley lately?" I interrupted.

We were walking toward the parking lot, trying to talk and keep an eye out for familiar faces at the same time so we could nod and smile and say "Hi there" and thus prevent our fellow Gravenhurstites from concluding we were a couple of snots.

"No," she said. "Why?"

"No reason."

"He's a nice boy," she said.

We'd been weaving along like kids, close together sometimes, separated others like when she happened to say that about Crawley so I had a chance to see her in perspective: the supreme compliment fresh on her lips, dome-shaped beaver jacket, white gloves, sheathed

thighs hinged to a hipless, static body, face raised in safe and per-
petual recognition, all traces of passion carefully concealed behind
this ass-operated, lip-fed, semiautomatic human mechanism known
as Nora Compton.

"Oh indeedy," I agreed. "So's his friend Hugh Godkin. So imagina-
tive."

"And what is that supposed to mean?"

"Nothing," I hedged. We turned into the parking lot.

"You're always so critical," Nora complained. "Why can't you say
something *nice* about people?"

"But I meant it. No really, I think you'll agree anybody who wants
a whore to beat him with a whip rather than go to bed is a very im-
aginative young man."

"Larry!"

"As well as being *nice*." I held the car door for her, slammed it,
then walked around, giving her time to think.

"If you must be obscene, then take me home and be so by yourself."

"But being obscene by yourself is naughty," I protested.

Nora chose to ignore me.

And I was destined to marry this girl?

Well it seemed as good a time as any to change all that. The
world closed in tight. Just me, the car, the grim struggle with traffic,
the private search for words and confidence: Well, Nora, I prepared.
Looks like this is the end of the line. I mean for us and all. I mean
it's better now, seeing as we don't get along and all, than it would be
later, or something like that . . . I recognized the need for revision
and was trying to brush it up a little as we approached the Compton
driveway.

"Larry, all our lights are on," Nora cried.

"Pretty."

"Larry, I turned them all off."

"Uh huh."

We were just about to turn in the driveway.

"Larry, the cars. Look at all the cars."

I woke up finally. "My God, she's throwing a party."

The driveway was full of un-Compton-like automobiles. An assortment of beat-up heaps none of which suggested even the second-
hand opulence of a college fraternity gathering.

"Do something," Nora suggested.

"What'll I do?"

"Aren't you supposed to know?"

"Sure," I said, backing up carefully. "I'll go call the cops."

Maybe I should have walked right in and thrown the whole bunch of them out. But I wasn't too sure how many it took to make a bunch. Looking back, I might have been braver had there been music and laughter coming from inside. But there wasn't. Only a sullen, sensuous silence which made me want to do nothing so much as get the hell out.

We beat it over to my house, called the police and headed on back to see what would happen. I must say they got there pretty fast. I'd just finished parking when two squad cars stuffed with beef screamed past and up the driveway. Nora didn't feel much like seeing what happened. At least so she claimed. But I, being a noble newspaperman and all, felt it my duty to find out what kind of a party it had been. As a matter of fact, I already had a pretty good idea and again was a little disappointed nobody had thought to invite me.

By then the house was beginning to look like a pinball machine. Lights were flashing off as the guests attempted to take leave of Miss Crump, then on again as the cops pursued. There was also a good deal of stumbling about caused, as I later discovered, by the fact that most of her guests had failed to get their pants completely on.

It was quite a sight. Apparently Mabel had taken a shine to the Compton couch. There she was, standing stark naked before it in a circle of adoring, semiclad admirers who in turn were surrounded by the boys in blue.

From other parts of the house I could hear such unfamiliar noises as "Ah lay off, fa Chrissakes," "Move along, lover boy," and "So we're here on invitation, so what's at to you, huh?"

Well there's nothing quite so silly as a group of half-naked males standing around like draftees. An invaluable collection of sunreddened arms and dank white bodies. I got to laughing and so did some of the cops, but it wasn't really so goddam funny. Banging a minor constituted statutory rape whether on invitation or not so most of Mabel's guests could look forward to some pretty intimate dealings with both city and county courts. At least if the police could establish what the law delicately refers to as penetration. Some of the guests were minors too and would probably get off with probation, but the others faced a few years of rock hockey at one of the state's penal resorts.

It was a pretty hot story and in the confusion I sort of lost track of the fact all this was occurring in the judge's stately Victorian manse. It meant a sure by-line and I was too busy congratulating myself on being at the scene. Then suddenly it occurred to me I was going to New York in the morning. There was no way out of that one so I ran into the library and called Jeff Collins. Being almost midnight, Jeff didn't sound too pleased to hear my voice, but you could smell a good story like this one right through the phone and he came over quick.

By the time Jeff got there Miss Mabel Crump and friends were already being hustled off, but it didn't matter. The gory details were yet to come, when they got everybody down to the station and began taking statements. I filled him in and headed back to Nora. Reluctantly.

She was sitting in the car, crying slow, patient tears.

"Hey! What's the matter with you?"

"I'm not going into that house. I'm not going into that house tonight."

"You can stay with us. Abby'll fix things up."

Nora said nothing more until we got home and I had a chance to make her a nice hot whiskey and milk.

"Here," I said. "This'll make you sleep."

She just took it. Then after a while she asked, "What was it like?"

"What?"

"Oh you know! Everything at home."

"I didn't think you'd want to hear about it."

"I ought to know."

"Well I guess you'd say Mabel was entertaining."

"That way?"

"Uh huh."

"Were they all . . . you know . . ."

"Naked?"

"Yes."

"Mabel was," I said. "Her guests were in various stages of undress."

"How horrible," Nora said. "Had they . . . you know . . ."

"I'd say that they had."

"All of them?"

"Most of them."

"How disgusting."

"Yeah."

"While the others watched?"

"I guess so. They didn't look like a very modest crowd."

"How revolting."

"I'd better get Abby," I said, but Nora grabbed my hand and pulled me against her and moaned a little and rubbed me with her body.

The stairs creaked.

"What do you need me for?" Abby asked. "You're doing fine."

We came apart like frightened dogs.

"Hi Abby," I said. "We were just going to call you."

"Why?" Abby asked. "Do I have the only bed or something?"

Nora seemed to be considering a new flow of tears.

"Listen, Abby," I said. "This is serious."

"Congratulations," she said.

"No, I mean. Oh come on, listen," and I filled her in on the details.

"I can see Nora's upset," Abby said. "The poor dear."

"I have to get up early, Abby. How about fixing Nora up with a toothbrush or something so we can all go to bed."

"Oh, is that all she needs?" Abby asked. "I was wondering."

"Good night, Nora," I said. "And don't worry. It'll turn out all right."

"The house will never be the same again," Nora said.

Not until she was halfway upstairs did I remember my speech. "Oh say, Nora."

She turned, looking like she had that night at Frank's. Lost, baffled, appealingly dependent. "Yes, Larry?"

"Try to get some sleep," was all I could say.

"Thank you, Larry. I don't know what I'd have done without you."

I smiled and watched her go, my thoughts a mixture of compassion and regret. Perhaps I should have told her anyway, but the Nora I could never marry had, for the moment at least, disappeared and what remained seemed the picture of sweet and tender dependency. It took a crisis to put me in the driver's seat but once there I was the very image of a man, she the female essence, warm and whole and waiting, except for maybe being a little too curious about the Crump party. But what was I to do between crises, make periodic dashes to the Fun House to remind myself what a rollicking, dominant, sword-slashing knight-errant I really was underneath it all? Way down deep underneath, below the heaps of "Yes, sweetie, no, sweetie, you know best, sweetie, and I'll be working late at the office tonight, sweetie."

Was I?

I was like hell.

Or was I?

I had a pretty good idea what the answer would be unless something decisive were done to stop it and wished I'd told her after all. But there'd be another chance and all too soon, probably. I waited until things were quiet above, then went to my room. With everything sort of calmed down I began to realize there were a few political and personal side effects to the Crump orgy which I hadn't properly considered. Ned Polk would be having another field day and I'd be taking the rap again. It was all getting sort of repetitious. Tomorrow's headlines slammed through my imagination:

JUDGE'S HOME SCENE
OF SORDID SEX ORGY
With the Judge Away
His Ward Will Play

But though I realized this didn't appear to be exactly in Pa's interests, or mine either, trying to stop it was about the last thing I would have considered. While the big three were off bartering their favors in the clean cool Catskill air, life seemed to be taking care of itself pretty nicely. Obviously this was all Ned needed to destroy what remained of the judge's influence. And whether he was fired from or quit the *Daily Watch* as a result, couldn't have mattered less.

Just why all this pleased me is a little hard to explain. The apparent result would be a clear victory for the *Enterprise* and the end of our political influence. Also it meant the probable loss of our municipal contract and a good deal of commercial advertising in the bargain. But it would clear the air and that to me was worth all the losses. The *Daily Watch* would no longer be hobbled to the favor exchange, no longer dragged through the muck of Ned Polk's political ambitions. It was a hell of a price to pay for freedom. We'd be damn near dead. But at least we'd be free to fight and that in itself far outweighed all the losses.

I slept smug and dreamless as a baby that night and left for New York earlier than necessary in order to avoid having to hide my guilt from Nora or discuss everything with Mother. It was like the Fourth of July. The fuse had been lit and I took off hell bent for cover with the fingers of anticipation snipping at the back of my neck.

As is frequently the custom in New York, there was a longshoremen's strike, so I spent my time taking pictures of the students carrying their own suitcases in order to avoid having to carry some myself. The place was swarming with the hobbledehoy set. I never saw so many kids in my life. Not all of them going to Gravenhurst, of course. Some were Americans coming home after a summer's dunking in the cultural dip of Europe. Some were European exchange students like our bunch on their way to strangeness. All of them were busy as hell in the private world of semichildhood, happily unaware of the adults surrounding them, except for an occasional frightened face which would look up suddenly and stare at the enemy with sad surprise.

The girl in charge of the Gravenhurst group seemed about my age, but apparently this did not strike her as grounds for friendship. She was being difficult as hell. I had to ask a lot of stupid questions about the kind of crossing they'd had and anything out of the ordinary which might have happened in order to get a little human interest into my story. But instead of answering right away and getting it over with, she'd look at me for a while as though trying to measure whether I was worth the bother. She finally got me so nervous I had to ask, "Hey what's the matter with you, anyway?"

"Nothing," she said. "It's just that I've been in Europe for a year and was wondering whether it had been a good idea to come home."

"What's the decision?"

"I don't know. What's it like these days?"

"About the same, I guess."

"That's too bad," she said. "It's nice in Europe."

About that time a little gypsy-haired girl began drifting away from the group.

"*Oyeme, chica, ven aca.*"

"What's that?" I asked.

"Swahili, stupid. What'd you think?"

That got an enthusiastic laugh from the little foreign bastards who could speak English.

I turned and walked away so everybody'd know my feelings had been hurt. The stupid thing was I'd studied Spanish in school for about eight years and knew what it was right after I'd asked. But obviously an American couldn't be expected to speak a language after only eight years. Not even the teachers could do that. At least I should have been able to recognize it though. But it sounded so different from classroom Spanish I thought it might have been Portuguese or something.

I looked around and found she was watching. My sulking act must have looked pretty ridiculous so I decided to go back and laugh it off. "That's a pretty sassy little tongue you've got there," I announced.

"I'm sorry," she said. "Guess I'm a little touchy about our language problems."

"Well I don't speak anything but English. It's sort of the accepted thing around here."

"I said I was sorry."

I laughed and felt comfortable enough to look her in the eye.

"Were you studying?" I asked. She had a subtle beauty.

"Part of the time."

And a penetrating sadness. "What about the rest?" I asked.

"I wrote a book."

Still tawny from the sun and she moved with an easy feline freedom.

"Hey great," I said. "Did you get it published?"

She shrugged and smiled and pointed toward her suitcase. "It's in there." Her eyes were steady, sure, close to mocking and her hair tumbled with careless, auburn beauty.

At least I knew better than to ask what it was about. People used to do that at college when they caught me writing a short story or something. It's an impossible question.

"Well good luck," I said, hoping she'd appreciate my not having asked.

"Thanks." That was all she said, but her eyes were smiling, curious, unaware their behavior constituted staring.

"Fifty-nine cents a pound," I said. "I'm a very good buy."

She laughed, then turned away and started counting noses while I watched, still trying to absorb her beauty.

It would be a waste of time right now to describe her perky little breasts—which I couldn't see, by the way, because of the loose-shaped tweed coat she was wearing—or her lips like ruby wine, or the subtle pressure of her behind against the overcoat. None of the established methods for processing visual impressions of beauty into neat little semantic sketches could be employed to describe this girl.

Not because her beauty was so exceptional, so painfully radiant words were inadequate; but because it was something personal involving only my dreams and no one else's. To me she was the image of gentle searching pride. A secret place in the mountains. Love beside a cool, black silver stream. The bitter sweet reward of a long day's searching. Soft warm giving and moonlight and summer beaches and driftwood fires and love and contentment for the right to give. These were my realities. Corny, maybe, but that was my business. As to her vital statistics, I suspect a personal prejudice and would rather let others supply the data their dreams require.

"Where to now?" I asked.

"Exchange House," she said. "Before I lose somebody."

"Come on, I'll get some cabs."

"Hey," she said. "You may turn out to be useful."

"American know-how. You can't beat it."

She laughed and I ran ahead to fight the transportation problem.

Nora's image, sharp and unwelcome as the whiff of a sour washcloth, touched my senses and was gone.

"Here's two," I shouted. "Tell them where to go. I can take the rest in my car."

"Okay," she said. "It's one thirty-five East Tenth Street. I'll meet you there."

Frankly, I'd sort of expected her to ride with me, but there was no time for discussion just then. It was not a particularly enjoyable trip without her.

"Exkuse me, sur, but could you tell where is Empeer Stati beelding?"

"I couldn't pin it down," I said. "Round Thirty-fourth Street, as I remember. But I haven't been down that part of town myself for a coon's age."

"Exkuse?"

I finally gave it in textbook English which most of them seemed to understand but speaking that way made me self-conscious and I almost cracked up the car a couple of times while trying to figure out whether I sounded as silly to them as I did to myself. It might not have been fair to call me an isolationist at that stage of life, but I was a bit insular.

It was a relief to reach Exchange House and hand the group back to its rightful owner. I still didn't know her name, but she didn't get out of my sight. I knew the kids were supposed to stay at the

Exchange and I assumed she would have to deliver them to Gravenhurst the next day so there didn't seem to be much chance of her
getting away.

"Are you staying here too?" I asked.

"Hell no," she said. "I'm going home."

"Where's that?"

"Seventy-second Street for the time being. It's my uncle's apartment."

"Oh," I said, relieved it was within my transportation potential.
"Well, I'll drop you by then."

She studied me again, but it wasn't a probe. Just friendly curiosity and I didn't mind. "Okay. Wait'll I get checked out of this
dump."

She sure wasn't the Girl Scout type you'd imagine would be in
charge of a bunch of students.

I waited in the hubbub and confusion like a frightened animal,
not understanding the disorder, but afraid to run away.

Finally she was liberated. I helped with her luggage which was
pretty simple seeing as she had only one piece.

"Not much to show for a year in Europe," I said.

"Try dragging it around for a while."

That was the time to ask her name, but I'd managed to get myself
into a bind over it. I've always hated trading names. It sounded too
much like dancing class or something. "My name's Larry Woodruff.
What's yers?" Not being able to muster anything more sophisticated,
I usually avoided the question. The result was a succession of
"Heys" and "Say nows" and "Uhs" which fell some distance short
of evoking the personal touch.

From Tenth Street to Seventy-second gave me exactly sixty-two
blocks to break with tradition and introduce an entirely new approach. By Sixty-sixth and Madison the matter was resolved, though
not quite as I had planned.

"What's your name?" she asked me.

"Larry Woodruff," I said. "What's yers?"

"Lucy," she said. "Lucy Delevan."

It was really very simple.

"Where do you live?"

"One-fifteen East Seventy-second."

"No, I mean home."

"Washington."

"D.C., I hope." But I knew it was. The name had already begun to nag my memory.

"That's right," she said.

"Delevan," I said. "Delevan, Delevan, Delevan."

"I'd never thought of it quite that way," she said.

"There's a Charles Delevan who writes a Washington column for one of the news services. Any relation?"

"My father," she said. "How'd you know that?"

"We run his stuff. I read it every day." He wasn't that well known and she was obviously pleased. Just in time too, because I was pulling up in front of her building.

"Well come on up," she said. "Anybody with your journalistic taste deserves a drink."

"I read the funnies too."

"Peanuts?"

"Yup."

"Two drinks."

"And Pogo."

"Keep the bottle."

"Your uncle might object."

"He's not here. Besides you've earned it."

"Okay," I said. "You win."

When we got upstairs she excused herself to go call her father and I wandered around, trying to figure out just where I was on the economic ladder.

The apartment was big and probably attractive, but dust sheets covered it in the musty sameness of summer abandon. It gave a queer feeling of adventure and loneliness to be there. Like finding a grave in the woods. But the loneliness was soon driven off by the sound of our voices and the friendly clattering crunch of ice.

"Thank God somebody knew I was coming," she said. "Cheers."

"Who did? The place looks kind of deserted."

"Daddy must have called the maid. She lives here."

"Kind of spooky," I said.

"I like it this way. Nice and cool and quiet."

"I meant for the maid."

"Oh well, she's been doing it long enough. They go away every summer."

"Where to?"

"The Island."

"What island?"

"Potters Island," she said. "You know."

"On the Chesapeake?"

"Where else?" She looked at me as though I might have been kidding.

"Oh yeah," I said. "We have some friends who go down there."

"You do? Who?"

"Uhh, hell, I can't think of their names now. They live in Century Park. You know."

"Century," she said. "Is that where you come from? Stuffy, isn't it. I used to go there when I was a girl."

"Well not exactly. We live near by, though."

"Where?"

"In Gravenhurst."

"Poor you. I thought you just worked there."

"What do you mean, 'poor me'?"

"Oh, you know, *Babbitt* and all that."

"Well poor you, too," I said.

"Why?"

"Oh, you know, *The Late George Apley* and all that."

"I'd rather be rich-type stuffy than ranch-type stuffy."

"Okay," I said. "You win again."

"Hey," she said. "Let's go to Coney Island."

"I could never find the way," I said hopefully. A nice quiet little lunch someplace was more in line with my plans.

"That's all right," Lucy said. "We'll take the subway. I know how."

"All right. On one condition: we have dinner together afterward."

"You drive a hard bargain," she said.

"Just let me call home. They're expecting me back tonight."

She pointed me into another room and I snuck in, closing the door behind me, as if somehow ashamed of the strange noises a Gravenhurst conversation would produce.

Several days seemed to have passed since morning and I was surprised to find Mabel Crump still on the front pages of Mother's mind.

"Teddy Pearson called," she said. "You and your father ought to be here."

"Is the paper out yet?"

"Of course not," she said. "It's only twelve."

"Oh is it? I'd sort of lost track."

"When are you coming back?"

"Tomorrow morning. How's Teddy playing it?"

"In all its scandalous glory. He's leaving everything to Ned."

"Wow, that takes care of the judge."

"And Mr. Ned Polk," Mother added. "That's why you should be here."

"Well there's no paper tomorrow."

"I know, but this way your father will blame Ted for the whole business."

"It's too late now," I said.

Mother laughed. "It's going to make quite a story. I can't wait to see Goldie Compton's face."

"And Pa's too."

"Yes," she said. "I'd rather not think about that."

"I'll see you tomorrow morning, Mother. Good luck."

I hung up and carefully crammed all thoughts of Gravenhurst as far back in my mind as they would go. Lucy was sitting on a couch, smoking and sorting herself out. I tried to pick up the conversation more or less where it had been dropped in order to forget the interruption of reality.

"So they're still on the island," I said. "How long do they stay?"

She hesitated, trying to remember what I was talking about. "Oh . . . Another week or so, I guess."

"It's after Labor Day," I said. "That's very naughty."

"Well my cousin's getting married there next weekend. So that's why."

"Okay," I laughed. "It's all right then."

"Which reminds me, I'm supposed to go . . . God, how will I ever get there? It's so *far*."

"You ought to be able to handle it," I said. "After just crossing an ocean."

"I know," she said. "You can drive me."

"You're nuts."

"Why not? It would be fun."

"I wouldn't know anybody," I said. Visions of gold goblets, champagne, servants in full livery and enormous, exquisite homes frightened me. Besides I doubted there was any such thing as a Woodruff Hill on Potters Island.

"Sure you would," she said. "Everybody knows everybody these days."

"That's what you think."

"Where'd you go to college?" she asked.

I told her.

"Where?"

I told her again.

"I guess you're right," she said. "Most of these are Harvard types."

"Porcellian?" That being the only one I'd ever heard of.

"Steeple."

"Is that good?"

"Oh veddy veddy," she said.

"I'd better not go," I said. "It might do something awful to the real estate values." I don't know where the chip came from, but it was sure there. All anyone had to do was mention Bar Harbor or Hobe Sound or Potters Island or any of those international watering holes and just as quick as that I'd start behaving like Teddy Pearson under the shadow of Woodruff Hill.

"Hey wait a minute," she said. "There *is* a boy you'd know. Oh damn, what's his name anyway?"

"Sort of an outsider, huh?"

"Oh stop it. Matt . . ." She began to snap her fingers impatiently. "Matt, Matt . . ."

"Richards?" I asked.

"That's right," she said. "See, you know one."

"He was in my class," I said.

"There, now won't it be fun to see old Matt? We'll get a keg of beer and some pretzels and it'll be Fall Carnival, or whatever you call it, all over again."

"How do you know so much about it?"

"I spent a football weekend there once."

"You did? When?"

"I'd rather not discuss it."

"All right now, take it easy. I'm very sensitive about my alma mater."

"Why?"

"The family wanted me to go to Princeton."

"Ugh, that's worse."

"How do you know?"

"Daddy went there and I have to go to the reunions with him. God, what drips they are."

"My father went there too," I said, pleased to have matched her at last, drips or no drips.

"Well, good. Then it's all right for you to drive me down."

"Maybe," I hedged. I'd have driven her anywhere she wanted to go but knew better than to admit it. Also I really was put off by the socially notorious "Potters," as it was called, I believe, by its intimates.

"You're pretty indifferent," she said. "If you hadn't told me I'd have said you went to Harvard."

I took that as a compliment, though it was hard to tell.

"Come on," she said. "Coney Island, remember?"

"How would your uncle like to lend me some old clothes?"

"Why he'd be delighted." She found me an old pullover sweater and a pair of gray flannels. I felt pleasantly and unusually sloppy. Normally New York turned me into a nervous dresser and I seldom strayed from suit with tie. I mean at home everybody knew who I was so it didn't matter but in New York I sort of had to watch my manners because there was nobody around to say "Oh that's all right, it's Larry Woodruff." But being with Lucy in New York was as good as being a Woodruff in Gravenhurst any day. Anybody who could be with a girl like her obviously stood above the conventions and restraints of ordinary men.

The New York subway system will always be a complete mystery to me, so I followed meekly as Lucy led us through the complicated ritual of getting aboard the Brighton Beach line of the BMT that went to Coney.

"How'd you learn to do this?" I asked. We were on the last leg by then and I wasn't quite so afraid of distracting her.

"We used to live here," she said. "When Daddy worked for the *Trib.*"

"That's not enough," I said. "You must have studied it in school."

"Even the best of us get caught sometimes," she laughed. "I spent four hours once trying to unlose myself."

"That doesn't surprise me," I said. "I could imagine disappearing forever."

Our car was sparsely settled compared, say, to the one or two rush-hour rides on the subway I'd had the misfortune to endure. There were some young hoods trying to talk like men, but managing to produce only whining, treacherous noises. Hollow chested, thick lipped, knees flexed partly for balance, partly as some sort of phallic salute to the girls who sat opposite. Girls with orange hair and green eye shadow and soft, Latin flesh trussed in toreador pants; begging to be freed; promising unknown ecstasy but delivering only a suffocation of grunts and sighs and sweaty disillusion. At least so I hoped. Old people with tired, faceless faces. The middle-aged who sat death still, staring at the advertisements, as if to move was to admit an awareness of life's indignities.

I too kept as still as possible, not wanting to let myself become a part of subway life. I stared out at the orderly desolation of crumbling brownstone. Miles and miles of resignation with nothing but the ominous rumble of a street gang to suggest men still dreamed in a twisted, crippled way.

Coney Island managed to deliver the usual inadequate pleasures of an amusement park. Not even Lucy could change that.

Pizza and beer. The false smiles and headachy fear of a roller coaster.

Crowds and cotton candy and dirt.

"Getcha red hots. Hey, getcha red hots here."

The boardwalk and the oily, dismal, now largely abandoned beach.

Crowds and frozen-faced laughter.

Dodge-em cars; "Ha ha ha, you son of a bitch."

And aching, tired knees.

"Comeon, pitch a winnah. Whaddya say. Three for fifteen cents. Pitch a winnah. Whaddya say, Johnny. Take a couple a free ones for the little lady."

The Tunnel of Love with its forced romance and chilly giggling and my arm around her in conventional style, but not touching except once when the car lurched and my fingers, stiff with restraint, speared her shoulder.

And finally sweet relief on the BMT back to Manhattan.

It was almost six by the time we got back to Seventy-second Street, so we confirmed dinner plans and I hustled off to find myself some shelter for the night.

My family always uses a hotel on East Forty-eighth Street so I had to move pretty fast to get parked, checked in, changed and back on the job by seven-thirty.

Hotels are a great luxury to the untraveled and even though damn few give the kind of service you expect, I am among their more ardent supporters. Therefore I will go to great lengths to hide their shortcomings from myself. Under my careful misconceptions the room clerk's unction and contrived suspicion turns to sincere regard for my well-being. The Negro elevator girl's refusal to return my good evening only emphasizes her startled gratitude for a kindness from the young white prince who, after all, might have chosen to climb ten flights of stairs rather than ride with her. And the bellboy's firm stand, having overrun the battlements of my room, has nothing to do with tipping, only a deep desire to serve. All for a mere fifteen dollars a day. Far too petty a stipend for such devoted attention.

Of course it wasn't possible to be totally blind to the shortcomings of our modern American hostel. Therefore my first act, once safely in my room, was to retaliate. I called every service available with grim efficiency and put them to work. There were shoes to be shined, a suit to be pressed, a martini to be brought, sent back for lemon peel and brought again, and so on. Naturally all this cost almost as much as the room itself, but it often had the side effect of suggesting one had been well-looked after and that, in a hotel, is nice.

I drew myself a thundering bath and settled down to drink my martini and think the whole thing over in a Roman excess of steaming luxury.

Could Lucy love Larry? A thrilling, premature and thoroughly unoriginal subject for bathtub speculation. Of course Larry loves Lucy. Somehow that fact has already been established. However, this would not be the first time I had involved myself in a rip-snorting imaginary romance which was not even vaguely suspected by the recipient of my silent passion. I could still remember a spring dance at prep school, for instance, the year before I graduated. I'd managed to fall in love with a pale blonde beauty belonging to some upperclassman. I'm not quite sure why, perhaps our cheeks had touched while dancing. Anyway, it was perfectly obvious to me something cosmic was going on. So obvious, in fact, that neither her disappearance before the last dance, nor the subsequent discovery she had been out on the terrace with her escort had the slightest effect on my serenity. It was not until several agonizing unanswered love letters later plus a chance meeting with one of her less tactful classmates—"Oh, you're the boy who wrote Pat all those drippy letters"—that I began to realize the extent of my miscalculations.

Though I have suffered similar indignities since, my ability to fall

in love at a given signal, real or imagined, has not altered in the
slightest. And when, by some misfortune, the signal turned out to
be imaginary, I never suffered much. There was always Nora to
hold my hand.

I don't know quite what I had expected Lucy to wear that evening, but for some reason it was a surprise to find her in prim black
with a velvet ribbon and a glow of virgin, private school simplicity.
At Coney Island she had worn dungarees and loafers and a man's
woolen shirt with the tails flapping. There had been an air of raped
pride about her which the leather-jacketed set had found most attractive, judging by the whistling and drooling and knee flexing
which accompanied us throughout most of the afternoon, and so had
I. But now she was propriety itself.

It was a disappointment at first. I saw her new role as something
less, not more, than unconventional. Not so different from Nora
after all. However, that impression lasted less than the time it took
her to open and close the front door. As soon as she began talking
the morning Lucy was back, full of gentle laughter and curiosity.

We went to a good, that is expensive, restaurant. Too good, that
is expensive, for a newspaper reporter's salary, as a matter of fact,
which I'm ashamed to admit was done on purpose to emphasize that
I was more than just a reporter. I was the publisher's son! Sing
Hallelujah! To my bewildered surprise, the news seemed to depress
her.

"Boy," she said. "You ought to try and get out of that place."

"I've considered it," I admitted. "But after all . . ."

Fortunately she interrupted before I had a chance to tell her
about the responsibilities of being a Woodruff.

"After all, nothing," she said. "Who wants to be a small-town
huckster all his life?"

"We're not exactly hucksters."

"Well all the same," Lucy said more gently. "It isn't much of an
ambition."

"What *should* I do?"

"I don't know," she admitted. "As much as you can, I guess."

"I can do that at home."

"Not when you're at the top of the pile. Then there's no place to
go but down."

"As a matter of fact we've just been finding that out," I laughed.

"There, you see?"

"But now we've gone down there's room to climb again. So why shouldn't I stay in Gravenhurst?"

"Wouldn't it be simpler to go somewhere where they have a longer ladder?"

"Maybe," I confessed. "Someday."

"I mean now."

"Where?"

"Well, like working for the *New York Times* or something."

"I'd rather be news editor on a small paper than obituary writer on a big one."

"News editor. Are you an editor?"

"It looks like I'm about to be."

"Boy, it really *must* be a small paper," she laughed.

"Thanks. Thanks a lot."

"I guess you're right about the experience," she admitted. "But gosh . . ."

"What?"

"Oh I don't know. All those clods."

Not being too familiar with Lucy's richly packaged world of Potters Island, Washington, and New York, I wasn't too eager to argue this point. Maybe we were clods by comparison. I didn't know.

"Want some dessert?" I asked, deciding to change the subject before my knees wore out.

"Just coffee."

"How 'bout a brandy or something?"

"My aren't we swish," she teased. "I mean for a country boy."

"Lordy," I said, but with admiration. "You get away with murder."

She shrugged and sparkled with mischief. "Lordy," she repeated and giggled.

Later we went to a place Lucy knew where somebody was supposed to be playing the piano, but about all I ever heard was a bunch of expense account celebrities trying to outsell each other. Hustling is our most important product.

It didn't matter, though. We finally got talking about *her* father which was a nice change, but she never gave me a chance to get even. Apparently he was quite a guy. Though brought up to worship New York's social trinity of prep school, the Ivy League, and Wall Street, Mr. Delevan soon rebelled against what he called the bother, the fun, and the holy coast and went to work for the *Tribune*.

This, according to Lucy, was a very heroic thing to have done.

"I should think it would be just like my leaving Gravenhurst," I suggested.

"Oh no," she said, horrified. "Wall Street's a very important place."

"So what?"

"It's much easier to justify doing what everybody else does if it's also supposed to be important."

"Oh. Well, what's wrong with doing what everybody else does?"

"Nothing, except it's usually too easy or they wouldn't be doing it."

"Who says?"

"Daddy."

I was beginning to wonder whether Daddy was a little too much of a good thing. "Not everybody who works on Wall Street is a clod. Why I'll bet some of them are as smart as your old man."

"I doubt it." She was dead serious too.

I decided it wouldn't do to laugh.

"Maybe we should go," she suggested. "Tomorrow's going to be a long one."

"Why tomorrow?"

"Gravenhurst."

"We'll try to make it easy for you."

"That's a tough assignment," she laughed.

"Try to be gracious. I'm about to request the check."

"Gravenhurst, Paris of the Connecticut Valley."

"That's nice, but a little confining."

"Best I can do if you expect me to say it without laughing."

"All right. Then you can leave the tip."

"Paris of New England," she corrected.

"That's fine," I said. "Beautiful."

"If you say so," she laughed.

The cab ride back to Seventy-second Street reminded me of our little trip through the Tunnel of Love. Somehow the fact of being tired seemed to curdle the day's intimacies and make us strangers again. Also the cab's wretched bouncing warned that cracked teeth would be the most likely reward for any attempts at love making. We sat in tense silence while I reassured myself the matter could be resolved over a nightcap at Lucy's apartment.

"Why don't you keep the cab," she suggested. "I'm so tired I can hardly see."

There was no time to protest. She was already on the street.

"It's been a wonderful day," I called hopefully, foolishly.

She turned and waved. "Call me in the morning."

The cab shot from the curb, dumping me back in the seat before I'd had a chance to answer.

"It's a tough life, ain't it, Mac?" the driver said.

I didn't answer.

"So wud it cost ta find out there was no action?"

"Listen," I said. "Just shut up, all right?"

"Broads," he said. "They're all alike."

"Shut up," I repeated and he did, which surprised me so much I nearly over-tipped the bastard. Issuing commands was a fairly new experience for me, but having them obeyed as well was downright uncanny. So uncanny, I found it necessary to drop by the hotel bar and order up a scotch and soda. Something I'd never have done alone before. Not in New York, anyway.

CHAPTER XIV

The next morning I phoned home to say there'd be one more for lunch which didn't please Mother much since Pa was back from the Catskills and not in one of his more hospitable moods. Then I called Lucy to tell her it was too late and we'd better meet at the Exchange House. And I gave Tommy a ring, but he didn't answer, which was just as well because I don't know just what we would have talked about. Sally Polk maybe.

Fortunately, three Gravenhurst ladies who must have been particularly bent on martyrdom had driven to New York and were already waiting at the Exchange when I got there. That took care of the transportation problem and allowed Lucy and I to drive up alone.

On the way I tried to give her some idea what to expect from Abby and Mother and Pa because for some mawkish, Sunday sentimental reason it seemed important. But she wasn't in that kind of mood and told me to dry up.

"Well, anyway," I said, "you'll like my sister, Abby. She's sort of a nut."

"I can imagine."

But most of the time we just listened to the radio. Lucy kept switching from one disc jockey to another as if she couldn't get enough of the stuff.

"If I had a grrrruul," the radio gurgled. "A liddle grrul lieek you oo oo, oo oo. A liddle grrul lieek you."

"Great," she said. "Terrific."

I thought she was kidding.

"It's funny the things you miss," she explained. "Now it really feels like I'm back in America."

"I thought you weren't in any hurry to feel that way."

"Well it's home. I guess you can't get away from that."

I'd have given anything for a good family performance that day, but unfortunately Pa was way off the mark and so was Abby. What was much worse, though, Mother had organized a reception for the students and their foster parents and the guest list turned out to include a pretty motley collection of social climbers. Not that student exchange programs and social climbing are necessarily synonymous, but it just so happened our program was sponsored by the Nepotan Club. Now if a lady aspired to membership in this exclusive little potpourri of Gravenhurst elegance it was considered a good idea to participate in the club's programs. However, it involved a lot of bother boarding a student all year long; a bother which those ladies most likely to be elected did not feel it necessary to assume. As a result, some of the foster mothers represented Gravenhurst's most socially pretentious and least attractive female elements. Of course there were one or two who had volunteered simply because it seemed like a worthwhile program but they were apt to be reasonable, unassuming types and their presence was soon reduced to crumbling obscurity under the barrage of pseudo-Continental chatter the others laid down.

"J'aim Paree tray byen mercy—ummm—J'etay on France—ummm —il ya deuks ans—Ohhh, hoo hoo hoo hoooo."

"That's very nice, Mrs. Parsons."

"Ooooh, hoo hoo, call me Mother, dear, please, sill vous plate."

"All right . . . Mother," followed by a look of horror from the youth whose only crime was to cultivate an ideal or, at worst, take advantage of one a little.

Since no one knew Lucy, naturally no one spoke to her, which she didn't seem to mind in the least. I did though, because almost all communities look pretty silly to the outsider and I hated to think what this group, being fairly silly even to me, would do to her preconceived ideas. I tried to liven things up by introducing her to Pa, though in the light of recent developments, that wasn't likely to be an improvement.

He was sitting by himself in a far corner of the room, his face dressed out in a harassed pout. When I introduced Lucy he just looked bored and didn't get up and asked what country *she* came from. I explained, trying to make a little joke out of his mistake, but he just grunted and made no effort to recover. About all you could say for him was he looked pretty regal off by himself in an aloof, princely funk. His suits were tailor made and on such semiformal occasions he often undid the sleeve buttons and rolled back his cuffs which achieved an air of frilled elegance I liked for some reason.

But other than his looks, I'm afraid Pa was in pretty sorry shape.

"I suppose you've seen yesterday's paper," he said.

That was about the last thing I wanted to discuss in front of Lucy.

"Just the headlines," I said. "I haven't had time yet."

"You should. You're mentioned."

"Me?"

"That's right," he confirmed. "'Larry Woodruff, a neighbor and son of Clarence Woodruff, publisher of the Gravenhurst *Daily Watch*, discovered the orgy and called police.'"

"Who printed that?" I asked. "The *Enterprise?*"

"No," Pa said. "We did. As a matter of fact, the *Enterprise* never mentioned it."

"Well," I said, trying to laugh it up a little, "so we scooped the *Enterprise*, eh?"

"That's right," Pa said. "Though unfortunately it's comparable to committing suicide as a matter of principle."

"Don't worry. Things will work out all right." Nothing pleases a father less than a pat on the head from his son, I've discovered.

"I've been on the phone all morning," Pa said, controlling his temper nicely. "And the impression is things will not work out all right."

"Couldn't we talk about it later?" I begged. "I wanted Lucy to meet Abby."

"We've as good as lost our municipal contract," Pa continued, flicking lint from his sleeve with an air of self-devotion. "Plus God knows how much advertising."

"What about Ned Polk?"

"We've lost him too."

"You fired him, eh?"

"No. He resigned this morning."

"Well at least he's gone."

"That's right. And how do we get along without him?"

"We weren't getting along too well with him."

"Things would have worked out," Pa said. "Once he'd lost the senatorial appointment everything would have been fine."

I could feel Lucy yawning beside me.

"Couldn't we talk about it later?"

"Why not?" Pa said. "Benjamin Rosenfeldt's coming to town Wednesday. Shall we wait until then?"

"What's he coming for?"

"Because I asked him," Pa said. "To discuss a merger."

"Oh Pa, that's crazy."

He shrugged, turned and stared out the window.

"Come on," I said. "Let's go find Abby."

Lucy gave me a confused nod.

"I'm sorry," I said. "Things are in sort of a mess."

"Sort of," she agreed.

Abby wasn't much of an improvement. I'd looked forward to their meeting, Lucy and Abby, and the friendship which was sure to blossom from the union of wit and beauty. But instead Abby seemed to go into partial eclipse. Like plate silver, she looked fine until you held a piece of sterling alongside and compared. Then what had once been vitality turned shrill and hectic and second best. There was a strident note of panic in her humor and if the sought for laugh was not granted immediately her eyes would jump and skip and her mouth would begin spilling words in a splatter of minor indiscretions and consequent apologies.

Apparently Abby had suffered some new setback and, since she seemed more or less resigned to the disillusionment of Pa, I could only guess this had something to do with Jesse.

I asked if she'd seen him lately and her eyes flattened, preparing to lie; something Abby had never bothered to do before. "No," she said. "That is, not much."

"What's the matter, lover's quarrel?"

"Hardly."

I should have dropped it because Lucy was there, but kept after her instead, hoping she'd say something funny, I suppose.

"Fellow named Jesse Rosenfeldt," I explained with the patronizing air of an older brother. "Abby's latest love interest."

"Ha," Abby said. "That's a laugh."

"He's the publisher of our rival paper," I continued. "And not too popular around here as a result, which is why Abby's being so mysterious."

"Oh dear," Lucy laughed. "That's a tough one all right."

"I suppose you've heard that Jesse's father called this morning," Abby said.

"I thought Pa called him."

"Pa? Doing something on his own initiative? Come on, Larry, wake up."

"Well, what about it?"

"You won't believe this, but right after the phone call a funny thing happened."

"What?" I asked.

"Pa got this great idea. 'Abby,' he said. 'Let's get your friend, Jesse, over for dinner sometime.'"

"It's not such a bad idea," I said. "Know thine enemy. You said so yourself."

"That's not what bothers me," Abby said. "It's whether I should take him to bed before dinner or after." She turned to Lucy. "Would you know which is proper?"

Lucy produced a nervous laugh. "No," she said.

Abby pretended to laugh and then left us. I watched her wander off to exchange banalities with Mother and a group of ladies. It was obvious from her eager nods and smiles that Abby was ingratiating herself for a change, practicing to be a matron, I supposed.

After the guests left, Woodruff morale seemed to improve considerably. If the truth be known, it was no real improvement; only a mechanical graciousness lavished on those guests fortunate enough to share our table. None of us cared very much about the student exchange ladies. Also there had been enough of them for us to misbehave without being caught. But now only Lucy remained, and a special effort was required.

Right away Pa bestowed one of the world's more coveted honors by stating that he remembered Charlie Delevan at Princeton and

as if this news wasn't enough for one day, he added that Charlie, in
his opinion, wrote one of the finest columns coming out of Washington.

But most charming of all was Mother. Nor was there anything
mechanical in her manner. She seemed to be thriving on our mis-
fortunes which I guess was just as well seeing as Pa had begun to
slide after his initial effort.

Lucy tried to keep things going at lunch by telling him how
much she admired his paintings and all that; especially the Monet.

"Oh I'm awfully glad," said Pa, "but it's really Mrs. Woodruff you
should be talking to. She's in charge of that department."

"Oh?" from Lucy.

"Yes, I'm just the old plow horse around here," Pa explained.
"Leave moneymaking to the menfolk, culture to the womenfolk, I
say."

Lucy looked at me, I looked at Mother, Mother looked annoyed,
Abby looked at Pa, Pa looked as though he really believed it.

"Yes," Mother agreed. "I like Monet too. His colors are wonderful,
don't you think? So unnatural, yet so effective somehow."

"Uh huh," Lucy agreed, looking vaguely disappointed.

Bollard came in with the roast beef.

"My God," said Pa. "That must have cost an arm and a leg."

"But what I like best about him," Mother hurried on, "is that
marvelous instinctive quality he had."

Lucy brightened.

"Don't you agree?" Mother pursued. "One feels he relied almost
entirely on intuition rather than tradition and technique."

"Oh yes," Lucy said. "That's what made him such a genius and so
much better than people like Pissarro. He didn't have to bother
about form. It was all right there inside him."

"But even a genius should learn the techniques, shouldn't he?" I
asked. "I mean he'll be just that much better off if he does."

"What time are we supposed to be at the Healys?" Pa interrupted.

"Six o'clock," said Mother.

"Don't you think so?" I tried to ask Lucy, but she was intent on
catching an elusive roast potato.

"Well, I suppose we'd better go," Pa said.

"Don't you think a genius should learn the techniques?" I insisted.

"Yes dear," Mother agreed. "I suppose we should."

"Where did you go to college?" Abby asked.

Lucy released a sigh, or so it seemed. "Radcliffe."

"Is my blue blazer pressed?" Pa continued.

"I don't know dear," Mother said. "I'll see *after* lunch."

Pa pushed back his chair, hung an arm over the back and seemed entirely satisfied with this line of conversation. "I suppose Bollard can press it if it isn't," he surmised.

"Yes dear," Mother agreed. "I wouldn't be surprised."

"Gosh," Abby said. "Radcliffe, what a grind."

"Oh, that's a myth," Lucy corrected. "It's really not so bad."

"Maybe not if you're smart," Abby said. "But I'm glad I didn't go there."

Lucy took a long, unladylike pull on her wineglass.

"Abby's just being modest," I said. "She's almost normal really."

"Normal," Mother laughed. "Why, don't you believe it, Lucy. She's absolutely brilliant."

Abby seemed to perk up, then catch herself. "I wonder where I got it from," she said.

"Why from your mother, of course," Mother prattled bravely.

But Abby refused to play. "Oh?"

"This knife wouldn't cut butter," Pa claimed.

I considered asking once more whether anyone agreed with my theories on genius, but gave it up in favor of these more interesting topics.

"Well for heaven sakes, don't use it," Mother suggested too heartily. "I'll ring for another."

Bollard appeared.

"Bollard, Mr. Woodruff says his knife wouldn't cut butter. Have you got one that will?"

"Not bloody likely," said Bollard and at long last we had a legitimate laugh.

"He's getting entirely too fresh," said Pa.

"I hadn't noticed any changes," Abby mumbled.

"Oh dear," Mother laughed. "Neither had I," and she turned to Lucy. "It's a terrible thing to be dominated by one's servants, dear, but I'm afraid we are."

Lucy chuckled. "Aren't we all," she'd apparently been taught to say.

"But we don't really mind," Mother continued. "It's rather a comfort to know someone is looking after us."

"Especially these days," said Abby.

Bollard returned.

"Never mind," Pa said. "I'm all finished."

And he withdrew, but not without pausing long enough for Pa to turn and silently question his presence.

"Dear me, Clarence," said Mother a trifle stridently. "You are a one."

Yes, I guess Mother was the most charming of all that day, but it was more our doing than hers. We'd simply crumbled and washed away, leaving her to tower above, a monadnock of grace and charm and competence, the only one to retain her shape and character as we continued our delicate erosion. It was a phenomenon requiring a certain hardness which, while noteworthy, was not altogether appealing, as when she schemed the *Daily Watch's* future without Pa's knowledge, but it could be useful, there was no doubt about that.

All this fascinated me, but I was a little nervous about Lucy's reaction. Getting involved in our family problems and topping it off with a bus trip back to New York didn't strike me as recommended courting procedure. I was driving her to the depot trying to figure out how to apologize without actually apologizing when Lucy came to the rescue.

"I had a good time," she said. "It's nice being with a family."

Somehow that particular attraction had not occurred to me.

"What do you mean?"

"Oh you know," she said, fidgeting. "Sunday lunch and all."

"Don't they do that in Washington?" I laughed.

"My mother's dead," she said. "So there's just the two of us."

"I'm sorry."

"Dad's great," she said. "But, you know, it's not the same."

"I'm glad you had a good time, but sorry you had to get involved in all our problems."

"Oh I didn't mind," she said. "But I wish you didn't have them."

We were at the bus stop by then and I had begun to panic.

"When will I see you?"

"Next weekend," she said. "The wedding."

The bus was coming and we had to scramble.

"I'd forgotten. When would we have to leave?"

"Friday morning."

"I'm supposed to work," I said. "Friday and Saturday both."

"Live a little."

There was no time.

"Things are in such a mess."

She climbed aboard.

"Call me."

"Okay. I'll try to make it."

She smiled and I backed away, waving, trying to make time hold still for once.

On an impulse I drove down to City Hall afterward to see how the cops were getting along with Mabel and her friends. They were still taking statements when I got there and the judge, in a fit of pique unbefitting of a public servant, had refused to grant bail so the forces of law and order were in some confusion. I watched through the one-way glass while a detective translated the statement of one gentleman caller into his interpretation of legalese.

"So what happened then?"

"So I banged her. Whatsat a crime or what?"

"You was in her, huh? And you got yer rocks off. Is at right?"

"Yeah. So what?"

Which under the detective's careful treatment would come out:

I, Joseph Hood, eighteen years old, of 144 Front Street, being of sound mind and body, do hereby testify that on the night of September 16, nineteen hundred and etcetera . . .

". . . that I achieved penetration and climax with the aforementioned Mabel Crump . . ."

"How 'bout your buddies. They get some too?"

"Sure, we all took a ride. Whaddya think, I got queer friends or somepin'?"

". . . that to the best of my recollections the following persons also enjoyed"—scratched out—"also *had* intercourse with Mabel Crump."

I turned to a nearby cop.

"Boy she sure took on a bunch of them, didn't she?"

"Comes natural to her," the cop said.

"How so?"

"Her mother's a who-er. Works down to the Fun House."

"Oh yeah? I thought her mother was an invalid or something."

"Who tolt you that?"

"Judge Compton, I think it was."

The cop gave me a funny smile, then wiped it off.

"No," he corrected. "She's a who-er."

I wanted to ask more about her, but he remembered something pretty important and had to leave. I don't know why, but a suspicion I couldn't quite define was nagging my memory.

I was just about to go when who should appear but Mr. Ned Polk, former news editor of the Gravenhurst *Daily Watch*.

"Well well well," he boomed. "If it isn't Clarence Woodruff, the Fourth, formerly of Woodruff Hill but currently in transit to Front Street and Sewer."

"Thanks to you," I said.

"Don't mention it."

"I won't again."

"They tell me you're going to be news editor now," Ned said.

"So I hear."

"Well say now, Mr. Editor. How about giving me your endorsement for the State Senate."

"Which is something you'd better start worrying about," I said.

"If there's a *Daily Watch* around to endorse me."

"That's right," I said.

He laughed, but it was more of a sneer. "Somehow the possibility doesn't worry me too much." He turned and walked off, waving at the cops in a genial, political kind of way.

"Afternoon, boys. How's Gravenhurst's finest?"

That's one of the troubles with dealing in human currency. You can't store the stuff in a bank and it has to be watched all the time. I didn't envy him the politician's life.

Back home I found Mother wandering the dying paths of her garden.

"Lucy's a lovely girl," she said.

"Who? Oh yes," I said. Already she seemed far away.

"Such nice manners."

"It's sad when everything goes," I said, changing the subject back to her garden.

"Hmmm? Oh. Actually I was thinking about next year. Too many hollyhocks, don't you think?"

"I don't know. They look pretty nice to me."

"Well it's good to have a change. I think I'll do the whole business differently."

"How'd Pa take it all?"

"He was relieved to be in the Catskills."

"Why?"

"So they couldn't blame him for what happened."

"Suppose he decides to sell?" I said.

"Well," she said, "the stock's in my name."

"It is?"

"That's right. Tax advantages, you know."

I started to bubble with laughter.

"And I don't feel like selling just yet," she said.

"Mother, you're terrific."

"Thank you, dear. How about more peonies along here? They're lovely in the spring."

"Whatever you think's best," I laughed. "You're the boss."

"I don't know. They're so messy when they die."

"Well, you figure it out," I said. "I'm going hunting."

"Have fun," she said.

There wasn't really much chance of bagging anything without a dog. Only pheasant was in season—at least it was for us because we had a special raiser's permit—and I'd have to step right on one to make him fly. But it didn't really matter, there were plenty of other reasons for going hunting that day.

I cut through the woods, planning to work toward the stream and follow it back to the lake. I could hear its earnest rushing. Only a tiny part of the lake's total but loudly self-important. A woodcock routed from his secret place, wings *peep peep peeping*, and headed down the stream, ducking, feinting, supremely unaware I had no intention of shooting.

The trees crackled with an early touch of fall.

I followed the stream to a spot where two stone walls cornered forming a little fortress on two sides. It was a good place for hunting deer. I had used it often enough, huddled with the cold stones and the rattling chill of a November dawn and the black iron clouds lying heavy on an orange sky.

I decided to sit there awhile and have a smoke and see what, if anything, might be crossing. It was getting along toward evening and the deer should be coming down for water soon.

I could hear the deep *hoof hoof* of a big dog, probably running deer. He wouldn't be catching them now. Not until the snow came and his quarry was confined to beaten, traveled trails. In the confusion of bare ground a deer, though short-winded, can usually escape the senseless fate provided by man's best friend. The dog runs him awhile, becomes confused, starts after another, becomes confused, and so on, allowing his quarry to spell each other. But in deep snow a deer is confined to his narrow trail and the relay system is not so easy to employ.

It was less than ten minutes before I heard the delicate step of an approaching animal. I listened doubtfully for a while, suspecting a squirrel romping in dry leaves, but the step came again, closer now, following a trail I knew was being used. I raised my gun, just for the hell of it, to prove I'd have got him had the season been on. I smiled, pleased with being able to outsmart an animal on his own ground. A deer doesn't move all that quietly, but he's very careful. Two or three steps, then stop, then two or three steps more, so unless your ear is on one you'll lose his sound in the turmoil of forest noises. But I was with him this time. Coming right toward me and not so cautious either. If nothing else I'd soon teach him to be more careful. Crunching along like a Borsch belt indian. A disgrace to the animal kingdom.

I sighted down the barrels and waited with a silly grin to inform him he was bang bang dead all right. There he was. A flash of brown through the maple saplings. Just a few more steps and . . .

Dead in the sights was my sister, Abby.

"Boy," I said. "You'd make a hell of a deer."

She jumped a foot off the ground.

"That's better," I said. "Now waggle your tail and snort."

"Oh," she said. "My God, you scared me."

"Wear that coat in the deer season. And you're a goner."

Abby couldn't be bothered bantering, just climbed into my fortress and sat down. "This is nice," she said. "Do you use it in deer season?"

"Sometimes."

"I'd like to go out one day."

"You'll be at college."

"That's right," she said. "Wednesday."

"Still sore at Pa?"

She shrugged. "Ah."

"What's that mean?" I laughed.

"I'm through worrying about him."

"Jesse then?"

She looked away.

"What's the matter? Doesn't he love you any more?"

"Sure," she said. "That's the trouble."

"But you don't love him?" I suggested.

"Who said so?"

"Well, do you?"

"I don't know . . . What's that?"

The big dog's steady *hoof hoofing* had come closer.

"Damn dog running deer."

She shuddered.

"If he comes by here," I said, "we'll pepper his ass for him."

"Good," she said. "I hope he does."

"So you don't know whether you love him or not."

"What?"

"Jesse."

"I did," she said. "Until all this trouble started."

"Well, that's his fault."

"I don't care whose fault it is," she said. "The result's what bothers me."

"Which is?"

"All of a sudden I'm scared what people will say."

"About what?"

"About Jesse being Jewish," she said. "What do you think?"

Hoof hoof hoof.

"Shh," I said. "He's working the same trail you did."

"Will you kill him?" Abby whispered.

"It's just bird shot."

Hoof hoof hoof.

"But I'll sure sting him."

The struggle came closer until his barking was no longer background music, but a part of Abby and me and suddenly the deer burst into sight, eyes wide with fright, caution gone, almost graceless with exhaustion. A button buck, maybe, still too young to raise a crop of antlers, but more likely a young doe, driven from the sweet, tiptoeing hesitancy of her nature to this present state of ugly terror.

She never saw us, but took the stone wall in a headlong plunge and disappeared.

And seconds later came the big, hang-jowled pursuer. He'd left the pipe, the slippers, the roaring fire and the man behind.

I let loose a blast that doubled his hind end under, turned his steady stride to a scramble, and sent him *ki-yi-yi-ing* on the homeward trail.

"What will happen to him?" Abby asked.

"He won't do much sitting up for a while."

"That's all?"

"Most likely. He was pretty far away."

"I'm glad it won't kill him," she said. "He looked like a nice old thing."

"Well I don't know about that," I said. "But anyway, it won't."

We sat without talking for a while, trying to recapture some measure of calm.

"Then why don't you stop seeing him?" I asked, getting back to Jesse.

She seemed to settle into the gray stones. "That's the awful part," she said. "I *can't.*"

"Why not?"

"He's so insistent," she said.

"Just say no."

"Oh you don't know him," Abby said.

"No?"

"No. You just can't refuse him."

"Why not?"

She threw her arms in the air in a sprawling, helpless gesture. "He just goes right on making plans."

"You can still refuse," I said.

"Then before you know it," she continued, "he's got tickets for something in New York or he's made reservations for dinner or he's got us invited someplace we're not wanted. I don't know. He just wears me down."

"Well, it won't be so bad when college starts," I said.

"I hope not."

We sat for a while longer, feeling the evening close in and the night chill approach.

"I don't know," Abby said, as if something in the woods had asked. "I'm just scared, that's all."

"About what?"

"And self-conscious too. As if it really mattered how I behaved and what I said."

"About what?" I repeated.

But she didn't answer. I stood up and the force of my waiting made her hand reach out for mine. I took it and gently helped her up.

"Relax," I said. "He's gone for the time being."

"Who, the dog?"

"Jesse."

"I know," she said. "But he'll be back."

When we got home there was a kind of screwy message for me: Miss Nora Compton had called to say she would not be at home in case I was interested.

Abby laughed. "She's been dying to tell you all day, you louse, why didn't you call? Now you've gone and spoiled her fun."

I tried laughter too, but lacked the defiance. An absurdity, no doubt, but Nora was tradition itself to me; a lifetime of stockpiled memory and emotion, and though I wanted it to end between us, there was more involved than just that. I was tradition's suitor on the one hand, her son on the other, thus the break would have a double significance and I preferred to remain in limbo, unwilling to accept the past, afraid of the future. My solution, therefore, was as usual to do nothing.

Mother and Pa were supposed to be at the Healys so it was something of a surprise when the old Lincoln came wheeling up around six-thirty, Mother driving, Pa staring at nothing with childish serenity. I went out to meet them.

"What happened, party called off?"

"Evidently," said Mother, stewing.

"Can't understand it," said Pa, more bewildered than annoyed. "I was sure they said six o'clock."

"Of course they did," Mother snapped.

"Nobody home, eh?"

"Precisely," said Mother. "Nobody home," and she hurried her humiliation into the house, Pa trailing unconcerned.

The family was getting to be more than I could take so I drove downtown, grabbed a hamburger at Chick's Diner and hit the flicks at the Palace: *Hiroshima Mon Amour*. Very uplifting.

CHAPTER XV

Monday was my first day as news editor and though I enjoyed some measure of success, it was far from total. Everything went pretty well until around noon when the copy began to flow so fast it was all I could do to write the heads and get it off my desk, never mind edit it. Fortunately Ted had been checking up and managed to rescue some of my more flagrant oversights. Carl Robinson, for instance, had got confused and glued one of the pages from a church supper story into a roundup of weekend auto mishaps. Another guy managed to get a couple of carbons mixed in with the original copy, thereby imparting a somewhat repetitious aspect to his story. When these were returned to my desk I felt the need to surrender a certain amount of obviously undeserved self-confidence and the result was panic. Stories got speared on the wrong spindles, headlines were lost, the dummy page one disappeared under a maze of rubbish which had once been useful copy, the clackety-crunch of the teletype machine as it spewed its endless tongue of news behind me made my neck ache, and I finally went up in a cloud of confusion.

Teddy wandered over about then, sat down beside me and quietly doodled his way through the mess, occasionally asking: "Did you want this for page one?" or "How about making the satellite story a two column head? It'll give the page more balance." Until somehow, to my great bewilderment, the desk suddenly stood empty, it was a quarter to one and a newspaper had been made.

A few minutes later one of the men from the back shop came in and tossed me a copy of the first edition. I picked it up, weighed it, looked at it, recognized the scribbling I'd sent out had somehow been translated into printed words and pictures and symmetry.

"So that's what I've been doing," and my surprise wasn't entirely feigned.

Ted laughed. "You'll be all right. Just as soon as you convince yourself it's really possible to produce newspapers this way."

"That's just what was bothering me," I said.

"Well those guys out back've been setting type a long time," Ted said. "They can usually figure out what you're trying to do before you can."

"Lucky, because I'm still not sure."

"Come on," Ted said. "Let's have some lunch."

On the way out somebody said, "Hey Larry, nice-looking paper."

"Yeah," said another. "Real sweet layout."

Gentlemen, may I present Clarence Woodruff, the Fourth, one of our nation's leading editors.

"Thanks," I said, and almost tripped on the goddam stairs.

At lunch I told Teddy about Benjamin Rosenfeldt's coming to town and we decided it might be a good idea to do a little research on how things stood between the *Enterprise* and us. Pa had started off keeping a fairly accurate account, but these days he really preferred ignoring the existence of a competitor rather than tracing its progress and thereby admitting such an evil had come to Gravenhurst. Therefore, Ted and I stayed up most of Monday and Tuesday night tabulating the hodgepodge of information which had accumulated.

The results we included in a new report for Pa to look at before he laid his sword at the feet of this real estate vendor whose visionary dreams and capitalistic instincts seemed bound together in what—at least up until now—had been a most rewarding philanthropic package.

According to us the *Enterprise,* in its three months of operation, had managed to achieve an average daily circulation of 5000. Not bad, to tell the truth. However, this had been done through a combination of curiosity, puzzle contests, and special subscription rates, none of which gave the circulation figures an aspect of permanency. Similarly, the *Enterprise's* advertising volume, though impressive enough on the surface, represented a harvest of rate cutting and bad credit risks which were not quite so rich and creamy as they looked. At least according to Ted Pearson.

But best of all was the confirmation of what we already suspected: operating costs, despite their genius for cut-rate competition, were not much lower than ours. It was comforting to know our enemy's secret weapons were not so deadly as had been claimed. All they had, in effect, was a larger pot of gold, but how long could a man like Benjamin Rosenfeldt watch his pot drain, and, according to a disgruntled *Enterprise* accountant, it was draining at the rate of some $4000 a week, without feeling compelled to replace the plug?

At breakfast Wednesday morning I presented the report to Pa, but he was too preoccupied with Abby's imminent departure to concern himself with such vulgarities. I guess he couldn't be blamed for trying to set things straight before she left, though it did seem he was being overly solicitous, overly grand about the whole college procedure. Everything but a couple of suitcases had been sent on ahead so there was no real reason for Bollard to drive her down in the Lincoln. But Pa flung out the gesture and waved it about with such determination Abby was unable to refuse. Then he produced his billfold and proceeded to disembowel it while Abby stared with the bored eyes of a prostitute and I drooled.

She and I have never been very good at saying goodbye to each other. Too much emotion from one or not enough from the other was a complication we never liked to face so our system was to pretend nobody was leaving; at least nobody was going any great distance in time and space. I just gave her a peck on the cheek and a "See you, Bones," and we called it a day.

Pa drove down to the office with me. I gave him the report again, having rescued it from abandon.

"Ummm," he said. "Thank you."

"What time's the meeting?" I asked.

"Three."

"Well I wouldn't be too hasty. Things aren't as bad as we thought."

"Ummm."

I'd been staring for some time at the red lights of the car in front of me before realizing they had something to do with brakes. I jammed on mine and lurched to a squealing stop. Somehow Pa made me self-conscious and clumsy. As if it were my first lesson.

"Let's concentrate on our driving, shall we?"

I no longer felt qualified to advise him on the future of his Gravenhurst *Daily Watch*.

The meeting with Mr. Rosenfeldt hung over me like the promise of half holiday at school. My brain clogged with dreams of glorious clashes with the enemy. Capture the flag and Larry Woodruff creeping with catlike cunning to snatch the coveted scrap of cloth and sprint past a bewildered and outclassed enemy to glorious victory. And now capture the Rosenfeldts with Larry Woodruff hiding the knowledge and skill of shrewd bargainer behind his boyishness, waiting to leap on the idealistic Mr. Rosenfeldt and batter him with facts about his supposedly indestructible *Enterprise*. Too much television, that's my trouble.

By a slightly suspect coincidence, that afternoon the *Enterprise* gave its endorsement for the State Senate to Mr. Ned Polk, "former news editor of the Gravenhurst *Daily Watch,* and a man whose concern for the welfare of Forest County would not only manifest itself in words but *deeds* as well."

Think of that!

Teddy and I took a couple of deep breaths and climbed to the publisher's office around two-thirty with the idea of organizing a little strategy before the battle. But Pa was busy discussing plans for our annual baby edition with the picture editor, even though it wasn't scheduled to run until January, so we had to wait until quarter of.

When we finally got into his office, Pa seemed so intent on reinforcing his own self-confidence that he didn't have much time for our practical trivia. There was a big oak table at the far side of the room which he used for board meetings, if they could be called that. Pa was sitting at one end when we came in, but didn't seem convinced it was the right one. He tried the other to see how the positions compared in relation to the door. Apparently this had something to do with the impression he intended to transmit when Mr. Rosenfeldt and his entourage arrived.

"Perhaps it would be better if I were at my desk," he said.

"I think so," Ted Pearson said. "Then it won't look like you've been waiting for him."

"Uhh, yes," Pa said. "Now let's see, water, glasses, pencils, paper. Everything seems to be in order."

"Except us," Ted said.

"What?"

"Except us," he repeated. "What's our position supposed to be?"

"Don't know," Pa said. "Haven't heard their offer."

"But shouldn't we have some sort of counteroffer?" Ted asked.

"Not today," Pa said. "Let them do the talking."

I began to feel Pa might know what he was doing after all.

About then the door cracked open and Mother's head appeared, smiling, gracious, at odds with the market place.

"May I join the conspiracy?"

"Alice," Pa said. "What are you doing here?"

"Thrill seeking," Mother said. "Does anyone object? Hello, Ted, how are you?"

"Just fine, Mrs. Woodruff."

"Why no," Pa said. "Of course not."

"I thought the presence of a lady might hold Mr. Rosenfeldt to a more gentlemanly approach than is his custom."

"It might at that," Pa laughed. Ted and I joined him, but the effect was of conspiring children whose little plot had barely missed discovery.

Pa's buzzer rang.

"Yes, yes," Pa said. "Ask them to wait, Jane, would you please."

"Why?" Mother asked. "Aren't we ready?"

"It's good strategy," Pa said.

"Oh fiddlesticks," Mother said. "Tell them to come in."

"Alice," Pa warned, "I said it was good strategy."

"Childishness," Mother said, but she sat down and prepared to ignore his disobedience.

"Would you like to have a look at this, Mr. Woodruff?" Ted asked, pushing our report his way.

"No time for it now," said Pa.

He drummed his desk awhile and finally gave up.

"All right," he buzzed. "Send them in."

Mr. Rosenfeldt came first. He was more than parchment paper and chicken bones. Considerably more. Behind him was Jesse and another man who, judging by the size of his briefcase, must have done a good deal of the dirty work. They all wore light topcoats, the Rosenfeldts' being gray while the dirty worker had a blue gabardine suggesting a taste suitable to something less than ten thousand a year, New York City money. Therefore he got no handshake from me, the poor boy, only a nod.

All three had a slightly preoccupied look about them, like actors on opening night fearful of forgetting their lines. It was comic the way these efficient, hungry-looking fellows marched in, bumped into Mother's presence and dissolved. Jesse saved the day by having something of a gracious manner about him and employing it to hurdle the problem of introductions.

"Papa," he said. "Papa"—as if to verify the relationship—"this is Mrs. Woodruff . . ."

"How do. Delighted."

". . . And Mr. Woodruff . . ."

"How do. Delighted."

". . . And their son, Larry, news editor, I believe . . ."

"How do. Delighted."

". . . And uh . . ."

"Ted Pearson, executive editor," Ted offered.

"Mr. Pearson, their executive editor," Jesse repeated.

"How do."

"And this," said Jesse, indicating his dirty worker, "is Mr. Mc-Carthy, our newspaper broker."

Everybody nodded and Mr. McCarthy gave us an enormous smile. He must have had a hundred teeth in his head and seemed terribly proud of each one.

Pa made a gesture toward the table. Our guests shed their coats and jostled themselves into chairs, grunting with self-importance as they did so.

I sat myself diagonally across from Mr. Rosenfeldt and watched him with such care that one might have thought I expected a momentary display of violence. He was an unattractive-looking man with none of Jesse's compensating charm and dignity. Slug-eyes and jowls that hung in gray, pasty tribute to an unattended body, and his hair was rotting seaweed. While we waited for the negotiations to begin his hands caressed each other, cobras in love.

"Well," said Pa.

"Uh huh," said the dirty worker.

"Yuh," said I.

Mr. Rosenfeldt finally grabbed the ball and began to run, but toward the sidelines, as if he intended not to gain yardage but to take it home with him.

"Yes, well uh, perhaps I should begin?" And his head bobbed from one to the other of us in what was intended to be an ingratiating way. He must have been around sixty, though it was hard to tell. One got the feeling he'd looked more or less the same always. Then his attention settled on Pa.

"Mr. Woodruff," he began. "The reason for my call last week was a report recently completed by Mr. McCarthy." He nodded and the dirty worker showed us his fine teeth again. "On the advisability of forming a newspaper chain based on the editorial principles and cost ratios with which we have recently been experimenting."

Pa bent an ear, but smiled to compensate for his handicap. "I'm sorry," he said. "The advisability of what?"

Mr. Rosenfeldt repeated the information. A little impatiently, it seemed to me.

"Yes?" Pa said.

"And the findings are most encouraging. But before going into detail, Jesse, would you outline the motives behind our little study?"

"Yes, Papa," Jesse came in on cue.

"Thank you," Mr. Rosenfeldt said.

"Now, as you all doubtless know," Jesse said, "my father heads Ventures, Inc., a company established for the purpose of promoting worthwhile business and industrial enterprises which the average businessman might find somewhat risky . . ."

"Oh really," Mother interrupted. "How useful."

"Yes." Jesse cleared his throat, being unprepared for an interjection at just that point. "Yes," he repeated. "We feel there is a journalistic vacuum at the small-city, big-town level. Because of increased production costs the smaller communities can no longer support a competitive newspaper climate . . ."

Mr. McCarthy nodded, pleased, as if the phrase had been his creation.

". . . Because of the high costs and resulting lack of competition, those papers which have survived usually find themselves with a virtual monopoly. This, quite naturally, leads to neglect of local coverage and increased reliance on the large wire and feature services."

Mr. Rosenfeldt nodded rhythmically throughout his son's discourse, as if to lend an air of authority.

"We consider this a threat to democracy," Jesse continued.

"Oh dear," Mother said.

"By packaging the news through national and international wire services, the opinion of the entire country becomes dependent on relatively few sources for its understanding, and on occasion, *mis*understanding of current events."

"Excuse me," Ted Pearson interrupted. "But you're not suggesting every small newspaper in the country send a man to Korea, Laos, the Congo, etcetera, every time there's a news break."

"Of course not," Jesse said. "But I am suggesting they might better concentrate on local coverage and leave the bigger news to the big newspapers, most of which have been made available to the smaller community." He paused to allow this far from original ideology to sink in.

"The result," he continued, "would be to re-create a local point of view and produce a greater variety of thought, action, and reaction. In short to revitalize the nation's heart and mind.

"Furthermore," Jesse continued, "we feel that an editorial vacuum exists in all papers, large and small, due primarily to an arbitrary division between editorial and straight news coverage. Thus it is our . . ."

"This is all terribly interesting," Pa interrupted. "But I'm not quite sure what it has to do with us."

"Mr. McCarthy," and Mr. Rosenfeldt thereby set another tactical weapon in operation, leaving Jesse a little miffed, apparently, but I guess he was used to it by then. Most sons are.

"Indeed," Mr. McCarthy had somewhere learned to say. "Uh huh!" And he leafed through the mound of papers before him, talking with an air of quiet confidence all the while. "As a result of considerable study," he began, "I believe we have come up, Mr. Woodruff, with positive proof that a daily newspaper"—all this had the singsong quality of a sermon—"when properly managed, can afford to compete at the small-town level."

"How unpleasant," Pa said.

"Here before me"—and he began passing out reports to his right and left like a farmer scattering corn—"are the figures to prove our techniques will cut production costs by as much as twenty-five per-cent, thereby considerably increasing profits. Hmm?" he added for no reason other than personal satisfaction.

Teddy and I glanced over the figures. The initial costs gibed pretty much with ours, but their operating expenses were way down.

"According to this," I said, hoping my nervousness wouldn't show, "you're almost breaking even."

"Quite right," Mr. McCarthy agreed. "And after only three months."

"According to us," I said, "you're losing around four thousand dollars a week."

"Yes, well uhh," the dirty worker began. "We've run into a few uh shall we say unexpected hurdles?" It all seemed more question than statement of fact. "These, however, are the projected operating costs once the kinks of getting a new business going have been worked out."

"The actual costs might have been more to the point," Pa said.

"On the contrary," Mr. Rosenfeldt said. "Eventually *these* will be our actual operating costs. These are the figures you will have to compete with."

"All right," Pa said. "Let's assume for the moment you can do what you say. What"—and he paused—"about it?"

"It is my intention," Mr. Rosenfeldt began, "to form a company which will establish and operate a chain of small competitive dailies throughout the country . . ."

"Competitive until the other fellow goes broke," I mumbled.

He ignored my interruption.

"On the strength of our performance here in Gravenhurst," he continued, "I intend to make each potential competitor the following offer: Sell or die. Quite simple really." He chuckled, wet his lips with a pasty tongue and seemed suddenly to be driven by a force over which he had no control. In all fairness, it was difficult to say whether this was pure enthusiasm or pure greed but in either case it was frightening in its intensity. "In the end"—and he smiled, partially satiated by the prospect—"I expect we will control quite a sizable newspaper empire." He nodded to himself, gorged with satisfaction. "And quite a sizable political force as well."

"How idealistic," Mother said.

This brought him from his reverie.

"Yes," he said, smiling vaguely. "It ought to be quite a help to the profession."

Mother looked at Pa but his mind seemed to have strayed and he apparently had no comment.

"You mentioned the strength of your performance here in Gravenhurst," Mother said. "What exactly did you mean by that?"

Jesse began to fidget. Then he scribbled a note and shoved it in front of his father. I imagined it said *"Watch out for her. She's a tough old bitch,"* and I smiled with pride.

"Yes," Mr. Rosenfeldt said. He read the note and crumpled it. "Excuse me. Now, let's see. Oh yes, the strength of our performance here. Well, uh, we'd like to see you come in with us as proof of our effectiveness. That's why we came to Gravenhurst, you see. Not because your paper looked like an easy mark, but for precisely the opposite reasons . . ."

Mother stared at Jesse, but he declined to notice. Pa began to appear interested and pleased, apparently eager to reject Jesse's earlier explanation with its reference to our journalistic incompetence.

"Really?" he asked.

"Of course," Mr. Rosenfeldt said. "We wanted to establish ourselves by competing with a first-class daily."

"I see," said Pa. "Sound thinking."

"Now if you come in with us we will have proved our effectiveness and be able to give future competitors something to think about when we offer to buy them out."

Jesse was busy scribbling another note, but if his intent was to correct the inconsistencies between his own idealistic declarations and Papa's less esthetic concern for the buck, I'd say he was a little late.

"What kind of an offer did you have in mind?" Pa asked, apparently not too concerned with these distinctions.

"Thirty percent of the chain," Mr. Rosenfeldt said. "In exchange for the *Daily Watch*."

"Hmmm," Pa said. "And it could grow into quite a little empire, as you say."

"It most certainly could," Mr. Rosenfeldt said.

"And if we refuse?" Mother asked.

"Then we will stay here and bleed you to death," Mr. Rosenfeldt said, abandoning any further pretense of idealism. "Which, though it may take a little longer, will serve our purposes equally well and leave you with a hundred percent of nothing."

"Comforting thought," Mother said.

"And what would my position be?" Pa asked.

"Executive publisher," Mr. Rosenfeldt said.

Pa nodded, obviously pleased. "Of course I'd have to think it over," he said. "Yes indeed, quite a political force. I admire your way of doing business, Mr. Rosenfeldt. You and I seem to be cut from the same tree. Not many of us left these days."

"Fortunately," Mother said.

Mr. Rosenfeldt stiffened but Pa stepped in manfully.

"Now look here, Alice. These gentlemen have made us quite an attractive offer. Could conceivably lead to Hartford. Even Washington."

"Even infamy," Mother suggested.

"May I ask"—Mr. Rosenfeldt tried to smile—"may I ask why you find our offer so objectionable?"

"It's quite obvious," Mother said, "that your only interest is profit. I'd have no objection to that, had you been frank about it, but to cloud the issue with all this talk of restoring competition to small newspaper publishing, well, frankly, I find it extremely distasteful."

"I'd like an opportunity to prove you've misjudged me," Mr. Rosenfeldt said. "Our record will show my past efforts have not been purely for personal gain."

"Perhaps I'm not very bright," Mother offered, "but didn't your son begin by saying you were interested in restoring competitive journalism to the small-town level?"

"Uh, that is correct," Mr. Rosenfeldt confirmed.

"Yet you intend to propose that the other fellow sell or die, as I believe you put it. That is hardly my idea of the way to restore competition."

"Ah yes," Mr. Rosenfeldt agreed. "An understandable confusion. I did not mean to suggest that the *Daily Watch* or any other paper with whom we might compete would be, uh . . . liquidated."

"Of course not," Pa interrupted. "I understood that."

"Only merged under one ownership, but with each paper allowed to go its own way editorially."

"A benign despotism," Mother suggested.

"If you will," Mr. Rosenfeldt conceded. "But I think you'll agree it would be more fruitful than the one-paper monopoly existing previous to our inception."

"Perhaps," Mother said. "Though I can't see that a chain would be any more stimulating to the American press than a scattering of individually owned newspapers."

"Ah but the chain is only financial," Mr. Rosenfeldt insisted. "Editorially speaking it would not be a chain at all."

"Mmmm," said Mother. "As long as you chose to leave it that way."

Mr. Rosenfeldt smiled, as though he had detected a slackening in Mother's objections.

"Certainly would be nice if we could work out something together," he said. "I feel as if we were all old friends, don't you know. Heard a good deal about you and your lovely daughter from my son Jesse."

Mother stiffened.

"That's beside the point right now, isn't it, Papa?" Jesse asked.

"Well, under the circumstances," Mr. Rosenfeldt said, "this little meeting shouldn't have to be all business and no play."

"Anyway," Pa interrupted, "before we get carried away with family affairs, if you'll permit me to think this offer over and look

into a few facts and figures of my own as well as those contained in
Mr. McCarthy's report, I should be able to give you an answer sometime next week."

"Oh I don't think that will be necessary," Mother said.

"Why not?" Pa asked.

"I'm sure these gentlemen are very busy with other more pressing
matters," Mother said. "I'd hate to keep them waiting."

"You can't expect me to decide right this minute," Pa said. "That's
absurd."

"Well, you see," Mother said, "there's one item which hasn't been
considered as yet and I think it might clear matters up considerably."

"Namely?" Pa asked, obviously impatient with the female mind.

"The fact," Mother concluded, "that all *Daily Watch* stock is held
in my name."

"Of course," Pa said. "What of it?"

"Just this," Mother said. "I refuse to sell my paper either to you,
Clarence, or to you, Mr. Rosenfeldt."

"*Your* paper," Pa began, then bit his lip for control.

There was a confused silence. Apparently the prospect had not
been considered and consequently not properly rehearsed.

The dirty worker cleared his throat, but there was obviously nothing for him to say. Mr. Rosenfeldt looked from Pa to Mother, from
Mother to Pa, but apparently the ocular exercise produced no new
persuasions.

"Perhaps this is something for the Woodruffs to discuss privately,"
Jesse suggested.

Mr. Rosenfeldt found his tongue. "Yes," he agreed. "My offer
stands, Mr. Woodruff. You can give me a call next week."

Pa nodded, torn between the bad taste of publicly abusing his
wife and the bad show of one of America's foremost capitalists
humbled by the whims of a woman.

There was a general shuffling of papers and chairs and more
inconsequential grunting until the Rosenfeldts and their squire
were coated and ready to depart the field of battle.

"It's been a pleasure," Mr. Rosenfeldt said. "I look forward to
your call."

"Yes," Pa said doubtfully. "I'll be in touch."

Jesse said nothing. He stared at the floor, as though thoroughly
embarrassed.

"Nice meeting you all," the dirty worker said, nodding vigorously in the hopes of transmitting his dubious enthusiasm.

"You bet," I said.

And they departed midst the gentle patter of forced farewells.

"What the hell," Pa began, then caught himself again. "Larry, I won't be needing you and Ted for a while."

Ted went first and I followed slowly, hoping to catch the trend of things to come.

"There's no point discussing it," Mother said. "I'll have nothing to do with the idea."

"Oh you won't, eh?"

"Give up the *Daily Watch* to be a cog in somebody else's wheel?" she asked. "Hardly."

I closed the door and let loose a long sigh of relief.

Ted was waiting for me. "Will she stick to it?" he asked.

"When Mother makes up her mind, that's it."

"Boy," Ted said. "I could use a nice long vacation about now."

"Oh my God. That reminds me."

"What's the matter?"

"I forgot. I'm supposed to go away this weekend."

"So what?" he asked. "It's only Wednesday."

"Well it's kind of a *long* weekend," I explained. "And I was supposed to call her."

"A girl, huh."

"Listen, Ted, could you take the desk Friday and Saturday both? I hate to ask, but it's kind of important."

"Sure. Go ahead."

"Boy, you're a saint," I said.

He laughed and I scooted for the phone booth, pulled Lucy's number out of my wallet and gave it to the operator. It seemed impossible such an insignificant piece of paper could bring us together and I began to feel ridiculous for even trying such foolishness when the buzzing stopped and Lucy was there instead.

"Hi. It's me, Larry Woodruff."

"Hey, I thought you'd forgotten or something."

"Oh no," I said, and laughed to hide my horror of such a possibility, true as it almost was.

"You coming?"

"Tomorrow night," I said.

"Okay," she said. "Come straight to the apartment."

"Great." But there didn't seem to be anything else to say.

"I'll see you tomorrow then," she said.

"Yuh," I said. "I'll see you tomorrow then."

"Well goodbye," she said.

"Well goodbye," she had to say again.

"Yuh," I said. "I'll see you tomorrow."

And Lucy was gone. All so quick I could hardly tell she'd been there.

I came out of the booth in a state of dazed confusion just as Mother was coming down the stairs.

"What's the matter?" she asked. "Don't you feel well either?"

"I'm all right. How's Pa?"

"He's a little upset," Mother admitted. "But likely to recover."

"You were terrific," I said.

She laughed. "It was fun," she said, and waved me goodbye.

"I'll be home soon," I called.

I wandered over and sat down at my new desk, thumbing the notes which had come in for tomorrow's paper. There was one from Jeff Collins reminding me the county executive committee would be meeting that night.

"Hey Jeff," I called. "Is there a file on Ned Polk?"

"Must be."

"Take a look and see how we're fixed for photos," I said. "I've got a hunch we'll be needing one tomorrow."

About that time Pa came down, but he didn't even look at me. Just went right on by, too preoccupied with the humiliations of a fallen capitalist to discuss operations with his new news editor.

CHAPTER XVI

Pa must have been angry with Mother but he didn't show it. His attitude was more "All right, if you don't like the way I run things, then let's see how you can get along without me." And his opinion of the outcome was fairly obvious. Meanwhile, if the night following our meeting with Mr. Rosenfeldt was to be any indication, he was determined to fiddle. This took the form of a few too many martinis before dinner and a slightly miffed air and a refusal to discuss anything concerning the *Daily Watch* or associated problems, but otherwise his mood was fairly genial. At least on the surface. Unfortunately, however, I'm a worrier by nature and so was able to find this very complacency disturbing enough for my needs. There wasn't much I could do about it, though, except try minding my own business for a change, whatever that was. After Mr. Rosenfeldt's "sell or die" pronouncement it was beginning to look as though I might do well to find out.

My lack of experience in the news editing department evidenced itself again the next day when we discovered Ned Polk had indeed succeeded in snatching the senate post but also that Judge Compton had consequently resigned as chairman of the executive committee. Not to have anticipated this development wasn't very serious, but it showed a lack of foresight which I, in my new anxiety, could not afford.

Anyway, I ran both stories under the same head which seemed a fitting way to record the replacement of one favor seeker by another. But though that was the lead, it wasn't half as important to us as a small box insert on page one which announced the municipal printing contract had been awarded to the *Enterprise*. Mayor Healy, with such obvious pleasure it was almost laughable, had called with the news around ten o'clock. I buzzed Pa to tell him but he didn't seem very concerned.

I was delighted when one o'clock rolled around and prospects for getting the hell out of Gravenhurst were my only concern. The idea of seeing Lucy Delevan again made me corny with excitement. I can't quite explain the feeling. It was a cross between the last night of school before Christmas vacation and receipt, at the age of fifteen, of a perfumed letter which begins "Dearest Larry." The fact that no one at home seemed to share in my good humor made it even more priceless and by the time I was ready to leave they were all pretty glad of it. For Hilda I generously bestowed a swat upon her great granite ass which she didn't seem to appreciate in the least. She couldn't be blamed, really, seeing as I had hardly said two words to her in all the months she'd been with us. And for Bollard a couple of not especially clever remarks about what that granite ass might be good for if he had half a mind to try. Bollard was a little old for such humor, as was Mother who happened to be within hearing distance. That left only Pa who was neatly dis-

patched by a statement to the effect that maybe Jesse Rosenfeldt
ought to be named Gravenhurst Man of the Year.

Thence to the showers.

I'm not quite sure just what my plans for Lucy were that night.
Something romantically unpretentious, probably, like the week before. With perhaps a kiss or two in the name of progress.

Anyway, whatever I'd planned was in for major revisions. The
Delevan apartment on East Seventy-second Street, though still
shrouded in summer abandon, was very much alive when I arrived.
Apparently Lucy had been placed in command of invasion forces
from the Northeast and, judging by the condition of the apartment,
I'd say she'd met the challenge, but only barely. Suitcases, most of
them with dinner jackets fresh from the cleaners dashed across their
tops, decorated the entrance hall and a shambles of conversation
filled the air. Since the front door had been wide open, I walked in
with a peering, may-I quality which might have gone completely
unnoticed but for the sudden and thoroughly unwelcome cry of
"*Wombat!*"

I'd nearly managed to forget that charming nickname.

It was Matt Richards who had apparently come down with part
of the Boston contingent for the express purpose of making me more
uncomfortable about my social debut than I already was. Abby
may have been used to this Social Register stuff, but I wasn't and
though I told myself being a Woodruff was just as good as being
from Potters Island, somehow the message never quite sank in.

"Matt," I said, "you old son of a gun." And I decided, but only by
the barest margin, not to run away.

"Wombat," he repeated, though it hardly seemed necessary. "Say,
this is great. Lucy told me you were coming but I couldn't believe
it."

I managed to keep smiling, though it seemed obvious to me his
doubt stemmed from a certain lack of confidence regarding my
social position.

"Quite a shock, huh?" I sympathized.

"I'll say," he admitted.

"Hi Lucy," I called weakly. She was on the phone but managed a
smile and a wave.

"Come on," Matt said. "Let me introduce you."

He did, but there were four other guys and as many girls and I
couldn't remember a single name by the time he was through.

Everybody smiled hard and looked me in the eye, as though they'd been practicing.

Probably it was because of my social discomfort, but they all seemed much glossier than the people I was used to. The men were in their shirtsleeves, all but Matt and me, sporting orange and black suspenders which I gathered represented the Steeple Club or whatever that place was called. And the girls, though not chic by any stretch of the imagination, looked sleek and well-attended. There was such an air of confidence and complacency everywhere that I began to wonder whether these people knew something the Russians and I didn't.

Because I didn't know anybody, Matt took it upon himself to be host, offering me a drink and chattering about good old college days. I half-listened and half-answered and half-eavesdropped in the hopes of establishing some common ground. It didn't look too promising.

Somebody yelled at Lucy, "Say, Dell, tell Old Scotty to wear swimming trunks under his tux *this* time."

Followed by a gentle chuckle of appreciation from all hands. Dell, apparently, was what they called Lucy and the fact I neither knew this nor felt comfortable with the name drove the wedge just a little deeper.

"That Scotty?" A tall, gentle-faced fellow whose name was, I think, Peter, got up and made his way to the phone with an awkward grace. "Say, I've got to have a talk with Old Scotty."

Lucy gave him the phone and he laughed in it for a while, mumbling "Oofly funny" and "Uh Guud" and things like that. He had the kind of soft, like-me face you see in bars from time to time, usually trying to pacify old drunks and, if necessary, denouncing Mother to do it. Not because they were cowards, just out of damn niceness. Had I known him we'd probably have been friends, but I didn't so he seemed sort of asinine.

"Tell him hoy," one of the girls requested.

"For me too," another one said.

"He'll be here in half an hour," Lucy said. "Control yourselves."

"Oh muveless."

"Scott still with the Guaranty?"

"Far's I know."

"What a wild man. Never thought he'd stick it out."

"Neither'd I."

"Long's it been now?"

"Almost a year."

"Say, that's something."

"Never know, do you?"

There didn't seem to be an opening so Matt and I continued to work on our own old times. He had always been sort of an arrogant bastard at college, but I liked him anyway, primarily because of his slightly morbid sense of humor.

But after talking to him awhile, I began to suspect Matt had lost a good deal of his undergraduate confidence. He seemed much more agreeable than I remembered and, when addressing his summer friends, almost obsequious. However, more than likely this was only another manifestation of my own discomfort, for as the whiskey began to do its job I found such subtle changes of character more and more difficult to detect. Pretty soon I was even talking to people, with Matt's help, of course.

"Hey Dolph, Wombat here's got wheels, so if you want to drive down with us there's plenty of room."

Dolph was a thick, blond-browed character named Randolph Edwards. "Sure," he said, but I could see he was hedging for a more companionable offer.

Then after a while I succeeded in starting a few conversations all by myself. Trying to match Gravenhurst lore with tales of Potters Island and Harvard-Yale games and the Stork Club wasn't easy unless the truth was pretty heavily salted with comic fabrication so I considered it quite a feather in my cap when any of them listened at all.

Lucy was on the phone almost continuously, offering rides and giving directions and otherwise making herself unbearably useful, so I decided there was no choice but to make an effort. That's something I haven't had to do much. Not before or since freshman year. But I couldn't see just tagging along all weekend with people wondering who the hell the quiet little provincial was, so it seemed like a good idea at least to make a bid for group comedian.

Therefore, when a girl who seemed to be one of those amateur psychiatrist types, asked me what I did I told her I was a junky. Apparently that drew a blank because she nodded mysteriously and asked if I found it interesting. Luckily Dolph was one of those easy laughers because I realized it was a three-drink joke and not good for much.

"Hey, Wombat," he said. "Ha ha ha."

"Just call me Bat," I said. "It's friendlier."

"Hey what *do* you do?" he asked. "I mean besides take dope and hold up gas stations."

"I work on a newspaper."

"Reporter?"

"News editor."

"No kidding." He was impressed, also baffled. "In New York?"

"No. It's just a small-town paper in Connecticut."

"Oh," he seemed relieved. "Well don't worry about it. Maybe someday."

"And you?" I asked.

"Me? I'm a trainee in a Boston investment firm."

"Well don't worry about it. Maybe someday."

"He's not worried," Matt interrupted. "It's his old man's firm."

"Well I'm not either," I said. "It's my old man's paper."

"Great," Dolph said. "Now we've got something in common."

"Wassat?"

"Lack of ambition."

Which seemed a very desirable thing to have, or rather *lack*, because everybody laughed in a warm conspiratorial way obviously meant to include me.

"I'll drink to that," I said.

By then we had formed a little group on the floor next to the bar and I guess we were beginning to develop status because pretty soon the tall one called Peter drifted over and sat down midst a gurgle of "Say nows" and "Uh oh, looks like trouble" and the like. Then a girl or two. Then three or four, until pretty soon the whole gang had regrouped except for Lucy who sat chained to that damn phone. It seemed like a good time for making points so I went over to ask if she wanted a drink or something. Halfway there this Dolph character had to steal my action.

"Hey Wombat," he called. "See if Dell needs a drink, will you?"

"Dolph, you're an angel," Lucy called back. "I'd love some bourbon."

How do you like that?

Then we got to talking about Abby whom Peter had met at some party or other, though he was absolutely positive *his* Abigail Woodruff came from Century Park.

"*Near* Century Park," I corrected. He seemed a bit upset.

I never really did get a chance to talk with Lucy all night. Not because she was on the phone continuously, but people kept arriving. Scotty, for instance, who offered to put the stags up at his place, including me, if one of us didn't mind sleeping on the floor. I had a pretty good idea which one. And there were some bridesmaids who'd be staying with Lucy and some others who just dropped by to chat before the Big Weekend.

By around ten o'clock most of the male members of our little group were pretty cockeyed and not in much shape to talk to anyone but each other. Somebody got the idea of going down to the Village to meet a Beat and I, in my hyper-cooperation, had to volunteer to call one whom I happened to know personally.

Unfortunately Tommy Compton was home and feeling pretty chipper, I guess, because he offered to meet us at a place where you could get authentic pizza and Beatniks. His being so chipper should have made me suspicious right off, but it didn't. When we finally got organized there weren't too many of us. Just Dolph and Matt and the one called Peter. None of the girls seemed to think we were such a good idea. Even Scotty, our future host, declined with the warning that we for Guud's sakes be quiet coming in because the landlord was a thoroughgoing buustard.

On the way down to the Village I began to get self-conscious about Tommy. After all, whatever he did would reflect on me and despite the carelessness which is supposed to accompany an overdose of whiskey, I was, shamefully, still uneasy about my glossy new friends.

The pizza place was big with high, breezy ceilings and a certain charmless charm. The only apparent effort on the part of the proprietor to decorate his establishment was consummated in an occasional Japanese lantern dangling from lofty naked girders. Other than that, it was up to his patrons who, judging by the abstract art covering the walls, seemed to have tackled the job with considerable enthusiasm, if nothing else. You can't blame people for trying to find some new means of expression, I guess. It's too bad they couldn't have been a little more successful, that's all. But since we were dressed in suits and such accompanying oddities as ties and socks and the like, I felt pretty touristy and not up to sharing my opinions with the Bohemia at large now languishing around us.

We found Tommy, alone but for an avant-garde magazine or two tastefully arranged in front of him.

I made the introductions, listening carefully for any signs of discord which might result from this blend of bluejeans and flannel. But fortunately alcohol had revitalized the democratic myth and my Potters Island friends were not even a little patronizing. I was proud of them.

"Well," I said, not quite matching their love for the Common Man, "this is quite a nice place, I guess."

"Hey," Peter yelled. "What are you supposed to order in a dump like this, coffee or something?" Then he looked around carefully, not prepared to back up the bravado.

Tommy didn't answer. Instead he moved one of his magazines a careful two inches to the left.

"There's a bar," I said after a brief search.

"What you got there?" Dolph asked, poking at one of the magazines.

"Magazine," Tommy said.

Dolph looked at him as if he had just discovered a creature heretofore believed to be extinct.

But Tommy seemed unconcerned, apparently sublimated by a source of satisfaction greater than public approbation.

"That's what I figured," Dolph said. "Could I see it?"

"Christ, let's eat," Peter said, his pleasing manner definitely on the wane.

"Sure," Tommy said without offering the magazine. "If you want to."

Dolph picked the thing up and started thumbing through, but it didn't seem to hold a message for him.

"Very interesting," he said and returned it.

Tommy didn't say anything.

"Hey," Matt said, "I thought people recited poetry and things like that."

"Tell him they do," Tommy said to me.

"When?" I asked.

"When they feel like it," Tommy said.

"Oh," I said. "They do," I told Peter.

"When?"

"When they feel like it."

Peter nodded, gave up trying. "Hey you," he called to what looked like a waiter, though it might have been a customer on the way out. "How about getting something to eat, huh?"

"What's his trouble?" I asked.

"Poor bastard sells mutual funds," Dolph said. "So he's got to take it out on somebody."

"Oh sure," I supposed. "That figures."

The place was kind of dark, but you could see brown clumps of people through the gloom, hunched in talk or languishing in a state of aloof contemplation. There was something nice and safe about it all, like being back in college.

Then suddenly somebody started reciting. At least I assumed that's what he was doing. Our waiter was taking orders at the time and in the confusion of talk about pizzas and beer and the distance and the darkness I thought at first there was a fight going on or something.

Whatever it was didn't sound much like poetry and I guessed maybe he was reading some of the more exciting passages from his latest novel.

"We give beauty, mysticism and meaning to the dull soul of life," he read, and: "You shit too, if you eat regular."

And suddenly the recitation was over. Nobody applauded. They just stared at him awhile, as if unaware he'd stopped, then turned back to their own conversations.

"What the hell's that?" Peter yelled. "Some nut?"

Finally the pizzas arrived. My fellow tourists and I were so hungry we forgot about the Beatnik message and buried ourselves in a gooey salvation. Peter, who still appeared slightly suspicious of our new surroundings, was the first to notice Tommy had quietly climbed onto his chair.

"Hey look out," he said. "He's one too."

We all stared with pizza hanging off our chins.

Tommy cleared his throat and began.

"Boom boom boom boom. Blood on the ground and beasts in the womb. Boom boom boom boom. Big bombs, little bombs, bang baroom."

And then he sat down.

None of us knew just what to say.

"Well," he said, sort of relaxed and easy. "That ought to hold the bastards."

"Huh?" I asked.

"It's sort of the thing to do," he explained. "Some of my friends were getting a little worried about me."

Peter leaned across. "He all right?"

Tommy laughed. "I'm sorry," he said. "I was kind of nervous."

"You do it often?" Dolph asked.

"First time," Tommy said.

Somebody shuffled out of the gloom. "Nice, man," he said. "Real nice," and shuffled off.

"Who was that?" I asked.

Tommy shrugged. "A friend."

"Well it's good to know you're only crazy part of the time," I said. "I was beginning to worry."

"*You* were," said Dolph and showed his concern with a long, sighing whistle.

"Hey, if you're not really a beat," said Peter suspiciously, "then what the hell are you?"

"I don't know," Tommy said. "What are you?"

"I'm a goddam mutual fund salesman," Peter said. "Anybody knows that."

Tommy laughed but said he guessed he had to go, and did without saying so long, it's nice to have met your or any of that, he just kind of wandered off. I had the feeling at least three different people had been in his seat.

"Boy," Peter said. "You sure got some nutty friends, Wombat."

"That's Harvard for you," I kidded.

"Harvard?" Dolph asked.

"Sure," I said. "Class of fifty-five."

"God Almighty," Dolph said. "We were *class*mates."

"I'll be damned," Peter said. "I thought he went to Williams or someplace."

"Well anyway, I'll bet he wasn't in a club," Dolph said.

"Hell no," Peter said. "Of course he wasn't."

That seemed to straighten things out pretty well.

It was after three when we got back to Scotty's place and going on four by the time we got through placating the landlord. Dolph, apparently, had rung all the doorbells in the building and the results were fairly unpleasant. Scotty was quite correct. The landlord was a thoroughgoing bastard all right. But he forgot to mention the tenants. They didn't seem like a very agreeable lot either.

CHAPTER XVII

The next morning was a re-enactment of college hangover days. Scattered clothes, piles of change and keys and Life Savers, an early edition of the *Daily News* somebody'd picked up on the way home. These things formed the background for an unrelated flow of semiconscious conversation concerning the internal disorders we attributed to our underfried eggs and stale coffee.

On the way to Lucy's we took time out for a couple of Bloody Marys and stopped at a delicatessen to buy some beer for the drive down. When we reached the apartment everybody was feeling fairly pleased with himself again. If nothing else, this compensated for Lucy's lack of approval. We were supposed to be in Maryland by midafternoon and it was already close to twelve.

I wanted to cooperate but the importance of this information refused to penetrate. "Have a drink, Dell, old girl," I suggested. "Put hair on your chest."

"The name's Lucy," she hissed, after all the effort I'd made to become one of the gang. I don't think anybody else heard her but the effect was just as devastating. It was as if I'd stepped on a nail. My stride was broken and the others went trotting by.

Fortunately, since I was busy with the driving, nobody noticed I'd fallen behind. That did nothing to explain why she'd done it, though, which was my real concern. Pretty soon our beer did its job and the boys needed a head call, so I got a chance to ask her what was wrong.

"I'm sorry," she said. "I just didn't want you to be like everybody else."

"Well, right now that's exactly what I want to be," I said. "This is supposed to be fun, remember?"

"I know," she said. "I'm sorry." Then Lucy did an extraordinary thing. She leaned across and kissed me which proved to be a most miraculous cure.

As a result, the rest of the drive was quite pleasant. By then we were beyond the murky stink of Jersey flatlands, pushing into summertime again at the rate of more than a mile a minute and, except for the occasional sharklike appearance of a parkway police car, I felt downright invincible.

They told me plenty about The Island. Dolph even managed to make fun of the place a little. For instance, he claimed a lot of people referred to it as Potters Retreat because most everybody who went there belonged in a funny farm. But it was easy to see he wouldn't have appreciated such wisecracks from me or any other outsider.

We left the car in a little town south of Annapolis and took the ferry from there. I felt somewhat emasculated without my convertible, but they all assured me I'd get along all right.

From the instant we were on board life became a delicate, wishful fantasy of ante-depression days. There were quite a number of slightly used, but well looked after Golden Girls who hid their years behind careful tans and gay summer dresses with husbands who wore ascots and tweed jackets and managed to combine elegance with a touch of suspicion. And there were others: sensible, tweedy round women and open-faced class reunionists who probably sailed a lot and looked their best after a wet day of racing. Only a few children were along. What with the summer being officially over, I guess most of them had previous engagements back home with Nanny. Everybody knew everybody else, including the local people who apparently supplied the many services needed to maintain so complicated an anachronism.

The crossing took about half an hour, most of which was spent exchanging greetings and establishing an atmosphere of warmth and friendship which seemed so deep, so firmly rooted in time that I could only suppose it too had been inherited.

Our bridesmaid friends of the night before were on the same ferry, having driven down with Scotty and some guy I hadn't met. This gave me people to wave at too, so by the time we reached the Pot, I was beginning to feel quite at home. However, it proved to be something of a delusion.

The ferry sidled in through a jumble of fishing boats while Lucy explained what everything was all about. "See those big ones," she said. "They're oyster boats. The little ones are for crabbing."

"Crabbing?"

"Soft-shell crabs," she explained.

"God," I said. "Pa'd go crazy here."

"We all do," she laughed.

"What are those things?"

"Crab sheds. That's where they keep them until they lose their shells."

"Will we be able to get any?"

"Just frozen ones. Now's the oyster season." She took a deep breath. "Doesn't it smell good?"

It was a rich sea smell, faintly fishy but sweet and fresh.

"God, I love it here," she said.

The ferry scraped to a gentle stop and we began to scramble ashore midst a smattering of talk about the weather and such things which seemed intended to give the weekenders a feeling of year-round participation in the island's life.

"Croker, I think it's time something was done about this old ferry. Turning into a bit of a relic, don't you know."

"Well it's the onliest way you kin get here."

"That's just the trouble, my good man. Time people got together and thought about replacing it."

"It's a mighty small place for people," said Croker. "Don't expect you'd find many as could afford such doings."

"Well something should be done."

"Yup," said Croker. "Something should be done all right."

But it seemed to me our next mode of transportation needed up-dating far more than the ferry. After following the gang a little ways I found myself in the courtyard of a stable. Surrounding us were phaetons and victorias, hansom cabs, gigs and sulkies, broughams and buggies—in short, every conceivable form of horse-drawn transportation.

"Uncle Paul was supposed to have made arrangements for us," Lucy said. "Wait'll I go see."

I must say she seemed alarmingly at home.

Dolph and Peter went with her to find out what if anything was available for them.

"Hey Matt, doesn't anybody have cars?" I asked.

"Oh sure," he said. "The local people have a few. And most everybody has a Volks or something at home in case of emergency. But we try to limit it to bikes and buggies."

I just nodded and watched doubtfully as the colored stable boys led the various carriages to their owners. The *clip clopping*, the sweet stable smells, the slap of reins and rustle of harness and soft commands of "Whoa, boy, easy boy, whoa now, whoa." It took a little getting used to.

Some of the more elegant carriages had drivers—nothing fancy, just the gardener or handyman—but most were handled by the men of the family or, in some cases, the women. It was just that lack of pomp which supplied an air of authenticity and turned what might have been a futile gesture into something warm and genuine.

After a while Dolph made an appearance on a sulky drawn by a high-stepping mare obviously in a hurry. "Meet the family hot rod," he shouted and clattered through the gate, slightly out of control, it seemed to me.

A few minutes later Lucy came out followed by a couple of four-wheelers, each drawn by matched chestnuts. Peter offered to drive one and she took the other and the rest of us piled in, suitcases and all, as casually as a turn of the century family on its way to the country for summer holidays.

"See what I mean?" Lucy asked. "I'll bet Gravenhurst was never like this."

"Not for quite a few years," I admitted.

Then she laughed, but with a touch of triumph meant only half for me, it seemed, and half for the thrill of returning to Potters Island.

I don't know what I expected to follow. Perhaps we would gallop off to a fairyland of time past, but the fact that we departed at a rather bored trot along roads no different from modern country roads anywhere else helped to maintain a measure of reality.

The houses we passed all seemed remarkably unimpressive. At least from the outside. Not one of them, happily, would have been a likely *House and Garden* selection. They had none of that over-manicured quality which can make a naturally beautiful piece of property look more like the reception room in an advertising agency. Instead they seemed to blend with the natural disorder of maple and birch and scraggy pine which gave the island a rough New England countenance.

The first house we came to robbed us of three bridesmaids. Next was Peter's which, though marvelously located on a cliff jutting over the ocean, was embarrassingly small by Gravenhurst's rule of status, and a prefab to boot. Then to make things even more confusing, Matt had to live in a house which looked more like a Maine summer camp than the southern spectacle I had for some reason imagined.

That left only Lucy and me, so I climbed into the driver's seat with her and began horsing around, pretending the orange sky behind us was actually the burning of Atlanta. It couldn't have been a very convincing performance. I just kept mumbling "Miss Ske-eyahlet, A don know nuffin bout burfin babies," and looking back for the flames of Tara. All of which had nothing to do with Potters Island, as far as I can see, and not a hell of a lot to do with *Gone With the Wind* either.

But I was enjoying myself.

Then Lucy gave the reins a good thwack which caused us to depart Atlanta at a much faster rate than seemed consistent with the rules of safety, so I shut up.

A few minutes later we arrived at the Delevans and their house turned out to be the biggest surprise of all. From in front it seemed to be about the same size and style as Matt's place, being made of shingles and surrounded by a terrace of rough pine. But though it seemed only a two-story house from the inland side, from the ocean it looked like a seaside resort, having continued down the cliff for two more floors. At the entrance level was a big living room and study, with the dining room, kitchen, and maid's rooms one floor down, and bedrooms at the top and bottom.

Of course, on arrival I knew none of this and thought it was just a nice little summer cottage like the others. By discovering it was something more, I became aware of the first Potters Island commandment regarding wealth: hide it. It was a nice law. The Woodruffs would have approved. In fact, as far as I could see the Woodruffs would have approved of just about everything about Potters Island and its summer inhabitants. Therefore, I don't understand why they made me so damned sensitive. Unless it was because I wasn't sure whether the Potters Islanders would have approved of us.

Lucy didn't get much of a reception. Everybody was too busy getting into everybody else's way. I dropped our bags in the hall and followed her onto a side terrace where most of the noise seemed to be originating. The project, apparently, was to raise a large papier-mâché leopard, which I later discovered to be the Steeple Club symbol, to the top of the orange and black striped marquee pitched for Saturday's reception. The workmen who were bouncing around on top of the tent seemed to be having more fun than the rest, but the paying customers were enjoying themselves too.

After a while they succeeded and people who until then had been making little waving motions and nodding at us, the way they do in church, were free to come over and say hello.

I met Lucy's aunt, but she was too busy to tell me her life story just then. She appeared to be one of the Golden Girls and somewhat past her prime.

Uncle Paul had more time to spare due, he claimed, to a real talent for delegating authority. "Ho ho, how 'bout a little drink?"

And I was introduced to the others, parents of the groom and assorted relatives including Lucy's father, Charles, pronounced Cholly, Delevan. He was something of a shock to me. I must have expected a tall, hollow-cheeked pundit who would stand at the fringes of humanity and watch with benign disapproval. The fact that he seemed not very different from the others was quite intolerable. However, there were compensations. He was about my size, including the ears, I'm sorry to say, and except for a touch of gray along the temples, his hair was a thick brown helmet still. In short he might very easily have been nicknamed Wombat too. Naturally I liked him immediately.

"'Lo Woodruff," he said. "Glad to meet you."

Possibly he greeted everyone that way, but at the time it didn't occur to me and the use of my surname had a brusque, conspiratorial quality which seemed to set us, as members of the working press, high above ordinary people.

I hitched my pants and considered adopting a look of tolerant cynicism. "Same here," I said.

"How's your old man?" he asked. "Haven't seen him in years."

"He's fine. Sends his best," which wasn't really a lie because I'm sure he would have, had his own problems not been or seemed so pressing.

"Didn't think he'd remember me," the great man said. "I was a couple of years behind him at Princeton and he was big campus editor in those days."

"Sure he remembers you," I said. "We run your column."

"Still publishing the old what's-it-called, eh?"

"*Daily Watch,*" I said, trying by the tone of my voice to inject a note of importance which I really didn't feel. "He's still at it all right."

There didn't seem to be anything to say after that. The pundit watched me awhile, apparently not bothered by the silence. Then he nodded, said, "Well," smiled, and walked off.

Before my social life had time to progress further Lucy's aunt sailed by chanting "Rehearsal, rehearsal, rehearsal. Wedding party, wedding party," until I was afraid she'd never get the egg laid.

Then Lucy came over to explain I'd have to go it alone for a while, at least until the rehearsal was over. She told me where my room was and I went down for a little nap before my Potters Island debut.

Actually I didn't sleep, but lay listening to the house sounds of a make-believe world which had somehow come true: the brittle crunch of carriage wheels in the driveway, the hesitant tinkle of an old-fashioned grinder telephone, voices and laughter of people I didn't know but already envied, though I wasn't quite sure why. When you thought about it the only real difference between this place and home involved matters of taste. Nevertheless, the effect of this seemingly trivial difference was a powerful one. The interior of the house, so unlike the outside, with its delicately gay chintzes and white wicker furniture. The soft blue wallpaper and gentle paintings of local scenes obviously done by friends, yet pleasing in color and mood. Occasional pieces of French Provincial furniture upholstered in fresh, bright colors, and rag mats splashing across the floor. These visual signs of taste blended with the manners of the people: laughter tuned to quality rather than volume, a friend's cigarette lit not to make a point of it, but as part of the conversation. No social games were being played here. There were no mayors on the make, no call for the kind of mannered graciousness which conceals an envious heart, no social prostitution, none of the stuff— stinking or otherwise—of which Gravenhurst was made. Why should there be? These people weren't going anywhere.

Perhaps it was only a mask they wore, but at least their purpose was to hide the relentless face of time and how much better this method than the golden-ruled righteousness of Gravenhurst! Better even when not wholly successful as with the Golden Girls whose colors had tarnished somewhat, for in their failure was a touch of gallantry rather than dreary resignation.

At least so it seemed to me, but at that point I was still a some-what impressionable witness.

From outside came a new wave of chatter and crunching of

gravel which probably meant the rehearsal was over so I got up and started dressing. Old sun was just finishing up in a blaze of promise. An offshore breeze gave the Chesapeake a look of hammered silver and, as I watched, lights from the mainland began to show in the approaching dusk. The gulls homed in twilight silence and it seemed time might stop its relentless onslaught after all. I turned away, saddened by something not quite clear to me when the bathroom door began to rattle and bang.

"You sure are slow," Lucy called. "Is there really so much to be done with a face like yours?"

"You ought to see it before it's been fixed up," I laughed.

"No thanks."

"Are we neighbors?" But though the question was meant to be offhand, I'm afraid a certain husky quality crept in to betray my eagerness.

"That's right," Lucy confirmed. "Sexy, huh?"

"Yuh. Oh yuh."

"Are you decent?"

"Some people think I'm downright genteel."

"Good," she said, and the door was opened. "Well, well, don't you look ravishing." She grabbed the sash of my bathrobe and gave it a yank which was almost disastrous.

"Hey, careful," I said.

"I just wanted to see if you were comfortable," she said, her face a blend of teasing and flirting.

"That's a hell of a way to find out."

"I didn't mean that," she said, coloring.

By then we were both leaning against the bathroom wall, not quite touching, tempting each other.

"Oh," I said pointlessly. "I thought maybe you did."

"No," she said. "I didn't."

"Well what makes you so full of the devil?"

"Full of the devil?"

We kissed and a torrent of longing burst inside me in a cascade of wonder and love and sweet relief. We held each other and kissed and touched and tried to share and then she pushed away. I could feel a hesitancy in the linger of her fingers and see it in the secret sadness of her eyes. The door swung open and the light fell across and she was gone.

CHAPTER XVIII

My first impressions of Potters Island were favorable enough, but they were doubly so shortly after our arrival at the bridal dinner given by Lucy's grandmother. The atmosphere was so informal I couldn't help but relax, yet due to the simple elegance of her furnishings, not informal to the point of drabness. The women were dressed pretty much in accordance with the custom of their winter communities, Boston and Philadelphia entries being inclined to pointedly styleless creations while the high-stepping New Yorkers displayed a bit more chic. Most of the young men wore black dinner jackets, while the older and more privileged were apparently permitted the indulgence of a special island outfit. It consisted of a crimson blazer, bow tie representing some club or other, but most of them the orange and black of Steeple, and white ducks usually a bit frayed at the cuffs. One had the feeling such casualness had not been easy to come by. Nor had the color combination which, while not in perfect harmony, apparently more than compensated by being *right*.

But right or wrong, chic or shabby, it was all very jolly and by the time dinner got announced the three or four martinis I had put away were dancing somewhat recklessly on my empty stomach. With Lucy in the wedding party I looked forward to a fairly lonely interlude, but the dinner worked out all right because Matt was at my table and so was Mr. Delevan and the girls looked just like those bridesmaids from Boston. There was only one other male at the table and he seemed a bit surly, as though he might very well have come from Gravenhurst too, so I felt right at home.

As a matter of fact it was sort of nice not sitting with Lucy, because then I could spy on her to my heart's content. Fortunately, her taste in clothes was of the New York school and she looked terrific. Her evening dress was bell shaped and seemed to encase her in a fragile, wistful delicacy, and the auburn gold colors of her hair glowed in the candlelight and she sent a secret smile my way from time to time.

The orchestra played with misty nostalgia, whispering of a past and sweet silver memories and I longed to be caught in its spell, but was caught instead in the obligations attending it. There was dancing between courses so I offered my services to the girls on either side of me on the theory it was easier to dance than enjoy myself.

The rest of the time was passed gulping champagne and roast beef as a means of ignoring those painful lapses in the conversation. But as the meal progressed it was the lapse of lapses which became more painful than the lapses themselves. To put it more plainly, as Mr. Delevan got drunker he got ruder. Some of his remarks, though not at all complimentary to Potters Island, at least had the grace to be funny, but unfortunately I laughed nervously at whatever he said, whether it amused me or not. This only made the surly member of the group surlier and eventually caused a considerable rift in our little dining alliance.

Later, when everyone else at the table happened to be dancing or otherwise occupied, the surly one launched an attack by asking where I had gone to college.

When I told him he looked enlightened, as if it explained many things, and took pity on me. He even managed to smile and say he thought there was one like me right there on the island.

"Matt Richards?" I asked.

"Who?"

"Matt Richards," I repeated.

"I don't know him very well," he said. "But it could be."

Then he leaned forward and with a surreptitious glance to left and right announced: "Do you know there are twenty-nine members of the Steeple Club on the island?"

"No," I said. "Really?"

"That's right. And only three Fly."

"Well I'll be damned."

He studied me carefully to see whether I had fully appreciated the import of his remarks. Apparently I had for he then said: "My name's C. Dudley Morehouse," as if it were some sort of astral sign.

"Larry Woodruff," I said, though it didn't seem relevant.

"You're a friend of Lucy's, aren't you?"

"Yes I am."

"Well her uncle is Steeple," he said.

I decided he was either drunk or nuts and was considering a call for help when someone began rapping on a water glass.

I'd assumed there would be toasting, but it had never occurred to me there would be so much. Whereas I am inclined to twitch nervously at the very thought of a public speech, these people seemed to welcome the challenge. Almost everyone made a contribution, including many of the women, and astonishingly enough most of them were pretty good. Especially the Steeple Clubbers who seemed to make a hobby of after-dinner speeches, recitations, songs, and the like. Mr. Delevan, father of the bride, made one of the more memorable contributions.

"I hope these young people will love each other," said he, "as much as I love . . ." And he paused for a suitable comparison, studied his wife as if considering her candidacy, then concluded: "As much as I love Potters Island."

After him came a mounting crescendo as each person who spoke thereby obligated two or three others to do likewise, and through it all the bride and groom sat glazed in smiles. I'd met them before dinner and could, if pressed, still remember their names. His was Ham Elliott, Hamilton Kingsley Elliott, known as the Kingfish, and she was Leslie, a delicate little thing on first impression but not on second. If it seems an oversight not to have mentioned them sooner, the fact is, until after dinner, they hadn't played much of a part in the proceedings. But both finally managed to toast each other, a ritual which consisted of revealing their impressions on meeting for the first time. The groom's confessions were brief but amusing because of an air of bewildered innocence. He was tall and dignified beyond his years, with a piercing nose and a mouth neither soft nor strong, but elegantly controlled. He said almost nothing, but left the definite impression something terribly worthwhile had taken place.

Leslie, for her part, put the confessions in poetic form:

> "Twas the twelfth of November,
> Though cruel to remind,
> Fair Harvard had lost
> And the Kingfish was blind."

And so on with a few intimate details about what the back seat of a car is for. There were times when it got a little rough for my provincial ears, but not for anyone else's, apparently.

Until that point I'd been enjoying myself, sitting back with an outsider's critical immunity, measuring the proficiency of each toast, but as more and more people took to their feet it occurred to me I too might be expected to make a few pithy, postprandial remarks and complacency turned to terror. From that point on I sat numbly listening, heart pounding, searching for other toastless ones, finding fewer and fewer, until thoroughly convinced I was the only one who hadn't done his duty. The whispered references to my rude, rustic, and ungrateful ways seemed almost audible and I suddenly found myself wondering what Jesse Rosenfeldt would have done under similar circumstances. How absurd can you get?

Finally, in a boil of rampant fright and confusion, I prepared to rattle a glass and take to my feet. Then, thank God, there was a general scraping of chairs, dinner was over and I was spared the embarrassment. About half the people began heading downstairs to what could only be a bar and the rest stayed to dance. I saw Dolph had cornered Lucy so Matt and I chose the bar. The mantle of gentle manners had been raised a little, revealing a roughness of laughter and conversation somewhat more reminiscent of a Gravenhurst social gathering than one might have suspected and I began to feel more comfortable. On my way to the bar I brushed past Lucy's father who was locked in combat with my friend Peter.

"I'm a poet, goddam it. You may be a goddam journalist, but I'm a goddam poet."

"I had some idea you were in the mutual fund business."

"No, no no, I'm a goddam poet."

"I see. Well all right then."

I lost Matt somewhere along the line and wandered back upstairs to see how Lucy was getting along without me. She was still dancing with Dolph so I cut in with as masterful an air as I could muster.

"Wow," she said. "What's got into you?"

" 'Bout half a gallon," I admitted.

But that was as far as we got because right away somebody cut in. I returned to the fringes and watched and envied. She seemed to be giving herself so completely to the enjoyment of her partner I was afraid there would be nothing left for me. And since her inviting me to Potters in the first place had been little more than a whim, this might easily have been so.

After a while I tried dancing once more, but that time we only got as far as: "Golly, I haven't seen any of these people for years," before I was sidelined again. It wasn't even good exercise so I finally gave up and headed for the bar, leaving Lucy to her reunion. Dolph was there, having an angry conversation with some guy I hadn't met. I listened for a while, but it didn't seem like quite my cup of tea so I wandered into another room and found the Delevan brothers with a large group of the younger set who had given up the pretended indifference of their elders and gathered around in hopes the pundit would spout a wise old political adage or two. He was spouting all right.

"All you do," he was telling his brother, "is collect new evidence to support old ideas. Why not collect some new ideas for a change?" He smiled at his own cleverness and drank without listening.

"Wait," his brother insisted. "Wait jus' a minute now. I happen to know the undersecretary intimately so don't tell *me* I don't know what's going on in Washington."

The pundit shrugged, unimpressed.

Heads swiveled, confused, not quite sure who was serving.

"Now look here, Cholly, if you're so damned smart perhaps you knew he and I went shooting every fall."

"No," the pundit said. "You're not serious."

"Well I can't think of a better way to get to know a man's thinking."

"About ducks?" the pundit asked.

"About everything," his brother said. "And I know well z'anybody in Washington this is jus' the goddam New Deal all over again, only worse."

"Did the undersecretary tell you that?"

"Not 'zactly," Paul Delevan said. "But he said things could get a lot worse before they got better."

"Well, well, well."

"Listen," Paul Delevan said. "That's a straight from the horse's mouth."

"You're quite sure it was the mouth?"

"Now wait a minute, Cholly," Paul Delevan seemed to plead. "This is a serious discussion."

The pundit began to fidget, but more in anger than boredom.

"The trouble with you, Paul," he said, "is you think you run the whole goddam country on the strength of a duck-hunting expedition once or twice a year with the people who do." And again he laughed at himself generously.

"Goddam it, Cholly, you're an arrogant bastard."

The pundit continued laughing, got up and toppled off in the direction of the bar.

His brother tried to wipe the anger away but succeeded only in smearing it into a drunken mess. Then he turned to a young man whose age required politeness and set out to restore his shattered ego.

"I had dinner last week with the Secretary of the Treasury," he explained. "That is he happened to stop by the club around dinnertime. Now I've known Winthrop since we were boys. Don't care who he is. Just Old 'Winner' to me. He said the very same thing. I'm absolutely serious about this. He said things could very easily get a lot worse before they got better. Now coming from him . . ." And on and on he went, begging us to agree his life had served a purpose simply from having been garnished with a flavoring of greatness—someone else's. I'd have been willing to help him with his lie, but there didn't seem to be any way.

It occurred to me the problem might not be his alone. Considering the opportunity which now lay abandoned here on Potters Island, souring in the dampness of time, it seemed hard to believe so little *had* been accomplished. Here were the vintage wines of America, carefully nurtured through the seasons. The best schools, the best colleges; bottled in Brooks Brothers' finest, stored in the cool cellars of taste, refinement and money, yet what was the result? A Secretary of the Treasury here, a pundit there, but not very much really, considering the investment. Perhaps the vines themselves were impure, unworthy of so much attention, or perhaps the very care they received had somehow sapped their power. Both possibilities were tragedies, one for the grower, the other for the grown, and I began to suspect these people knew it. There was a frustration about them which, nurtured in alcohol, had now grown to a tentacled, soul-eating monster. A tremble of violence became part of the night. Drunkenness had carried too many people too far beyond the boundaries of custom and it seemed even the slightest difference of opinion could spread like fire through the complicated scaffolding of which this community was made.

Had these people built their gracious and magnificent tower for some purpose other than simply to honor itself, then perhaps this would not have been true. But they hadn't and therefore, instead of a tower reaching for achievement, theirs was a necropolis honoring tradition, the past and death. Except in the arrogance of style, not so different from our Gravenhurst architecture.

I glanced at my watch. It was after two and I went to find Lucy. She was still dancing but not with Dolph, happily.

"Where've you *been?*" she asked with such sincerity I immediately became suspicious.

"You seemed to be getting along all right," I said.

"That doesn't mean I wouldn't have rather been with you," she said.

Haunted, I suppose, by a deep conviction of my own inadequacy, I pushed away to see her face. The teasing I'd expected to find was not there.

"Really," she smiled.

I pressed her and she came against me in sweet submission. Her cheek touched softly and we became one.

"Couldn't we go?" I asked. "Before someone steals you again."

"Sure," she said.

"I didn't think it would be that easy," I admitted.

"Enough's enough," she explained.

I started to pull back, but she held me for a second. I wasn't sure she'd meant to, but it was nice anyway.

As we left a cluster of men in black and red jackets hovered near the front door. It looked like there'd been a fight or a sick drunk or both and all the king's men were working feverishly to put Humpty Dumpty together again. We hurried off before their broken rhythms became ours.

The night was warm and moonless black, the better to hide in. There were stars but no shadows. The horse clopped his own way home. I took the reins, though it wasn't necessary, and we grumbled slowly through the past on a lullaby of love and hope.

On the way we told each other such secrets as were fit for sharing in an effort to lay the foundations of intimacy. And we talked about people and what was wrong with the way they did things and how maybe we could do them better. Not very romantic, I guess, but in its way more important because the ideas were only half-cooked and we knew it and there was a certain intimacy in our willingness to share them, to risk seeming absurd.

And then we were interrupted by a clamoring and clattering fit to wake the dead. People from the party in a discordant, sour medley of confusion. They came fast, shocking in their hectic joy.

The rattle clatter-crunch of horse and buggy. The *yaaahoooEEE* of bottled exuberance. Suddenly a sulky went past, pacing high and whiplashing to avoid us. And another following with the blond head and raw whoop of Dolph Edwards and just behind him a carriage rattle banging like a stagecoach in Injun territory, barely managing to squeeze by. I could see the outline of a man standing like a charioteer driving his steeds, while behind him four or five men and women hung on in doubtful revelry, emitting occasional squeaks and grunts of courage.

Lucy and I, stunned by the shock of them, *clip clopped* along in silence, working with careful concern to regain our privacy. My lips brushed her cheek, soft and cool and sweet as morning mist. We hesitated, to tantalize rather than torment, then kissed gently, hopefully, asking that this be more than reality, that this be the wishing dream children have, the sweet wishing dream of perfect love.

"Lucy," I whispered. "Sweet Lucy."

She began to laugh then, but in a quiet, intimate way which brought no embarrassment.

"What's funny?"

"I used to have a *horse* named Sweet Lucy," she giggled.

"Boy," I said. "Just leave it to me."

"Poor Wombat," she said, but the way she said it—the intimate, silly, happy way she said it—mended the broken mood and brought a new tenderness.

By then we had reached the driveway and a tinkle of music and laughter from the house brought a new threat to our privacy.

"Let's not go in just yet," I said. "Couldn't we take this thing down to the beach or something?"

"Sure," Lucy said. She took the reins and directed our reluctant steed down a narrow trail which branched off from the driveway. It led along the cliff's edge, angling down to the sea where a little backwash of sand lay almost hidden in the black, protective shadow of rock. There were no lights on the mainland now, only the occasional probing of an automobile as it crept a country road. The steady lapping of waves was a part of the night silence. I took off my shoes and rolled my pants up and we went down to the water's edge and stood unseen and unseeing in the blackness. The enormous power of the night and sea settled on our souls, urging us to cling more closely than before.

We wandered back to a dry place and sat down. We were close, but not touching and our dreams and fears sifted back and forth in silent sympathy until yearning was not enough and the caressing began again. We fell back on the warm sand and our lips clung and our bodies touched secret places. I had never felt so safe, so sure, so unconcerned.

When I woke a faint gray light was settling like mist on the beaches of morning. Lucy lay beside me, her head resting on my arm, and in the coming light she seemed a sweet dream crossing to reality. I touched her cheek and traced a wave of hair. She stirred, moving closer.

"I love you, Lucy."

She looked at me and smiled. "That's nice," she said in a vague, sleepy way, then sighed and closed her eyes.

"We ought to go," I said, "it's daylight."

She seemed unimpressed.

"Lucy . . . it's daylight."

"Nice," she said.

"We'd better go."

"All right," she said and with an effort brought herself awake. "Did you say you loved me? Or did I dream it?"

"I said it."

She yawned and shook the sleep away. "And did I say it back?"

"No. You didn't."

"Well then, I do," she said.

"Thanks," I smiled, wondering why it seemed funny.

She got up. I rolled onto my knees and there was that old horse criticizing with blinkless eyes.

"He must think we're nuts," I said.

"She," Lucy corrected.

"All right. *She* must think we're nuts then."

Lucy yawned, untied the reins and led her around.

"Could be he's right," she said.

"She," I said. "Could be she is."

Lucy smiled and took my hand and we climbed the hill, tiptoeing through the stillness to our separate dreams.

CHAPTER XIX

At first the wedding day looked like one I would probably remember as well as my own, not for anything specific, but for the total feeling of social perfection. That I would remember it turned out to be true but for quite different reasons. I had to hand it to these people, though, they may have been fooling themselves, but they were making one hell of a good job of it. Even nature was in on the caper, for not a cloud could be seen all day and the sky was a gentle, Caribbean blue with this mild, soft fall I had never known before. But even if it had poured, I think the impression would have survived. Somehow all the king's horses and all the king's men had managed to put Humpty Dumpty together again and it was hard to believe he had ever been other than whole.

There was an informal brunch at Peter's house on the lawn overlooking the ocean. White sails spattered the blue and gulls swooped, probing the rocky coast.

The women wore bright garden colors; slacks and summer dresses and scarves and soft cashmere sweaters and their laughter tinkled gaily while the men, each burdened with the special responsibility of his hangover, managed to evoke a hazy, conspiratorial, childlike good humor.

And Lucy was mine.

Once as I watched her shivering with delight at some whispered indiscretion and flirting openly, playfully, as was the island's custom, I was reminded of Mary Kowalski, the little farm girl who first taught me the art of wanting. Probably it was the summer dress which did it; light and breezy and soft fitting. I liked seeing Lucy that way, warm, provocative, and full of life as the earth itself.

Because she was mine.

The day rambled sweetly by. Brunch, change of clothes, church, the reception; everything carefully planned, carefully tuned to perfection. Whatever sharp edges there may have been remained wrapped in the mists of nostalgia until the final anachronism of all: the newlyweds heading into the setting sun on a buggy to the rear of which some thoughtless twentieth-century soul had tied a string of tin cans.

For some time before they left I'd been wandering alone at the edges of Potters Island life, thinking champagne thoughts about the Future and the Meaning of Existence and all that and wondering where everybody went to. I had simply gone to the bar for a refill and returned to find all my friends gone. Later I discovered it was a Steeple Club custom to gather in the groom's room while he changed, singing sad songs, writing do-it-yourself directions on his chest for the bride's edification and otherwise carrying on. Since the Island population consisted, in part anyway, of twenty-nine Steeple and only three Fly and since I knew none of the latter, the conversational pickings were pretty slim. Even Lucy was gone, probably penning a few well-chosen words of her own for the groom's convenience. I had no idea. Anyway, that's why I'd wandered off, dunking my nose in the portable champagne font and thinking big.

It was a mistake, I guess, because when I did get back, drawn by the send-off noises, the mood was broken and the differences, imagined or otherwise, between these people and me were exaggerated to such an extent I began wondering whether it hadn't all been a mistake, whether perhaps I wasn't supposed to be here at all and might soon be asked to leave. Even the return of Lucy and my Steeple Club friends failed to stem the wave of self-pity. I kept the champagne flowing in an effort to change the nature of the flood but that only added to my confusion and brought the sickly fear of making a fool of myself. Why this was so I can't imagine. Everyone else was just as drunk—maybe drunker. In fact the Idyl of Potters Island was beginning to crumble again and a touch of chaos, warm and sweating, had become a part of the evening. Nothing to worry about, of course, just some more of that Humpty Dumpty dissonance I found so admirable: a stagger here, a hee haw there, a girl sprawled, but attractively, on the dance floor. Nothing to worry about if you knew the rules. Knew the rules. Perhaps that was the trouble. Did I know them? But weren't they the same here as Gravenhurst or anyplace else? Maybe so, but the fact was I didn't know for sure. How could I? I'd never been an outsider before.

Tables had been set up under the marquee and I was seated at one with Lucy and Dolph and the others, my chair tilted back precariously in the soft turf as though welcoming a chance to topple over backward and call attention to my pathetic self. I hadn't really seen much of Lucy all day, except from a distance, which was kind of nice being as she was mine and all that, like sharing a terrific secret with somebody, but not half as nice as being right with her. Dolph was whispering something and she was laughing, looking sort of wild as though maybe she'd had a little too much champagne too and I happened to notice the collar of her dress was turned up and looked funny so I reached out and fixed it. She turned, looking sort of annoyed, as though a fly had been buzzing her or something.

"What's the matter?" I asked.

"Nothing," she said. "Except I'm still quite capable of dressing myself, thank you."

"It didn't look that way. Your collar was turned up."

"It's *supposed* to be," she said, sighed, and turned back to Dolph.

I was a little confused as to what it was I'd done to deserve all this affection, but only for a minute or two. Pretty soon she turned around and said she was sorry, it had just sort of spooked her having someone fool with her dress and not knowing who it was.

"Let's dance," I suggested.

She hesitated. Dolph and Peter were laughing like crazy about something and I guess she wanted to get in on it.

"Okay," she said when it became obvious they wouldn't be fit for conversation in the immediate future.

As soon as we started dancing it was the night before all over again.

"Know something?" she asked.

"What?"

"You dance pretty well for a country boy."

"Oh thanks," I said and started a lot of twirling which I noticed everybody else doing.

"That's right," she said. "Given time and a little luck we might be able to make something out of you."

"Oh?"

"You know," she went on. "So you don't look so store-bought."

I pushed back and had a look at her face.

"You're not kidding, are you."

She smiled and sort of cocked her head. "Maybe," she said, then tried to come close again. "Oh come on," she laughed. "Don't be so sensitive," and I let her come.

"I thought we might go down to the beach later," I suggested.

"I'll bet you did," she teased.

"Okay?"

"Much later," she said. "There's a party at Dolph's."

"Let's skip it."

"Why?" she asked. "It'll be fun."

"Let's sit down," I said.

"Oh dear. Now you're in a puss."

"A what?"

"You're mad."

I sulked.

"You don't own me," she said. "Not yet anyway," and she turned away, headed for our table, me following confused, shaken by her warning, encouraged by the time limit she'd put on it. If "not yet" then when? Tomorrow, the day after? But all the same it wasn't as encouraging as some conversations we'd had and I went back to the table with every intention of taking up my sulk right where I'd left off. No sooner had I settled down when someone intent on adding to my sorrowful condition snuck up behind and tipped my chair, thereby deftly slopping champagne down my shirtfront. Instead of saying anything I just turned on a sour expression and refused even to recognize the incident, which I don't suppose was very sporting of me but seemed to suit my mood pretty well. Then Lucy sputtered "Oh Daddy, now look what you've done" between bursts of laughter and that brought me around a little. Since he was the one guy with whom I felt any link at all, I finally managed to perform a lip-raising ceremony which could have been mistaken for a grin and hiked my chair over so he could sit down.

"Are you all right?" she asked, as though afraid I'd start a fight or something.

It was my turn to sigh and I did so wholeheartedly.

Then Dolph, his curiosity aroused, leaned forward for a better look. "Uh oh," he warned. "Looks like Wombat's getting cockeyed again."

"Shut up," I said.

But Dolph was laughing too hard to be offended.

"Well now," said the pundit who had apparently managed to get himself pretty drunk too. "Z'nice friendly lil group we got here."

There was a nervous, unappreciative sprinkling of laughter followed by a general turning away and I began to realize Cholly

Delevan was just as much of an outsider as I. Yet for him it must have been even worse since Potters Island was his home, at least his summer one, and its people supposedly his friends. I don't know why this was. Perhaps because he no longer shared the agony of their particular struggle with inconsequence. He had his own. When people did talk to him it was in a halting kind of way because his problems had nothing to do with theirs. The best they could do was ask glorious questions concerning the world situation, then listen painfully while he tried to answer, mumble "Interesting, very interesting," and drift away.

Loneliness, I decided, that was the temporary link between Mr. Delevan and me.

"How you doing, Woodruff?" he asked, eyes wide, fixed on a point in space clearly unoccupied by me.

"Okay," I said inadequately. "How's yourself?" It was an awkward expression, as unnatural to me as to any of them. I don't know what made me say it.

Mr. Delevan squinted at me suspiciously, then started laughing.

"How's yourself," he gurgled. "How do you like that?"

I knew it was all in fun but it was also kind of loud and I wished with every available ounce of self-pity that he'd lay off.

"Come on, Woodruff," he said. "Snap out of it."

And the funny thing was I did just that. His apparent insight must have had as much to do with it as anything else. The element of surprise bounced me right back on the track. I looked up and started to laugh and he did too. Sort of half-talking, half-laughing. Nothing he said was very funny or even intelligible half the time, but it didn't matter. The sweet joy of laughter lifted me up and away from my sulk, and the two of us laughed and we laughed and we laughed until you could see people were becoming annoyed and we laughed some more.

"You two are bad for each other," Lucy told us when we finally managed to bring things under control.

And she may well have been right, but the whole idea of being considered co-mischief-maker with Charlie Delevan, Washington columnist, almost started me off again.

"All right, Woodruff, that's enough of that," said the great man. "Let's go find ourselves 'nother lil drink."

"Right with you, Cholly," said I.

Lucy caught my sleeve as I got up. "Stay here," she whispered. "Daddy'll just get you in trouble."

But was trouble, if you got into it with Cholly Delevan, really trouble?

"Don't worry," I told her with a secret and very important wink. "Be back in a jiff."

She gave me a look similar to that one back on the docks when I had asked her what language she was speaking. Then she turned back to Dolph and seemed to forget about me.

By that time the pundit was way ahead but I managed to catch up just as C. Dudley Morehouse was introducing him to a fat, red-headed, sluglike fellow with a superior air about him and no apparent reason for it.

". . . The Count de Duroc-Jersey," C. Dudley was saying as I approached.

French, I told myself, knowledgeably.

"And this is Mr. Woodruff," C. Dudley continued, took a deep breath. "The Count de Duroc-Jersey."

"*Enchanté*," said the Count.

"Been in this country long?" asked Cholly Delevan.

The Count seemed baffled by that one.

"Ten years off and on," said C. Dudley. "Extremely well thought of on the street."

"Has a real command of the language, too," said Cholly with a touch of awe so convincing the Count began to nod happily. "How d'you like the Pot?"

"Count Duroc-Jersey likes it very much," said C. Dudley. "He's thinking of taking a place here."

"Ah, that's nice," said Mr. Delevan, giving the Count a friendly pat on the arm. "Thinking of going into stud are you?"

The Count grinned happily and looked to C. Dudley, interpreter, but C. Dudley, interpreter, was too busy trying to liquidate the pundit with a brown frown.

"Which reminds me," Cholly continued, unconcerned. "How's your mother, Dudley? I haven't seen her this weekend."

I hadn't the slightest idea what that meant, but it appeared to be well beyond the boundaries of propriety. C. Dudley lunged. He didn't swing, but heaved himself onto the pundit and began to shake him in a series of lurching jerky spasms which seemed more an expression of his own pain than an effort to hurt Mr. Delevan.

And to confirm this his attack was accompanied by a pent-up squealing, as if the agony were being squeezed out of him, broken by a series of "God damn you, you sonofabitch, God damn you, you sonofabitch."

Then just as suddenly as the attack had started it was over. C. Dudley let go, turned and walked off with an air of casual unconcern which, under the circumstances, was downright admirable. I looked around and found to my amazement either no one had noticed, or else didn't care to let on, except the Count, of course, who had managed to disappear. I finally located him sitting suavely at the farthest end of the marquee, as if he'd been there for hours.

Well that was that. It was all over and no harm done. I turned to the pundit in an effort to pick up where we had left off. The great Cholly Delevan and his good friend, the up-and-coming young news editor from Gravenhurst, Connecticut, were gonna have a lil drink.

"Now," I said. "How 'bout that trip to the bar?"

"Shut up," he told me.

"Oh come on," I said. "Don't let a little thing like that bother you."

"I said *shut up*." He really yelled it too. I took a step back. This time people *were* noticing.

"I was just trying to . . ."

"Just trying to what?" he shouted. "Just trying to kiss my butt, weren't you?" He advanced on me, his face contorted like a man watching an accident. "Who the hell do you think you are, you . . . you *pip*squeak?" I started backing away, but it was like one of those nightmares where you run and don't go anywhere. The faster I backed, the closer seemed that twisted, writhing face. "Punk," he screamed. "Think you can walk in here and take over. Get palsy-walsy, fool around with my daughter." And here his mouth flung open, completely out of control. "Any goddam thing yer lil heart desires."

He was crying, too. That was the last thing I noticed before tripping over one of the tent ropes and sprawling on my ass.

Then Lucy was there. "Daddy, Daddy." She slapped him hysterically. "Stop it, Daddy. Stop it. Stop it." Then she turned to me. "You fool," she shouted.

The rest is a mystery. I got up and ran. It must have been a pretty silly sight, old Wombat Woodruff hurtling through all that elegance

like a rat at the Westminster dog show but I was in no mood to
care. At least not until a half mile or so later when my flight had
slowed to a jog and the huff puffing required to maintain this road-
eating pace did not seem justified by the distance covered. I slowed
to a walk, feeling better already. This road, the soft sandy shoulder
flecked with weeds, crumbly bits of tar, an occasional beer can; it
was another world, a world ignorant of Steeple Clubs, pundits,
ooofly nice accents and all the rest of it. That their world could be
so small was the greatest comfort. I took a deep breath. Already
they seemed a long way off. Even Lucy. Just an episode, a pebble
tossed into the blackness. And though I wasn't sure that was the
best way, it was the way I wanted it for the time being, until the
pain burned away and I could try again.

The stars gave off just enough light for me to see where I was
going, but left me to decide where that should be. Then the night
sound of a car engine reached through the stillness. I looked back as
a pair of headlights probed around the corner, hesitated, speared
me, slowed, shuddered, stopped. I could see from the outline it was
an old thing, not one of those snappy little Volkses the Delevans
and everybody else were supposed to have tucked away for emer-
gencies. As if I qualified as an emergency anyway.

I walked around and opened the door.

"Where you going, young fella?"

"To town," I said, wherever that was.

"Hop in," he said.

The upholstery was that old-fashioned, fuzzy, velvetlike stuff. The
windows were closed tight. It smelled like a farmer's kitchen in
midwinter. Warm, not just lived in but worked in too.

"Thanks," I said. " 'Preciate it."

He didn't answer. I could see he was crouched over the wheel,
an old guy giving all his attention to the job of staying on the road.
Or most of it anyway, some was going into a chaw of tobacco he was
working on. With the windows rolled up the way they were I was
beginning to wonder how he'd managed to master the spitting problem when he let fly into an old gallon can on the seat next to me.
After that I stayed pretty close to the door.

"Would you have any idea," I asked, "how I could get over to
the mainland?"

"Boat," he said.

"Uh huh," I agreed.

"Ferry leaves in the morning," he offered.

"Well I was thinking of tonight."

He only chewed.

"I was thinking maybe somebody could take me over in a fishing boat or something," I suggested.

"Maybe."

"Oh that's great," I said.

"It'll cost you some money."

"How much."

"Dunno," he said. More chewing. "About ten dollars."

"That's okay. Do you know anybody who'd do it?"

"Yup."

At that point a car came up behind us and he was so busy looking both ways at once, besides his chewing, that I didn't want to risk asking any more questions. Finally whoever it was pulled out in a whine of little car noises and zoomed by. That time it *was* a Volkswagen and looked like Lucy driving with maybe Dolph or somebody with her. I was beginning to enjoy myself.

"I thought there weren't supposed to be any cars around here," I said, mostly for conversation.

"There ain't," he said.

"You suppose something's happened?"

"Looking for you, most likely."

"Oh I don't know," I said. "How come you have one?"

"One what?"

"Car."

"That's just summer people," he said. "Rest of us got no time for such foolishness."

I laughed.

"Traveling kinda light, ain'tcha?"

"Excuse me?"

"No suitcase."

"Oh, that's right," I admitted. "Friend of mine's got it."

"Uh huh," he said.

More silence.

We came into town, pulled up behind the Volkswagen, empty now, and turned right down a bumpy, once-paved hill to the fishing docks. I still didn't know who was taking me across, but was beginning to get the idea.

He got out, crossed the street and went into a little diner on the corner. To tell them where he was going, I guess, because he was right back out again.

I followed him down some rickety stairs, out onto the dock and down a line of fishing boats slapping gently at their berths. I could hear Lucy or somebody calling my name. Whoever it was seemed a long way off.

His boat was what you'd call a skiff, I guess, long and low on the water, the kind Lucy said was used for crabbing.

"Lucky the weather's holding," he said. "You'd be here all night."

I agreed.

The fisherman had his lines cast off almost before I got aboard and the engine glubachugging at about the same time. Before I'd even given up looking for a place to sit down we were easing our way into the channel. I looked back at the other boats silhouetted against the soft glow from town and as we went past the ferry landing I saw a car swing by and disappear. I couldn't tell if it was Lucy or not.

It was over an hour to the mainland. We didn't talk. You couldn't over the engine anyway. But there was plenty to keep me occupied. I watched the channel markers slipping by our left side—port side, if you want to get technical—and the occasional lights of a small freighter or pleasure yacht, maybe, stealing down the bay. The engine's pulse was steady, reassuring, only a whisper of breeze crossed the water, barely ruffling its oily calm and as I stood next to that fisherman, watching the shore lights blossom, it seemed there were more than words between us. I resisted the temptation to draw some mystical conclusion, great, good, and true, about why there should be any communication at all between this unknown fisherman and me and decided instead there were more than words between any two human beings if they'd shut up long enough to listen. Then it occurred to me these wordless conversations weren't always friendly, judging by the unconscious chat I must have had with Mr. Delevan.

Could he have known about Lucy and me and our little beach party? How the hell did I know?

"Any place . . . ?" the fisherman asked, but I couldn't hear him over the noise.

"What?" I yelled.

"Any place special?" he shouted.

"Near the ferry landing."

And that, except for "Thanks" and a wave, was the last exchange we had.

I found the car. It was ten o'clock by then, but I decided to go all the way. It would take a good purge to get the rest of Potters Island out of my system and you couldn't ask for anything better than an all-night drive.

Sometime soon I'd have to sit down and figure out whether I could have Lucy without being had by her old man and the rest of them. But I wasn't in the mood to think about it just then. The hell with Potters Island.

CHAPTER XX

I got home around five o'clock, running on smoke and coffee mostly but feeling pretty good, considering I'd worked my way through one whole hangover, driven seven hours and been two days with almost no sleep at all. But I couldn't go to bed right away. Not until the fact of being home was totally absorbed. I went into the kitchen first, got myself a glass of milk, wandered around the house slurping away and humming a quiet tune, found a magazine and went up to bed. But I didn't do too much reading.

Next morning—or afternoon, to be exact—I discovered the *Daily Watch* fortunes had reached a new low, but this time the catastrophe was so absurd I almost laughed in Pa's face. We had an arrangement with the Columbia School of Journalism whereby once a year they would take over the *Daily Watch* editorial department and turn out the paper for a couple of days. It was a pretty confusing practice but we'd been doing it for years and kind of a nice tradition had grown out of the arrangement. Well, apparently Columbia found a paper closer to New York and so the whole deal was canceled. It had nothing whatsoever to do with our competitive problems but a certain amount of prestige was involved in the university tie and Pa seemed to consider this pretty important. I watched him run around for a while, cursing and brandishing the blunted sword of his indecision, but it was hard to get very excited. There were more important things to worry about. Besides all his righteous gesticulations seemed more like the futile efforts of a Sunday golfer than the soldier god he was supposed to be.

I made a couple of tries to get him on more important topics but he seemed sick of the *Daily Watch*. Maybe just a little sick of himself as well because he dodged my questions not with reason or even indignation but by pleading a headache and asking to be left in peace for once. That was a new one.

I looked a little incredulous, but Mother came to the rescue.

"Don't bother your father now," she said. "He's really feeling *awful*."

Pa groaned and stole off to his study.

Lucy called in the evening to apologize, I guess, and tell me she had my suitcase. I . . . well, I wish she hadn't called just then. A couple of days later and maybe I wouldn't have been quite so sullen and indignant, but at the time I was in no mood to let bygones be bygones. She tried but I answered everything with grunts and I don't knows. When she finally threw in the towel and hung up after a particularly long silence even the suitcase problem hadn't been solved. That meant the next gesture of reconciliation would probably have to come from me, a fact which in itself threatened to spoil the fun of having been treated unjustly.

However, for the time being, anyway, I was too busy with the paper to worry about my love life or my suitcase either.

From that day on I took Mother's advice to heart and left Pa in peace as far as the *Daily Watch* or anything else was concerned and, for the most part, he'd managed to repay me by staying there. In fact, most of the time he stayed home, partly in pain and partly in apathy, for though the headaches seemed real enough, they had a way of coming and going almost at will. As a result, Ted Pearson and I were free to do pretty much as we saw fit just as long as it didn't cost too much money.

God, it was a great feeling to be able to run free and unencumbered by politics and favors and indecision and the great web of trivia which had bound us up to that point. The whole staff seemed to sense we'd been cut loose from the past and there was a rustle of enthusiasm I could feel the minute I walked through the door. And with it came a new vigor and a new strength which made our people so eager to fight we had a hard time cooking up enough battles.

Not even the arrival of that damn suitcase, sent with no note or comment of any kind, could limit the extent of my new confidence and enthusiasm. I still felt the lack of her, still felt the need to patch things up. But time was a lost concern and I thought of almost nothing but the *Daily Watch*, or rather the *Enterprise* and how it might most effectively be destroyed.

By the end of October things were shaping up nicely. I wouldn't say we had the *Enterprise* on the run. Far from it. In fact the results of our changes hadn't begun to show materially at all, but it was inevitable they would. The home delivery tubes were almost completely installed, each one with a nice big fat *Daily Watch* printed on it, and we'd been working to figure out a legitimate way of running separate country and city editions in order to divide our circulation and allow limited advertising at limited rates. As for the paper itself, Ted and I had managed to brighten up the typography with some new combinations, but the big changes had nothing to do with us. As if by magic the reporting style seemed to freshen while the volume of local news and feature material pretty near doubled. What the editorial department needed, apparently, was not a bonus, but simply a chance to stand up and slug it out, free from the shackles of political expediency and Polk's derision.

We also pulled one other little stunt for which the motivations were not quite so honorable as they may have appeared. It involved the establishment of a *Daily Watch* Advisory Board of eminent local citizens who would meet with us once a week to discuss ways and means of improving the paper. The idea was mine and, I modestly submit, constituted an act of pure genius. It was a ten-man board plus me including our four department heads and six prime movers of community machinery. Though we didn't pick them on the basis of their business potential, the fact that a leading citizen would likely have some influence in the business world was not entirely lost on us. But more important was the good will, the enthusiasm, and the loyalty these gentlemen would generate among their friends once they became involved in the *Daily Watch's* destiny, and if their advice was helpful too, why so much the better.

But as I've said, the effects of these innovations were necessarily slow to develop and by the end of the month no real change of fortune was apparent. Except, of course, to the experienced newspaperman. And that's the reason it was so reassuring of Ned Polk to drop in for a visit. He had been sending us news releases from the Office of the State Senator with singular lack of success. Now I'm willing to admit a newspaper shouldn't carry its private feuds into editorial policy, but it seemed to me Senator Polk had evidenced certain qualities which were less than desirable in a servant of the people. Therefore, I wasn't about to do him any favors and publication of his news releases would have amounted to just that. During a political lull such as occurs in the fall of a non-election year, the local vocals are in the habit of pumping a steady stream of trivia through the communication pipes in order to keep their names on the public mind, or conscience, as the case may be. Thus most of the Polk releases were nothing but rehashes of dormant issues, announcements of public-speaking appearances, and sentimental bids for popularity through endorsement of this or that charitable project and I wasn't about to run them.

But though encouraging of him to stop by, frankly the sight of my old boss, his great bulk yawing my way, shivered the junior Woodruff timbers ever so slightly. Fortunately, as a politician, his manner had become a little more supplicant than before, but not much.

I told him we'd be happy to cover any real news the senator might generate and added it was more than likely we'd make an editorial comment or two in the bargain. From the look of him I was under the impression he understood exactly what I meant. Anger bubbled up from deep in the slimy coils of his soul, but happily it didn't overflow and he left without achieving his goal for once.

Otherwise things were going pretty well. I had an interesting time keeping tabs on the results of the Mabel Crump episode. Not that we played up the story. But once the legal gears begin to turn there is very little one can do about those who happen to be caught in them. When the grand jury meets that's news and when an indictment is handed down that too is news, and when the trial begins it has to be covered. The fact that all this festered like boils on Judge Compton's political neck was unfortunate but scarcely our concern. I found it interesting to note, though, that even the judge wasn't above a little political reconciliation. Not with me, needless to say, but with Pa. Apparently he'd made quite an interesting discovery, namely that while Pa could not get along without him and Clem Harper, neither could they get along without Pa. The broken alliance had shattered the myth of their separate prestige and no one carried a whit of influence without the other two. But I think the judge failed to realize there was a fourth horseman, namely the *Daily Watch,* in his political backfield and without it the old razzle dazzle was somewhat more difficult to come by. Worse than that, though, there had been a fumble and even with the *Daily Watch* support, an unlikely possibility at best, I doubted the old guard would have a chance to renew their offensive. Their days of glory were finished. Still, the reconciliation had its useful aspect. For example, how much fun could only two of them have sitting around the fire and discussing the tough old sonsabitches of yesteryear? Not much I wouldn't think.

Pa tried to get me off the Crump story entirely as a favor to the judge and a token tribute to their joyful renewal of friendship, but his heart was only half in it. Even Pa was used to subtler forms of back-scratching so when I objected he didn't press me. I don't know whether Judge Compton sensed this or not but I do know he suddenly rediscovered up-and-coming young Larry Woodruff. That he managed this by means of Nora seemed less than noble, but then how could it have been otherwise? She called one evening to announce I was forgiven. I don't mind saying it was about the most alarming bit of news I'd heard in a long time.

"I am? What for?"

"For what you did to Daddy," she said.

"Oh. That's right, you were sore too."

"Of course," she went on. "That's why we haven't seen each other."

"It is?"

"Yes. But now Daddy feels you didn't mean any real harm."

"Just sort of muddle-headed, huh?"

"That's right. He thinks we shouldn't be angry with you any more."

"Golly, I don't know what to say."

"And he wants you to come for dinner tomorrow night."

"On such short notice?" I asked. "Gosh, Nora, I'll never be sufficiently grateful by then."

"I beg your pardon?"

"I feel unworthy. Couldn't we put it off until, oh, let's say next year sometime?"

"I don't understand," she muttered.

"Or even the year after. If it would suit you better."

"Larry," she scolded. "Don't make jokes." But I was pleased to note a trace of uncertainty in her tone. Pleased, and also a little contrite. The telephone, after all, was no way to solve the problem.

"All right," I agreed. "I'd love to come."

"That's better," she said.

"Better?"

"Yes. This is hardly a time for joking."

"Why not?"

"After all, it was a terrible thing to do to Daddy. You should be grateful for his forgiveness."

Goddam her anyway. Besides, who said I wanted to be forgiven, sort of socially castrated just because I happened to be more useful that way? I liked being in hot water. It reminded me I was alive. "Nora," I began, but somewhere inside me was an ounce of discretion or compassion or some such foolishness, and the words refused to come.

"Yes?" she asked.

"Nothing," I hedged. "I'll see you tomorrow."

"Six-thirty," she said. "And you know how Daddy feels about punctuality."

By damn, that was just too much for me and I started to laugh.

"Well," she huffed, "you certainly are acting strangely."

"Oh boy," I agreed. "If you only knew the half of it."

"Goodbye," she said. "I've no more time for your foolishness."

"I should think not," I laughed. "You've got all you can handle." But she beat me to it. She'd already hung up.

The reality of Nora, my private symbol of indecision, pulled me up short with the realization that almost a month had gone by since I'd seen or heard from Lucy. Dedication to the *Daily Watch* cause was all very well, but if I kept it up to the exclusion of everything else Nora might turn out to be the only one left. Well, I wanted to be successful as much as the next guy, but that seemed like a pretty steep price to pay, so I put in a call to New York but Lucy wasn't there. Then I tried her person-to-person in Washington, having no desire to chat with my old friend Cholly Delevan, but he answered and said she was out. He wanted to know who was calling and I didn't want to tell him so the whole thing was a waste of time.

It was cold as my love for Nora that next night, but I decided to walk to the Comptons' all the same. The sun had set and there was no moon to cast its icy glow. The land was hard and still and bare, resigned to the winter death which would follow close on November's heels. Somehow the coming of cold weather always managed to take me by surprise. Either that, or I simply preferred to ignore it as long as possible. Therefore, I wore no overcoat that night and suffered accordingly, shuddering from time to time, unable to ignore the chill and wondering whether, by God, it might not just start snowing after all.

On arriving at the Comptons', however, I found phenomena even more extraordinary than the weather. Apparently the judge, either from ignorance or a cunning I'd never suspected, wasn't one to quit easily, for there before me, panting with pleasure at my surprise, was Mr. Jesse Rosenfeldt. Judge Compton, it seemed, was determined to fill that backfield of his. But how foolish can a man get? He no longer had any players worth trading.

Whatever the judge was up to became no clearer as the evening wore on and I was pretty certain his invitation to Jesse constituted an act of panic rather than profundity. If his purpose had been to scare me then he'd either already talked to Jesse and now realized the *Enterprise* had no intention of betting on a dead horse, or else he'd figured it out for himself. Either way, the revelation had apparently been achieved, for he made no effort to suggest anything but the social pleasures had been on his mind when he'd decided to invite Jesse and me.

The result was a pretty sticky evening. There was Nora, fuddled by an apparent loss of sovereignty, for such things are usually pretty obvious. And Judge Compton, stripped of his purpose, and Mrs. Compton dashing hither and thither in a vain attempt to shore the crumbling walls of her top-heavy pretension. And in the midst of it all, Jesse and I smiling in polite and baffled silence.

As I was leaving Nora managed to ask whether I'd be dropping by soon and I told her we were pretty busy. It wasn't an ideal time to talk about it. Jesse waited and the Comptons hovered, batting portentous glances back and forth, but Nora seemed to understand, which was all that really mattered. At least for the time being.

Fortunately the cold weather chilled Judge Compton's hospitality and he didn't bother to escort us outside. As soon as we were alone Jesse offered to drop me home.

"Well it's not all that far," I said.

"I know," he said. "But I've got something for you."

"Oh?" I asked. "Then you knew I'd be there tonight?"

"Sure."

"I wonder why they didn't tell me about you."

"Didn't think you'd come," Jesse said.

"So you were in on the plot, eh?"

"If you could call it that."

"What was he up to?" I opened the car door and jumped in, impatient for the heater's assistance.

"He had some crazy scheme for forming a local group to buy into the *Enterprise*," Jesse said. "Thought it would remove the outsider's stigma or something like that."

"What's so crazy about that?"

Jesse shrugged. "Has-beens and outsiders don't mix."

"I guess not," I admitted.

Jesse started up the car and cruised down the driveway. "Besides, I'd still like to keep the door open for some kind of a deal between our two papers."

"Getting scared?" I laughed.

"No," he said. "It isn't that."

"Well we'd never accept anything like what your old man offered before."

"I know," he nodded. "I didn't mean that either."

"What did you mean?"

"I really don't know. I'd just prefer not to rule out a chance for some sort of negotiation." Then he laughed, but with a touch of embarrassment, as though his motivations were sentimental rather than practical.

"Heard anything from Abby?" I asked.

Jesse turned, looked at me with feigned surprise, and almost missed our driveway. The transparency of his confusion made him abandon any further pretense. "As a matter of fact, I have," he laughed.

"What?"

"Well I saw her last weekend. We went to the Harvard-Columbia game."

"How'd it go?"

"Fine," he said. "Harvard won for a change."

By then we were home. "I didn't mean that exactly."

"Oh?"

"I meant with you and Abby."

"Fine. Everything's just fine." But obviously it wasn't. He looked at me. Then looked away.

"Good," I said, letting his lie trot on by. "I'm glad to hear it."

"Well good night," he said.

I was just about to slam the door.

"Oh I almost forgot," he said, reaching into the back seat. "This is for you." He thrust a manila envelope through the door. "It's about your father. I'm not sure how much longer I can hold up publication. Unless, of course, someone took steps which would render the story useless." He laughed at himself again, then with a "Well," a nod, and a baffled smile he drove away.

The hall light was on, a lonely warning that meant everyone was asleep. I flicked it off and tiptoed upstairs in the dark. There was a letter on my bed. Without seeing the handwriting, I knew it was from Abby. We hardly ever wrote. She had a theory it only reinforced the fact of being away and since I hate to write letters anyway, the theory was a welcome one. However, when a letter did come from Abby it usually meant trouble.

I forgot my manila envelope for the time being and went to work on Abby's letter. I was right. She was having her troubles, all of them traceable to the publisher of the Gravenhurst *Enterprise*. It seems Jesse had turned the courtship into a chase and the results weren't doing either of them any good.

"He's driving me nuts," Abby wrote. "And I don't mean slang nuts, I mean really and truly crazy nuts."

The way she put things made it hard to take seriously what she wrote, but apparently Jesse *was* sort of getting her down. I mean even worse than before college. He was calling every night, trying to get her to do this or that, usually something fairly lavish and extravagant which, aside from being a little rich for her blood, had the effect of steadily increasing her commitment.

"El Morocco, for God sakes. *Me!*"

And besides, he was as tough and relentless in his courtship as he was in business. According to Abby's letter, the few times she did scrape up the courage to say no, they'd have to stop seeing each other, he simply ignored her and went right on calling.

"Anyway, maybe I *do* love him. Oh Larry, I'm just so mixed up and scared and confused I don't know what to do."

The gist of it was she thought maybe I could help.

"Couldn't you tell him to go away or something? Maybe he'd listen to another man."

But apparently she didn't want that either because she took it right back.

"Not go away exactly, but just sort of stop all this pursuing so I can have time to think."

By that I guess she meant think about whether or not she was up to the challenge of marrying a Jew because right after that she added: "Oh God, how I disgust myself," and signed off.

While my thoughts were sorting I opened Jesse's envelope and absent-mindedly leafed through the pages until repetition of the name Woodruff finally drew my complete attention and I turned back to the first paragraph.

"Clarence Woodruff, owner and publisher of the Gravenhurst *Daily Watch*, was under investigation today on conflict of interest charges related to his activities as chairman of the Gravenhurst Redevelopment Committee.

"Purpose of the probe, according to municipal authorities, is to determine whether Mr. Woodruff's ownership of much of the property slated for redevelopment is by coincidence or design. In either case the Committee Chairman and not Gravenhurst would appear to be the program's chief beneficiary."

It wasn't necessary to read the rest. Whether justified or not, the charges could do nothing but harm in those very departments Pa cherished the most; for his reputation and prestige would suffer far more than his pocketbook when the story got into print.

Or rather *would* have suffered, had Jesse not warned us. Now all Pa had to do was resign in a cloud of civic righteousness, a move which could very likely earn him the respect rather than distrust of our local citizenry. As every red-blooded, loyal American knows, to stand up like a little soldier and tell the truth when one is about to be caught red-handed demands immediate forgiveness. Thus, it didn't matter whether Pa was consciously trying to feather his own nest or not. Either way, by confessing—that is by resigning—he would not only be forgiven, he'd be praised.

The story itself, therefore, was fairly easy to deal with. What really interested me was Jesse's motive for revealing it to the enemy. The only possible reason, as far as I could see, was Abby, yet it seemed hard to believe he'd compromise his newspaper or any other business obligation for the sake of love. I mean who ever heard of a Jew, or anyone else for that matter, doing a thing like that? But there didn't seem to be any other explanation. It occurred to me that the tougher and more relentless his wooing, the gentler and more sentimental his business techniques and I couldn't help but laugh at the irony of that. Maybe little Abby would turn the trick after all and though I told myself not to minimize her difficulties simply because they might prove helpful in solving mine, the truth is, looking back on it, I'm not sure I didn't.

I undressed and got in bed and lay thinking about the two of them for a while, trying to decide just what, if anything, I should do. It seemed so illogical of Jesse to have done such a thing purely for emotional and private reasons. But then come to think of it, most of the important decisions people make *are* for illogical, or at least ingenuous, reasons. For instance, though justifiable maybe, how much inductive reasoning was involved in my decision to hurdle the walls of convenience and run away from Nora? Or Mother's decision to defy Pa in the Rosenfeldt merger? Or take right now. Just how much attention was I giving to Abby's problem compared, say, to the agonizing mental gymnastics I could perform over whether to go to the movies Tuesday night or Thursday. Boy, that's a tough one. I mean Thursday you've got The Untouchables on TV, though of course by going to the early show I could catch The Untouchables too. But didn't I say I'd drop by the Pearsons' Thursday night? No, it would be better to go Tuesday, except Tuesday was YMCA night and the Palace Theater would be full of screaming kids. Or was that only the seven o'clock show? Oh hell, I didn't want to go Tuesday anyway. What about Wednesday? That might be the best solution. And so on and on.

But would I exercise that much mental muscle over Abby's problem which, from the tone of her letter anyway, sounded pretty serious? Certainly not. I told myself, with a superior smile, it was nothing but a case of juvenile histrionics, rolled over and went to sleep. As I say, I'd hate to think my lack of concern was motivated, at least in part, by the expediency of keeping Jesse in a state of confusion. But I don't suppose that would be any worse, really, than the other possibility: the secret, subconscious pleasure Abby's suffering gave me.

CHAPTER XXI

I got up early the next morning to answer Abby's letter. However, as the innocence of sleep faded, so did my honesty. While I'd first been inclined to offer my services in personally calling Jesse off the chase, what went down on paper was something quite different. Instead I patronized her with the obvious clichés about young love and its attending hardships—all this despite only two years' seniority—and even managed with unconscious deception to lead her away from my real motives by making a little joke about her charms and how helpful they had been in our newspaper struggles. However, at least I answered her and that, considering our non-existent letter-writing habits, was something of an accomplishment.

It was still too early for breakfast so afterward, more to kill time than anything else, I wrote Pa's letter of resignation from the Gravenhurst Redevelopment Committee, then puttered around my desk for a while until it finally occurred to me Lucy might know how to read and I wrote her too. It was a nothing letter; a gesture thanking her for the suitcase but lacking the courage to mention love or longing or any of that. Just a polite hint it would be nice to see her again and the unwritten hope she could sense some of the feeling I was so careful to hide behind the façade of careless chatter.

After that I got dressed and went downstairs, armed with the evidence of Jesse's weakness and the resulting draft of Pa's letter.

I was just starting a cup of coffee when Mother came in.

"Hi," I said. "I've got something . . ."

"Good morning, dear," she interrupted. "Is Bollard in the kitchen?"

"He was a minute ago. Where's Pa? I've got something . . ."

"He's not feeling well again. I want Bollard to take up a tray," and she was gone before I could steal the scene. When she came back I tried again.

"*Mother*," I said with an urgency which might have contained just a touch of hysteria. "Mother, I've got something kind of *urgent*." The idea that I couldn't capture her attention even when in possession of important information somewhat rattled me.

"What is it?" she asked, trying to temper her impatience.

I held out Jesse's envelope. She sighed at my melodramatic ways and accepted the offering. When she'd read enough I handed her my letter.

"Oh dear," she said. "Of all days."

"All he has to do is sign it," I said. "And the sooner the better."

"I suppose," she agreed. "You say Jesse Rosenfeldt gave you this?"

"That's right."

"But why?"

"Because of Abby."

"Really?"

"That's right. I guess he's in love with her and doesn't want to dirty up the game."

"But he's the publisher," she pointed out. "All he had to do was refuse to print it."

"Maybe he'd rather do it this way. To be sure we'd know."

"I saw you received a letter from Abby yesterday," Mother said. "Is everything all right?"

"She's kind of upset. Jesse's courting tactics are pretty high-powered."

"It's strange she hasn't mentioned it to me."

"Well, I guess she'll survive," I said, with a superior smile.

Maybe Mother wasn't satisfied, but some urgent shouting from Pa stole her attention. "Come upstairs when you're through break-fast," she said and hurried off to tend our fallen idol.

When I went up later Pa was lying on the bed fully clothed, Jesse's envelope beside him, but with those black sleep patches pasted over his eyes. He could have been asleep, but there was something rigid in his position which suggested he was not. Either dead, or hiding, but definitely not asleep.

Mother was at her dressing table. She turned toward him when I came in. "Clarence," she said. "Clarence, are you awake?"

No response.

"CLARence," she shouted.

He reached out a languid hand and removed the patches.

"Darling, Larry's waiting for the letter."

He made no sign of interest, only pointed to the phalanx of pills guarding his bedside table. "May I have another Codeine," he said.

Mother sighed and fetched the required pill. "You'll have to sit up to swallow it, dear," she said.

He did, reluctantly, his hair scattered in gray wisps. He seemed fluttery and fragile, like a pinned moth. "Now," he said, as if making a special effort for my benefit. "What seems to be the trouble?"

I repeated the whole business though obviously Mother must have just finished telling him much the same thing. He seemed to be listening but not especially interested.

When I had finished he looked at his hands for a while. Not thinking, I don't believe, just sort of passing time. Then he began rubbing the back of his neck to remind us there was something much more important to worry about. Tiring of that, he reached for the letter and signed it.

"I probably won't be down today," he said, as if that were news. I nodded, took the letter, picked up Jesse's envelope, being careful to drop it by my room for safekeeping, retrieved my letter to Lucy, and went down to the office.

As November unraveled so did my patience. No matter what happened to our newspaper fortunes, Abby and Pa seemed to lead each other farther down the prickly path of pity; not one for the other, but each for his own. Had somebody been able to leave off licking imaginary wounds long enough to note the fortunes of the fourth estate were at last favoring us, I might have been able to produce a little more sympathy. But even Mother was too busy nursing them to notice Ted and I were making headway. Oh, I suppose she had reason. Especially as far as Abby was concerned; our delicate plaster icon crumbling in the dampness of her abandoned temple. Confusion, fear, and disgust ravaged her symmetry as inevitably as wind, weather, and time and the expressions now occupying her face had routed beauty, replaced it with the leprosy of doubt. Like a dream of searching and horror each door she opened produced no beautiful, shining Sir Clarence, but only the dogged, lolling, horribly caricatured face of Jesse Rosenfeldt. And when she ran away to college, he followed, but still worse, when she ran home he not only followed there too, but contaminated her whole being with the reminder he had destroyed her god. And though the *Daily Watch* continued to grow stronger, Abby wandered, faltered, crumbled into someone quite different from the girl he'd loved at first. Obviously Jesse would have preferred it the other way around for now he too seemed somewhat off his stride; hurt, bewildered, a little halting in his manner. But if this gave me some consolation, it offered no solution.

Consequently, when Friday afternoon rolled around I wasn't overly eager to meet the bus and pick up Abby's psychic remains. As it turned out, though, for the moment, anyway, she was sort of in between horrors, being neither at college nor home, and her mood was comparatively cheerful. We even managed to kid a little about this and that, so long as it had nothing to do with Pa or Jesse. The fact that she had any spark left at all put me in a Tweedledee,

humming kind of mood and I went sashaying through town without
noticing which copy of the *Daily Watch* she'd picked up off the
back seat where I keep a fairly helter-skelter and unintentional
assortment of reading material.

"What's this?" she asked, unwrapping a nice fat, forty-eight point
headline. I gave it a quick glance and almost went off the road.

PUBLISHER STEPS DOWN
AS RENEWAL CHAIRMAN

Woodruff Declares
Private Interests
Imperil Project

"What's what?" I asked.

Abby started to read:

"'In a surprise move hailed by city officials as forthright and
statesmanly, Clarence Woodruff resigned from chairmanship of the
Gravenhurst Urban Redevelopment Committee today in order to
avoid compromising the group's effectiveness.

"'Mr. Woodruff, publisher of the Gravenhurst *Daily Watch* and
owner of considerable real estate both in and around the renewal
area, felt the committee risked conflict of interest charges while he
was its chairman and chose to resign rather than let the project be
damaged by what he called "the vicious, false charges of political
opportunism."

"'In a letter of resignation submitted to the *Daily Watch* this
morning . . .' Well that's about the size of it," Abby concluded.

"Oh that," I said, beginning to realize there was no reason for
Abby to see this as anything but a noble gesture. "Pretty good stuff,
eh?"

"I didn't think he had it in him," she admitted.

"Oh Pa's really taken hold in the last few days," I lied. "You'd
be surprised."

"How come?"

"Well the *Daily Watch's* been showing some progress and I guess
he's beginning to feel maybe we can lick 'em after all."

"It's about time," Abby said, but it was more prayer than criticism
and I didn't bother to tell her the *Daily Watch* improvements had
nothing to do with Pa, in fact were probably unknown to him.

I don't know just how I expected to hide the fact Pa hadn't changed at all, except possibly by working Abby into a state of enthusiasm turbulent enough to blur her vision and make him look as if he had. I played this angle for the rest of the drive, describing those improvements and signs of spirit which seemed suitable to reality and generally working up such a tizzy of deceit there was no time to consider the dangers.

Actually, it began to look like I'd get away with it, for when we got home it turned out Pa really *was* in a better mood. Not a great deal better, but enough to trigger Abby's enthusiasm which in turn improved Pa's frame of mind more than even he probably cared to admit.

To dare hope such a combination of chance and illusion might set our world right may seem pretty silly, but all the same, I did. One illusion, after all, is as good as another and I saw no harm in filling up a new balloon to replace the one Jesse had popped. Of course, that isn't exactly progress and maybe Abby should have learned to get along without balloons and such similar childhood appurtenances, but at that stage of the game anything which succeeded in improving family morale seemed worth the risk.

It was quite a night. Between them, Abby and Pa managed to pump each other up to the bursting point. And though there was a touch of hysteria in their efforts to reconstruct sullied and disproven myths about the courageous Clarence Woodruff and his bold daughter, Abigail, we were all too eager to accept the gaiety as a sign of recovered health and ignored any indications to the contrary. It was hard to believe all this could blossom from my little batch of lies, yet apparently such was the case. By creating the impression of order I had somehow brought order itself.

The effects of all this optimism kept us hopping until past midnight, even though Abby and I both knew we'd be up talking half the night.

She was in my room even before I got there.

"Well," I challenged. "Now how do you feel?"

"Pretty good," she admitted. "Pretty good," and she meant great.

"God's back in his heaven and all that," I said.

She smiled and looked away, as though embarrassed by all the foolishness, and ashamed even to talk about it any more.

"Hey, what's new with that girl of yours?" she asked. "Lucy what's-her-name. I haven't heard you mention her in a while."

I wasn't ready for that one. It was the first time Abby had taken an interest in anyone else for months. Besides, I really didn't know the answer. "Be right with you," I said. "Nature's calling," and I ducked into the bathroom to brush my teeth and all in the hopes she'd forget about Lucy. Not that I wouldn't have welcomed a chance to tell her everything. It was my turn for self-pity, by then. But the trouble was I hadn't really prepared my sad song and didn't want to spill it until I was sure the lyrics would be suitably touching. Besides she hadn't answered my letter so I couldn't even tell for sure whether my song should be a sad one or not.

I could hear Abby moving around amusing herself, I supposed, with those pictorial records of my not so glorious athletic career.

I smiled, gave my face a quick splash and was just reaching for the doorknob when the desk chair shrieked, there was a rustle, a sob, and the sound of my door slamming.

I fell out of the bathroom, looked around in brief confusion, then saw the contents of Jesse's envelope flung across my desk in an angry proclamation. On top of the pile was a copy of the resignation letter I'd written for Pa plus, conveniently, a penciled note explaining it all which I had attached afterward with the officiousness characteristic of someone suffering from a mistaken idea of his own importance.

Well, that did it. One lie to restore the balance and another to knock the whole works over again.

I made a hopeless sortie, but Abby's door was locked and she didn't seem very interested in any of my red-faced theories.

"What's wrong?" I asked stupidly.

"Wrong?" she repeated. "Have I done something wrong?"

"Not you. Come on, Abby, open the door."

"No. Go away."

I tried to wrench the doorknob but it wouldn't give and anger began to mix with my frustration. "Open the goddam door," I snarled.

She didn't answer and I banged it a couple of times with my fist. She wasn't impressed.

"For Christ sakes," I tried to whisper but kept losing control. "Don't you want to know what happened?" I sputtered. "Pa didn't know anything about it until the whole business was almost done."

I rattled the door again. "It was Jesse who really did it," I shouted.

"Because of you. And I helped him. Because of *you*. You, you you and your goddam tender soul."

I was seething by then, twisting the knob and pushing against the door in nearly uncontrolled fury. "Will you open this thing?" I demanded. "Or am I going to bust it down."

But even that didn't get a rise.

"All right," I said. "Okay." I backed off, lunged at the door. It splintered and made a hell of a bang but held. "Bitch."

I hit it again and that time it flew open with a crash and clatter of scattered screws and splinters. There we were, Abby kneeling on the bed, frightened but scrappy, and me standing there, my mission accomplished, forced now to say something which would justify it all.

"Now that you're here," she said, "what am I supposed to do, thank you for saving Pa's precious reputation or something?"

I wasn't entirely sure what she was supposed to do just then. Or me either.

"Maybe I should," she said. "Now everything's all straightened out it won't be necessary for me to marry Jesse, will it?"

That was all I needed. "Listen," I said. "If you haven't got guts enough to marry a Jew that's fine, but don't try an' blame it on me and Pa."

"Guts," she said, half to herself. "Where in the world would I have gotten those?"

I was just going to tell her when a hand closed on my shoulder.

"All right," said Pa. "That's enough."

I turned, still locked in the private world of fury, absolutely amazed anyone could have overheard me.

"Hadn't you better go to bed," Pa suggested. He stood in the doorway, gently firm, controlled, not at all the sort of man who needed help from anybody.

"She found out about that favor Jesse did us," I said. "The papers were on my desk."

Pa just nodded and stepped out of my way. I turned back to Abby.

"Pa was sick when that happened," I said. "He wouldn't have done it otherwise."

"All *right*, Larry," Pa said. "That's enough."

I started back to my room. Mother, wearing only her nightgown, was sailing down the hall, a grim white spectre of concern.

"Honestly, Larry, what on earth is the matter with you?" And she sailed past.

That surprised me so much I just stood there staring after her, not seeing anything, just staring, dumb-faced.

"Now look here, Abby," Pa was saying. "What is it that's bothering you?"

Abby snorted. "That would take all night," she said.

"Then let's take all night," Pa replied.

Abby didn't answer.

"Apparently I've done some things you don't approve of, Abby," Pa continued. "Now, aren't you going to give me a chance to explain?"

"There's nothing to explain," Abby dodged.

Mother hovered uncertainly, fidgeting.

"Well now," Pa said, "obviously there is." He waited but she refused to cooperate. "Apparently you don't approve of this resignation business," he said. "Or anything else I've done since the *Enterprise* came to town."

I heard nothing from Abby.

"And perhaps you're right," Pa continued. "I certainly haven't been at my best."

"Ha," said Abby.

"Now that doesn't help," Pa argued gently. "This campaign of disillusionment . . ." But that was as far as he got.

"Oh God," Abby moaned. It was as though she couldn't reconcile the inconsistencies between her simple bumbling caricature of the fallen idol and this human being who stood there, flawed, soiled yet far more gallant than a god too perfectly endowed.

"But Abby," Pa insisted. "People make mistakes. You must realize . . ."

"No," Abby screamed, then I heard a scuffle, she burst through the door, hesitated in an instant of wide-eyed, flaring confusion, raced past me and down the stairs.

I stood watching, paralyzed by surprise and indecision.

The front door slammed.

"For Heaven sakes," Mother demanded in a whisper of rage. "Catch her."

I ran then, reached the front door just in time to see Pa's white Lincoln swing down the driveway, turn, squat with power and lunge into the night.

I started to go after her, was restrained by the fear of precipitating an accident, and tried to decide what we should do next. A light rain was falling. I scuffed the gravel to see if it had started to freeze. It didn't seem so but I couldn't be sure.

They were just coming downstairs when I got back inside.

"Where is she?" Mother demanded.

"She took the Lincoln," I said.

"Well don't just stand there," Mother said. "Why didn't you go after her?" There was so much rage in her voice I could hardly bring myself to answer.

"I didn't want to," I said, unable to look at her. "I was afraid she might get rattled and have an accident."

"And isn't she rattled enough as it is?" Mother demanded.

There was nothing to say.

"Honestly, Larry, how you could have been so . . ." She hesitated but not for very long . . . "So utterly stupid as to leave those papers around, I can't imagine."

My eyes begged Pa for a little help.

"If anything happens to her," Mother said, "I'll never forgive you."

"Now now, Alice," Pa insisted. "It's as much our fault as Larry's."

"I don't see why," Mother said.

"Don't you?" Pa asked.

"Most certainly not," Mother said.

"Well perhaps that in itself is an explanation," Pa said.

"And that is supposed to mean?" Mother demanded.

"All right," Pa said. "Let's not argue now. We'd better think what to do about Abby."

"We could call the troopers," I said. "Maybe they'll pick her up."

"And have the whole town find out about it?" Mother asked.

"The whole town wouldn't have to know," Pa said. "But I'd rather not, Larry," he continued. "Just as you said, I'd rather not rattle her."

"Well, I suppose we're just going to sit here and wait then," Mother sneered.

Pa ignored her. "What's it like outside?" he asked.

"Raining," I said.

"Freezing?"

"No, just raining so far."

"Well, go have a look at the temperature," he said.

I went in and looked out the kitchen window.

"Thirty-four," I called.

"It's already one o'clock," Pa said. "Shouldn't get much colder."

I heard steps on the backstairs, then Bollard's sleep-fattened face peered through the kitchen door. "What's the matter lad?" he demanded.

"It's Abby," I said. "She got upset and went off in the Lincoln."

He grunted, pushed through the door, swathed in a crimson silk brocade robe which must have been Pa's once, and padded by me. "Would you like some coffee?" he asked Pa. "Or some hot milk?"

"Thank you, Bollard. I think coffee."

"Yes please," said Mother, behaving herself.

"Was there plenty of gas in the Lincoln?" Pa asked.

"I filled it this morning," Bollard said.

Pa nodded vaguely, as though not sure whether that was a help or hindrance.

"I wouldn't worry about Miss Abby," Bollard said. "She's a fine driver."

"You taught her yourself, didn't you, Bollard?"

"Yes sir, I did."

"Then I don't suppose there's much to worry about, is there?"

"No sir."

And the missed opportunity to tease Bollard served as a measure of Pa's concern.

We settled in the living room after that to speculate over where she might have gone, a return to practical matters which calmed Mother enough to tell me she was sorry.

Which was all very well but insufficient to erase the bitch fury I'd seen in her earlier, mostly directed at me, or perhaps at the collapse of order for which she held me responsible. Either way left me appalled at the apparent disintegration of love, that love of hers which seemed to cover such a vast area, yet had no depth.

Bollard brought our coffee, then went back to the kitchen where I found him later, sitting hunched at a table, sipping his own brew, only waiting.

"Where would she go, lad?"

"I don't know."

"What started it?"

"I don't know," I lied. It was too complicated to explain. "Love problems mostly."

"With that Mr. Rosenfeldt?"

I nodded.

"You might call him," he said.

"She'd never go there," I said. "It takes over an hour."

"Wouldn't hurt to call him," he repeated.

"Well, don't say anything about it," I said. "They're worried enough."

He nodded, still hunched, back to me slurping his coffee.

I went up to my room and called Jesse, got the wrong Rosenfeldt home, judging by the hacking, mucous voice, hung up and tried again. That time it was Jesse who answered, slow-witted with sleep, out of control, quick to panic. He wanted to call the troopers, go out after her himself and God knows what all, but I finally got him to do nothing except call us if she showed up. It was almost two o'clock by then and I told him she'd be due there in a half hour or so.

Downstairs Mother and Pa were still speculating between long silences, but had yet to light on Bollard's theory. They thought she might have gone back to college, just driven around, stopped at that dreadful place, what's it called?

"Frank's?" I asked.

"Yes," they said and I gave him a call, just going through the motions, knowing she'd only go there on the upswing.

And we went back to our waiting, disaster seeming more inevitable with each passing minute.

By two-thirty Mother was ready to start calling all the hospitals, convinced Abby lay crumpled and broken in one of them, and Pa was too unsure to stop her.

It took almost an hour to find them all and when she finally gave up there was a hopelessness about her, a real disappointment, as though finding Abby in a hospital but still alive was the only alternative.

Five minutes later the phone rang. I beat them both to it.

"She was here an hour ago," Jesse told me, half-screaming with frenzy.

"Why the hell didn't you call us?" I demanded.

"The goddam phone," he shouted, and I realized it was more frustration than frenzy. "It's been busy the whole time."

"Oh that's right," I said. "Well, what happened?"

"I don't know," he admitted. "Everything seemed all right when she got here. Abby was quite calm, even . . . well . . . even affectionate really." He paused, embarrassed or confused or both. "I just went out to get her some coffee, and . . ."

"And what?"

"When I came back she was . . . well, she was gone."

"Gone?"

"Yes. Oh God, everything was all right and then she just ran off."

"What do you mean all right?"

"Well I mean that she'd come to me," he tried to explain.

"Oh."

"But then she ran away again, don't you see? Then she ran away again."

"Okay," I said. "All right, I'll call you if, I mean *when* she gets back," and I hung up.

"What in the world was she doing there?" Mother asked.

"I didn't know it was that serious," Pa said.

"No," I said ambiguously.

"How long was she there?" Mother demanded.

"I don't know," I answered. "Not very long."

"I should think not," she said.

"He tried to call," I explained, unable to resist discrediting Mother's hospital idea. "But the phone was busy."

"Well, did he expect us to sit here doing nothing?"

"He didn't have to call at all," Pa reminded her and that was the end of that.

Armed with the new developments, we went back to our speculation but soon ran out of anything to do but wait. I made drinks for Pa and me and we sat there, eyes stinging with smoke and sleep, mouths velvet and bad tasting, minds and bodies numb.

Four.

Four twenty-five.

Four-forty.

Four fifty-five, and the sound of a car engine droned through the distance, swelled to a roar and scraped our tender nerves until we were jarringly, painfully awake. I ran to the front door, Mother and Pa following, and stood watching, somehow prevented from going to help her by the dull, mechanical, lifeless way she disentangled herself from the car and sleepwalked toward the house.

She reached me first and stopped. Her eyes, slack with disgust and futility, flickered from face to face with total disinterest, then settled on me.

"You're right," she said. "I don't have the guts to marry a Jew." Then she toppled by us and up the stairs. Not even Mother could think of anything to say or do.

I started up to bed.

"Larry," Mother called.

I turned.

"I *am* sorry, darling."

"Sure," I said. "Me too," and kept on going, remembering to call Jesse before I spilled into bed. That he didn't answer surprised me, but I was a little too punchy by then to figure out why, guessed maybe he'd cut off his phone and was just beginning to drop off when it began to filter through that someone was feeling his way up the backstairs, shufflingly, haltingly. I lay still trying to listen over the pounding of my heart, finally heard a whispered, "Abby, Abby, is that you, Abby?" and the reason Jesse's phone didn't answer became all too apparent. I lay there for a minute or two, hoping what was happening might turn out to be a dream, but the longer I waited, the more obvious it became that I wasn't asleep. Finally I heard Abby's door creak, saw the glow from her lights and went out to referee. It was Jesse all right, but not the sleek and well-attended Jesse I'd first met at that Jaycee cocktail party. He was sick-eyed, gulping, jerky, as though each gesture somehow burned his fingers. There he stood in sweatshirt and baggy flannels, trying to talk, rejecting each attempt before the words could form, staring down at Abby who lay fully clothed and all the more crumpled because of it, wide-eyed, seeing nothing.

He saw me, but it made no impression.

"Abby?" he asked again. "Abby?" But she said nothing, moved nothing.

I waited, wondering whether to interfere, waiting for him to do something with which I could interfere, but he did nothing; just stood there bewildered, watching. Had she moved he might have found the word, the gesture, but she didn't. The Abby of his pursuit, his love, had died, and as Jesse became more aware of this his concern seemed to falter, his eyes began to wander about the room, his hands grew calm. Then without a word he turned, loped off toward the stairs and disappeared.

"Bones?" I asked, but she still made no response and I wondered whether perhaps my Abby had died too. "Bones, are you okay?"

She dipped her head in a half-nod and I left, as much afraid to leave her as to face sleep with its tangle of thwarted instinct, twisted morality and terror.

CHAPTER XXII

Abby managed to miss breakfast next morning but so did everybody else, except me, which wasn't too surprising. I'd have been all too glad to miss it myself but for the unhappy fact we published Saturdays. Maybe Abby's low jinks should have been my primary concern but I was blurred from lack of sleep and a little resentful for her having caused this condition and therefore not too inclined to sympathize. Instead I told myself maybe she wouldn't be so goddamed superior and high strung now she'd managed to be a damn fool along with the rest of us and let it go at that.

I was more interested in my own problem than Abby's anyway. That look on Mother's face had been so close to hatred it was difficult to apply the balm of reason; to tell myself it had only been a flash of anger and no kin at all to what it seemed like. But as I picked my way through the scrambled eggs and bacon, mulling for the usual scraps of self-pity and resentment, I found these tender by-products, while there, no longer satisfied. Instead a cold, confident defiance rose like musk and settled on my soul. The need for their approval, their sanction of everything I did was strangely absent. And not only absent, but totally unwelcome. What, after all, was so precious and inviolable about their opinions?

Bollard came in with a pot of fresh coffee.

"Thanks," I said.

"It's the early bird gets the worm."

But I didn't feel like bantering, said nothing, poured the fresh coffee and drank it black, feeling the tissues in my mouth and throat scorch, cool then scorch again as I continued gulping, forcing the body to accept a whim, gaining a grim kind of pleasure from this tortured, perhaps masochistic and certainly needless exercise in self-discipline. My body, my spirit driven by my will, judged by my mind; these were the ultimate concerns and to hell with seeking approval from anyone other than myself.

That this theory might hold no place for love, other than the perversion of self-love, was not apparent to me at the time. I was interested only in a formula for my own survival and would alter it to fit new aspects when and if those aspects arose. Meanwhile I'd be for me and me alone. I gulped the last of my coffee, scanned the metropolitan papers for an idea of the kind of day we could expect and was just getting ready to go to the office when the front door opened and closed, followed by the sound of hesitant footsteps.

"Yes?" I called.

And Nora appeared at the dining-room door.

"Oh," she said. "Is your mother up?"

I shook my head.

"I have her, uh . . . I have her tickets for the Thanksgiving Ball."

"Oh?"

"You know, at the Armory."

"Sure. Would you want to leave them with me?"

"Well," she said. "I guess I could do that," and she took a tentative step into the room.

"How 'bout a cup of coffee," I said, breaking my new rule already but she looked so sort of lost and everything.

"I guess so. If you're not in a hurry."

"I can be late. It's Saturday," and I buzzed for Bollard. Nora sat down. I couldn't think what we might talk about and neither could she.

"Got any more coffee cups?" I asked Bollard when he came in.

" 'Twouldn't surprise me," and he went in search.

"Sorry Mother isn't up. We had sort of a late night."

"Oh," Nora said and shrugged, as though that had been just an excuse anyway, then unbuttoned her black wool overcoat, let it flop open revealing the dress beneath, its crimson textures clinging to the soft curves of her abdomen, creating an effect both menacing and seductive.

Bollard was back with the cup.

I poured. One lump or two, Mrs. Woodruff, and shuddered at the thought.

"Here," I said, pushing the cream and sugar her way. "Help yourself."

"Thanks," she said, reaching, spidery arms poking from the black sleeves. "Tommy's home, you know."

"No," I said. "For the weekend?"

"Uh huh."

"Well, maybe I'll see him."

"I doubt it."

I raised my eyebrows.

"He's been very strange," she explained.

"He's not the only one."

"Didn't get in until after four," she said.

"He's not the only one," I repeated.

"But I thought you hadn't seen him."

"No, not me," I corrected. "Abby was kind of late last night."

"Oh?" she asked.

"But I don't think there's a connection," I hastened to add.

"It's a funny coincidence," she said.

"Now don't go jumping to conclusions," I laughed. "I happen to know where Abby was."

"Well where was she?" Nora insisted.

That pulled me up kind of short. "What business would it be of yours?"

She began to swell.

"Oh now, come on, Nora," I said. "After all it really isn't any of your business."

"I was just trying to be helpful," Nora said.

"Well, that's nice," I said. "But actually there isn't any way you *can* be helpful so far as Abby's concerned."

"None of my business," Nora repeated, not quite concealing the hint of a gasp. "How can you say that?"

"Because it isn't," I insisted.

"But how can you? After all these years."

"We're not married," I said, wallowing. "What are we talking about, anyway?"

"Oh," she said. "Oh Larry," and curled up tight in the chair, beginning to cry in a high-pitched, constipated kind of way.

"Oh balls," I said, but apparently that was not the secret word for then she really let loose.

"What's the matter with us?" she sobbed. "What have I done?"

"Nora please," I said, alternately getting up, sitting back down, finally getting up. "You haven't done anything."

"Uhhh huh huh huhhh," she sobbed. "Shush shush shush," went the nose, and "Huh huh huhhh," the chest.

"Come on, sweetie," I begged, squatting down beside her, trying to find her face in the huddle of arms and coat and wrenching shoulders. "I'm sorry for what I said."

"What?" she asked.

I tried to remember. "Ah, that it was none of your business," I repeated triumphantly.

"Oh, it isn't just that," she said and her sobs took on a bubbling permanence.

I was afraid it wasn't but didn't feel up to discussing the real reason just then. Bollard started through the pantry door and I waved him off.

"Say, I'm glad you came over," I said. "I've been meaning to talk to you about the Thanksgiving Ball anyway."

"Talk to me?" she asked. "What about?"

"Well, whether we were going or not."

"Going?"

"Yuh. You know, you and me."

"Oh!" She sat up straight, then began to gather her lost composure.

I leaned over and kissed her wet cheek, feeling strong, competent and, for some reason, aroused. My lips seemed to slink and finally pounce on her soft, wet, still slightly trembling mouth and there was an almost irresistible urge to grab a fistful of hair, twist her into submission. But rather than submit, Nora seemed to be gathering, clenching beneath my kiss and suddenly I found myself seated on the floor still quivering like a hungry dog.

"Don't you start patronizing me," she said, patting herself together.

"Doing what?" I asked, still a trifle put off.

"You don't have to feel sorry for me," she sniffed. "And it just so happens I'm going to the dance with Sam Crawley."

"Well fine," I said, getting up. "That's just fine and from now on you can do your crying over at his place."

"Maybe I will. And maybe I won't."

"In any case you won't be doing it over here any more. That's for sure."

She got up at that and we faced each other, her eyes ducking, feinting, probing for the truth of what I'd said. "You seem awfully eager to build this into a crisis," she hedged.

I laughed. "And what else is it?"

"If you can't be serious, perhaps we'd better discuss it later."

"Nora," I insisted, "there isn't going to be any later."

She looked at me with a mixture of impatience and panic, as though I were a child grown too big to spank.

"Well, we'll just have to wait and see about that." She sniffed and marched off.

I looked at my watch. It was eight-thirty. Already a half hour late. I pulled out a cigarette, lit it, heard her car go down the drive, and hurried out.

Well, that was it, as far as I was concerned, and the sense of freedom was so overpowering, so intoxicating I hardly knew where to begin enjoying it.

Mr. Quincy was just coming down from the barn carrying his leaf rake and looking less than delighted as I wheeled out of the garage.

"Good morning," I called.

"Ain't nawthin good 'bout it th'all them leaves t'pick up."

I laughed for lack of a suggestion. "How 'bout putting out some birds tomorrow morning," I said.

"Suits me," he said. "Your Pa going?"

"No, just me. So far as I know."

"All right. I'll be by."

I waved and swung down the drive, telling myself not to scratch off as I turned into the main road, but doing it anyway in a sizzle and yaw of sand and gravel and grabbing tires.

"Don't let 'em fool you," I laughed. "Growing up's for kids," and I took off down the road giving Nora the old Bermuda bell as I whipped by and laughing out loud not at Nora or anybody else. Just laughing.

When I got to the paper Ted already was working my desk which didn't surprise me at all being a Saturday when everything was screwed up anyhow. It turned out the troopers had picked up a guy in connection with one of those big New York gang killings so Jeff was out at the barracks getting a picture and I took over for him. City Hall even *looks* dead on Saturday with only the cops open for business but I checked the blotter to see if anybody illustrious had been admitted to the drunk tank. Nothing, not even the usual bunch of bums. It looked like just one of those days. Except for Jeff's story and a couple of auto accidents there wasn't anything doing so we sat around drinking coffee and writing heads for the wire copy and otherwise fooling the morning away. Spaulding of Yale began reciting limericks while he typed which I understand is

one of the first things you have to learn up there at old Boola Boola
if you want to be somebody, and of course everybody does, but they
were pretty funny so I managed to keep my private prejudices
private.

Then Ted made the mistake of asking Jeff what he had on the
New York hood and got a play by play complete with dialect which
must have set us back another fifteen minutes.

"That's very interesting," said Ted. "In fact, it's the lead so don't
forget to write it, okay?"

"Don't you want to hear the rest?" Jeff asked.

"I'd rather read about it," Ted admitted. "In the *Daily Watch* if
possible."

"Oh come on," Jeff laughed. "Don't be so competitive."

"A handsome young bishop of France . . ." Spaulding began.

"All right, all right," Ted interrupted.

Spaulding shrugged, went back to drinking coffee with the rest of
us.

Needless to say it wasn't much of a paper that day but we needed
a break every once in a while after the pressure of those last few
months so I guess it wasn't anything to be ashamed of.

I gave Hal a call to ask if he was interested in flying that afternoon
seeing as we wouldn't be able to once the snow started and he said
he would be and then I got to talking with Jeff about hunting. He'd
been out a couple of times but no luck so I asked him how about
coming out with me in the morning and he said sure. Then we all
went over to Frank's Place for a sandwich and a few beers and a
couple of rounds of shuffleboard so I was feeling pretty mellow
when it came time to go home and downright convinced Gravenhurst was the garden spot of America or at least no worse than any
place else, Potters Island included. I figured this theory might be
pretty severely tested just as soon as I got home, but it turned out
things weren't so bad after all. On the surface anyway and that was
all anybody cared about. Abby, in fact, was downright apathetic,
as though she'd decided to accept being a slob along with the rest
of us, and by calling it serenity instead of apathy it got to be almost
virtuous. First she came to my room and apologized for her perfectly frightful behavior as though she were talking about her little
girl rather than herself. Then she smiled with rather patronizing
tolerance and said: "Oh dear, you know poor Jesse proposed to me
again last night."

I was reminded of Nora. "Yes," I said. "I thought he seemed upset."

"Did he?" said she. "I'm so sorry."

"And you declined?"

"In effect," she said. "I left."

"But you didn't say no?"

"I think it amounts to the same thing," she snipped, carefully crossing a leg and watching her hand smooth the dress from thigh to knee.

"In fact you've never actually said no, have you?"

She smiled gently. "It's hard. They're so sensitive."

"Oh they are are they?" I snorted.

"You know it perfectly well," she said.

"Well *they* seem to compensate for it," I said, "by living pretty interesting lives." I'd been lying on the bed, arms behind my head, watching Abby try to be a schoolmistress and mother to our secret souls.

"Interesting?" she asked, smug-voiced, and at that I rolled into a sitting position ready to rant again, then remembered she was no longer any of my business.

"Well it's not such a bad life," I said, almost defensively. "Living all over the world and doing all kinds of different jobs and just being the kind of guy Jesse is."

"Oh I guess he's not so wonderful as all that," she said. "Nobody is."

"He's alive," I pointed out.

"Who isn't?"

"He's alive all over. Not just the bowels."

"That's disgusting."

I shrugged, flopped back on the bed.

"Besides," she said, "everybody's alive."

"Some more than others."

"And in Gravenhurst some less than others, I suppose."

"You're the one who thought it was such a dump," I said.

"One has to grow up sometime," she said.

"Speak for yourself," I laughed.

"Honestly, Larry, you're such a child."

Ah, but there was nothing funny about Abby.

"Listen," I said. "Since when has growing up got anything to do with acquiescing? Everybody sits around here waiting to turn into a pig and when it happens the excuse is 'I've grown up, what's the matter with you?'"

Abby didn't say anything, just looked away. She wasn't that impervious yet.

"Well?" I demanded.

"I saw Tommy Compton last night," she said, as though it were relevant.

"So."

"Speaking of not wanting to be a pig," she said.

"At least he's trying," I said.

"Don't you want to know where I saw him?"

I got up and dug in the closet for my flight jacket. "Where?"

"Coming out of a motel about four this morning."

"So?"

"With a girl."

"Well I'm glad it wasn't a Boy Scout."

"Know who I think it was?"

"Nora!"

"Sally Polk."

I came backing out of the closet hauling my jacket free of the debris. "Are you sure?"

She nodded. "The motel lights were pretty bright."

"They're crazy. Where was it?"

"Way over near the Hudson. A very discreet little motel."

"That's nice."

"I guess they just don't want to be pigs."

"No," I agreed. "Nor baboons either."

"And what's that supposed to mean?"

"Nothing. I have to go." I started for the door.

"You ought to tidy your bed," she said. "It's a mess."

"Yes, Nora," I said, but Abby just smiled her brand-new don't-be-childish smile and let me go. On my way out Lucy's face appeared again, incredulous, slightly mocking, the way it was when she'd asked, "You don't really live in a place like Gravenhurst, do you?" I rattled down the stairs and almost ran to get off where the new Woodruff, champion of Number One, could function freely without the clogging effects of sympathy and love.

It was pretty chilly out but I rolled down the car windows and let the wind shiver me, force me to think only of my body, my discomfort, my defiance. "Screw the whole bunch," I said to nothing and no one, to everything and everyone. "Including the pallbearers."

Some jackass was crawling along in front of me about twenty miles an hour and a truck coming at a pretty good clip but I dropped into second and swung out, engine howling and scrambled past him just ahead of the truck and how do you like that? Damn fool's gonna kill us all. And what if I do? The thought of death, pious and threatening as a Sunday sermon, swelled over me.

"What do you want?"

But it just stayed, threatening, frightening, bringing me to heel.

"You would, would you?" And I pressed down on the gas carefully, deliberately so there'd be no mistake, and death said don't be fresh. The red line pressed to sixty, seventy—over the top of Birch Hill and down—eighty—down with the wind a fist now, beating—eighty-five, eighty-seven, ninety, ninety-four. Death grinning.

"You want me, do you? Well, come on."

I lifted my foot and jammed hard on the brake, mashing death and fear and hesitation. The car screeched, lurched, dove left across the line, phone pole looming as I spun the wheel, yawed and dove hard to the right, trees now, and back left, then right until strangely all motion was gone and I sat panting, a quiet country road stretching harmlessly, and death nowhere to be seen.

"Well, isn't that too bad," I said. "But you be sure and try again."

I saw a car coming, waited, recognized Hal James's Jag, gave him a toot and pulled out to follow.

When we got there I noticed he was looking kind of pasty.

"You look awful," I told him. "What's the matter?"

"Little trip to Mother Murphy's," he said. "I'm hung to the rafters."

"You ought to get a season ticket, Hal."

He laughed. "You'll never guess who was out there last night."

"Your old man."

"No but you're close."

"Your old lady?"

"Don't get funny."

"Who?"

"The judge."

"Compton?" I was delighted. "No kidding."

"Scout's honor," Hal promised.

"How'd you happen to see him?"

"Didn't . . . I heard him talking."

We pushed through the door into Pete's office and dropped the subject. He was at his desk, feet propped up on an open drawer.

"What are you, nuts?" he demanded. "It's cold up there."

I shrugged. "It's cold down here too."

"Yeah?" he asked. "It'll seem like Miami when you guys get back."

"Don't worry about it," I said. "We're a couple of rough boys, right, Hal?" and I gave him a good teenage punch on the arm.

"Hey," he said, flinching. "What's the matter with you?"

"I'm no good," I said, turned and walked off. "Come on, let's go flying."

"I know that without being hit," Hal said, rubbing his arm and following.

I was in first so Pete started me up and I was just about to move off when Hal's face appeared at the door and he started making open-up signs.

"What's the matter?" I yelled.

"I'm all jittery," he shouted. "Lemme go up with you," and he crawled in behind me.

"I'm the last guy on earth to fly with when you're feeling jittery," I laughed.

Hal laughed back but a little grimly. "I need the fresh air. Too goddam hung."

I started downwind along the runway, the engine stuttering with cold, pulled off to rev her up, began to ease her around for the take-off.

"Give it a couple more seconds," Hal said. "It's cold out."

"No fooling." But that wasn't the day to tell *me* what to do. We swung around and I opened up on the throttle and down we went, the extra weight making it sluggish at first but okay once we got a little speed up.

Things were still a little sticky during the climb, though.

"I'd forgotten what it's like with two people," I shouted.

"Feels like a balloon," Hal agreed.

But it was better when we leveled off.

"Where to?" I asked.

"Suit yourself."

"Let's go buzz Mother Murphy's," I laughed. "Shake up the matinee."

But Hal didn't seem in the mood, so I swung west, heading for our house. We came in high along the south side of the lake and I could see someone out on the dock. Abby most likely. I pointed for Hal to see.

"Looks like Abby," he shouted.

I nodded, felt like fooling around a little and went into a long bank over the Comptons', dropping down all the while, then cut the throttle, coming in over our house and across the lawn. I wasn't more than a hundred feet up and could see Abby plain as day standing on the end of the dock, west wind lashing her hair and dress. I was going to get right on top of her, then gun it and take off down the lake.

"Be sure you get a look at her face," I laughed and shoved on the throttle and—Oh, sweet Jesus, if you're not too busy—the engine sputtered, went cold dead.

"Goddam carburetor heat," I yelled. "Forgot all about it." We started gliding in over the lake.

"Christ sakes," Hal muttered. "Get it up."

I could feel him hauling on the dual controls. "Keep your god-dam hands off," I yelled.

He did.

Nothing but windy silence.

The lake was hourglass shaped with a pretty good meadow on the north side of the narrows. If I could just stay in the air long enough to get there. That water looked close, though, and the stick was already feeling mushy. Or was it? I inched back a little, still had control.

"Well?" Hal demanded.

"Keep your pants on."

"Those wheels catch and we're diddled," said Hal.

I couldn't stop a yawn. "None of that life insurance for me," I said. "I'll take mutual funds any day."

"Up yours," said Hal.

I eased back a little more. She was still flying. "We're gonna make it," I said.

"Then what?"

"Few stone walls," I laughed, but there weren't, thank God.

"Swell," he said. "The old man can save a couple of bucks on the tombstone."

I got to giggling and hauled back all the way and she started to mush. It looked kind of bumpy and I hoped to God we wouldn't flip. Then we touched, came up, teetered left, bumped, then dropped for good and bundled to a stop just beyond mid-field.

"There we are, chaps," I said. "Everything ticketyboo."

"Everything ticketyshit," said Hal. "How do we get out of here?"

"Same way we got in," I laughed. I turned around and patted Hal on the cheek. "How's the old head now?"

"Just fine," he grumbled. "Except I need to get drunk all over again."

I unhooked my belt, got the door open and wiggled out. Abby was coming across the lake, oars flapping like a wounded duck.

"Hurry up," I called to Hal. "You don't want to miss this."

He stuck his head out, then scrambled after it. Abby washed out and nearly fell off her seat.

"Who's rescuing who?" Hal snorted.

She turned around, saw we were all right and kept coming at a more leisurely pace. I went down to the edge and hauled her ashore.

"What in the world are you two doing here?" she demanded.

"Waiting for you," I said.

"But you could have been killed," she said.

"It wasn't exactly our idea," Hal admitted.

"What happened?" Abby asked.

"I think the technical term is pilot error," said Hal helpfully.

"Are you trying to make me look like a jerk?" I asked.

"That shouldn't be necessary," he said.

Abby had climbed out by then and was looking from one to the other of us as though we were a couple of crazy Martians. "Weren't you scared?" she asked.

"No," I said. "We're too dumb."

"No really," she demanded.

"Well there wasn't much time," I said. "But I am now."

Hal held out his hand and we watched it tremble. "Not me," he said.

Abby laughed at him and his mouth fell open from the shock of it. I guess she'd never done that before.

"And now what?" she demanded.

"We better take the thing back," I said, sounding a little doubtful. It looked sort of silly sitting there in the middle of nowhere but I wasn't too eager to move it.

"Can I go?" she asked.

"No room," I said.

"Well somebody stay here," she insisted. "I want to go."

"It's against the rules," I said.

"Why?"

"We're students."

"You must have broken most of the rules already," she said. "What's one more?"

"You have a point," I admitted.

"Well, which one?"

"Which one what?"

"Which one takes me?"

I shrugged, still reluctant.

"After seeing your brother fly," Hal spoke up, "I shouldn't think there'd be any question about it."

I raised my eyebrows.

"Why not?" he asked. "Pete'll cool off by next spring."

"Field's kind of bumpy," I said.

"You game, Abby?" Hal asked.

She nodded.

"Your funeral," I said.

"Come on," Hal said. "We only die once."

"I've been dying all day," I pointed out. "Without any luck." They both looked at me sort of funny but decided it was a joke and started walking toward the plane. I followed.

"Put your foot right there," Hal was saying, steadying her. "It's a tight squeeze."

Abby wormed her way in and sat down. Then Hal helped get the seat belt on and climbed in, got himself set, gave me a nod and I spun the prop. It started first time.

"I'll be damned," I shouted, jumping back out of the way.

"Nothing to it when you know how," Hal yelled, slammed the door and started back toward the water.

I decided to have a look at the rest of the field and headed off at a trot but it seemed smooth enough so I waved them on from the far end and squatted down as the plane came at me, lifted off and pulled away easy as pie with the two of them waving. Once in the air it didn't seem like anything at all had gone wrong and I felt a little confused about being on the ground. Not half as confused as Pete would be, though, when he saw Abby come crawling out of that plane.

I laughed and started back for the boat, feeling slightly heroic

and therefore foolish. Landing that Piper Cub in a meadow wasn't
quite the same thing as getting a crippled jet back to the carrier,
maybe, but I found the distinction a difficult one to make. Thus I
rowed back to the dock, admitting one minute I was a damn fool
and imagining myself a pilot ditched at sea the next.

Mother and Pa were in the living room.

"Well, dear, did you have a nice lesson?"

"Not bad," I said, "considering."

"Must have been a little cold," Pa suggested.

"Yes it was, as a matter of fact." Then I decided it might be a good
idea to wander outside and intercept Abby and Hal so they wouldn't
spill the beans. Mr. Quincy was there and I told him there'd be two
of us shooting in the morning so he could put out a few more birds
and about that time they came crunching up the driveway, Abby
first looking flushed and competent, the future of her sad little soul
already forgotten.

"Well how was it?" I asked.

"Great," she shouted. "I'm gonna start taking lessons next spring."

"Shh," I laughed, thumbing at the house. "They don't know anything about it."

"Oh," she shrugged carelessly.

"And I'll look like a liar if they find out."

"Oh," she said. "Okay."

"Pete sore?"

"Didn't even see him," Hal laughed. "Out in the hangar someplace
so we just hustled on through and disappeared."

"The perfect crime," I said. "It's as if the whole thing didn't
happen."

"That suits me," Hal said.

"But I was a hero," I said.

"You were also a jerk," Hal reminded me.

"That's the price you pay. Without war a man's got to be his own
damn fool."

"You've mastered the art," Hal admitted.

"Even with a war sometimes. I knew a guy in college got the Silver
Star for holding off a bunch of coolies when everybody else'd beat it.
Turned out his foot was asleep. Couldn't move."

"I see the connection," Hal said. "Your brain was asleep."

"I was a hero," I insisted.

"What do you think?" Hal asked Abby.

"I think it's still asleep," she said.

I gave up.

"Hey," Hal said. "There's a good flick at the Palace. Let's have dinner at the club and catch it."

"Sure," I said. It never occurred to me to ask what was playing.

"I don't know," said Abby, catching herself with Hal maybe, or just having a good time in Gravenhurst. "I shouldn't."

"Oh come on," I said.

"Please Abby," Hal said.

"Well, all right," she said and managed to smile at his sincerity.

"It's six now," he said. "Meet you up there around seven."

We waved and started for the house.

"He's changed," she said.

"How?"

"I don't know. Not so smart alecky."

I hadn't noticed he was so smart alecky or that he'd changed either but didn't say so.

We were halfway upstairs when Mother yoohooed. Abby spooked and took the other half two at a time.

"All right," I laughed. "I'll go."

I went and parked myself in the living-room door.

"Yes?"

"Oh," Mother said. "I thought it was Abby."

I said nothing.

"Well," Mother stalled. "Are you going to be in for dinner?"

"No," I said. "We're going out."

"It's a little late to be letting us know," she said.

"I'll tell Bollard," and I turned to go.

"Where are you going?" Mother asked.

"Change."

"No, I mean for dinner."

"Club," and I turned again.

"Would you like a drink first?" she asked. "You and Abby?"

"No thanks. We're late."

"How is she?"

"Who?"

Pa dropped the paper he'd been hiding behind and peered out. "Your sister," he said. "Who did you suppose?"

"In the pink," I said and went.

I could picture them sitting there staring at each other, wondering, perhaps asking what was the matter with me. Why was I so uncommunicative all of a sudden and so . . . well, so apathetic? And of course they'd decide it was because of last night; because Mother had hurt my feelings which was partly true, but only partly. I wasn't retaliating, as they probably thought, but simply apprehensive lest I again be privileged to peek over that jewel-incrusted parental façade at the little piglets scurrying within.

I went and told Bollard we'd be out. Then hurried upstairs, shaved, changed, collected Abby and got the hell out.

Once safe in the car—my very own car, never mind who payed for it—I felt better.

"There seems to be an insurrection in the making," I said.

"Oh?" Abby asked. "Who?"

"Us."

"On the contrary," she said. "I just quit."

"It's the same thing."

"What?"

"They liked you being a rebel; now you've stopped. That's an insurrection too." I started the car, let it loosen up for a few seconds, turned down the drive.

"But it's sort of a negative one," she said after a while.

"Passive resistance," I laughed. "It's the latest thing."

"Why?"

"I don't know," and I didn't. "No place for direct action any more, I guess. Countries do it they get blown off the map. People do it they get lost in the coils of super justice and win or lose it's not their doing."

"I don't know either," Abby said.

Hal was out front when we got there, having what looked like a pretty heated conversation with his old man so we waved and went on in and staked out the quietest corner.

Hal came in after a while looking sort of rattled.

"What's the matter?" I asked.

He dropped himself in a big armchair and became part of it.

"Oh, the old man's in a sweat," he said. "What're we drinking?" He raised an arm just in time to catch the waiter sneaking out.

"I don't know, martini, I guess."

"Me too," said Abby. "On the rocks."

"On the stem for me."

"The same," said Hal. "With a twist all around."

"What's the matter with him?" I asked.

"Who?"

"Your old man."

"Oh hell. You know the Barclay place?"

"Up the street from you?"

"Yeah, well it's for sale, Healy was handling it."

"I'd heard."

"And now Rosenfeldt's handling it."

"So?"

"Son of a bitch—excuse me, Abby—son of a bitch showed it to Louis Abrams. Supposed to be a restricted neighborhood."

"Who cares?" Abby asked.

"The old man," said Hal.

"Do you?" she asked.

Hal slumped further. "It's a free country," he said. "But . . ."

"But what?" she persisted.

"Well, it raises hell with property values," he said, sort of pleading. "And that's a fact."

Abby and I looked at each other, not sure what we saw, then the drinks came and we rested our consciences in the oily look of gin and guaranteed oblivion.

"Besides," Hal insisted, "what kind of a jerk does the old man look like getting forced out of his own house? I mean being in the real estate business and all."

"Forced out?" I asked.

"Sure. Those goddam Blockbusters'll drive us out so fast you won't know we were there."

"And do you think that's right?" Abby asked.

Hal started, hesitated, looked her in the eye. "No," he admitted. "As a matter of fact I don't."

"Then why don't you say so?" she asked.

"None of my business."

"You live there," she insisted.

"It's not my house," he said.

"But you can still tell him what you think."

"I could quit my job and move out too," he said.

"Well?" she asked.

"Look, Abby," he said, "that's just the way it is," and he took a long pull on his martini. "You can't change the way people think. Better just forget," and he followed it with another sip.

I joined him.

"Pretty good movie," he said. "About that Indian who put the flag up in Iwo. Know the one I mean?"

"Oh yeah," I said. "The lush."

"Let's eat pretty soon," Abby said, flat-voiced.

I was kind of surprised she'd stayed.

On the way out I gave Abby a poke, whispered: "Still think he's changed?"

"I didn't see you starting any crusades," she said.

"Well hell, Hal's my best friend." We hurried after him.

It turned out we were wrong on the movie. It was about a guy who hated phonies so much he died of it. What you'd call a misfit. It also happened to be about that Indian who helped raise the flag on Iwo and later on drank too much fire water, but these facts were relatively incidental. Anyway, everybody sighed at the injustice of it all and felt lots better.

We ran into Tommy Compton on the way out of the Palace.

Abby stared at him as though she'd never seen one before and I guess I did too. He was the first seducer I'd ever known—or at least the first one I ever knew I'd known—and a more unlikely candidate I couldn't imagine.

"Hey," I managed finally. "You still reciting poetry?"

Tommy laughed, kind of rolled and flexed his shoulders like a cat; but an alley cat. He was still pretty skinny. "Wasn't that a crazy deal," he said.

"I was beginning to think you were a little crazy too," I admitted.

"What's this all about?" Abby asked.

"This guy reciting poetry in a Beat night club," I explained.

"Really?" she asked and began exploring with her eyes, like when she first met Jesse.

He laughed confidently.

"Had to," he explained.

Hal shook his head, but with admiration. "I swear, Compton, you're the nuttiest guy I ever met."

I guess that went for me too. He was somebody else every time you saw him.

"Well well," I said. "Look where we are," and sure enough we'd managed to reach old Frank's Place.

"Didn't think you were going home, did you?" Hal laughed and shoved at the door, gave it a push so it would stay open long enough for Tommy and me, then followed Abby into the smoke and dark-ness.

They were stacked three deep at the bar. All kinds. Politicos, off-duty cops, teachers, businessmen, reporters, lawyers, hotshots from the community college. The works, all sucking on Saturday night as though it were the last one they'd ever get. We followed Hal as he maneuvered Abby through the crowd, deftly clearing the way with a "Hey Joe, smatter, you got no manners? Can't see there's a gentle-man trying to get through," and a lot a laughs and friendly shoving and Abby playing the game too, looking polite and proud as though she were running for public office or something.

I don't know, they sort of made sense together, it seemed to me, but then so did Nora and I.

Everybody was standing for fear they'd miss something so we didn't have any trouble finding a table and first chance I whispered to Tommy he should be more careful, Abby saw him coming out of the motel. There was no pretended perplexity, no anxiety, confu-sion, nothing. Just: "Pah, what's the difference?"

"Plenty," I said. "If Polk catches you."

"And if he does?"

"I'd hate to think."

"Who cares?"

"How 'bout Sally?"

"She knows what she's doing."

"But you wouldn't want her to get hurt," I argued.

"No, but I couldn't stop it."

"You could stop seeing her."

"No," he said. "I couldn't do that either."

"Why not?"

"No point," he said. "No point to anything."

"That sounds like you're an existentialist or something."

"I am," he said.

"Well you picked a convenient time for it," I said and just for a second there I was pleased to note a crumbling, a trace of doubt, a wondrous welcome sign of confusion.

"I'm thirsty," he said. "Let's get drunk."

We waved down the weekend waiter, some kid from the com-munity college who came over and hung around, doglike, as though he'd already been hit once too often that evening. But he managed to take our orders without crying.

"Boy," I said in his wake. "What a sad sack."

"Somebody must of stepped on his tail," Hal laughed, but Tommy didn't.

The thought of Lucy, light and silvery, tinseled with love and laughter, opened inside me, fluttered and was gone. I tried to hold her, set her down at a checkered table in Frank's. Cardboard coasters by Schlitz, swizzle sticks, emptied glasses and heaped ashtrays from the previous occupants, "She had a dark and a roving eyeayaye and her hair hung down in ringelets" spilling from the juke. Everything for my lady, but she wouldn't materialize. I knew it wasn't the place or the music. Lucy'd been in worse, heard worse. I was sure of that. But I couldn't seem to bring her across the forest of noise and laughter and familiar tones, faces, movements. Perhaps if I'd been a stranger too, sitting alone she could have come and been with me but not now.

"On the rocks?"

"Huh?"

"Who had bourbon on rocks?"

"Oh that's for me," I said.

"Dream a little dream of me," Hal suggested.

"No thanks," I said.

"What'd you all think of the movie?" Tommy asked.

"Not much," I said.

"Why not?"

"I'm sick of the good guy losing," I answered. "It's un-American."

"Well, doesn't he always?" Tommy asked.

"Not if he's smart," Hal said. "That guy was just dumb."

"He was sick," Abby contradicted. "Alcoholism's a disease."

"But he didn't die of alcoholism," I said. "He died of exposure."

"Because he was drunk," Abby insisted.

"Because he climbed to the top of the mountain," I said. "Instead of crawling under the bed or someplace."

"He was dumb," Hal said. "He should of worn a coat or something."

"He was just trying to get away from all the crummy people down below," Tommy suggested.

"Well he succeeded," I had to admit.

"Is that the only way?" Abby asked.

Tommy looked at her, then back to the cigarette he'd been dabbling on the edge of an ashtray. "I don't know. Is it?"

"You figure it out," Hal suggested. "I happen to like crummy people."

"Well," Tommy started, "it seems to me you of all people ought . . ." He stopped, the insult torn from his lips and tossed into oblivion.

I looked up. Ned and Sally Polk had just come in.

"Here we go again," I said.

They came our way, Ned a little gentler, quicker to smile but still overbearing enough for two and Sally trailing, hand in his now, smiling at no one, but smiling. Such a handsome couple. He's in politics, you know. When they got to us Ned looked down, barely hesitated, reached out a stubby mit and patted Tommy on the cheek.

"Baby's up late tonight," he said.

"Keep your fairy hands to yourself," Tommy said. "I'm not one of your Little Leaguers."

The hand flinched, threatened to become a fist. Sally's eyes crumpled, seemed nearly to close, but the smile remained. Ned withdrew his hand. "Baby's getting brave," he said and went off waving but at no one.

We each of us fumbled in separate silence, moving our drinks a few inches one way or the other, sucking the swizzle sticks with pretended relish, lighting up, then snubbing out that cigarette we'd already lit. Finally Tommy asked: "Whatsamatter? How come everybody's so quiet?"

"You better watch out," I said. "One of these days he won't be so hesitant."

"I have to live with myself," Tommy countered.

"Well try and be a little subtler about it, or you might not have to for very long."

He didn't say anything to that, just drank.

"I got in a fight once in the service," Hal mused. "Some guy didn't like my face so I told him to change it."

"What happened?" Abby asked.

"He did."

"It looks the same to me," I laughed.

Hal peeled back his lower lip revealing a long pink ridge. "Not on the inside. Five stitches."

"You never told me about that," I said.

"I never told anybody. Nor have I ever asked anybody else to change my face."

"You never asked anybody to do anything but buy insurance, as far as I know," Tommy said.

"So?" Hal smiled, but with only one side of his face, as though the other had had enough.

Tommy shrugged. "There's more to life than that."

"When you find it let me know," Hal laughed.

"If there isn't I'd just as soon be dead," Tommy said.

"Suit yourself." Hal turned away, staring at the table, smiling in a secret kind of way. Abby and I watched him, curly black hair and soft handsome features, sideburns carefully cut, cheeks still pink from the afternoon shave, carefully sloppy as though he knew we'd be going to Frank's. A male model but for the subtlest insufficiency his face never quite concealed; a slackness round the mouth, eyes quicker to hide than see, a likable touch of confusion. Then like tennis spectators we turned to Tommy, sprig of blond hair flying, eyes soaring one minute, flitting and darting the next, mouth defiant, serene, cowed; a fever of inner turmoil blended to doubt and fear. Was it one or the other? we seemed to be asking.

"One more drink," I said. "And then I'm folding."

"Party poop," said Hal.

"Got a shooting date in the morning," I explained.

"I wish I'd learned to shoot," Tommy said. "It must be sort of interesting."

"I wish I'd kept it up," Hal agreed. "But we've been so damn busy."

One or the other, I rambled to myself, or compromise. But that means giving up one value to gain another. What about balance, moderation, the power to let each flourish, atrophy or die if it must; nursing the roses, ravaging the weeds, tolerating the rest? Why couldn't life be that instead of this either-or stuff; this corn patch of Hal's on the one hand and Tommy's tender hothouse on the other? Well, maybe it could.

"How's the writing going, Tommy?" I asked.

"So so," he said.

"Do you have a schedule? I mean a set time every day when you work."

"No. I don't believe you can write by the numbers."

"Then how do you?"

"Just when it comes."

"Boy," Hal laughed. "I'd sure like to be able to sell insurance that way. You know, just to the clients you knew were going to buy."

"Well, why don't you?" Abby asked.

"Unfortunately it doesn't work that way," Hal replied. "The big accounts don't just come in out of the blue."

"No?" she asked.

"No. They come piece by piece. Personal contact here, little auto insurance there, some free advice on a guy's personal property floater, a few breaks self-made or otherwise and after a while maybe you'll end up in the president's office with a chance for something big."

"Well, writing isn't like that," Tommy insisted, but he declined to tell us why. Instead he preferred to stare across at Sally, as though reminding us she would most certainly agree and she would therefore most certainly be right. Whether she agreed or disagreed or felt anything at all was hard to tell from looking at her. She just sat there, eyes squinted to ease the strain of smiling, head cocked in pretended sympathy as the patronage hounds sidled over, sniffed and freshened their scent lest the big man forget.

I was about to leave when Spaulding of Yale, who had apparently been honing his considerable ability to meet people and be liked, came over dragging Bill Wilbur, a young lawyer I knew from here and there, plus Clammy Sammy Crawley and a guy named Steve Brooks whom I'd gone to school with way back but hadn't seen much of in recent years. It struck me funny when Spaulding introduced us all as though this was *his* town or something.

Well, we sort of kidded him about that and he managed to look a little sheepish until I asked Wilbur whether he was still with Lowe, Harper & Dale only to discover he'd quit them two years before and was now working for the City Planning Commission.

"Even I knew that," said Spaulding of Yale, recovering, "and I only just met you, didn't I, citizen."

"How about you, Steve?" I asked. "Still burning the candle at both ends?"

"Well no," he admitted. "Not since I got married."

"Married?" I asked. "Say, that's right."

"Ha," said Spaulding of Yale. "I knew that, too."

"You know everything," I said, only half-kidding. "You're a regular Ward McAllister. It must be terrific knowing who everybody is and what they're doing and all. Especially when they never heard of you."

"Hey," Abby said. "What's the matter with you?"

"The matter?" I asked. "Nothing. I just think it's great somebody could know so much more about what we're doing than we do."

"It wasn't too hard," said Spaulding, not being quite so nice.

"How 'bout you?" Wilbur asked. "Still doing the police stuff?"

"As a matter of fact I'm not," I said. "I've been news editor for some time now."

"Hah," said Spaulding. I found it hard to look at him.

"Well, I was on my way when you fellows came over," I said, getting up. "Nice to see everybody," and I sidled from my seat. "Ought to keep in touch, eh?" I tried a smile, sort of flubbed it, and left.

I guess it was from being sent away to school and college. I don't know, but whatever the reason, even after a year's work and street-seeing all these people every day I sure was out of touch. Practically a hermit and in no position to judge the relative merits of living, working, loving in Gravenhurst, Connecticut.

CHAPTER XXIII

"This town's a dump and you can have it."

"Huh? Wha?"

"I said this town's a dump."

No, I thought. I'm dreaming.

"Are you awake, Larry?"

"No, I'm not," I said.

"Well it doesn't matter," she said. "Just so we can talk."

I rolled over, shook, got myself placed reasonably close to reality.

"For God's sakes, Abby, what time is it?"

"Shhh. It's only two."

"Oh hell. I have to be up at six-thirty."

"I'm sorry. I didn't know."

"Going hunting," I said. "Remember?"

"Oh that's right."

But by then it didn't matter. I was awake, sitting up, aware she was there on the bed and there to stay. "Well what's the trouble?"

"Oh, no trouble."

"You got a cigarette?"

"Sure." I could hear junk jangling, fingernails shuffling as she fidgeted through her pocketbook. "Here, right here." She poked around for my hand, gave me the cigarette and matches.

"Thanks," I said, found the filter end, lit up, watched the yellow light scatter across her face, catch a sadness which could have been hers, could have been caused by the light itself. "What the hell have you been doing the last two hours?"

"Going 'Ha ha' and 'Oh, is that so' at regular intervals."

"Oh please, Abby," I yawned. "Your sad stories are getting me down."

"Sad stories? What's sad about going 'Ha ha' and 'Oh, is that so'?"

"They seemed like pretty nice guys to me."

"But *you* didn't stay."

"I wanted to."

"Uh huh."

"As a matter of fact it's true," I said. "I was just beginning to realize how out of touch we were in this place."

"For good reason," she insisted.

"Listen, if you knew those people better everything would have been fine."

"Oh Larry, honestly. Who wants to be funny all the time?"

"Maybe they were put off by you," I suggested. "Did you ever think of that?"

"By me? Why, for heaven sakes?"

"Don't know you."

"Don't know me, they've known me for years."

"Not really. We've both been away for years."

"Well I'm glad of that. And I'll go away again first chance."

"Oh you will, will you?"

"Yes."

"With Jesse?"

"With Jesse," she confirmed. "If he asks me again."

"Don't get humble or I might throw up."

"Humble?"

"If he asks me again," I mimicked. "You know damn well he will."

"Oh, I do?"

It was kind of hard talking in the dark, not enough light from my cigarette to read her face, only the tone of voice and body movements to guess at.

"Don't you?" And I began to realize maybe he wouldn't. There was something kind of final about the way he'd just sort of turned and padded off.

"Maybe," she admitted. "But if he does I will," she repeated, trying to convince us both.

"Just to get out of Gravenhurst, huh?"

"Just to get out of Gravenhurst."

"I don't get it," I said. "You and Hal and Gravenhurst seemed to be getting along a little better today."

"Oh boy," she said. "Mr. and Mrs. Hal James and their six children spent Sunday visiting the Larry Woodruffs. He's her brother and our good publisher, as you all doubtless know, and a good time was had by all." She finished up with a series of well-executed retching noises.

"Okay," I laughed. "All right."

"I just can't live like that."

"Just because some idiot happens to write it that way doesn't mean it's the way you're living."

"I didn't go to college for that," she said.

"No?"

"No! Maybe I'm no career girl but I learned enough to make this place look like a dump."

"Oh I see."

"Don't sneer," she said.

"Who's sneering? There's just one thing I don't understand."

"What?"

"The difference between raising six kids in Gravenhurst and trying to bring up six little Jew babies in Pakistan or Paris or someplace."

"Boy, you put it nicely."

I kept quiet.

"Anybody who would say a thing like that couldn't be expected to understand," she announced.

"Understand what?"

"That I'd be doing something . . . well, something important just by marrying him."

"Something noble, huh? Something romantic and self-sacrificing and virtuous as all hell."

She kept quiet that time.

"So you're going to marry this suffering Jew, are you, and sacrifice yourself to a life of bigotry and hatred and, oh sure, travel too. I forgot about that. Boy, I wish I was as unprejudiced as you."

"Is this a conversation," she asked, "or a diatribe?"

"Then maybe I could get myself a little black girl," I continued. "Doesn't matter what she's like or whether I love her or get along with her or anything like that. Just so she's good and *black* and wants to travel where there's lots of foreigners because foreigners aren't really people, you know, and therefore can't be slobs because only *people* are slobs and won't life be grand?"

"My God," Abby said. "Are you through?"

"I guess so."

"Is that what I'm really like?"

"I don't know," I admitted. "Sometimes it seems that way."

She sat silent and invisible. I stubbed my cigarette, wondered if I'd said anything right.

"Tell you what," she said.

"It's late," I said. "That's what."

"You marry Nora. And I'll marry Hal."

Another yawn.

"Yes sir," she laughed, and slid off the bed. "That's a deal."

"Sure thing," I said. "Nighty nighty."

"Oh I can just see *that* happening." She went out of the room laughing all over the place.

"What's so funny?" I mumbled but not loud enough for her to hear.

Next morning was gray inside as well as out. I felt washed and dried just once too often but managed to haul my limpness from the bed, wash, shave, dress, and make the kitchen before Jeff or Mr. Quincy arrived. In fact I nearly got the coffee on before Jeff came peeping through the kitchen door, trying to figure out where I was.

I went over, rapped on the window and waved him in.

"Hey, Larry," he greeted. "Howsa boy?" It was falsely cheerful and I guessed maybe he'd had a late one too.

"Hi," I said. "You had any breakfast?"

He nodded. "Just give me some of that fine old country coffee you got over there."

"It's just fine old warm water so far. You'll have to wait."

"Sure thing." He propped his gun in the corner and sat down. "Boy, this is the greatest."

I was just getting some eggs and stuff out, turned and looked at him. He looked away. Something was fishy. I heated up the pan and cracked a couple of eggs. He said nothing. I looked again. He flashed a candidate's grin.

"What's the matter?" I asked, and right away he dropped it.

"Well, I was out to Pearson's house last night," he said.

"So?"

"Dave Wright dropped by. You know, Clem Harper's assistant."

"Yeah?" I kept on fooling with the stove.

"He knows everything goes on."

I turned around for another look. Jeff was shaggy-haired and a little pasty from working too hard but with bone and muscle features, the kind of guy who's so loyal it almost hurts. He looked up at me, hand spiderwebbed over his face, staring.

"It's a mess," he said.

"What is?"

"In fact Dave would never have told us except it's so crummy."

"*What?*"

"Well seems like the judge was in to see Harper day before yesterday. He thinks Polk's a winner. Wants to get him back on their side of the fence."

"How?"

"Run the son of a bitch for Congress," said Jeff.

"You're crazy. Clem Harper hates his guts."

"Not half as much as he hates being an uninformed political circle."

"How the hell can they swing that?" I asked. "We don't control the Congressional district?"

I slipped my eggs on a plate, grabbed the coffeepot and sat down.

"There's nobody else at the moment," Jeff said. "Old Chester, he ain't a gonna run for re-election. We haven't had a Congressman from this end of the district in over ten years, Ned's a fighting journalist and all that." Jeff shrugged, reached for the coffeepot. "It's practically a sure thing."

"If he wants it."

"Are you kidding?"

"I guess so," I admitted. "Anyway, so what?"

"You haven't heard the worst."

"No?"

"They figure he needs a little more class. Just being a newshound isn't enough. Something with dignity, style, responsibility."

"Like?"

"Like publisher of the Gravenhurst *Daily Watch*, for instance."

"You *are* kidding." I dropped everything, not just dropped, forgot, went numb with a mixture of shock and fear. "They wouldn't."

"No?"

"Is my father in on this?" I asked.

"Not yet," Jeff admitted. "Wright said it was all speculation so far."

"Well, he'd never do it," I insisted.

"He's your father," Jeff said. "All I know is those three have worked pretty close together in the past."

I could hear Mr. Quincy stomping on the back porch.

"Never," I said as he came through the door. "Mr. Quincy, you know Jeff Collins, I guess."

"Shu-ah. Seen your name in the papah anyway so seems though I know ya."

"Morning," said Jeff. "Looks like a good day for it."

"Euh," and he sat down, sliding the coffee mug his way and pouring at the same time.

Well, we finished up pretty quick, or so it seemed to me. I had no awareness of time and not much consciousness of anything but fields, various kinds of cover, dog, cold, gun. Everything subtler than that had been filtered out and while I knew there were two other people with me it was only in terms of where they were so's not to shoot too close. There was no gracious hosting, no "Watch Triumph, he's working," no thought of giving Jeff first shot. Only a simple predator numb with shock, stalking, staring, eager to kill. When the first bird flushed I dropped it, teeth clenched, dropped it from the hip too close, messing it up before Jeff even got the gun to his shoulder.

Mr. Quincy said nothing, waited for the retrieve, held the splattered bird for me to see. "Hamburgah," he said. That's all, but it was enough to bring me to a little and let Jeff have the next shot. Even at that, though, I was pulling up on every bird, following with grim certainty, waiting for Jeff to miss, and he did a couple of times, so I could have the joy of killing. And no matter how far off that bird seemed to get I'd drop it in a ritual of rage and defiance, my senses sharpened, not dulled, by this threat of impotence and in-justice, quite a different animal from Larry Woodruff, golfer.

By the time we'd had enough and started back I already had a scheme, or at least the essence of one. It was so beyond the rules and regulations of orderly Gravenhurst I'd never have conceived, never mind considered, such an idea under other circumstances. But this was a matter of survival—mine—and I wasn't too concerned with rules and regulations.

"Hey Jeff," I said. "Let's take a little walk, huh?" As though we hadn't walked enough already.

"Sure," he said, so we thanked old Quincy and wandered off toward the dock.

"I'm going to break the Fun House story," I said.

"You're gonna what?"

"Or at least get ready to," I corrected. "Collect the necessary info."

"You're crazy," he said. "Christ, it'll blow the whole town."

"Maybe we wouldn't have to print it," I said. "Just so the right people know."

"Like?"

"Judge Compton. He was out there Friday."

"How do you know?"

"Friend of mine heard him."

"Sure?"

"Positive."

Jeff giggled. "My my, what a beautiful story that'd make."

"I can see it now," I laughed. " 'Whoremonger backs Polk for Congressional bid.' Nice, huh?"

Jeff shivered. "Christ."

"We'll never have to use it," I insisted.

"Maybe not. But once those things get started . . ."

"It'll never get started," I said. "Just the pictures."

"You hope."

We walked down to the end of the dock and sat down. The wind came whistling through the narrows, hammered the water, rustled the frosted marsh grass. I shivered from the sight of it more than the cold. "I figure next Friday'll be a busy night," I said. "We can drive out any afternoon, get some shots of the place in daylight right from the car. Then Friday night comes the dirty work."

"How do we handle that?"

"You ever been out there?"

"I'm a married man," he laughed.

"So?"

"I'm a nonconformist. No key swapping, no feelies, no nights out. I'm no fun."

"Well, they have an attendant, see. You drive up to the back door, he parks the car and gets it for you so nobody'll know who's there. Meanwhile he waits inside for the next guy who drives up."

"And?"

"I have a Minox," I said. "We'll get some shots of the license plates."

"We?"

"I need company."

"I see."

"Besides, maybe we could bring another camera. Sometimes the big shots come by taxi, sneak in through the front door. We could get a shot of them going up the steps, then run like hell."

"I think we ought to take the daylight pictures after the others," Jeff said. "Just in case we get spotted. Otherwise they'll start getting extra careful at night."

"Okay," I agreed.

"This gets interesting," Jeff admitted. "Any chance of some inside shots?"

"It's down in the basement," I said. "Kind of dark and you'd never get out in one piece after popping a flash."

"How 'bout upstairs?"

"The rooms?"

"That's what I mean. Action shots are the best."

"Might miss it with the Minox. Then we'd end up with nothing even if I got out."

"I guess so," he agreed.

"There's a big maple right near the front door," I went on. "One of us gets behind that they'll never know until it's too late. The other waits up the road, lets off the brake and comes rolling down just after the cab turns around. Then comes up fast when the flash goes off."

"Cops and robbers," he said. "Okay, you work out the details and I'll go along."

We got up then and started back, me so enmeshed in the intricacies of our plan I'd almost forgotten the cause and Jeff laughing to himself, shaking his head, mumbling, "Oh boy, will this ever rock the bastards."

But for the time being anyway life remained quite normal so I said goodbye to Jeff and wandered back to the house for some more coffee. They were all having breakfast together and behaving like nothing had ever gone wrong between any of us so I joined the game, suspecting the longer I played that maybe they were right; nothing ever *had* gone wrong. Trouble sure ran deep in our family, buried under the silty demands of peace and harmony. We were pacifists by instinct.

Thus we sat around, chatting, reading the Sunday papers, Pa playing the humanist wherever he could afford to—or had to, like when Abby blew her fuse Friday night—and Mother tinkering with her latest project, a raffle with the winners to be drawn at the Thanksgiving Ball, first prize an Austin Healy Sprite, proceeds to buy Christmas packages for the needy. And through it all Abby and I kibitzed, joked, reveled in the peace and quiet of a cease-fire. Too bad every day isn't Sunday. It's like a lobotomy. I couldn't even get very excited when Pa announced after dinner he thought he might drop by Judge Compton's for a little chat.

That long-awaited letter from Lucy arrived on Tuesday telling me she'd moved to New York and had an apartment and was going to work in the research department on *Time* and why didn't I get off my fat you-know-what and come see her?

Well, why didn't I?

Especially seeing as she took the trouble to explain about that Potters Island nightmare. This isn't exactly relevant, but it was funny reading about something serious and even sort of grubby in that round, careful boarding-school handwriting. I'd always associated it with "love love loving" to come to the spring dance and "you're just the most terrificest football player in the whole nation" and stuff like that and now it was telling me about how Daddy had sort of a problem with the bottle and she didn't mean I was a fool in the sense of being stupid but only for not knowing enough to stay away from him when he was crocked. In other words, she'd meant "You poor sap," which I suppose is a little better than the way it had seemed.

Anyway, I was delighted with the promotion and called her to say so. It was great. Lucy really sounded glad to hear from me and we actually made a date for the Saturday after before it occurred to her that was Thanksgiving weekend, she was going to Washington. I asked her "How about changing your mind, coming to Gravenhurst for the dance and all," but she just laughed and said, "A dance in Gravenhurst? Oh no, Larry, I don't think that would be my cup of tea, thanks ever so." But aside from that she sounded great, her voice fresh and gay and welcome as a second chance the way she talked about New York, the job, herself, as though all three were just a little absurd to take themselves so seriously, yet charming. The sound of her made everything seem possible again and I sat afterward in a reverie of pleasure, building an imaginary life around us, filling it with perfect homes, perfect friends, perfect children, as though determined to keep us as far from reality as possible. For Lucy and me, it seemed, life would be one long night on the beach and I barely noticed we hadn't taken the precaution of making a date for any time, never mind Thanksgiving.

Then came a couple of strategy meetings with Jeff and suddenly, palpitatingly, it was Friday.

Pa was out that night, attending the annual GOP City Committee dinner, which took some guts considering his late fall from political grace and power, so Mother and I had dinner alone. I guess she'd been waiting to get me that way but Friday sure was a poor night for it. All I could think about was would somebody spot the car if we came in the back way from above the Fun House and parked in one of the snowplow turn-arounds? And was there really only one attendant or did Mother Murphy have some bone-crushers hidden around the place? Anything seemed logical at that point and I found it very hard to play the at home game with Mother. She didn't seem to notice though; just went sailing along.

"Goodness me," she was saying. "The Thanksgiving Ball less than a week away and I haven't even planned a dinner yet."

"Dinner?"

"Well, I thought it would be nice," she said. "We might ask the Comptons."

"Not this year."

"But why not?"

"Nora and I have had a little disagreement," I explained.

We were sitting at opposite ends of the table like man and wife and I had to peer round the elaborate silver candelabra to see her face. It all seemed slightly Victorian and more than a little foolish.

"Oh for heaven sakes," she laughed. "You young people are always having disagreements."

"Well, we young people really had a corker this time," I said. "I don't think you grownups would enjoy our company. You're much too civilized."

She tinkled with laughter. "I'm sure everything will be patched up by then. A whole week, goodness me."

"I'm afraid not."

"Well at least you can behave like a gentleman if she comes."

"As a matter of fact it doesn't matter. I forgot, she's going with Sam Crawley."

"Oh?" Mother asked. "And who are you going with?"

"No one. If I go."

"Pity," she said.

Well, indeed it was, but under her chatter lay a sense of urgency, almost a yearning to part the curtains of propriety and really talk. Yet either because she couldn't think how to begin or couldn't face risking disorder, the prattle went on. And this, it seemed to me, was even more of a pity.

I excused myself as soon after dinner as I could and hurried down to the newspaper office.

Jeff hadn't got there yet so I sat down at my desk and fidgeted around, finally pulled Lucy's letter out of my pocket and began reading it again, hoping by this intangible intimacy to conjure an image of the two of us together someplace but it was always a fairyland of cobblestone streets and gaslight, easy joy and secret beaches; never reality.

CHAPTER XXIV

I heard the office front door slam, then footsteps, and pretty soon Jeff came in looking about as preoccupied as he would for any night assignment.

"I was supposed to cover that GOP dinner," he said. "Forgot all about it." He laughed, shook his head, uncased a .35-mm. and began setting up the flash attachment.

"That's all right, Jeff. The old man's there. He can give us the story."

"Well, I called Robinson. He went out to take some pics."

I opened up my desk, got the Minox out, took a couple of shots to be sure the flash was working.

"Looks like we're in business," Jeff laughed.

I took a deep breath to ward off the pre-game nerves.

"Well?" Jeff asked. "We ready?"

"As we'll ever be." I reached for the light switch, flipped it, and we were off.

Getting there by the back way was a real test of navigational skills, a maze of dirt roads all looking alike, all looking wrong, but finally we came to a sign marking the township line and I knew we were only a quarter of a mile from dear old Mother Murphy's. I doused the lights and idled along to within a few hundred yards, pulled off and backed up a little side road I'd forgotten was there. A real break. It was inclined enough to roll out and a lot better than the snowplow turn-around where we could be seen by any passing car.

"Okay?" I asked.

Jeff shrugged, buttoned his jacket. I did the same. It was cold but not too and dark, thank God. No moon, no stars, but a glow to the overcast so you could at least see the silhouette of buildings, stone walls, trees. We crawled under barbed wire into a pasture some two hundred yards above the house and stumbled onto an old wagon trail likely to lead down through the barnyard where they parked the cars. There was a fair breeze coming our way and I knew from hunting nobody'd be able to hear us more than ten or fifteen yards off but that didn't help my nerves much. Stalking people is just different from deer and that's all there is to it. We left the wagon trail and hunched in behind a stone wall some fifteen or twenty yards from the barnyard itself. From there you could see the driveway and back door as well as the parking area.

"It's almost eleven," I whispered. "Still kind of early."

"I wish we'd thought of that back where it was warm."

"There's cars in the lot all right. Let's just wait and see how careful the attendant is."

Jeff poked me and whapped something in the palm of his hand. "What'sat?"

"Sap," he whispered. "Blackjack."

"He better not be too careful."

Lights poked at the bottom of the drive, probed, swung up.

"Customer," I said.

The car door slammed, light spilled from the house as someone came out, car door slammed again and the headlights crawled up toward us, engine hollering, sighing, finally dying as he backed, filled, finally got it parked. I raised up slow and easy to watch how he operated, see if he waved to a lookout in the barn, maybe, or stopped to talk or even looked around. He did none of these, just slammed the door and wandered back whistling.

"It'll be a breeze," I whispered. "All he's thinking about is getting inside where it's warm."

Jeff nodded, produced a hopeful smile.

"Me too," he said.

"Must be half a dozen cars in there."

He nodded again. I heard an engine working way off.

"Number two?"

Jeff thumbed over his shoulder.

"Oh Christ, it's on our road."

He nodded. We sat still as death as though somehow that might help get the guy past my car without seeing it. The lights swung round and down and a rattle-trap clamored by.

"Wow," I sighed. "Just some country boy."

Then another one coming up.

"Here we go," and I ducked down as another car pulled up, unloaded, gunned and crawled for the barnyard. The attendant got out, started back as before, hesitated, turned and started toward us.

I shoved down on Jeff's shoulder and hunched trying to get as low as possible and still be able to move fast if he spotted us.

What the hell made him come this way? My heart thundered, body turned to slush and I wondered if I'd be able to move at all.

Footsteps.

Silence.

Sound of splashing.

Ahhh, zzzip, and footsteps going away.

"That's the first time I ever got worked up over a guy peeing."

Jeff sighed his relief. The back door slammed shut. I checked the Minox.

"Okay, keep me covered." I ran down through the barnyard, crouched low, knees bent to cushion my footsteps, scared as a deer.

Flash.

And, oh my God, the world must have blown up.

Flash, and I got number two.

Stumbling.

Flash.

Fumbling.

Three more and I was done, panicked, running for the stone wall, crouching just long enough to grab Jeff, ready to go all the way when he reached out and held my arm.

"Take it easy, take it easy," he soothed.

And I let myself settle down.

"Okay, okay, everything's fine," he whispered. "Smooth as glass."

I looked down at the house. Nothing. I shuddered.

"It's cold," I said.

"Want to take another batch?"

"You're crazy."

"Sure you got them?"

I nodded, sure I wasn't going back anyway.

We headed for the car, got Jeff's camera, rehearsed.

"Big maple right in front of the house," I reminded him. "Get between that and the stone wall. I'll start rolling down while the cab's turning."

"Okay," and he started down the road sounding like Sherman's army.

"Shhh!"

And he moved onto the shoulder.

I got back in the car, rolled down the windows, front and back, and listened so hard breathing was a luxury, ready to pull out in a hell of a hurry if Jeff got spotted. The night silence roared. It didn't seem like I could hear anything.

And then the waiting set in. One car, but bound for the parking lot, then another and after a while one more, but all three going up the driveway and sometimes a half-hour wait in between.

It was twelve-thirty, Jeff must have been frozen stiff. I was.

Then it came. I could see the cab light on top, watched it stop, pull up, turn around and I let the emergency go easy, its snapping like steel cables, and rolled for the road, front wheel in and up over the ditch, back wheels in and *uuuuup*, no not quite, she rolled back down and stayed there.

Oh God, I almost laughed, jumped out and tried for a push. Nothing doing. Seconds flying. Jeff halfway up the lawn by then ready to flash and me out there grunting, getting nowhere. I piled back in, started her up, saw the flash go and came roaring out of there, no lights, no silence, slamming down the road, skidding just as Jeff barreled out, shadows behind him moving fast, and dove at the window, forcing me up against the wheel, him half in half out.

"Move it," he shouted and I scratched out of there just as some growler dove for Jeff's dangling legs, missed and caught a face full of fender.

He dropped his camera on the front seat and scrambled the rest of the way in and sat down, laughing like a nut.

"Oh daddy," he said. "Where were you?"

"Wouldn't clear the ditch," I said. "Had to drive it out last minute."

"Last minute and then some," he said. "I've been playing tag with those bastards all over the goddam lawn."

"Who was it?"

"I don't know," he laughed. "The attendant and some little guy. One of the ones in the cab."

I saw a light behind us.

"Uh oh," and I switched mine off doing fifty at least and only a dim gray cut through the blackness to show me the road, then onto the main drag and tore for about two hundred yards, U-turned, put on my lights and went cruising back at a genteel thirty miles an hour. They came slithering out, cut in front of us and went like hell after the only pair of taillights in sight, about a quarter of a mile ahead. I dimmed my brights politely and followed until they got over a hill, then swung around and headed back to town.

Jeff watched for a while, saw nobody coming, relaxed. "Magnificent. A master of deception."

"Piece of cake," I said, and we let the fear run out of us in bursts of laughter. "Got any idea who it was?"

"Christ no," he laughed. "I was sort of rushed."

"We'll soon find out."

"But there were two of them," he said. "I know that much."

"Well, let's get 'em developed. See who we got."

"Not at the office," he said. "They'll be around there sooner or later."

"Then where?"

"I've got a darkroom. That'll do the trick." And we settled down to a little private reminiscing, letting the sights and sounds of normalcy relax us; road signs, billboards, cars crawling, turning, doing their humdrum tricks until pretty soon it seemed unbelievable that what had happened had happened not just in dreary Gravenhurst but anywhere I could ever be.

By the time we got to Jeff's house he and I were relatively calm but the sight of us started his wife off on stage one so pretty soon the three of us were nuts all over again.

Jeff was laughing and sputtering and trying to tell what happened, trying to make it more funny than scary and his wife—she was a pot of scrambled energy anyway—ran around fetching drinks and popping questions, making us tell it again and again, liking it better each time, until finally we had to practically tie her down to get at the darkroom and find out what we had. I guess the thought of missing something calmed her and she came in after us, quiet as a mouse except for an occasional offer of assistance to prove she was as capable of performing rationally as we were, which wasn't saying much.

I didn't know beans about darkroom operations and still don't, so I just propped myself in a corner, letting the red glow soothe me, and continued to unravel.

"Tell me when you get something," I said.

"Will do." He sounded super-busy.

Then after a while the lights came on, but Jeff didn't say anything so I stayed where I was, half-snoozing.

"Got somebody," he said. "Can't see who until we make a positive."

"How 'bout the license plates?"

"So goddam small, can't tell for sure. But they look all right."

"Whadjou expect?"

Jeff laughed.

"Listen to him, Bess. Pretty cocky."

"I heard," she said happily. "I heard."

"Okay," he said. "Let's see what we got." I went over, watched the white paper sloshing, graying slowly, conjuring a scandal. You could see there were two people.

"We're in business," I laughed, and winked at Bess.

"Keep an eye on it, honey," said Jeff, and he turned to fool with something.

"Okay, sweetheart," I said.

"Not you, idiot."

I laughed, looked at Bess, saw only a mask of horror and bent over the pan.

It was my father.

"Well whaddayou know." I looked again, fascinated.

With Clem Harper, only it was just his back.

Jeff was looking over my shoulder by then. "I'll destroy the negative," he said.

"No, don't, I want a copy."

Jeff looked at me.

"He knows somebody's got a picture," I said. "It might as well be me."

"It might as well *not* be you," Bess said.

"Well it *is* me," I said. "And I want a print."

Jeff fished for it, put some stuff on, hung it up to dry.

"Need a drink," I said and ducked out, eyes souring, belly clutching, I made the kitchen, pressed up against a wall. "Oh Jeeezus. Oh Jesus Christ," and then nothing but the sound of my breath catching and sniveling and the most appalling sense of loss and then a long shuddering sigh and I shook myself, grabbed the bottle, took a long pull, not needing the whiskey, only the pain of it to distract me. And after that I got control, went back.

"Guess there's no hurry," I said. "Might as well do the Minox prints, bring it all down tomorrow morning."

He nodded and Bess took my arm, walked me to the door. I wish she hadn't. I hardly knew her and it started me feeling sorry for myself again.

"Night," I said as I turned toward the car. I felt sick and tried to think of only that.

Pa's car was parked in front of the house so I guess he'd picked it up and come home in a hell of a hurry. Only the hall and kitchen lights were on.

As I came in Mother backed through the pantry door with a glass of milk.

"What's wrong?" I asked. Milk at night is a symbol of trouble for us.

"It's your father," she sighed. "One of his headaches again."

"Too bad. What do you suppose caused it?"

"Oh those dreadful political dinners," she said. "They're so tedious."

"Yes," I agreed. "They must be." I followed her upstairs.

Looked like the poor bastard was really sweating it out.

I went about the business of getting undressed, washed, and to bed in a charitable haze of shock. It all seemed far away, impersonal, and I found myself mostly concerned with this apparent lack of emotion, feeling, caring, rather than the opposite. I switched off the light and lay there staring, wondering why I didn't care more, reminding myself I'd cried, hadn't I, wanting to cry more but not succeeding. It was as though the ability to feel had, in an instant of pressure, burst through the silt and sludge of propriety, only to be covered over almost immediately and I wondered whether emotions, like muscles, could atrophy with disuse or whether they'd simply been overpowered by an excess accumulation of surface weight.

"But you did cry once, jackass," I reminded myself. "What are you supposed to do, sob all night?"

Or maybe I just *didn't* care. The idol was dead, long live myself, but then I thought of Pa, arm around me, showing me how to hold a tennis racket and "There we are, that was well stroked, Larry, well stroked, old boy" and Pa thumbing the newspaper, "Well well well, what have we here 'YMCA Celebrates Centennial by Larry Woodruff,' looks like we've got a by-liner in the family," and watching Pa on the steps of City Hall as he introduced Senator Somebody-or-other on a barnstorming tour and the two of them kind of kidding each other in that chummy, real-people way important people have and my eyes warmed with new tears, an easy crying that soon turned to sleep.

I dreamed of Anita that night, Anita coming to me full of want and the two of us not making love but coupling, two hot hungry beasts, and suddenly it wasn't Anita at all but Mother and Pa there too, laughing and Mother sighing, "Goodness me, with the Thanksgiving Ball less than a week away," and finally I woke up full of lust and disgust.

Maybe there was nothing wrong with going to a whorehouse or having a mistress but if so then I should have been brought up to believe it, and I lay awake, stark with resentment, sifting ways to get even, finally fell to fitful sleep, soothed by thoughts of spite and revenge.

CHAPTER XXV

Pa was on the hall phone when I came down next morning. "No, I can't explain now, Judge, but Clem and I'll stop by this morning about eleven . . . Right, fine, we'll see you then."

He followed me into the dining room.

"Morning, Pa. How'd the meeting go?"

"Meeting?"

"GOP dinner," I reminded him. "Things looking any better?"

"Oh." He sat down. "Yes, things are . . . things are looking better."

"Well good," I said. "I'm glad to hear it."

Pa kept glancing around, as though he wore glasses and couldn't find them. "Yes," he continued, "as a matter of fact I wanted to talk to you about that."

"Oh?"

Bollard came in with the breakfast, exchanged good mornings and left. Pa lost his thread.

"Talk to me about what?" I reminded him.

"Ah yes," he said. "Talk to you about . . . Oh dear . . ." He shook his head as though to chase reality away. "Perhaps this isn't the best time."

Feeling sorry for him wasn't what I'd had in mind. "You all right, Pa?"

"I suppose so." He let out a long, shuddering sigh.

"Is Mother up?"

"No, we . . . we didn't sleep well last night. I'm afraid I kept her awake."

"Pa."

"Yes?"

"Pa, I know what it is bothering you." He looked up, a blend of guile and innocence on his face, just as he had in the picture. "And I know what it is you can't tell me."

He said nothing.

"About making Polk publisher."

"Oh yes." He seemed to relax, forgetting I had mentioned two things I knew.

"That's why we took the pictures last night," I said.

"*You!*"

"I hadn't planned on taking yours," I said, close to tears again, almost apologizing. "That wasn't the idea at all."

"Oh Larry." He brought his hands to his face, dropped them immediately, as though ashamed of hiding. "Let's go into my study."

I followed him, knees rubbery as a schoolboy's, but determined not to let it get past the knees.

"Now," he said, sat at his desk, started to sink, leaned forward propping his head in his hands. "You'd better start at the beginning."

"Well, I happened to hear about the idea of making Polk publisher and running him for congress," I said, surprised it sounded so defensive.

"Yes?"

"It seemed like a pretty rotten deal."

"Rotten for whom?"

"The *Daily Watch*. And me."

"So you took it upon yourself to put things right, eh?"

"Now wait a minute!"

"Well isn't that what happened?"

"You don't seem to understand. In the first place, we've done plenty for the *Daily Watch* since Polk quit and it's going a lot better without him."

"That remains to be seen," he said.

"The hell it does. While you've been sitting around here feeling sorry for yourself we've made that paper go better than Polk ever did and you haven't even bothered to find it out."

"Oh?"

"I gave you our progress report before the Rosenfeldt meeting and you never even looked at it."

He said nothing.

"Well, did you?"

"There was no time."

"Have you since?" He didn't answer. "No," I went on, "you're just going to pull off some sweet little deal to regain control of the lousy GOP political machine and the hell with everything else."

"Do you realize to whom you are talking?"

I paused. "Aren't you the guy who was out at the Fun House last night?"

And he withdrew the question.

"How did you know?" he asked instead.

"I didn't. All I knew was Judge Compton had been there and I figured on collecting some license plates, getting a few pictures and scaring you off the Polk idea."

"That's blackmail."

"So it is."

"And what am I supposed to do now?"

"Forget about your plans for Mr. Polk," I said. "Unless you want me to run the story."

"How do you plan to run the story in *my* paper?"

"*Your* paper," I sneered. "All right, so it's your paper. I'll give it to the *Enterprise*."

He sighed, went limp, looked away.

"I'm sorry, Pa."

"Then why go through with it?"

"Not about that," I said. "I'm sorry it was you."

"Yes," Pa said, and wiped his hand across his face. "Yes, I suppose so." I had no idea what that meant and didn't ask. "All right, Larry, all right." For a moment he sat there pulling on his lip. "I'm going to give you a free rein. Let you run the *Daily Watch*, do what you want with it, but I'm running Ned Polk for Congress and we'll see . . ."

"In the first place," I interrupted, "you're not giving me free rein, I'm taking it."

"I beg your pardon?"

"How would it be if the publisher's son quit and went to work for the *Enterprise*?" I asked. "And in the second place, you can run Polk if you want to but we'll beat hell out of him."

"You're determined to make this a showdown, aren't you?"

"Well, isn't it?"

"Larry, about this business of last night. The picture."

"Yes?"

"I . . . I want you to understand it doesn't happen very often."

"Oh swell," I said.

"But your mother and I, well it's been some time since we've had . . . well, since we've been able to . . ."

"Please," I interrupted. "I know too much already."

"But you should know it all."

"All right, I know what you're going to say."

"Well, try to understand."

"I will, Pa, I swear I will." I got up. "It's just being taught one thing and shown another," I tried to explain. "You get disgusted."

"Oh and don't forget to destroy those pictures," he said.

I nearly laughed at the switch. "Okay," I said, and left.

When I got to the paper there was a brown manila envelope in my typewriter and Jeff's eyes stuck to it.

"Thanks," I said, pulling it free. "Looks like we won't be needing them after all." I shook the pictures down, folded the envelope and slipped it in my pocket.

Jeff didn't say anything but he wanted to.

"We had a little talk this morning," I said, staring at my desk, sorting the copy. "Seems like everything's all right."

Ted Pearson looked from one to the other of us, knowing the problem, not knowing how it had been solved.

"Devil's back in hell," I said. "And all's right with the world."

"If you're happy, I'm happy," Ted shrugged, and that was all there was to that.

It was another one of those foolish Saturdays, but with me at the helm, foolish as they were, I sometimes wondered whether there'd be news enough to fill a paper and that, despite the holiday atmosphere, could make any news editor a little anxious. Especially this one. But we keep a good supply of AOT, for any old time, copy on hand so the pages got filled after a fashion.

With the paper done we sat around chewing the rag awhile about how some of the stores were so mixed up they already had their Christmas decorations in the windows and here it wasn't even Thanksgiving and about a truck that turned over on Route 19 spilling cans of pineapple juice everywhere but there wasn't near so much to pick up as got spilled, according to Carl Robinson, and about how this kid over on Duchess Road got the first buck of the season and why was it always a kid instead of some guy who'd been hunting all his life? And how, according to Ted Pearson, the Gravenhurst Players were in trouble, some guy they'd hoped to get they hadn't been able to and did I know whether Hal James'd ever done any acting, seeing as how he was just right for the part? I didn't think so but said I'd ask him anyhow and what was it they wanted him for? It turned out they were doing *A Bell for Adano* and needed someone to play Lieutenant Livingston, this sort of stuffy Yalie who's in one scene and supposed to be funny, so I dropped by his house after lunch to see if he'd be interested, among other things. I was glad to see the Jameses hadn't moved yet and said so first chance I got.

"Don't be such a wise guy," Hal suggested. "We may be any day now."

"Why all the indecision?" I asked. "Your old man getting tolerant in his old age?"

"Hardly. It's just Abrams hasn't decided to buy."

"Boy," I said. "Hating's getting to be a real inconvenience."

"It keeps the old man busy," Hal laughed. "Like a hobby."

"Sort of a do-it-yourself crucifixion kit," I suggested.

"Except who's crucifying who?" he asked.

I was wandering around the living room while we talked, not really paying much attention, just wandering, hating the house which was sort of cute and fussy colonial with lots of frilled curtains and French windows, potted plants growing out of little ceramic pony carts and top hats and stuff like that.

"Let's get out of here," I said. "Let's go deer hunting or something."

"Woods are too dry," Hal said. "We'd sound like the Russian army."

"Then we'll sit."

"Too cold."

"Come on," I persisted. "Don't be so goddam lazy."

"Okay." He shrugged. "Seeing as you put it that way."

I went upstairs while he changed and told him about the Gravenhurst Players wanting him to try out.

"Me?" He laughed. "That's the craziest thing I ever heard of."

"I agree."

"Kind of a part is it?"

"It's an Ivy League lieutenant who's supposed to be funny," I said. "That's all I know."

"How come they want me? . . . I didn't even go to college."

"They're crazy," I said.

"Must be." He stomped into his boots, sat down to do the laces. "Now where the hell's my jacket? Oh hell, downstairs."

"Ready?"

"Yeah. Let's go."

We went back down and out to the rumpus room, where the guns and coats were, and on outside.

"Maybe I'll give it a try," he said suddenly. "Always had sort of a yen to act."

"Well I'll be damned."

"What the hell's wrong with that?" he demanded.

"Nothing. I was just kidding."

"I don't see why people shouldn't try something new once in a while," he argued, but not with me.

"Okay, okay," I laughed. "Just call Pearson if you're interested."

"Yeah," he said, realizing he'd overprotested. "Yeah, I might do that."

We went back to my house for a quick change and headed for the woods.

Hal was right. We didn't even see a deer, never mind shoot at one, but it didn't matter. I just wanted to get as much action as possible between me and recent developments so's to make it all seem like history.

Later on I headed back to the house, hoping to sneak upstairs and think things through a little but Pa heard me come in and called from the living room. I wouldn't have thought he wanted to see much of his son and heir just then, but . . .

"Oh hi, Pa."

He was stretched out on the sofa, feet crossed elegantly, tweed jacket, scarf, bourbon on the rocks, truly a man of extinction. "Any luck?" he asked.

"Too dry," I said, studying him, trying to measure his mood.

Pa waved me toward the bar and I went, wondering whether it was later than I'd thought. "Yes sir," he said, as though we were in the middle of a long talk. "Been doing some thinking this afternoon and decided it doesn't pay."

"What doesn't pay?" I asked, suspecting he was going to take the vows of chastity or something.

"Thinking," he said and burst out laughing, letting it cascade, pour and finally trickle down to a quiet, contemplative giggle. Then he turned and gave me a mischievous look. "Whadyou think I was going to say?"

I blushed partly at having been so far off the target, partly at the piety of my assumption.

And he burst out laughing again. "Oh you did, did you?" he sputtered. "Well fancy that now," and then buried his nose in the bourbon, came up talking. "Can't you just see it?" he asked. "Wouldn't it make a sweetheart of a human interest story?"

"What?" I asked, flat-voiced.

"Son leads Pa down straight and narrow," he explained. "Tells old man lay off the ladies." He rolled to a sitting position, winked at me. "Whoa boy," he told himself.

"This is a game any number can play," I said and finished off my drink in three long, sickish swallows.

"Be my guest," he said, gesturing to the bar again.

"Thanks," I laughed and started up.

"But I shouldn't have to tell *you* that, should I?"

"No," I agreed, still laughing, trying to keep it light.

"Been my guest for twenty-two years," he said. "Ought to know your way around pretty well by now."

"Where's Mother?" I asked and poured myself a hooker.

"Where's Mama, where's Mama?" he mimicked. "How the devil would I know?"

I started out of the room with my drink.

"Wait," he said. "Wait, wait wait." He got up and caught me at the door. "Wayyyt just a minute now, your old papa's a little loaded but otherwise harmless. You ought to know that."

I let him guide me back, arm on my shoulder and set me down on the sofa.

"Put up with you," he said. "All the way from screaming infancy on through the slack-faced pimples of puberty and now . . . Hey, jus a minute," he interrupted himself, "that's beautiful. The slack-faced pimples of puberty, 'The ghoul-haunted woodland of Weir,' Edgar Allan Poe, howdaya like that? Anyway," he continued, "now I hafto put up with all your goddam righteousness, least you can do is bear with me while I have a lil drink."

I was looking up at him through all this, watching the wispy hair shake loose from its usual precise resting place, bobbing to emphasize his point, providing a touch of absurdity instead.

"Okay, Pa," I said. "I'm bearing."

"Attaboy." He gave me a big wink. "Now . . ." He paused, shook his head, blinked. "What're we going talk about?"

But all I could think of was the Fun House. It rattled round in my head like rocks in a tin tub, crashing, crushing, obliterating everything. I barely remembered my name.

"Well there's always the *Daily Watch*," he suggested. "We can always talk about that sorry goddam mess, can't we?"

I remembered a guy in my class at school whose old man took him to a whorehouse Christmas vacation of his senior year. At the time it seemed like a pretty sporty thing for the old man to do and I remember sort of wishing Pa would take me some time. It was funny, but I never fitted the kid's mother into the picture at all. Never wondered whether the old man had a go too. Didn't matter whether he did or didn't. In fact it wasn't even an issue. I just thought it was a sporty thing to do.

"All right, so you don't want to talk about the *Daily Watch*."

"Sure, sure I do." I scrambled to catch up. "I wish you'd come down and see the paper, Pa, see what we've done."

"Oh hell," he said, "yes, yes, yes."

"Never mind. Not if it bores you that much."

He shrugged and waved his cigarette back and forth, watching it, smiling. "I'm retired," he said.

"Oh?"

"That's right."

"Well come down anyway," I said, using laughter as my excuse. "I'd be glad to show you around."

"Now why would an old fool like me want to put you to all that trouble?"

"All right. Suit yourself." I got up.

"Where you going now?"

"'Nother drink," I said.

"Attaboy," he said. "Chip off the old block."

"Lucky me."

"S'matter?" he asked, following me over. "You don't wanna be a chip off the old block?"

I looked up at him, down at my drink, watched it fill.

"What do you think of that, Alice?"

And sure enough, it was Mother back from a shopping trip, innocent as a lamb. Well, innocent anyway.

"Think of what, dear?"

"Larry here doesn't want to be a chip off the old block."

She gave me a quick look of irritation, realized there was no cause as yet and took it back with a smile.

"Oh? And why not?"

I burst out laughing. "Go ahead, tell her."

Pa put a finger to his mouth and made clownish, *shhh-ing* noises. "Nev-mind, dear," he said. "Have a nice day shopping?"

"Clarence, you're drunk."

"How'sat?" Pa demanded, bending an ear. "Lil hard of hearing, don't you know."

"My foot," said Mother.

"Well, we've had a lil snort," he admitted. "Larry and I."

"Really, Larry," she snipped. "You should know better."

"Me?" And my mouth fell open with surprise. "Who's the father around here anyhow?"

"I am," Pa said, "or so I've always been led to believe."

"Clarence, really," Mother warned, and to me: "I told you last night he wasn't feeling well." Then she marched out of the room to deposit her packages.

"Shame, shame," Pa said. "You've led me down the prickly path, thas what you've done." He started giggling at himself again.

"Well, I didn't have much trouble finding it."

"Oh no," he warned, finger shaking. "Don try weaseling out. You've led me down the prickly path and thas all there is to it." Then he wandered off as though I hadn't been there at all, laughing to himself. "Have to tap a kidney," he explained.

I ducked out and upstairs to change. Boy, it was going to be some evening. I took a bath, a nice long soak, anything to postpone going back down. I was almost dressed when Mother knocked at my door.

"Come on in," I called.

She did. "Sorry I was cross, Larry."

"That's all right," I lied.

"How long has it been going on?" she asked.

"The drinking? I don't know. He was like that when I came in."

"Which was?"

"Round five."

Mother sighed, sat on my bed. "Oh dear," she sighed. "Oh dear, oh dear, oh dear."

"He'll be all right in the morning."

"Will he?" And that was a sigh too, not really a question.

I whipped a tie around my neck, busied myself fixing it, fussed with my cuff links, feeling the warm, liquid texture of gold, welcoming its distraction.

"Sure," I said, reaching into the sleeves of my blazer, setting it with a shrug. " 'Cept for a little hangover maybe."

Mother didn't say anything and I turned to see why. She just sat there with wide-eyed resignation, staring across at one of my football pictures as though it were interesting. She had on a dark blue velvet teagown which should have been all elegance but under the influence of her present mood looked more like an old and tired wrapper.

"Everything seems to be collapsing," she said.

But it wasn't really. Just the walls. The rest had been gutted long ago.

"You're the only one I can rely on," she added.

Now if Pa had said that it would have been different.

"Don't be too sure." I tried to laugh.

"You *have* to be."

In return for what? I wondered. All the loving kindness and understanding lavished on me? Or Pa's approval and recognition maybe? Or . . . ah cut it out, I told myself, before you choke on the tears.

"Okay, lean on me if you like," I joked, took her hand, helped her up. "But I can't be responsible for the consequences."

She took my arm and squeezed it. "Ummm, nice and soft," she said.

"Heroes are supposed to be hard and sinewy," I complained.

She smiled and kissed me but all I felt was regret.

Pa was playing Music for Lovers Only on the phonograph and waxing sentimental when we came in but he got over that fast enough in his determination to be super-gracious one minute, super-snide the next.

I couldn't quite make up my mind what Mother's interpretation of family propper-upper amounted to. Was I supposed to discourage his drinking, and if so how, or should I drink him under the table, counting on his head start, and have my picture taken one foot on his chest, a fist on mine, jungle fashion? The latter, whether successful or not, had more appeal somehow.

As things turned out, it wasn't what he did but what he might have done which kept me constantly off balance. Not that it was an entirely unpleasant condition. Here we were, after all, the props and appurtenances of admiration tossed aside, just three old friends boozing it up, for even Mother had taken the easy way, and there was no reason why I shouldn't have enjoyed it. Except I didn't. And especially not toward the end of dinner when Pa reached that giggling, finger-pointing, head-shaking state in which everybody's supposed to understand what's funny but nobody does. Mother was no help at all from then on. She could handle his being tight or even drunk, but not clobbered. And I was no expert either, being forced to fall back on college fraternity experiences for the necessary reactions and finding few which suited, since I was almost positive Pa neither wanted to wrestle, slide downstairs on metal trays, nor indulge in anything so brisk and refreshing as a water fight.

Then he got nasty.

Not for any reason I could see. Or anyway, not for anything very important. Just because Mother yawned, that was all.

"Oh dear," he sneered. "Don't tell me I'm keeping you up."

"Hmm?" she asked, swallowing the end of it. "Oh no, not at all."

"Then I must be pretty goddam boring, zat it?"

"No, dear. It's just late."

"Don't patronize me, goddam it, jus wanted know ff'Larry was goin out on tha town, thas all."

"No, Pa, I'm not."

"Jus tryin make lil polite convsation with ma son an you yawn in ma face."

"Clarence," Mother insisted, looking scatter-eyed. "It had nothing to do with that."

"If yer so goddam fascnating then go ahead and talk," he insisted.

Mother could think of nothing to say.

"*Talk,*" he bellowed, and the force of it brought him to his feet. "Go ahead, say something, goddam it."

"Please," Mother said.

"Am I such a boring son of a bitch nobody can even listen to me?" He advanced to a place of attention in the middle of the room.

"Come on, Pa," I whispered. "Take it easy."

"Who the hell are you telling what to do," he hollered. "You, you goddam . . . You goddam back-stabber." Then he started to address Mother, changed his mind, turned back on me. "Min yerown business, you fff . . ." He let it go, spun around and fell in a chair, not passed out really, just pretending to be.

Mother and I sat there without saying anything for at least ten minutes, until at last it seemed the pretending was real. Then we switched off the lights and went up to bed, still without a word, each clamped in private shame and panic.

Next morning Pa came in while I was having breakfast, bathrobe awry, hair the same, one hand on his hip the other holding his forehead.

"Oh dear," he said. "Oh dear me."

"See you got to bed all right," I commented.

"Oh, did I?" he asked, then noticed his bathrobe. "Yes, so I did."

I went on eating, wishing it weren't Sunday so I'd have the office to hide in.

"My my," he said. "Better have a lil pick-me-up." He stumbled toward the kitchen, came back with a jug of tomato juice, took it to the bar and away we went all over again.

He didn't quite make lunch that day, or the next one either, but while Mother and I could think of absolutely no solution, we took some sustenance from the fact he at least stayed home, thus limiting the scope of his degradation to a large and heartening extent.

We were very grateful.

CHAPTER XXVI

Abby got home Wednesday evening and I met her, eager—if that's the word for it—to fill her in on Pa's latest tricks and find out in return how things had gone with her.

I tried a guess based on the way she looked but the hustle of traveling and being home, even though only Gravenhurst, and the cold snipping at her cheeks and people saying "Well well" and "Lookit Miss Pretty" and "Sakes, hasn't it been a while," either to Abby or their own relatives made it impossible to guess how she felt underneath.

"Well?" I asked when we got into the car.

"Well, what?"

"Jesse," I said. "What happened?"

"Oh God," she said with a whooping, half-hysterical laugh. "Don't even ask."

I didn't know what that was supposed to mean. She seemed more exasperated than hopeless. "Good or bad?"

"Search me," she said.

"Well, did he ask you?"

"Yup."

That surprised me.

"And did you accept?"

"Nope."

That didn't.

"Refuse?"

"Nope."

Neither did that.

"He didn't ask very hard," she added.

I said nothing. A hotrod had just passed me and I was wondering whether to fall back out of harm's way or risk their foolishness and keep my pride. They were restless, pulling out to pass, braking, honking. I fell back.

"Anyway, what's new at home?" she asked.

— So I told her. At least I told her everything but why and she didn't ask, probably assuming it was just part of the over-all pattern of disintegration.

"Seen anything of Hal?" she asked.

"Yeah, couple of times," I said, then remembered: "Oh say, he may be in a play."

"Hal?" She laughed. "You're kidding."

"Well, it's not definite," I admitted. "But Ted Pearson wants him to try out for *A Bell for Adano.*"

"Lordy," she said. "What next?" And after a while, "But does he really want to do it?"

"He wouldn't admit it, but I think so."

"Boy, if this keeps up Tommy Compton'll be joining the Junior Chamber of Commerce or something."

"Oh come on, it's not that out of character."

"Is too," she said. "And you know it."

"Can't be, or he wouldn't be doing it."

"People are funny," she said.

"You ain't seen nothing yet." I swung up the driveway.

"I almost forgot," she sighed. "How are we supposed to treat him?"

"As though he were big for his age," I suggested.

"Well, that's nothing new."

I laughed and reached back for her suitcase, dragging it out of the car, happy for some reason, soothed by Abby being home and Thanksgiving and all the nonsense it's supposed to signify.

Mother had taken the trouble to put little harvest wreaths in the windows and there was a cluster of Indian corn on the front door and the house lights glowed yellow and warm and I laughed and took Abby's arm. "Happy Thanksgiving," I said.

"Oh God," she retorted. "Don't make me laugh." But I already had.

Pa was in a lot better shape after four days of boozing than I'd have suspected. He wasn't sober, that was perfectly obvious, but neither was he red-eyed, slack-faced, and distraught, the way he deserved to be. Just a little irrational, his fire too bright one minute, flaring in a blaze of generosity—"Abby, seems to me time you had a little trip. How 'bout Easter in Bermuda, compliments of the old man?"—damping down to self-pity the next with a lot of soupy talk about how he was getting old, wouldn't be around forever, didn't want to be a burden on us young folks, and then an occasional, but only occasional, sputter of resentment usually aimed at me, or so it seemed, and stemming from advice first offered, then withdrawn. "But you don't need any help from me, do you?" he'd say. "Oh no, not you, you've got it all figured out." And if I said nothing he'd forget, then go right on to something else.

I'm not trying to suggest this was an ideal family arrangement but at least we could live with it and, after all, he couldn't keep the pace forever. Though we were beginning to wonder.

Needless to say that cozy little Thanksgiving dinner with the Comptons or whoever had been called off. Only Abby and I were still going to the dance—together, poor lil rich chillun that we were. Nobody'd thought to ask Abby being as she was away at college and I was Nora-less, currently playing fast and loose, or slow and sticky, with the eastern seaboard set. Very fancy. Very unrewarding. And Mother and Pa, of course, weren't going at all, or so Mother hoped.

But then there's nothing sneakier than a cockeyed anthropoid.

We made this discovery when Pa appeared for dinner in his tuxedo, all smiles and staggers, a wholly inauspicious sight.

Now Mother would put up with most anything but a public disgrace. That she simply couldn't abide. But abide it or not, there didn't seem to be much she could do to prevent it. "Clarence," she demanded, totally appalled. "Where on earth do you think you're going?"

"Going?" he asked with a mixture of piety and guile. "Why to the Thanksgiving Ball, my dear. Don't tell me you've forgotten."

"Oh no," she said.

"My my. You *are* slipping."

"Clarence, I forbid it." Which was just the wrong thing to say.

He smiled, winked at us to hide his determination, returned to the bar.

"Clarence, did you hear me?"

"Yes, I think so, dear," he said with enough sweetness to warn her off.

She sighed, went upstairs to change.

"My my," Pa said. "I *am* looking forward to this evening."

"Me too," I said, and that was true. I was fascinated, drawn to him like a crowd to the circus. Would the highwire man make it or would he fall and splatter?

Well, he made it through dinner, unfortunately, at least from Mother's point of view, and he didn't seem to mind Bollard's driving us over, in fact he quite liked it.

"Moy moy," he said, mouth all puckered and fake stuffy. "Aren't we being foncy tonight."

When we got there Pa most graciously ushered us in, tipped the man at the door five dollars, which was rather unusual since he happened to be a volunteer from the Rotary Club, and then grandly led us to the wrong table. But though a little late, Mother came to the rescue, got us aimed in the right direction. I don't think anybody noticed. After all, we weren't expected to be cold sober.

Once firmly seated we all felt a little easier about life. In fact, after a flurry of furtive glances to be sure we'd gone unnoticed, even managed to relax and practically enjoy ourselves.

The place was jammed. Must have been five hundred people, half dancing to a heavy dose of brass, the rest guzzling at their tables, plenty of them looking a lot worse off than Pa.

The place was an armory all right. That couldn't be concealed. But the walls had been draped with gold cloth and orange and black fliers hung from the girders, balloons struggled to hide the ugly ceiling, and life-sized cutouts of turkeys and Pilgrims and log cabins were propped along the walls. Also members of the dance band wore Pilgrim hats, as did a number of guests, so the whole effect was . . . how shall I say . . . well . . . colorful.

"Quite a turnout," I said.

"Ugh," said Abby.

I saw the Comptons, Tommy and Sam Crawley included, but they were too far away for a critical appraisal.

And what was his name? Bill Wilbur with his family, it looked like, and a couple of girls whose names I'd forgotten, and old Spaulding of Yale taking a free ride.

"And what would you like, Mr. Woodruff?"

"Bottle voldcrow do nicely," Pa opined, giving the waiter his most affluent smile.

Mother squirmed.

"Less of course you ladies'd like something else."

"No," Mother said, apparently fearing even the presence of another bottle. "That will do nicely."

"Soda, sir?"

"Finandandy," said Pa.

"Very good, sir," and that it most certainly was not.

Meg Brown of social-editing fame danced by under the guidance of Wesley Pierre, known to his intimates as "Lucky," a pudgy, middle-aged hermaphrodite who ran the local dancing school. Meg flickered her fingers at us and we flickered ours back.

Next came Ted Pearson and wife, bouncing by, but not before he leaned out of orbit and told us this was really living. I laughed and discreetly turned my back to the dance floor. It was too complicated.

"Who's that?" Abby asked.

"Where?"

"Over there. Just this side of the Comptons."

I squinted, made out Hugh Godkin and his fiancée.

"The girl?"

"Yes," she said.

"Hugh Godkin's bride-to-be, Amanda something-or-other. Simpson, I think."

"She looks sort of droopy," Abby suggested.

"You'd be droopy too," I said. "If you were engaged to Godkin."

"Oh? I hardly know him."

"As a matter of fact, neither does she," I laughed.

Then came a slap on the back. I looked skyward. "Hey," I said. "Howsa boy?"

"Bearing up," said Hal. "Got an extra seat?"

"Why certainly," said Mother with a rabbit-toothed smile. "Do join us."

"Hey, I got the part," Hal said. "I'm an actor." He started to sit down.

"No kidding, that's great," I said.

"Splendid to see you, old man," said Pa. "Solutely splendid."

Hal sized him up, smiled, asked Abby to dance. She shrugged, sighed, then, as though suddenly remembering a previous resolution, smiled back. "Love to," she said.

I wished I'd thought of that. It was a little lonely with just the three of us but Pa soon solved the problem. With a few hearty waves he drew the Clem Harpers and Sam Bryant, alderman from the Fourth Ward, the guy who took over Mayor Healy's slot.

I figured Mr. Harper might not consider me his best friend and excused myself just as the whiskey arrived. Bad timing, I must say, and Mother looked like she agreed. "Be back soon," I promised.

Just where I was going remained something of a mystery until Nora loomed dead ahead and I swerved, cut in on the first familiar face. It was my old friend, Mary Kowalski, now Mrs. Al Noonan. Noonan happened to be assistant coach of the Gravenhurst High football team; a large and jealous-looking chap known descriptively as Big Al.

"Hey, Al." I grinned and went off dancing.

"Well," Mary said. "This *is* an honor."

"Ah come on," I said. "You can do better than that." It was like we were still kids and I'd seen her only yesterday with nothing but a couple of meals and a night's sleep between kissing.

Mary laughed. "That's what they say in the movies," she explained. "I was just trying it out." She was still soft and supple as fur, still frisky, too.

"I want you, darling," I said because I felt like it.

"Huh?"

"That's what they say in the movies," I explained.

"Some movies," she laughed. "Where are they shown, at the Elks?"

"You're supposed to say 'take me,'" I corrected, "or something like that."

"Yeah, well keep me informed." But Big Al was back before I had a chance.

"You dance divinely," I said and waggled my eyebrows at Al.

"He's a nut," Mary explained, and the Noonans disappeared in the crowd.

That's what she thinks, I told myself, wandering off, happily steeped in her touch and scent and the memories they stirred.

Then before I knew it, Tommy reached back and aimed me to-

ward an empty chair. The Comptons were there, but so was Jeff
Collins and his wife so all I had to say was hello and yes I would like
a drink when Mrs. Compton asked. The judge was offering nothing
but his special brand of gray and ill-concealed disapproval, a gift he
apparently reserved for Nora's ex-suitors and those who know too
much but aren't likely to tell. Thus he could appear both indignant
and shamefaced at one and the same time. A singular ineptitude, a
remarkable incompetence. I snuck a wink at the Collinses, and
turned to Tommy.

"Gathering material for a novel?" I asked.

"Something like that."

"Well there ought to be plenty here."

"Ummm."

"Where's Sally?" I tried, sort of to prove my point.

"Over there."

I followed the direction of his nod, found her at a table full of
such politicos as Healy, Spanger, chairman of the Common Council,
and a couple other members of the "Young," or Renegade Republican set.

"Danced with her?" I asked.

"You crazy?"

"Well, I'll admit it's a little unconventional," I kidded, then
paused. Tommy said nothing. "But then so are you."

He still said nothing.

"Aren't you?"

"I'm a writer, not a fighter," Tommy said, laughing, watching to
see if I was too, carefully leading me away from his precious brood
of ideas.

"Sometimes I wonder whether you know what you are," I said.

"Sometimes I do too," he admitted, and took a drink. "Don't you?"

I took a little drink too. "Be here long?" I asked.

"Weekend."

"How's life in Beatsville?"

"Like every place else."

"It is?"

"Everybody's conventionally unconventional. It's a drag."

"How do they manage that?"

"Oh you know, nobody has television because it's bourgeois. Even
something they'd like to see off the one-eyed monster is bourgeois
on it. And all the girls buy the same far out jewelry and they all

make the same far out remarks on the same far out subjects like aren't the buses crowded and the Astral shop's all out of Zodiac earrings and if you don't happen to be interested, boy, you are *square*."

"I'm sorry," I said. "I thought it was working out better than that." He shrugged. "Oh hell. The slobs are everywhere."

"Oh, hiii hiii."

It was Sam Crawley with Nora.

"Case in point," said Tommy.

"Hello. Guess I have your chair, Sammy," and I hurried to vacate.

"No no," he said. "Plenty of room," and they proved it by sitting down in two empty spots.

"Yeah, well anyway, I have to . . ."

"Oh stick around," said Tommy.

So I did.

"For a minute," I said. "Got to get back to the family."

Carl Robinson came wandering by with his camera, looking like the only white man at a Black Muslim picnic.

"Hey," I called. "You working?"

"Free-lancing," he said.

"Oh. Hey listen." I motioned with my finger for a whispering session. He listened, gave me a reassuring nod, headed for the old man's table.

I caught Jeff's eye. "Watch this," I mouthed, thumbing over my shoulder.

Carl crept up on them, *bang* went the flash and, boy, you'd think Pa and Mr. Harper had been shot. I got laughing so hard and trying not to that it looked more like crying. And Jeff the same way.

Carl came by again, leaned over close, whispered: "They must of thought it was loaded," and joined the laughter, not knowing why, just glad to be in on something. Even only part way in.

After a while I calmed down and got to watching Nora. She looked surprisingly well. I mean getting all dressed up for a guy like Clammy Sammy wasn't much of an inspiration. Then the memory of Lucy materialized and old Nora didn't look quite so great under the strain of comparison. That is, if it was really Lucy. Not just the mating of memory and imagination. I couldn't really remember, couldn't really be sure, wished she was here with me, then thanked God she wasn't. It was such a lovely memory. Why ruin it?

"How've you been, Nora?" I asked.

"Oh pretty good. You?"

"Bearing up."

Yes, she did look well. Or else I was seeing her differently, no longer equating her to the Main Street cliché of dullness and bias and prying charity, the booby prize for conceding to inconsequence. Why the change I'm not quite sure. Partly because I was no longer harassed by the urgency of a decision, no longer afflicted with the resentment this stirred. But also because the very town she symbolized no longer seemed as ugly and impotent as before. Surface dullness it had aplenty. Bias and prying charity as well, though these were characteristics imposed mostly by reputation and no more typical of Gravenhurst than Potters Island, New York City, or anyplace else.

And beneath the dullness? I don't know, it seemed to me there was quite a bit going on. Not all of it charming and tastefully done, I'll admit, but far from dull.

"Nora?" I asked. "Want to dance?"

But the band struck a fanfare, priming us for a special announcement, then went dead.

Somebody blew in the mike. "We're going to have the raffle now," he said without ceremony.

Nora smiled, cocked a shoulder.

Clammy Sammy looked smug, as though he'd actually planned it. I managed to produce a gesture of mock concern which felt downright sophisticated.

Abby and Hal drifted by as the dance floor cleared.

Tommy nudged me. "Abby here with that Rosenfeldt fellow?"

I shook my head.

"No?" he asked. "What's the matter?"

"Search me."

"No Jews is good Jews?" he asked.

"And now, ladies and gentlemen," came the voice from the mike. I considered righteous indignation, a Woodruff substitute for lying, then decided this was as good a time as any to change the game.

"That's right," I said.

"Too bad."

"That's right."

"Don't tell me you're planning a merger with the House of James," he kidded.

"That's right," I said a third time.

"May I present our master of ceremonies, the honorable and illustrious Mayor Happy Healy."

Rattle of applause, clatter of chairs and whisper of settling bodies.

Mayor Healy took the stand. The band slumped behind him, instruments dangling soggily, a sweating troupe of Sancho Panzas.

"Guess there's folks here'll be glad to know I'm not planning on any speeches tonight . . ." Mild cheering. "No sir, way I see it the quicker we hold the raffle the quicker I win me a brand-new Austin Healy . . ." Some cooperative booing. "But why not?" he asked. "Brother Austin assures me it's in the . . ." But there was no need to finish. Everybody pitched in hissing laughing and booing. "All right," he said, hushing them down. "All right, I'm going, but first let me present a man whose honesty, integrity, and industry no one need question and no one had *better* question: our honorable high chief in the art of raffle running, State Senator Ned Polk." The mayor backed away, clapping, nodding, winking as Senator Polk passed him by and waited, one hand slotted, statesman-like, in his dinner-jacket pocket, for the applause to die.

"Thank you, Mayor Helium," he began, and while they laughed, directed two men who were carrying a large wire ball stuffed with raffle tickets to a spot near the mike. "Now," he began, "as a former newspaper editor, I'm naturally suspicious of politicians even though I am one myself and will therefore call on one of our more illustrious citizens, a man whose honesty and devotion to the public rather than private good has recently been witnessed by all. A man who would prefer to step down from the chairmanship of a project for which he and he alone was totally and completely responsible rather than jeopardize its future."

Oh my God, I thought. He must have seen Pa was loaded.

"A man with whom I hope to work closely in order that Gravenhurst may continue to stand second to none in this great state and nation."

"Correction," I groaned. "This must be part of that goddam new alliance."

"What?" Tommy whispered.

"I give you the owner, the publisher, the man behind the guns of progress, Mr. Clarence Woodruff."

Pa rose to the rumble of applause, blinked, nodded, swallowed, took half a step, arched his back in good-natured surprise and fell with terrible, tree toppling force.

I jumped up and ran, oblivious to the humiliation, sure he'd been hurt. A leaning, peering, wondering mass of would-be helpers had already gathered but I managed to shove and elbow my way through. Mother was still seated, clenched with indecision. Hal and Abby had got to him first, but could hardly move with the crowd.

"Gowan, please," I said, pushing at the wall of white-breasted onlookers. "Everybody sit down." They gave way but not enough. I hesitated, started to cut loose in anger and hysteria, caught myself, went round the circle from one to the other. "Please. Please sit down, he may be hurt." They turned away.

By then Hal had him rolled over, sitting up, dangling like an old, abandoned puppet, a trickle of blood from his nose.

"Let's get him the hell out of here," I whispered.

But he was dead weight.

"Christ," Hal grunted. "Step on his foot."

We did and using the leverage this afforded, managed to haul him up, each get under an arm and drag him the endless, head-lolling, shuffle-footed length of that ugly overlighted, overcrowded, thousand-eyed armory, Mother trailing, not looking one way or the other, I don't suppose, and Abby tossing little eyeloads of arrogance from side to side. Then, at last, the peace and charity of darkness.

We were out. So was Pa. Knocked out or boozed out, I didn't know which, but he just hung draped on Hal and me while Abby went after Bollard. Then Doc Grady was there, full of questions and concern until I admitted what the trouble was. But he decided to follow us home anyway, be on the safe side.

Getting Pa in the car was like trying to stuff a dead deer onto the back of a jeep. I finally had to climb in and haul while Hal pushed, trying not to hurt him, but more intent on just getting him inside the car and the hell out of there.

We finally did and I was sort of sorry. The agony of doing nothing, Mother still frozen, staring straight ahead, the rest of us slumped with the memory of it, was far worse. I was glad when we got home and could start our pushing and shoving all over again.

We tried getting him upstairs, almost gave it up, then made it, step by step by everloving, teetering, belly-grunting step.

And finally onto the bed.

When Mother saw him lying there, almost as though asleep except for the trickle of blood and disheveled hair, she knew exactly what to do, fetched a damp cloth, wiped off the blood, smoothed his hair and smiled, reassured by these apparent improvements.

He started rattling around a little then, mumbling "Whoa boy, easy now," and so forth. It was kind of embarrassing so Hal and Abby and I went down to get some hot broth as well as a few other things like a drink and away.

Bollard had already fixed the broth so we went into the living room and set to work on those few other things.

"You know we ought to go back," Hal said. "Give people an explanation before they start making up one of their own."

"Hah!" Abby said, and then, "Yes, I suppose we should."

"What'll we tell them?" I asked.

"To go to hell," Abby suggested.

"You're regressing," I said. A car pulled up then. Doc Grady, most likely. "I'd rather not go back," I said. "Makes it look more serious if we don't, less like he was just drunk."

I went to let the doctor in, came back to our waiting, unraveling, trying to see what had happened the way everyone else had, wondering what kind of an excuse, if any, would suffice or whether Abby was really right and the hell with excuses.

Doc Grady was back down in five or ten minutes and I walked him out.

"Far as I'm concerned," the doctor said, "your father's suffered a mild coronary. Nothing serious. Suggest a good night's sleep and moderation in all things." He smiled. "*All* things," and with that he was gone.

Well, that was fine with me. I went back and told them what the deal was and we decided I should stay, keep Mother company, but maybe Abby and Hal'd better go back, nip the rumors before they got out of control.

So I stayed all right, but it didn't do anybody much good. I was so dead sick of the whole mess my bones felt soft and my insides soggy, unsure, my whole being searching hungrily for nothing, a wonderful round and empty nothing, and not being able to find it, I offered Mother some halfhearted assistance, saw Pa was sleeping, and went to bed.

CHAPTER XXVII

Pa was just a little unsteady that next day and maybe a little shamefaced to boot, though it was hardly noticeable. In fact, he seemed not only relieved by Doc Grady's convenient diagnosis but actually convinced it was so. Thus there was something in his manner; something undeclared but obvious all the same which suggested we treat him kindly and with respect in this his hour of need.

Abby had about all she could stomach by then, went back to college with relief and resignation a day or two early rather than help Mother face the sympathy calls and I went back to work, busier than ever so as not to be a part of this restoration process. There wasn't much I could do anyway and I think they preferred having me out of the house rather than looking on while the grownups played coronary thrombosis.

In any case, there really was plenty to keep me busy on the paper. All our changes, though still imperceptible for the most part, took some getting used to and a lot of extra work resulted. Just as life still seeped under the frozen countryside, so change stirred under the congealed surface of our dull routine. As a result the November figures showed some pretty sizable gains; gains based not on novelty, sensationalism, and such similar sleights of hand, but on sound, practical journalism. We had to sweat long hours for every penny of it, pull every legitimate trick we could think up, but none of that mattered so long as things continued to improve. And they did.

The whole thing was kind of ironical when you stopped to consider, which I did occasionally. After all, the Rosenfeldts had come to town intent on introducing editorial and economic reforms in order to improve journalism on the small-town level and the fact was they'd succeeded. As a result of their efforts, the *Daily Watch* had improved considerably, both editorially and economically, and could conceivably put them out of business in the not-too-distant future. Maybe this was partly their own fault, seeing as the *Enterprise's* methods had never quite reached those heights of virtue and efficiency to which Jesse claimed aspiration. But no matter who was at fault, the fact remained that our fight for survival had trimmed the fat, quickened the pulse, honed the will to a point where their pursuit could very likely end in panting, slavering confusion. Since they hadn't been able to stop us during our fat and happy waddling days, it seemed doubtful they could do it now.

Or so I hoped.

In any case, whether they failed to restore competitive journalism or not, some good had come out of the conflict, I had to admit that.

Even their influence on my home life, while none too merciful, had at least brought a glimmer of reality. After a period of grace lasting several generations, the Woodruffs were now back in the struggle for survival, along with all the other creeping things that creepeth, and it didn't appear to be doing us any harm. On the contrary, we each seemed finally to be finding our separate wills and were far better off than the self-deluded sons and daughters of complacency who once crowned Woodruff Hill.

That is *if* we survived. And more than that, if we had sense enough to realize this struggle was as much a part of our existence as life and death, just as inevitable, just as vital to our ultimate deliverance, just as unimpressed by Lincoln Continentals, art collections, country clubs and all the other trivia in which we had been seeking to bury it.

Anyway, with things beginning to look a little more livable on the home front, I suffered a minor distraction from abroad—if New York City can be called "abroad" and I'm inclined to think it can. It came in a quilted envelope stuffed with all manner of engraved verbal festoonery, the purpose of which, apparently, was to secure my presence at the Stuyvesant Ball, New Year's Eve, Hotel Pierre, R.S.V.P., and all like that. To say I was totally overcome would be inaccurate. After all, having accompanied Abby to the Stamford Junior League Debutante Ball, Stamford Yacht Club, Stamford, Connecticut, I was not unfamiliar with this rather expensive form of selective breeding, but the fact is I'd never been invited to strut my stuff in the big city. Thus I'll admit to a mild dose of social perplexity but it lasted only until I discovered Lucy's name among the sponsors. After that an entirely new set of imponderables took over. First and least complicated, I was pleased she'd thought of me, wanted to go, wondered if I'd be going with her. But after that considerations got a little less reasonable. Was I ready to risk another social bludgeoning à la Potters Island?

No!

Was I interested in subjecting my store-bought, country self to Lucy's rigorous social improvement project?

No!

Would I be?

I didn't know, but there were indications: the amused and slightly patronizing air with which she had declined my invitation to the Thanksgiving Ball, for instance.

On the other hand, how much did all this matter when weighed against the possibility we might one day learn to love each other, had already clocked some mileage in that direction?

Frankly, I didn't know, though it had occurred to me this newly acquired independence of mine, this sudden severance from the past, must one day be trimmed to fit the contours of another body and soul. Otherwise the animal in me would surely shrivel and die and stink up the rest, whatever the rest might be, and I'd be left with a significance as crippled and unfulfilled as Pa's. But whether the psychic alterations necessary to fit myself to Lucy were reasonable or not was something I still couldn't answer.

There was only one way to find out, of course, but at that point I really preferred to let the whole thing ride awhile, not being overly eager to subject the brand spanking new Woodruff to such a formidable test just then.

So . . . well, I just tucked the old invitation in my pocket, along with another one which came next day, inviting me to dinner at the Delevans, and forgot about the whole thing.

Just a week or so before Christmas this routine of work, conquest, and unrequited love was broken by the weather. A blizzard stole in during the night and lashed out with cruel beauty, muffling the land under two feet of powder. Next morning when I looked out the window, with an eye to judging my chances of getting to work on time, they didn't look too promising. The air sizzled with driven snow, our driveway was piled to the fence tops with awesome, rolling drifts, the trees reared like chained sheep drenched in fear. Suddenly my world was strange, harsh, untamed as a northern wilderness and infinitely beautiful. But as I watched, a gray sputtering ghost appeared at the head of the driveway, thrust its snout into a drift, backed up and plunged through the swirling wasteland. Mr. Quincy and his trusty tractor were on the job and, judging by the private blizzard those two were creating, it looked like the driveway would be ready long before I was.

I love the tension and excitement of a storm. Especially a snow-storm. Hurricanes and the like have an aspect of waste and pollution about them; a deadly, malicious, wanton quality in their coming and nothing but rot in their wake. While the blizzard, though destructive too, has a clean crisp execution; harsh, perhaps, but above the wretched tactics of its summer cousin. Thus for many people, among them me, the weather is a source of entertainment, a relief from the chill of boredom.

I welcomed every aspect of a blizzard right down to such insignificant items as the matter of dress. It was great to break the monotony with heavy socks and boots and ski pants and the tough leather sheepskin jacket instead of my usual coat and tie routine. Even Pa's curiosity was roused enough to come down to the office in a flurry of puffing and fist pounding and cordial profanity.

Unfortunately, on reaching the office there wasn't much he could do, for though our changes weren't so copious as all that, their very recency demanded more attention than those other matters with which Pa was more familiar. But he took the unexpected strangeness pretty well considering such trifling matters as the Columbia contract withdrawal could knock him ass over tip. Instead of brooding, he spent his time wandering around the plant making hearty remarks about the weather and trying at least to look like his old self. I'll admit it didn't last. He gave up and went home around noon, but that didn't matter to me. At least he had tried.

A couple of days later—it must have been Saturday because I was home for lunch—Mr. Quincy came in and reported the inevitable. Dogs were running the snow-packed trails and cutting down deer "twenty to the dozen." He wanted me to go out with him in the afternoon, see just how bad the slaughter had been and whether we couldn't drop a few of our canine friends before they did any more useless killing. I accepted with pleasure. Having been too busy for much deer hunting that year, I resented the idea of those damn dogs getting out there and doing what I couldn't. But it was more than that. I guess a dog has as much right to kill as I have. Provided there's a reason other than the pure sport of it. Provided they at least fill their bellies. But that was the trouble; they had no other reason. Their pleasure was to run a deer, shred its hind legs, and leave it wasted, bleating in the bloodied snow. I don't suppose the dogs would be interested in my analysis of their sport, but it seemed such a futile and unnatural pastime to me. As if domesticity had somehow perverted the purpose of their instincts, for they hunted without hunger, without need, and their only pleasure came in the chase. Thus by destroying the quarry they destroyed their pleasure too. But try telling that to a dog. Or even some people. I've seen a dog stand over his kill, nuzzling, sniffing, even whining, as though trying to persuade it to get up and run some more. And I've seen men do the same thing, standing over their freshly killed buck, poking it with the gun, confused, slightly disappointed, and why? Well, partly they're a little nonplused by the killer urge still throbbing in their bellies, but also it's because they have to pack up now and go home. Too bad, Jack, no more hunting until next year, and off they go, one by one, dragging their deer behind them, wishing to Christ they'd missed.

It's funny. I mean sometimes it seems like there isn't much difference between the way a man and a dog do things. Granted most men at least eat their kill, thus giving the hunt some purpose, but there are plenty who don't; who stuff it instead, or give it away, or just plain can't be bothered to track it down and drag it out of the woods. But whatever is done with it, the fact remains men don't need to hunt any more than dogs do, not these days anyway, yet in one form or another, it's all we do. Being a hunter myself, I've got no drum to beat, only a sad little song to sing, and that concerns the way I feel after killing. Not during or just after when the turmoil in me can usually be mistaken for elation, but later on when the absence of hunger begins to cheat me of a purpose and no amount of persuasion can erase the fact that I did it for nothing. Then comes a sadness, more than that, a feeling of inconsequence, futility, hopelessness, for I realize nothing can be done—nothing—to restore the sense of purpose to an act which is as much a part of my nature as loving. The only solution, I suppose, is to know this, accept it, expect it, and not feel cheated when it comes. Or else only hunt for what we need. In the woods that's impossible, seeing as all game is food, so I guess all we can do is accept the futility of killing in return for the pleasure hunting gives us. But in the cities and towns where we practice most of our predatory skills, maybe it's not so impossible. With our coffers filled to the brim maybe it's time we went looking for food of another kind. Otherwise, like those dogs, each kill, each success, brings a new frenzy, a new futility, and a spiteful urge to kill again.

But what other kinds of food are there? Well, they say fish is good for the brain. Maybe I'll do more fishing next year.

After lunch Mr. Quincy and I rummaged through the pile of past necessities we kept in the garage loft and managed to come up with a couple of pairs of snowshoes.

It's supposed to be tough work dragging those damn cumbersome netted feet around, but the snow had crusted and settled a bit and we didn't find the going too tough.

There's an old logging trail circling the lake and we split on reaching it, with Mr. Quincy going left around past Mayor Healy's house and me to the right. The cold was pitiless and I wished to God somebody had invented earmuffs you could hear through. I cradled the gun and buried my hands in the warm jacket pockets. The lake, once Nature's womb, now crouched white and endless and dead. It seemed impossible life could still exist there, waiting for the chance to rise, struggle, atrophy, and die in its endless, infinite search for a creature just a little finer than the one before. But it did and as I watched a feeling of uneasiness came over me. It was no great comfort to realize I was a part of the same process, for unhappily only death could complete the cycle. Yet I suppose it was better than being a part of nothing. I could see the carcass of a deer, brown and shapeless in death and terribly lonely, out in the middle of the lake. And rounding a corner I found another plunged headlong into a snowbank in what must have been a last futile bid for safety, torn hind legs testifying to her lack of success. Then later three more, stiff, flattened, and frozen on the ice.

By that time, given the opportunity, I might have shot a poodle right out of his mink coat. At least so I told myself, but when the opportunity did arise my zealous concern for justice seemed to slacken. Sound carries a very short distance through snow-muffled woods and the howling confusion was almost on top of me before I'd heard a thing. I'd just time to step behind a tree when a young doe, floundering with fatigue, toppled past followed by a great urgent beast of a dog. I pulled up the gun, sighted, then hesitated just that instant necessary to consider this was a dog, almost a friend, I was about to kill, and during that pious lapse of reason my victim disappeared around a turn in the trail.

I came out from behind the tree and did some floundering of my own in an effort to catch up and correct my mistake, but the going was too slow. My only chance was to let him kill once more and hope for a shot while he performed his grim destruction.

I heard nothing.

Then the pitiful, half-human bleating.

"God damn it," I swore.

I came over a small hill and there was the death pageant not twenty-five yards below. The crying and thrashing and rip, snap, busy growl of the killer. I sighted fast, fired and slammed a slug into the big dog's straining rump. His *kiyi-ing* joined the doe's wail in a grim but satisfying duet of death. I'd hit him in the back end, paralyzing but not killing. Not yet. It didn't take an expert to see the doe lacked only an act of mercy, so I delivered it, shuddering almost as much as she.

I turned to the dog. He was done for too.

"You son of a bitch," I said.

But right away I was sorry for him. The killer was gone and nothing remained but a great bewildered, flop-eared, sad-eyed, panting sit-by-the-fire with about as much understanding of why he did what he did as a man might have on discovering his actions, though intended for quite different purposes, had brought misery and confusion instead.

"Well, I guess there's nothing we can do for you," and I blasted him out of his misery.

I stepped back, eyeing the two of them suspiciously because they were now dead and no longer part of the world I understood. Then I turned and headed back toward home, unable to forget the doe had died as much by my hesitation as by the devil possessing that poor dumb mutt lying there beside her.

CHAPTER XXVIII

Santa Claus came to the *Daily Watch* a full week early that year, but better still, he came laden with a few unexpected goodies. One of them we found especially enticing: the *Enterprise* had managed to lose its share of the Tompkins Sunnyside Supermarket account. Moreover Jesse himself was believed directly responsible. According to Ted Pearson, who on top of everything else was turn-

ing out to be a masterful rumormonger, Jesse and Ben Tompkins
had had one hell of a row—right down at the store, too, in front of
everybody—over why Ben didn't use the *Enterprise* as his exclusive
advertising outlet. Apparently Jesse had come to him with some
kind of a rate-cutting proposition or a kick-back arrangement or
something provided Ben go along with his idea for an exclusive
contract. Well, there were plenty of legitimate reasons why he
wouldn't. Not only was it kind of a shady deal, but just plain bad
business to boot. Had our circulation been way off—and by De-
cember it was far from that—the last thing Ben would want would
be to limit the scope of his advertising. Even if we had a circulation
of one, as long as the rate was equally modest, he'd probably want
to stay with us. And Jesse should have known this, in fact must have
known it. Maybe he was running scared, though, or maybe Abby
was getting him down. I don't know. Anyway, he not only made
the offer, but blew his top when Mr. Tompkins refused. According
to employees and customers alike it was quite an explosion. Not
just raised voices from behind a closed door, but the shouting of
threats and insults—mostly Jesse's—the length and breadth of Ben's
store. It seemed Jesse took the refusal as a personal insult, a manifestation of those prehistoric business techniques so characteristic
of our fair city and most shocking of all, a clear exhibition of anti-
Semitism. All this was bellowed over his shoulder as Jesse loped
through the market while Ben Tompkins pursued like a farmer
driving some stray dog from his chicken house, mumbling "Get the
hell out of here, you son of a bitch," and off to the parking lot where
a few last-minute sentiments were exchanged.

Well, from a business point of view we couldn't have asked for
anything nicer than that. Being accused of anti-Semitism, whether
true or not, was an insult to which the whole city could and would
take exception. In Gravenhurst we consider racial or religious hatred
a private affair; something to be done but not talked about, like
charity. And next to that in the mustn't-do-department comes making a scene in public. Plenty of people do it at one time or another
but they suffer accordingly until the vicarious pleasure of discussing
someone else's fall from grace has been replaced by a hotter item.
But for an outsider to commit such a crime was far more difficult
to reconcile since an outsider, by definition, has achieved no grace
in the first place and need only use his knife as a pusher to prove it,
never mind throw a fit in public.

Thus my first reaction was a joyous one but later, perhaps because I really did like Jesse or was still smarting from my Potters Island wounds, I began to feel sorry for him. He also roused my curiosity. This sort of thing was so out of character. I could see Jesse being methodical, unrelenting, even ruthless as he carefully crisscrossed the field of competition in his effort to put us out of action. But this was different. It was as if his love for Abby or his frustration at not being able to have her, had infected and spilled its poison into the rest of him. Except that the drive was desire rather than death, Jesse was like that dog I'd killed.

I decided to go see him that afternoon after Ted told me what had happened. Not for anything specific. Just because I was sort of sorry he'd been having his troubles, even though we'd been the beneficiaries.

I noticed the secretary looked kind of funny when she buzzed the intercom to tell him I was waiting. There was something slippery-eyed about her, as though maybe I'd arrived at sort of a bad time. But if that was so, she didn't let on, just told me he was downstairs and to wait in his office.

It wasn't more than a couple of minutes before he came in.

"Sorry," he said, as he tugged at his vest and buttoned his coat. He looked as though life was still very much under his control. "Had a little trouble in editorial."

"Oh?"

"Nothing serious," he assured me, but with enough mystery to suggest that wasn't so. "Just a little misunderstanding."

"Oh."

"Well," he said, and smiled as though I were a client or somebody he vaguely knew in a business way. "What can I do for you?"

"Nothing," I admitted. "Just dropped by to say hello."

That seemed to baffle him.

"What's the matter with that?" I laughed.

"These days, something's the matter with everything."

"What'd you expect? That we'd just lay down and quit."

"Beg pardon?" Then he thought for a second. "Oh no, I didn't mean that exactly."

I found myself a little miffed at not being the center of his troubles but managed to avoid saying so.

"No," he repeated. "As a matter of fact, Papa's been keeping me rather busy on a low-cost housing project he's been considering for Latin America."

"Latin America?" I asked. "Are you . . ." But at that point we were interrupted by a commotion in the anteroom.

"Wait hell. I don't care if the son of a bitch is celebrating Rosh Hashana. Ned Polk doesn't wait for anybody," and the door suddenly whipped open.

"What *is* this?" he growled, slapping a copy of the *Enterprise* with the back of his hand.

Jesse sighed, walked over and sat on the edge of his desk, as if he had put up with this kind of thing more than once.

" 'Polk to address Knights of Columbus.' Page sixteen, for Christ's sake." He spotted me about then but it didn't alter his attack in the slightest.

"Look," Jesse said. "I was just downstairs in Healy's office when you phoned. It seems to me he explained it pretty well."

"Explained it, my ass. This is a big story."

"With Congressional elections one year off," Jesse singsonged, carefully placing each word side by side with the apparent hope this would be the last time. "We do not feel your speculations on Congressman Chet Brown's successor have any news potential at this time."

"Don't patronize me, you kike bastard. I was editing a newspaper before you'd celebrated the bar mitzvah. If there's no story make one, but don't give me any . . ." That was as far as he got. Jesse had dropped his pencil, seemingly by accident, and was at the point of retrieving it when instead he came up with a floor-to-jaw punch which was so well-traveled by the time it reached the target that it seemed reluctant to stop. The effect was more like a blast than a simple punch. The combined *thwack* of fist, flesh, and cracking bone froze me with fascination. There was an instant of distortion, flying spittle and astonishment, then the enormous mound which had been Ned Polk melted, sagged, and plopped to the floor. There he sat, too fat to keel over, blood spilling joyfully from the corners of his mouth. He was out cold but still sitting up like a monstrous fat child doodling on the beach.

I noticed Jesse stuff his fist under the other arm, as though trying to hold it together.

"You okay?" I asked.

He nodded, picked up the phone, holding it with a hunched shoulder.

"Let me speak with Healy," he said. "Hello, Harvey? Listen, Polk's up here and he's hurt. Get hold of some reporters and run him over to Memorial Hospital." Then he laughed. "I don't know. Why don't you ask the senator for a statement?"

"I'd better get out of here," I said. "Things are confusing enough without having me around."

Just then Senator Polk groaned, shook his head and toppled over sideways.

"I think he's trying to tell you something," I laughed.

"Point of order, Mr. Chairman," Jesse suggested.

"I should say so." I started to go.

"You were asking about Latin America," he said. "The answer is yes, I am going there."

"I'm sorry."

"I'm not," he said. "It looks like quite an interesting proposition."

"That isn't exactly what I meant."

"Yes indeed," he said. "We've got this fellow who can produce shell houses—you know, those reinforced concrete things—cheaply enough to accommodate the working class."

"At a profit?"

"Oh yes," he assured me. "But of course we're more interested in the social ramifications. Battling Communism and all that."

"Sure," I agreed. "And the *Enterprise?*"

Polk sputtered, shook his head, threatened to rejoin the discussion.

"You'll have to discuss that with Harvey Healy," Jesse said. "Our new publisher."

"I see," I said. "And of course he'll be carrying on your fight for better newspaper standards and all that."

He hesitated but apparently declined to change the game. "Of course."

"Okay, if that's the way you want to play it," and I left.

Just what the senator from Gravenhurst felt about his little altercation was difficult to ascertain with his jaw wired shut. However, since support from the *Enterprise* was vital to his political career, one wouldn't have expected him to be overjoyed.

As it turned out, though, speechless or not, Polk was not at all inactive and neither, apparently, was Pa. Having recovered from his unfortunate attack of coronary alcoholosis my father must have been busily and secretly furthering his Congressional scheme, a project which I had wistfully thought might only have been a threat. But he apparently had not bothered to explain that his plan would have to unfold without *Daily Watch* assistance, or else why would Polk have come marching into the office, tossed a news release on my desk and marched out again without even staying long enough to watch me file it in the wastebasket? Why indeed.

I asked Pa as soon as I got home that night and he told me, I'm sorry to say.

"Had a little chat with Mr. Rosenfeldt," he said. "Seems you forgot to tell me he was leaving."

"I didn't forget."

"Rather an important matter, don't you think?"

"I guess so."

"Not something one just puts aside and forgets."

"Not ordinarily," I admitted.

"Especially since it tends to change our little agreement."

"It does?"

"I think so," Pa said. "Means we've pretty well got 'em on the run and . . . uh . . . so on and so forth."

"Pa," I said. "Ned Polk runs for anything he chooses with no help from the *Daily Watch*."

"That's absurd," he said. "After all, I am still the publisher, you know."

"Then retire," I said.

"I'd appreciate it," he snapped, "if you would not presume to advise me on how my life may best be managed."

"You can do as you please," I said. "I've already told you what I'll do if you try using the *Daily Watch* for your little political intrigues."

"Don't be impertinent," he warned.

"You can do as you please," I repeated and left him.

Well, I held the cards, I guess, but it was hardly a satisfactory arrangement between father and son and I sorely wished he'd lay off. But lay off he would not. News releases kept trickling from Polk's office to wastebasket with annoying regularity and for no apparent purpose except I suppose Pa was still stalling, still unwilling to admit he'd been checkmated. If he had.

Anyway, the family limped along under a cloud of bitterness and contempt with only the threat of an irreparable break to keep us civil. That plus the therapy of Christmas confusion and Abby's being home. I asked her if she knew about Jesse's leaving and she said no, but it didn't matter because he hadn't called since that last halfhearted proposal so she guessed whatever his plans were, they no longer included her. And she said as a matter of fact she was just as glad, but I could see *that* persuasion was more for her benefit than mine.

But Abby was pleasant enough, if a little too docile, too resigned. We went shopping together several times, slushing through the shabby tangle of municipal Christmas dressing, gray snow and shoppers, warmed by cadaverous Santa Clauses on each corner and pasty-faced Salvation Army ladies in between and the tarnished tinsel in a cigar-store window; warmed by these familiar sights seen only once a year but every year; nostalgic symbols of time passing; proof it was all right to cut another notch on the gun. We'd made it again.

Thus we struggled through our joyous yuletide season. Obviously this couldn't go on forever. Pa would have to put up or shut up one of these days, but I was hoping to postpone the inevitable at least until after the holidays. In fact I was sort of counting on Christmas Eve with its gentle blend of tradition and sentiment to solve the whole mess, and foolish though this may seem, for a while I began to think it might do just that. Somehow the soft glow of celebration seemed to draw us into our more harmonious—though illusory—past and thus restored at least the semblance of order.

Gramps was there in all his tinseled absurdity and we rallied round him, teasing, laughing, hiding our messy discontent so carefully we nearly forgot its existence.

Then there were such yuletide traditions as the annual photograph of Abby and me with Bollard in between, a trifle unsteady as usual, but upright enough to serve as the measure by which our miraculous growth had once been recorded. And of course the tree had to be decorated, there were party snappers to be popped, funny hats, presents, plenty of champagne, and all midst the time-worn patter of Christmas talk which may have been unoriginal as could be but at least had the advantage of a whole year under wraps.

Things weren't going too badly as a result, until around ten o'clock when the doorbell rang. I went to answer it convinced Jesse Rosenfeldt had arrived at last to provide a final touch of melodrama. Instead I found Tommy Compton, crocked but still navigating under a power the source of which even he must have questioned.

"Boy, have you got a snoot full," I said. There he was, decked out in a black turtle-neck jersey, gray tweed suit dating back to the days of respectability, and sneakers. His intention had obviously been to re-create the Beatnik but the effect was more like a devil's intern. He swayed slightly, though I could feel no breeze, and from each hand swung a bottle of champagne, domestic.

"Yes! That's right!" he said. "Wow man and phew!"

"I don't know the routine, Tommy, but come on in anyway."

"Man, you're beige."

I didn't know whether it was authentic hipster or not. What's more, though I don't suppose Tommy could have grasped the fact, I didn't care.

"Nobody told me you were home," I said.

He yawed past me, banging the grandfather clock with one of his bottles.

"Where'd you think I'd be Christmas Eve, playing back-seat bingo with Sally Polk, or something?"

"I wouldn't know," I admitted. "Sally Polk, huh?"

"Sally Polk," he repeated, then pretended to be even drunker than he was. "Zally Polk, Zally Polk, Zally Polk. Wonder how old Zally Polk's getting along. Haven't seen her'n a coon's age." He took off down the hall at a fast stagger.

But I caught up quick enough.

"When are you gonna knock off this Sally Polk stuff?" I demanded.

Tommy turned and faced me, grinning with secrets, the padded shoulders of his jacket flopping unsupported.

"Don't bug me, man," he said, then turned and almost skipped away, silly and smug as a freshly pinned prom girl.

"Hey take it easy," I called. "The family's a little the worse . . ." But there was no need to go any further, he had already joined the others.

Having to worry about someone as harmless as Tommy Compton upsetting us was a pretty sad commentary on the House of Woodruff, but in our present teetering state of convalescence anything was possible.

I reached the living room just as Tommy had sashayed once around, unable to shake hands because of his champagne burden.

Behind him was a litter of awkward silence which he tried to disperse by mumbling "Have a cool Yule, Daddy-O" and continuing to giggle, but more and more self-consciously, thank God. Then unfortunately his eye lit on Gramps. "Hey," he said. "Who's the old fream?"

Gramps was looking around birdlike, but didn't seem to realize he was being discussed.

"My father," Mother said, happily in the dark, as all of us were, with regard to the definition of a fream.

"Uh oh," Tommy warned himself. "Shoot low, man, they're riding Shetlands." Then he took a long pull on his bottle, some of which bubbled out of his nose before it could be properly swallowed.

"Here," Pa offered, steering him to the bar. "Let's put it in a glass, shall we?"

"Wizard," said Tommy.

After that he calmed down a little, as though Pa's gesture had reminded him there were some limits, and he began talking in a language we could all more or less understand.

"How's the writing?" I asked, once everybody had relaxed and started talking again, so he wouldn't be embarrassed.

"That must be your favorite question," he said.

"Any luck?"

"No no," he said, too quickly. "I'm just sort of gathering information, you might say."

"Oh."

"If you spend all your time writing," he explained, "pretty soon you run out of things to write about."

"I see," I lied.

We both took a long swig of champagne and regrouped.

"I hear Nora showed you the door," he said.

"That's right. I'm grief-stricken."

Apparently realizing he could cause no pain on this tack, he turned to Pa. "How's the *Daily Watch* going?"

Pa looked a little confused. "Oh quite well."

"How are your mother and father, Tommy?" Mother asked.

"I hear Ned Polk and Jesse Rosenfeldt are running you pretty ragged," Tommy said, completely ignoring Mother.

Pa looked at me with a mixture of helplessness and frustration, as though he wanted to be free of anything to do with the *Daily Watch* but realized he had no acceptable explanation for having achieved this state of unconcern.

"Your information is a little outdated," I said.

Abby laughed, but it was really a call for help.

"How are your mother and father, Tommy?" Mother repeated with careful anger.

"They're fine," Tommy said. "That is they're the same as ever."

"That's nice," Mother said, ignoring his innuendo. "I haven't seen Goldie in ages. Wish them both a Merry Christmas, won't you?"

"They need it," was his reply.

"Hey," I said. "We need some more champagne. Come on out to the kitchen, Tommy, while I crack another bottle."

"Use mine," he offered, the stupid bastard.

"I don't want to," I said, the tone of voice pretty well dissipating my efforts to be tactful. *"Come on."*

He shrugged as though to assure everyone it wouldn't inconvenience him in the least, and trotted out the door. The silence we left behind enraged me.

I waited until we were out of earshot, then booted him in the ass so hard we both left the floor. Fortunately he landed on a scatter rug, slipped and fell. I leaned over and had a word with him. "Stupid son of a bitch," I whispered. "Why don't you think of someone besides your lousy self once in a while?"

"Hey," he cried, absolutely baffled. "What's wrong with you?"

"You're screwing up our Christmas. That's all." I straightened up to get away from the musty, sour smell.

"Oh is that so." He didn't bother to get up. "And what do you think you've done to mine?"

"Me?"

"I come all the way over here to wish you a Merry Christmas," he sniffled. "And this is what I get . . . a kick in the ass."

"Oh for Christ sakes." I headed for the kitchen. When I came back he was sitting on the stairs, still sniffling. "Wait a minute," I said. "I'll be right back." I took the champagne in, popped it and stayed long enough to fill everybody's glass in hopes it would liven things up.

"Where is that nice young man?" Gramps asked, apparently untouched by the incident.

"He's right outside," I said, as though nothing could be more ordinary than leaving him in the hall.

"Fine people, the Comptons," Gramps remarked.

"I'm going to take Tommy home," I told Pa. "He's in sort of bad shape." But Pa was staring listlessly over the top of his champagne glass and didn't hear me. "Pa," I shouted. He looked up, bent an ear, but I couldn't explain it again. "Never mind," I said, and you could see he didn't.

"All right, Larry," Mother said. "You go ahead."

And I did, almost running to get free of this Christmas debacle. I could hear Gramps, on my way out, happily taking over the conversation.

"Who did you say Judge Compton married?"

Followed by Mother's automatic response.

I found Tommy still sitting on the stairs but feeling better, which didn't surprise me since he found only himself worth looking out for.

"Come on," he said, apparently forgetting our little disagreement. "Let's go find some action."

"It's Christmas Eve."

"Ah, don't punk out," he said. "Frank's Place'll be open."

"Maybe it will. But I don't want to go there."

"You're chicken."

"Chicken? Of what?"

"The frontier," he said smugly.

"Frontier?" I asked. "What the hell frontier are you supposed to find at Frank's?"

He was still sitting, elbow to knee, wagging a finger at me.

"That's where it is," he said. "Places like Frank's; the wild west of whiskey where souls are rubbed raw and righteousness gives way to honest desire."

He seemed to be quoting but I didn't bother to trace the source.

"Honest desire?"

"Sex," he explained. "But you wouldn't know about that."

"Why not? I used to take out your sister."

"That cow," he said.

"Well," I said, "it seems to me a cow's just what you need. I mean who ever heard of a frontier without a cow."

"Very funny," he said.

"Listen, Tommy. I've read all about this apocalyptic orgasm stuff where nothing matters so much as a good lay. If you haven't got the guts to be anything but an animal that's all right with me, but don't try an' tell me it's some kind of new frontier."

"I didn't think you'd understand," he said.

"Here's the new frontier," I said, tapping my head. "Not where you think it is. And I don't have to go to Frank's or any of your Beatnik clinics to find raw souls and desire."

"Brains," he sneered. "A lot of good they've done us. *Boom boom boom boom*, blood . . ."

"Please," I interrupted, "once was enough."

"Well, have they?"

"You've still got them," I said. "And pretending to be an animal won't make them go away."

"Maybe not, but it helps."

"Anyway, it isn't just brains," I said. "It's everything inside you."

"The soul, I suppose." He made a retching noise.

"What the hell's the matter with you, anyway?" I asked. "You're acting kind of funny."

"I'm drunk. Didn't you know?"

"It's more than that."

"Zat so?" He got up and started for the door.

"Where you going?"

But he didn't answer.

"Come on, Tommy. I'll drive you home."

"Don't bug me, man," he said, picking up the act again. "I got wheels."

"Well, where?" I insisted.

"Looking for kicks," he explained, his frail body so at odds with the hip talk it was laughable.

I followed him out, wondering whether to go along or not, but he seemed pretty sober by then and I had plenty of worries without listening to his sad song all night.

"Hope you have a grand time at Frank's," I kidded. "Say hello to all the cowboys for me, will you?"

He just climbed into his car and drove off, unamused.

I went back inside to see how the family were making out, found everyone sitting in stunned silence while Gramps led them up and down, back and forth across the face of Europe without missing one customs stop or forgetting the exact amount, in real money and foreign, of every single hotel bill.

I crossed over and sat next to Abby. "Where are we now?" I whispered.

"Gibraltar," she whispered back. "He just bought a watch for half the price it would have cost in America."

"Heading which way?"

"West."

"Thank God for that," I said. "It's getting late."

She giggled and we settled down for a quiet snooze while Gramps droned on. Boredom aside, everything seemed fairly peaceful for the time being. I thought of Tommy lurching through the night in search of oblivion and thanked God I hadn't gone along.

CHAPTER XXIX

It was quite a while before Gramps finally decided to pull down his flag, and Mother's announcement that I had been elected to take him home was most ungraciously accepted. It seemed as though my name only occurred to her in connection with the running of errands. But then Abby volunteered to go with me and I felt better.

Actually there wasn't time to feel much of anything. Not with Gramps along. For no good reason other than to indulge his powers of total recall, he decided my car reminded him of a camel and thus created the opportunity to tell us about the time he rode a camel in Egypt and how in those days a camel was a camel.

It was a long half-hour drive to his apartment and by the time we got there Abby and I were so congealed with respectful silence we couldn't even talk to each other. Partly to shake the mood and partly because Tommy was sort of worrying me I decided to go home through the center of town, maybe stop by Frank's.

"Hey," Abby said. "Where we going?"

"Through the center," I said. "Just for the hell of it."

"I couldn't think of a better reason."

I laughed and Abby stared out the window, pretending not to care, but pleased at having been silly.

"Thought we might look in on Frank," I said. "See how Tommy's doing."

"Boy," she giggled, "I never saw him like that before."

"He wasn't so funny out in the hall."

"He wasn't so funny in the living room either." Then she was silent again, apparently sorry she'd mentioned him.

I didn't want to talk about him much either, mainly because I didn't understand him any more. Tommy made a great rebel when tightly secured to the family stake. Then he could bark and frisk and charge his captives knowing the rope would hold and there could be no encounter. But let the rope break, as it had, and first thing he did was get lost.

We drove down Main Street, glowing now under a shabby arbor of Christmas lights.

"Merry Christmas," I said, half serious.

"It's sort of pretty," she admitted. "At night."

I started to turn into Railroad Avenue, past City Hall and the *Daily Watch* when a squad car bounded into the street, whined past me, its red light ticking, and tore out East Main. I pulled over, confused by this cacophony of law and order, just as another one skidded into the street and roared by.

"What the hell," was my best effort.

"Let's follow them," Abby suggested.

I spun the wheel and gunned her and off we went with a screech of self-importance and the working press was underway. Christmas seemed long gone. So did Tommy.

It took all my concentration to keep up with those reformed hot-rods and I had no energy left over for speculation, no idea where we were going. Finally I saw the squad cars dive for the curb and pulled in alongside. We jumped out and started running.

"Hold on there. Where do you two . . ."

I turned around so the cop could see my face.

"Oh," he said. "Okay, Larry."

And we kept on running, Abby holding my hand and mincing in tight dress and high heels.

Even after we got inside I didn't know where we were. The place was so full of cops and detectives it looked as much like City Hall as anything else except for occasional homey flashes through the jungle of officialdom: a wreath in the window, a small fake Christmas tree, a framed reproduction of Christ being removed from the cross, a vase of sweetheart roses.

I moved with the tide, dragging Abby as we maneuvered toward whatever had happened.

Suddenly the crowd thinned and I saw it. There flung in a cor-

ner of the bedroom, his neck broken, head twisted horribly, was
Tommy Compton.

I turned and faced Abby.

"We're at Ned Polk's," I said and tried to steer her back where
we came from. But she ducked under my arm and saw for herself.
It seemed a long time before she could bring herself to turn away,
as though a good close look might disclose some clue no one else
had seen; some proof it was all a bad joke.

Then she turned. "It's Tommy Compton, you know." And she
worked her way out of the pack. I followed and reached her just
as she let out a low kind of yowl, more of an echo from within, then
pressed against the wall and began pounding her head as though
pain thus inflicted might keep her from going nuts. "It's Tommy
Compton," she repeated, then stopped pounding but continued to
hug the wall. "What was he doing here?" she asked.

"Sally," I said.

"Oh," she said, remembering, though still not fully understanding.
"Where's Sally?"

"I don't know. In the other room, I guess. People are going in
and out."

Then she turned and headed for the closed door, not panicked
and running, but persistent.

"Are you all right?" I called.

She nodded, kept on going.

No one stopped her so I decided to follow. Aware of what had
happened only mentally, I was able to think clearly enough but
had no emotional reaction at all. I simply went through whatever
paces were available, wondering with monotonous objectivity what
the next step might be. So I followed Abby and found her sitting
on the bed beside Sally Polk. I don't think they'd even spoken. Abby
must have just sat down and taken Sally's hand and waited for whatever was going to happen. It wasn't an act of friendship, because
they weren't friends, but one of sympathy which helped remind the
interrogators they were questioning a human being with the misfortune of being something more than a mere disinterested witness to
murder.

Sally's reaction seemed similar to mine. She answered the questions in a steady monotone, as though reading the record of someone
else's tragedy and she seemed only tired.

Yes, she and Ned had seen and spoken to Tommy just as they

were leaving Frank's Place over an hour ago. He had been drinking, so had they, there were words.

What kinda words?

Ned said something insulting.

What?

But she didn't remember. Just that Tommy hadn't answered and they'd gone home to bed and pretty soon Ned thought he heard a noise, went to investigate and all of a sudden there was a lot of swearing and sort of yelling and then gurgling and Ned came in carrying Tommy and just threw him in the corner.

And did she know Tommy?

Yes, she did.

Intimately?

No—too emphatically—she did not.

The interrogators were sorry they had had to ask that, but they were sure Mrs. Polk would understand.

She would.

But why did she think he had come?

Because he was drunk, she supposed.

But she *did* know him.

Yes.

And he'd been living in New York recently?

Yes.

Had Mrs. Polk ever seen him in New York?

Yes.

Again the gentlemen were sorry to keep asking those questions.

That was quite all right.

And where did she think Mr. Polk had gone?

She had no idea. He just took the car and left.

But he had a broken jaw, is that not so?

Yes he did.

How about money?

Money?

Did he have any?

The house money. About a hundred dollars.

What kind of car was he driving?

And so on, while outside the system continued its digestive process destined eventually to remove all traces of Tommy Compton.

Abby and I, filled to surfeit with misery by that time, left just as Ted Pearson was arriving. I gave him a quick rundown.

"Christ," he said. "We ought to get out an extra."

That hadn't occurred to me, but the idea of staying up all night with something to do was better than lying in bed waiting for the horror to set in. On the other hand, I wasn't sure our employees would be quite so receptive.

"On Christmas?" I asked.

"I can't help that."

"How many would we need?"

"Just you and me in editorial. I'll rout out four or five for the back shop."

I must have still looked dubious.

"Bachelors," he promised.

"Even bachelors have better things to do Christmas."

"Shame on them," said Ted, and already we found ourselves laughing, relieved by the fact we had something to do.

"Let me come, too," Abby said. "I'll keep you in coffee."

"All right," I said to Ted. "We'll meet you at the office in a few minutes."

I drove by the house to make sure they were asleep and not worried about us. Abby went in to swipe some coffee, milk or anything else handy, leave a note and we were off.

"What'd you say?" I asked her.

"Just that we were at the paper," she said. "And to call us when they woke up."

"You were great with Sally."

"I didn't do a thing but sit there. I couldn't think of anything."

"Just being there was enough. You don't always have to do something."

"How horrible," she said.

I didn't say anything.

"Will they find him soon?" she asked.

"Search me."

I pulled into the parking lot and we hurried over to the paper. The Compton car was parked out front of City Hall. I was careful to lock the door behind us and draw the shades lest they or anyone else get wind of what we were up to.

Ted was on the phone talking to Carl Robinson, sending him out for pictures. "Who's gonna write it?" he asked.

"I will," I said. "I was there longer." The fact that it was Tommy

Compton, a lifetime friend, was lost on me for the time being. All I saw was a jumble of incidents to be sorted and put to words.

Abby dug up the coffeepot and electric burner and went to work sort of kidding around about how you make coffee, which may not have been all kidding, while Ted began clipping the scattered rolls of wire news, writing headlines and working up a page one layout. The atmosphere was filled with secrecy, excitement, and muffled good humor, like kids sneaking out to a midnight rendezvous.

One by one the backroom boys crept in, none failing to roll his eyes and wish us a Merry Christmas, some still a little loaded with the spirit of goodwill carelessly, but not neglectfully, protruding from their hip pockets.

It was nice having Abby in on things.

Ted and I had it wrapped up by five o'clock so we went out back to lend a hand as copyreaders or anything else they might need while Abby, unbeknownst to herself, stayed behind, sleeping on a desk.

But nobody needed our help. Somehow word had spread and it looked like the whole crew was there.

By six-thirty the pages were cast and fitted and the presses ready to roll.

One of the guys looked at Ted. He shrugged. The guy shrugged back, flipped the switch, pulled out his pint, took a long pull and passed it around as the machinery began to roll and the thundering rose to a steady, beatless, churning and the newsprint wound and folded its perilous way into a neat pile beside us.

Abby came in, awakened by the noise, and stood watching as the black monster spewed our reward:

POLK SOUGHT IN SLAYING
City Judge's Son
Dies in Beating
At Senator's Home

Gravenhurst Mourns
Christmas Tragedy

And as I watched, the meaning of those headlines began to sink in. I remembered the names belonged to people I knew and things began crumbling inside.

"Okay," Ted yelled. "Let's get this stuff onto the truck," and I started shoving bundles along the rollers to the loading platform. Tears were streaming down my face but I felt okay as long as there was something to grab and shove and grab and shove with all the hatred and frustration and momentary hopelessness that was in me.

Getting them delivered was something of a problem since we weren't likely to find any newsboys around at eight o'clock on Christmas morning and I guess we were a pretty awful-looking sight roaring through town, the drunkest of us yelling Merry Christmas, and dumping those stacks of horribly headlined newspapers at every corner.

But the profanity, at least so it seemed to me, was mostly revulsion at having to dirty the day and nobody could be blamed for that. Even Abby, riding up front with Ted, had caught the evil spirit and was hanging out the window, black hair flying, waving furiously at the early risers, laughing, touched with madness.

And within the hour we were on our way home.

"Well," she concluded. "The *Daily Watch* may be clumpy all right, but *working* for it's exciting enough."

I laughed, happy she'd made that discovery.

"Just like Gravenhurst," I suggested.

"Hope so."

"And Hal," I added.

"Oh? And Nora too?"

"Who says it has to be Nora?"

"Well then, maybe that Lucy Delevan?"

"Maybe."

"Oh boy," Abby laughed. "I can just see *her* deciding to live in Gravenhurst."

"I can't," I admitted, then remembered those unanswered invitations and, just as quickly, forgot them again.

"Well then?"

"All right. But it doesn't have to be Nora."

"Or Hal either."

When we got home Mother and Pa were still at breakfast.

"Well, where on earth . . ." Mother began.

"I've been calling the paper for an hour," Pa interrupted. "Where've you been?"

"We were out delivering the papers," I explained.

"The *what?*" Pa demanded.

I could hear the phone ringing as I started to prepare my explanation. "Something terrible happened last night," I began.

"What?" Pa asked. "Speak up, for Heaven sakes."

Maybe I should have written him a letter. "Tommy Compton was killed last night," I shouted. "Ned Polk killed him." Then I unfolded my copy of the extra and slapped it on the dining-room table.

None of us had seen Bollard come in. "Telephone for Mrs. Woodruff," he said. "It's Mrs. Compton."

"Oh God," Mother said, "and they must know he was here."

I'm sure that wasn't all that concerned her, but it was funny she mentioned it first.

Afterward she came back and poured herself another cup of coffee too calmly. "The funeral is tomorrow at St. Andrew's," she said. "Eleven o'clock." Mother seemed more preoccupied than grief-stricken. "Now Larry," she continued, "I want you to tell me exactly what happened."

I realized this was some sort of cross-examination. Like school when you're suspected of smoking.

"What do you mean?" I asked, automatically acting the part she had given me.

"Exactly what I said," she told me.

"Well it's all in the paper." I pushed my copy toward her.

Pa moved to a chair across from me where he could hear better and picked up the paper.

"Whose idea was this?" he asked.

"Ted's . . . and mine, I guess."

He didn't criticize it, though I had a feeling he wanted to.

"It was Ted's," Abby said.

"And mine," I repeated. "I could have stopped it." Then I lost my train of thought, said nothing.

"Well go on," Mother said. "Tell us what happened."

"You mean at the Polks'?" I asked.

"I mean from the time you took Tommy home," she said.

I was beginning to get the idea.

"Oh," I said. "I never did take him home."

"And why not, may I ask?"

"Because he had a car. I didn't know he had a car."

"And did you offer to drive it for him?" she asked.

"Mother, Tommy didn't want to be driven anywhere. He was in a very funny mood."

"He was intoxicated," Mother corrected. "That's precisely why you should have looked after him."

"Please," I said. "You can't make somebody . . ." But Mother was being logical and there seemed to be no defense. Besides the night was catching up with me. I pressed the heels of my hands against my eyes in an effort to hold back the confusion.

"After all, you and Tommy grew up together," Mother continued. "What's Goldie going to . . ."

"All right," said Pa, "that's enough of that."

Abby and I both pulled up and stared, hang-jawed, as though we were looking at a ghost.

"The hell with Goldie Compton," Pa continued. "Why did she let him out of the house if he was so damned drunk?"

"Hurray," Abby shouted, spilling over with relief. "Here comes the U. S. Cavalry."

It was so absurd I couldn't help laughing and once the gates were down out poured the tears again. I was turning into a regular male Margaret O'Brien.

I sputtered and laughed and cried helplessly and Abby was right there with me. Oh, we were a beautiful pair. And the look on Mother's face; that look of baffled righteousness, it was so funny I almost stopped crying. But it wasn't funny really. It was sad. And so it went until we finally pulled ourselves together enough to go up to bed.

On my way out I heard Pa still at it.

"Good God Almighty," he was shouting. "What are you trying to do, blame the boy?"

And Mother: "Why no, Clarence. I just wanted to be sure Larry did the right thing."

I gave Abby a swat and we took the stairs two at a time, both still blubbering.

"For shame," I said. "Don't you know it isn't right to cry when you're laughing."

"Oh foo," she said. "I'll cry when I please," and we tumbled into our rooms doing just that.

I was no longer naïve enough to think Pa's asserting himself like that meant all was right with the Woodruffs but whether it was or not didn't matter any more, we seemed to survive either way. Anyway one thing we'd both learned was not to rely on Mother and Pa for the answers because whatever those answers might be, they sure as hell hadn't found them. Maybe we didn't know what they were either but we had a pretty good idea what they were *not*, and at least that was a beginning.

CHAPTER XXX

Funerals provide the family involved with a grim form of occupational therapy and I suppose that in itself is enough to justify them. The ghastly preparations, the service, the burial, all demand such careful and concentrated attention to detail that anguish must necessarily be held in some degree of check. Otherwise who is going to call up friends, hire limousines, order flowers, select the burial plot and attend to all the other ceremonial horrors which fastidious and delicate death demands?

But therapy aside, it's a grisly business attended by sympathy and pity, to be sure, but by cold curiosity as well and perhaps just a touch of smugness on the part of those clever enough to be alive and involved only by reason of vague and distant friendships.

And I must admit, though my involvement was more than vague and distant, my sadness was contaminated at least by a touch of curiosity. And if there was any smugness hidden in the sorrow then let it stay hidden. But I couldn't help watching the Comptons. The judge had nothing to reveal, as usual, but Nora and her mother kept looking around, apparently measuring the turn-out and nodding to people and whispering to each other, as though they might be commenting on the flowers or some other matter of etiquette. If it took their minds off Tommy then who could blame them, but I couldn't help wondering at the kind of thing which seemed to give them relief.

"It was really a very nice service," Mother said as we were on our way to the car. "Weren't the flowers lovely?"

"And what a lot of people," said Abby.

Only Pa seemed to have found no time for snooping, but maybe it only seemed that way because he kept his mouth shut. Like me.

Then the long line of cars, lights on, snaked its way to the cemetery, sharing death with everyone it passed.

Something went wrong inside me when they started covering him up and I just stood fascinated as the dirt was piled in, wondering whether they realized Tommy would suffocate if they kept that up. Most of the people had moved off by the time I got hold of myself and I was just starting to go when Mrs. Compton came out of nowhere and kissed me and took my arm and walked me back to the car.

I guess it just isn't a good idea to dislike people. They'll always get you in the end.

Afterward I had to go back to the paper and give Ted a hand with the last-minute stuff. I picked up the page one layout to see what was left to do. Ned Polk was still making headlines, naturally, and would for some time to come. We hadn't had a good local murder in over ten years.

"What's new?" I asked.

"Nothing," Ted said. "Nationwide search continues. That's all we got."

"That's all we need," I said. "These days you could make headlines with his write-up in the class yearbook."

"Hey Jeff, let's go with that Polk lead. It's one o'clock," Ted shouted. "Hey, hey, hey, come on, you guys. Where's my court story?"

At that point it landed on his desk—my desk really. He checked the head written earlier to make sure it still held, tossed them both in the out basket, reached across the aisle, pulled Jeff's lead out of his typewriter and checked it over. It was the kind of Polk-like gesture which used to make everybody sore as hell but Ted did it without malice.

"What's the matter with you, Collins? Don't you know better than stop in the middle of a sentence?" Then he scribbled in a couple of lines to complete it and that was that.

Jeff just sat there, lighting a cigarette, relaxed, not seeming to mind. Sometimes you get bogged down even when you're good and Jeff knew it, so what the hell. As long as it was done with a joke instead of the insults Ned Polk thrived on.

The rest of the day we spent going through the files and calling up everybody we could think of who might contribute something to the Ned Polk story. It wasn't easy since both his parents were

dead and I didn't want to bother Sally. But we managed to find
a couple of cousins, some friends, and schoolteachers who could
supply enough for our purposes. And since Ned had been a schoolboy hero there were plenty of old engravings in the files showing
Piston Polk, the triple threat; Promising Polk, the Eagle Scout; President Polk of the student council, and so on right on up to Pious
Polk, better known as Old Fire and Brim, coach of the Little League
champs four years running. We were able to put together a nice
little biography of the All-American Boy on his way down.

It's funny the way things happen so unexpectedly sometimes
they're over and done with before you've even gotten around to a
proper reaction. I was sitting at my desk a couple of mornings
after Tommy's funeral, clipping the AP teletype news and scanning
an assortment of politics and disaster as though I were a professional dealer in human misery when a special bulletin to the *Daily
Watch* caught my eye. I began to read with only a little less detachment that THE BODY OF CONNECTICUT STATE SENATOR NED POLK, SUB-
JECT OF A NATIONWIDE MANHUNT FOLLOWING THE BRUTAL SLAYING OF
THOMAS J. COMPTON OF GRAVENHURST, CONN. WAS FOUND IN A VACANT
SUMMER HOUSE NEAR HERE EARLY TODAY, VICTIM OF AN APPARENT
SUICIDE. THE BODY WAS DISCOVERED WHEN TWO BOYS . . .

I continued reading with detached fascination, then tossed the
story on Ted Pearson's desk and watched as he, taken equally by
surprise, succeeded in mustering only a low whistle.

"Well that takes care of today's page one," he said, and tossed it
back.

I nodded, gave Jeff Collins the story to rework, called for the Polk
photo file and went back to clipping wire copy. My mind kept div-
ing for the proper sentiments—joy, horror, grim satisfaction, whatever they were—and coming up with nothing but cold curiosity. I
tried to piece together what had happened from the factual news
report, but more as a mental exercise than an expression of personal
involvement. He must have headed for Canada, then realized that
would do no real good and forced his way into a house instead.
The story was datelined South Pines, New Hampshire, which meant
nothing to me except it appeared to be somewhere between Gravenhurst and the Canadian border. I could picture him with that
jaw of his still wired shut, snorting and cursing between clenched
teeth as he squeezed through a forced window or pried at a back
door. Then, later, hiding his car in the garage and trying to cover

up those tire tracks left in the snow, storing food and finding ways to keep himself warm; things like that, after which . . . nothing. Nothing but the wait until food ran out or his jaw needed attention or he froze to death. There he'd be, the action of flight behind him, nothing but inevitable capture, disgrace, and prison. Under those conditions I couldn't imagine him coming to any decision but suicide and neither, apparently, could he.

But Ned Polk wasn't a man to quit with honor, and even in death managed to sow the seed of his malignancy. Those two boys who found him swinging from a rafter, pale and stiff with frost, wouldn't be likely to forget. Nor would the men who cut him down, packed and shipped him back to the senders, the people of Gravenhurst, myself and Pa included, whose false, deficient, and timeworn values had helped him achieve this pinnacle of loathing and malevolence. Not that the murder was our doing; only the murderer.

But no matter who was to blame, benefit or suffer, the New Mogul was dead now and Tommy Compton along with him and the rest of us—the walking wounded—well, we'd been lucky enough to win a second chance and maybe we learned something in the bargain.

Maybe.

But whether we had or not, there was still a newspaper to get out and some doubt as to whether it would.

Since Tommy's death we'd been pretty harassed by the wire service and syndicate boys but that was nothing compared to what they did to us that day Senator Polk turned up swinging. Those who couldn't come called or cabled their regrets like the gentlemen they were and asked a few hundred questions besides, but it seemed like most of them managed to make it in person.

What a rat race!

And each one wanting to see the news editor, raising his eyebrows in awe, wonder and downright disbelief when that turned out to be me; but not one above asking for the moon no matter how busy we were with our own problems or how insignificant I seemed to be.

Well, we put up with it as best we could but I don't guess there's a man alive who knows less than an out-of-town newsman, nor is there one in more of a hurry to correct this lamentable condition, so: "Where'd this Polk character live?"

"Fifteen Highland Avenue."

"Yeah? Well, where's that?"

"Okay, you go out West Main to King Street, see, then take a left down four blocks to Hollow Spring Road . . ."

"Hold it, hold it. I'll take a cab."

"So this Polk, he's forty, huh? How old was the Compton kid? Is it Ned or Edward? Was he working here two years or two months? Well, whaddaya suppose happened? I mean what's with the guy's wife and all that? Nothing, huh? Nothing, my foot."

And on and on and on.

It was a miracle we managed to get the *Daily Watch* out at all, but we did. After deadline Ted and I were trying to organize things a little but without much luck.

"Listen," I was saying, "why don't you guys wait until the two o'clock meeting upstairs? We'll answer all the questions . . ." Jeff pushing through, tossed a copy of the *Enterprise* on my desk. "So what?" I asked, seeing nothing but the Polk story.

"Down at the bottom," he said.

And I saw it:

ROSENFELDT STEPS DOWN
ENTERPRISE CONVERTS TO
MORNING PUBLICATION

"Two o'clock, for Christ sakes," somebody moaned. "I gotta deadline."

"Can't help it," I said. "Read the back issues. They'll give you all the information you need anyhow."

"How about that?" Jeff asked.

Phone rang.

"Takes 'em out of direct competition," I said. "Running scared. Hello? Yeah, speaking. What we got's on the AP wire. What do you mean 'it's not enough'? Oh, is that a fact? Well listen, Jack, I don't care whether you're *Time* magazine or *Izvestia;* you want any more information come up and get it." I flashed our switchboard.

"Give me the City Police, will you please?" I covered the mouthpiece. "Hey Spaulding, do me a favor, get these guys four or five copies of the first edition. Let 'em see what we got." The operator was babbling away about something. "Who? Oh, my God, sure I'll speak to her. Lucy? Hi, how're you? Not so good? What's the matter? What dance? Oh, my God, wait a minute, hold on . . . No, no, not 'the former City Judge,' for Pete's sake. He still is. Read the paper, why don't you. Hello, Lucy? Listen, I'm awful sorry, we've been so damn busy. You see this friend of mine . . . Never mind, it's too complicated, but I'd love to come. What? Wait a minute, somebody's yelling at me . . . Well, as a matter of fact, it is sort of a bad time, but I'll see you tomorrow. Tomorrow night. Okay, bye bye."

"Hey, Johnny, do me a favor, will ya?"

"Woodruff's the name," I said. "Larry Woodruff."

"Yeah, okay, Larry, listen, do me a favor, will ya? Anybody calls looking for Eddie Griscolm tell 'em they can get me down at the whatchamacallit diner."

"Chick's," I said.

"Yeah, yeah, Chick's. Be back at two, arright?"

"Okay."

"Eddie Griscolm."

"Okay," I said. "Okay.

"Who's checking the first edition?" I asked.

"It's okay," Ted said. "I already did."

"Jesus, what a rat race," I laughed.

"You think this is bad," some guy with a camera advised me. "You should see New York."

"The hell with New York," I said, then remembered Lucy. "I'll take that back," I said.

Goddam phone again. "Yes? Who?"

"Louise Cullen out to the Memorial Hospital."

"Yes, Mrs. Cullen. What can I do for you?"

"Well, I just wanted to remind you tomorrow's New Year's Eve."

"Yes," I said. "So it is."

"And you'll have a photographer out here, of course."

"We will?" I was puzzled.

"The first baby born in the New Year," she said, sounding a bit snippety. "You always take a picture of the first baby born in the New Year."

"Oh yes, yes . . . of course we do."

"Well," she said, "I just thought I ought to remind you."

"Yes," I agreed. "Yes, you certainly should."

"This will be the tenth year we've had a picture," she went on.

"Hold it," I said. "Hey Jeff, where's Meg Brown?"

"She didn't notice anything unusual going on," he said, "so she went home."

"Well, stick a note on her desk or I'll forget. Baby picture, Memorial Hospital, New Year's Eve."

"Yeah, sure."

"Jesus Christ," the photographer groaned. "What is this, the Junior League, or what?"

"It's a small-town newspaper," I said. "Okay, Mrs. Cullen, Meg Brown'll be out there."

"Oh, I'm so glad," she said. "You know, we've had four little boy first babies and five little girls so this is sort of exciting, don't you think?"

"I should say," I said. "Well, thank you very much for calling."

"I do hope it's a little boy baby," she said. "Don't you?"

"Just so it's a baby. Goodbye now."

"Keee-rist," said the photographer.

I let it go, tried to remember who the hell I'd been calling in the first place. Oh yeah, the city police. Well, there was no hurry. Enough was enough and I shoved back my chair, cocked a foot on the desk and prepared to unravel, then realized nobody'd thought to tell Pa about Ned being found. Or about Jesse either and the *Enterprise's* switch to a morning daily. Maybe I should have let him find out for himself, but with Polk out of the picture we really had nothing more to fight about. Seemed like as good a time as any to start putting things right.

I reached for the phone, then changed my mind, decided it might be better to go on home and tell him myself.

"How about some lunch?" Ted suggested.

"No thanks," I said. "Just thinking maybe I'd go home and fill Pa in on the latest developments."

"Do what?" Ted asked.

I shrugged, unable to go into details with that photographer and everybody else hanging around. "He ought to be at the meeting," I said.

But Ted didn't seem inclined to buy that.

"After all, he's the publisher," I offered.

Ted nodded once, waited for something more substantial.

"He's also my father," I said, and walked out without waiting to discover whether that was considered good enough or not.

It seemed pretty good to me.

healthy fever pink. Her eyes dropped to her left hand where trembled the engagement ring, its modest diamond and setting looking like nothing so much as the eyestalk of a lobster.

"Congratulations," I said to one or both. "Where is your home, Miss Simpson?"

But the lost composure continued and I began to suspect it was a permanent condition.

"Amanda's from across the Hudson. Center Falls, New York," Hugh interpreted.

"Well, what do you know," I said, disgusted with myself for bothering. "And what brought you two together?"

"Amanda plays the organ for Father," Hugh explained.

"Isn't that nice," I said, straight-faced, and: "Awfully glad to have met you." I gulped, gobbled, paid, and ran.

Outside I felt better immediately. The town's soft summer rhythms simmered and cooked the harshness from reality until nothing remained but a vague and gently recognizable spattering of colors, faces, objects, sounds, all blandly reassuring from a distance, all confidence and comfort until a closer inspection revealed the various components in their separate tedium, insufficiency, and drabness. The trees lining Main Street were beautiful, not in themselves alone but because they sprang from cement, fed on dust, grit, urine, scraps of sunlight, and managed in their struggle to cast a spell of gallantry and hope. In the woods where they belonged one would have noticed only that they were a trifle scraggly. The cars, false-fronted buildings, traffic lights, billboards, neon signs, all of little consequence separately, together made that special aggregate which was Gravenhurst, Conn., not New Milford, not Gravenhurst, Nebraska, but Gravenhurst, Conn. A dubious achievement, perhaps, but an achievement nonetheless.

And the people, what of them? Also of no consequence separately? I suppose so. If they chose to be.

And if they didn't? Well, they could always leave town and go to New York or one of the other metropolitan achievement centers. Hal James and I ought to know. We'd talked that subject over often enough. Right from childhood on up, he visiting me or vice versa, lying flat on our backs in bedroom privacy and darkness, me with an arm curled tight across my face for increased seclusion and Hal the same way, talking until dawn grayed and the birds tattled about how someday we'd do something and be somebodies somewhere.

But always somewhere else. Never in Gravenhurst. With us it was axiomatic that to stay in Gravenhurst was to achieve a sort of permanent somnolence, an unquestioning reliance on instinct and custom, a loss of self.

Yet here we were.

I turned off Main and down Mill Street toward the slum section. Smells from the fish market rolled across my senses, sweet and powerful and somehow touched with mystery; a colored boy and three whites loitered on the corner, bored, trouble seeking. I started to cross the street, stopped in disgust and walked them down, eying each one back, being careful not to break the rhythm of my strolling gait, pleased with my performance and the fact that I'd made it without incident.

Then up Front Street, slightly unnerved by the sudden closeness of life; the rows of shacks so thin-skinned you could hear a bed squeak from across the street, porches bordering on the sidewalks their shadows filled with voices and laughter and secrets barely hidden, like pooping in a public lavatory, laundry pink and stained and unashamed lolling gently in the evening breezes.

I hurried on back to the crowded, light-flicking, traffic-filled order and routine of Main Street, got my car and went home where, except for Abby and me, and Hal on an occasional martini call, no one ever thought about Gravenhurst in terms of leaving any more, only of coping.

CHAPTER IV

Abby never took much of an interest in the Gravenhurst *Daily Watch* because, as she put it, "the damn thing's so clumpy," but when she got back and discovered a small-scale war looming on the horizon her attitude toward journalism changed considerably. She wanted to know all about Jesse Rosenfeldt, a name which was fast becoming dirty around our house, and even went so far as to ask a couple of questions about the *Daily Watch* which was not like her at all.

But at that stage knowing anything about the *Watch* was practically irrelevant. We were more interested in fortifying the ramparts of Woodruff good will and prestige, both aspirations in which Abby had a singular lack of interest. Pa's first move was to promote the Gravenhurst Urban Redevelopment Program which, to the surprise of almost no one, earned him banner headlines in the *Daily Watch:*

PUBLISHER SPARKS URBAN RENEWAL
Woodruff Seeks Federal Funds

Over the years Gravenhurst had not done much to help itself in such areas as urban improvement and industrial expansion. Consequently these were quite challenging and all-encompassing fields. Just about everybody in town could thank Pa for his noble and forward-thinking project. But the best part was whatever the town invested for housing projects in slum areas or the reconditioning of rundown business sections would be matched by federal and state funds. Now if there is anything the far-seeing citizens of Gravenhurst like it's getting something for nothing. And if they can't swing that then getting it at a third of the price is next best. Of course the fact Pa owned a good slice of the property proposed for redevelopment was not mentioned in the *Daily Watch* article, nor in subsequent editorials praising Clarence Woodruff, "Gravenhurst's man of tomorrow." In defense of family decorum, I must say Pa made a point never to proof read editorials about himself. Theoretically, therefore, they could be either favorable or otherwise without interference from above. However, I don't believe this theory has ever been thoroughly tested.

The redevelopment committee, though most important, was only one of many prestige pots Pa set boiling. Charity drives, school improvement drives, God-fearing editorials on why we should buy from our dedicated local merchants, nothing was beyond the vision of our enterprising little daily. Even Mother resumed her newspaper skills by reviving a long dormant weekly column on the New York theatah and assorted subjects of interest to Mother. Most of them went something like this: DON'T MISS DESIRE! New York: You really mustn't miss the charming production of Eugene O'Neill's *Desire Under the Elms* now playing at the Shubert. Your dear publisher took me the other night and it was one of the loveliest evenings I've ever spent in the theater. We dined at Sardi's and saw such a mob of interesting people. Elsa Maxwell was there and John Wayne and that charming Cyril Ritchard, but best of all . . .

She seldom got around to what the play was about because obviously nobody cared very much. Then there were some horrible ones about Abby or me and what cute things we had done as children. Yuk yuk. I finally had to edit those myself to avoid becoming the town clown.

Mother would be first to admit it was a pretty nauseating journalistic performance, but the good ladies of Gravenhurst took to it like addicts to their must dust so that was all there was to that.

Other areas of self-preservation included such matters as a promise by Pa to repair a certain store front which had been left peeling and paintless for several profitable years, or to reduce a rent commensurate with the reduction of living standards in a certain neighborhood.

By the time Rosenfeldt and his gang were ready to roll, the *Daily Watch* was more firmly entrenched than ever, as far as we could tell. In fact the day they printed their first edition we felt confident enough to carry the story, although I must admit putting it on page twenty-two under a number ten headline (which is not much bigger than an airmail sticker) was something more than an oversight.

NEW DAILY IN CITY
A daily newspaper published by Jesse Rosenfeldt, son of Benjamin Rosenfeldt, the real estate king, began printing in this city today.

Pa seemed to think that about covered the situation and most people on the *Watch* agreed with him. Nevertheless, there wasn't a one of us who didn't sneak out and buy a copy of the *Enterprise*, as Jesse and his father modestly called their little effort. Without even bothering to read it you could tell one thing right off: it sure was different! In the first place, it was tabloid size and inclined to let photography do the job, while we are standard and lean pretty heavily on the printed story. But the big difference was style. The *Daily Watch* is a classic example of the reserved approach to American journalism. A lot of people think that's too bad because it makes pretty dry reading most of the time, but we run a conservative newspaper devoted to fact rather than flair (sort of like the *New*

DATE DUE

DE 6 '76	JA 4 '83	JA 21 '8	
MR 30 '77	FE 18 '83	AG 9 '88	
JE 24 '77	MR 3 '83	SEP 1 2 '94	
SE 10 '77	AP 2 '83	NOV 20 '96	
OC 31 '77	MY 14 '83	NOV 29 '96	
MY 25 '78	AG 19 '83	MAY 5 '97	
SE 15 '78	SE 6 '83	OCT 1 3 2000 ILL (VDX)	
OC 4 '78	SE 19 '83	67228 67226(m)	
DE 2 '78	OC 21 '83	MAR 08 '06*	
MY 21 '79	FE 22 '85		
JE 15 '79	MR 15 '85		
SE 24 '79	JUL 28 '86		
AP 25 '80	SEP 24 '86		
NO 30 '81	JUN 22 '88		
JE 18 '82	AUG 25 '87		

31870

Wetmore, William

All the right people

MILLBROOK LIBRARY
Millbrook, N.Y.